The Complete
Fifty Shades of Jezebel

The Complete Fifty Shades of Jezebel

Melinda DuChamp

A Fairytale for Adults

Contents

Part 1

Fifty Shades of Jezebel and the Beanstalk

Chapter 1

A Dreadful Date

I'd rather stick a fork in my eye than continue with this terrible date.

Jezebel once again nodded politely at the young man sitting across from her. That was really *all* she'd been doing the entire hour.

His name was Chet, and a friend from her job at Burger Barn had set them up. He was supposedly a good catch because he was: 1) single, 2) not ugly, and 3) manager of a book store. But practically everyone Jezebel knew read ebooks. Bookstores were closing faster than birthday cake disappeared at a fat kid's birthday party. Jezzy couldn't see how Chet's career was solid at all.

"So I told the woman she shouldn't read that popular garbage," Chet rambled on, "and pointed her to some of my favorite Dostoyevsky translations. I so much prefer Magarshack's interpretation to Garnett's..."

Jezzy sighed, smiling politely and wishing she were at home reading an unending, impenetrable Russian novel instead of being stuck there. Chet barely stopped talking long enough to swallow his food. He was completely self-absorbed, and men like that were terrible in bed.

"And if she read Uncle Vanya, she could Chekov that from her list. Get it? Check off? Aren't puns funny?"

Puns weren't funny. Her needs would never be met by a young man who was deathly amused by his own lame attempts at humor, and she'd had more than her share of selfish lovers.

Jezzy wanted someone who would sweep her off her feet and be everything she'd dreamed a true love should be. Prince Charming. Mr. Right. Or better yet, Christian Grey from that kinky bestselling novel she'd read on her Kindle. A panty-drenching story, even though it was overpriced. There was plenty of good erotica under three bucks.

Unfortunately, Chet was no Christian Grey. Jezzy bet he couldn't get her off while armed with a boxful of battery oper-ated devices and an annotated copy of the Kinsey Report.

As she watched him talk, she tried not to look at the rather large bit of broccoli stuck between his two front teeth, and had to turn away to avoid smelling his drugstore cologne, which reeked like bug spray. She gazed at the garden just be-yond the patio, and tried to focus on the scent of the wild roses that grew there.

At least they were sitting outside, thank goodness. She tried to listen to the conversations of others on more interest-ing dates. Jezzy looked over at a young couple sitting very close to one another. The attractive man's hand was sitting high on the woman's bare thigh, her already short dress hiked way up. The woman closed her eyes, her lips slightly open, as his hand slipped between her legs.

Jezebel squeezed her thighs together and shivered, wish-ing she could change places with the lucky girl. A warm breeze lifted her freshly washed and straightened hair from her bare shoulders and kissed her skin. She'd worn her prettiest red peas-ant blouse with a long, summery, tiered skirt, for easy access. She so longed to be touched, to be kissed. That most definitely was not going to happen now. Jezzy had enough broccoli with her own dinner. She wasn't about to share Chet's. And though he knew his Tolstoy, Jezzy doubted he could find her clitoris, even with Google Maps and a magnifying glass.

She looked at the table on the other side of them, at another attractive couple kissing and groping passionately, completely oblivious to the waiter who delivered their food. The woman had opened the man's fly, and was stroking him beneath the table. The man had a hand inside the woman's bra and was caressing her breast while licking her ear.

It was so bold, doing that in public. Such a turn on.

Why doesn't anyone touch me that way? Why were all of my lovers so selfish?

She glanced back at the first couple. The woman's eyes were closed as the man pleasured her under the table. Her fists were clenched, and Jezzy noticed the engagement ring on her hand.

She checked the other public display of affection. Both wore wedding bands.

Was that the key to satisfaction? Commitment?

Of course, before commitment, there had to be love.

But love seemed even more elusive than an orgasm from a hand other than her own.

Maybe I should start small. With mutual affection.

Jezzy decided that she would not have sex with a single other person unless she was absolutely certain that they liked her, and that she liked them. No more sex until there was at least a spark of something. No more bad dates which ended in her being treated like a receptacle, rather than a human being with feelings and needs.

And above all, no more talk about fucking Russian literature.

A waiter appeared at their table, looking first at Chet, then at Jezebel, giving her a pitying look. This wasn't the same waiter that had served them earlier. But she had seen him before, at this restaurant, many times, and he was painfully cute.

Brooding blue eyes and curly hair. Broad shoulders and narrow waist. Big feet.

And you know what they say about big feet.

"Is everything okay?" he asked. His name tag read Jack.

She gave him a look that said, *how can things be okay when I'm stuck with this insufferable idiot?*

"Have you ever been tied up and licked until you couldn't stop screaming?" Jack asked.

Jezzy blinked, unsure if she just heard what she thought she heard. Chet continued to drone on, oblivious to the question.

"Pardon me?" she asked the waiter. She studied him closer, realized he was even more attractive up close.

He was also quite aroused, his erection straining the front of his pants.

Am I imagining this? Have I started to fantasize because this date is boring me out of my mind? Or is some perverted server with a hard-on really talking dirty to me?

"I suggest the beans, Miss," he said.

Chet still hadn't noticed the waiter, or if he did, he didn't care.

"Beans?" she asked in a wistful way, almost entirely sure this was a daydream.

"I really think you'll like these beans. They're magical."

"No, thank you," Jezebel said. "I'm really not hungry."

"Of course, he didn't want to be a novelist when he was younger," Chet continued. "He just needed a little Pushkin. Get it? Alexander Pushkin? Aren't puns funny?"

The waiter gave her a serious look, penetrating her eyes with his blue gaze. "Forgive me, Miss, but I really believe you should try them. You will not be disappointed. In fact, I'll bet you will be completely satisfied."

Jezebel was struck by the intensity of his gaze, by his insistence, and by the bulge only inches away.

Maybe it's not a daydream. Maybe it's a real dream. I'm home, asleep in bed, and the blind dates I dream about are as boring as my blind dates in real life.

But this dream had taken an interesting turn.

Jezzy decided to go with it, see where it led.

"Okay, I'll try the beans."

Chet continued to talk. "Blah blah blah Nabokov, blah blah Solzhenitsyn, blah-dee-blah blah, but then that pun is rather Brodsky. Aren't puns funny?"

Jezebel sighed. "So where are the beans?"

"I have them right here." Jack stared down at his groin. "Reach in and take them."

Jezzy stared at the lump in his pants and chewed her lower lip. She'd just met this waiter, and moments ago she'd promised herself never to get involved with anyone if there wasn't mutual affection.

"By the way," the waiter said. "You're very beautiful, and I like you very much."

"Good enough for me," Jezzy said, and with one deft movement she unzipped his fly. His penis sprang free, and it was lovely; thick and long with...

Three beans balanced on the head.

"You have beans on your dick," Jezzy said.

"Magic beans. That's what I've been trying to tell you."

She raised an eyebrow. "Let me guess. I'm supposed to suck them off your erection?"

"No. You just take them and throw them onto the ground in the garden over there."

"Oh." Jezzy said. She was somewhat disappointed.

"Don't you know the fairy tale?" the waiter asked, his penis bobbing.

"You mean with the Beanstalk?"

"That's the one."

Jezzy frowned. "I preferred Alice in Wonderland. Did you know there's an erotic version of it called Fifty Shades of Alice? I really liked it."

"Perhaps you'll enjoy this one as well."

"I'm not sure I want to climb a beanstalk and have sex with a giant. Anything bigger than eight inches tends to hurt." She stared at Jack's penis again. "Yours, however, looks like a perfect fit."

Jack placed a soft hand on her shoulder and smiled. He really was adorable.

"A whole world of adventure awaits you. But if you'd prefer to stay here with Chet, I believe he's about to launch into a lengthy dissertation on the alleged plagiarism of Mikhail Sholokhov's *And Quiet Flows the Don.*"

"I'll take the beans," Jezzy said, snatching them immediately.

The moment they touched her skin, the beans began to glow and vibrate, causing a tingling in her palm. The tingle worked its way all the way up her arm, and down her chest and belly, into her loins.

"Ooooh," Jezebel breathed. "They feel nice."

Becoming light-headed, she reached out for something to steady herself, grasping the waiter's sizeable erection. Touching it, she went from tingly to full-blown horny as hell.

But Jack gently held her wrist and removed her hand from his throbbing manhood.

"Hey!" Jezzy complained. "I can't even get laid in my own dream?"

"You said it yourself, Jezebel. There must be mutual affection before you sleep with anyone again."

"How do you know my name?"

"I have watched you come into this restaurant many times on many bad dates. Listened to many lame guys' feeble attempts to woo you. Watched as your patience turned to disappointment. I apologize for eavesdropping, for my clandestine voyeurism, but I can't help it. I've grown very fond of you."

"That counts as affection." Jezzy reached for his boner.

Jack danced out of reach. "But you have no affection for me."

"I'm sure I could. I'm sure I could like you very much."

"Perhaps. But first you must learn to like yourself."

"That's not true. I like myself."

"Then why are you still sitting here with Chet?"

Jezebel glanced at Chet, who continued his non-stop talking, something about Fyodor Dmitrievich Kryukov and Venyamin Alekseevich Krasnushkin.

She frowned. "So this is going to be one of those fairy-tales where I travel to some strange land and go on an epic adventure only to realize that what I really wanted was within me all along?"

"Yes. And also, you're going to have a lot of orgasms."

"Done. So where do I plant the beans?"

"The garden is right behind you. Simply toss them onto the soil."

Jezebel got up and left the table—Chet not even noticing—and threw the beans onto a patch of dirt between some calla lilies. Within seconds a *whooooshing* sound engulfed her and three thick stalks sprang from the earth, swirling around each other and shooting far, far up into the sky.

"It looks like bad CGI," Jezzy said.

"What did you expect for a $2.99 ebook? Now climb the stalk, get to the top. Just one warning. Do not stray off the path. You may be tempted to go into the woods, but do not, for the wicked witch Lucinda lives there. Follow the path."

"Why do these fairy tales always have stupid rules? We all know I'm going to stray off the path."

"Do you want to get to the dirty parts or not, babe?"

With that, Jezebel turned and began to climb the beanstalk.

"Beautiful," Jack called up to her.

Jezzy stared down to see that the waiter was standing directly beneath her, looking up her skirt. She'd forgotten that she'd gone without panties—a lame hope that if her blind date turned out well it would have facilitated getting to third base. Jezebel grinned lewdly and opened her legs a bit, giving him a better view.

"Actually, maybe you should come back down here," Jack said. "I'm rethinking my advice."

"Too late," she called down. "I'm committed to an adventure. You had your chance and now... ooooh, my goodness."

A velvety leaf from the stalk slipped between her thighs and caressed her most private place. Jezebel paused, allowing the leaf to fondle and caress. It stroked her slowly, sensually, like a lover's tongue.

She closed her eyes, picturing Jack's cock, so thick and hard, her hand wrapped around it.

Maybe I should climb back down.

Jezzy tried to descend, but the leaf increased its tempo, lapping and sending a wave of dizzy pleasure through her. She was forced to cling to the stalk so she didn't fall.

Then there was a rushing, vertigo sensation, and Jezebel realized the beanstalk was lifting her skyward like an elevator. The combination of hurtling upward and being stroked by a soft leaf was a strange, wonderful thrill, and Jezzy's hips began to grind involuntarily.

She couldn't remember the last time she'd had an orgasm with a lover. And while masturbation always brought her release, it often took a bit of time. But at that moment Jezzy was extremely aroused, very close to coming, and she was chewing on her lower lip about to scream when the beanstalk, and the stroking, abruptly stopped.

It was, unfortunately, a feeling she was very used to. By the time she was just getting into it, her partner was usually finished. She half-expected the beanstalk to turn on the TV and then start snoring.

Jezebel caught her breath, buried her disappointment, and looked around. She found herself standing in a very strange place indeed. A long strip of land that hung in the air like a floating island, green and lush with a cobblestone road which led to a huge storybook castle in the distance, surrounded by fluffy clouds and blue sky. On either side of the path there were lovely, gigantic flowers, which reached out for Jezebel as she walked toward the castle. An enormous violet reached over the path toward her, large leaves reaching, stretching and shivering to touch her. Other giant flowers joined in, bending toward her, and a low hum of whispers began lilting in the breeze.

"Cooooome Jezebel. Come to ussss. We will make you feeeeel soooooo gooood."

Jezebel loved getting flowers, even though it didn't happen often. They made her feel special and romantic. The last time she'd gotten roses, she had sniffed one and ran the bud along her lips, her neck, down her breasts, loving the sensation and wanting to go further but feeling silly.

Right then she didn't feel silly at all. She wanted to stretch out and let the flowers have their way with her. Jezzy was just about to lift up her dress and nestle in a particularly sexy-looking bed of orchids when a harsh male voice said,

"What do you think you are doing, young lady?"

Jezebel Makes a Friend

S tartled, Jezzy spun around, taking a quick, sharp, breath. Before her stood a lithe, slender man who shimmered in the sunlight. Blond waves curled just above a set of the clearest green eyes Jezzy had ever seen. Pointed ears poked through his curls, and a devilish smile curved his lips. A wooden bow and a sack of arrows were slung on his shoulder.

Wow, was he hot.

"I repeat, what are you doing?"

"I was... um..." Jezzy felt too ashamed to go further.

"You were going to lie in my flower bed and let them ravage you," the man answered for her.

She nodded, blushing and staring at the ground.

"They are quite good at it," he said. "I've taught them many ways to pleasure a woman. Can you imagine being caressed and stroked everywhere at once by thousands of succulent, velvety petals, forcing you to climax over and over?"

"I can now," Jezzy said, feeling herself get wetter.

"Perhaps I should allow it. You are quite pretty, and the moans of a beautiful woman are the sweetest music."

He walked up to her, his lips suddenly at her ear and his strong hands cupping her buttocks, pressing her against him.

"The problem is, dear Jezebel, those flowers are insatiable. They do not know when to stop. They'll keep you there, forcing you to come and come and come, until you die of ecstasy."

"Doesn't seem like a bad way to go," Jezebel managed to croak. She ground against the handsome stranger, and found he was as aroused as she.

"I would enjoy watching it. Watching you wiggle and scream. I would stroke myself as I watched."

He cupped her ass, and ran his tongue over her ear. Jezzy squealed, once again on the verge of orgasm.

Then he abruptly released her.

"But, alas, you were summoned here for someone other than me. And we must be off." As Jezzy watched, a set of huge, black feathers unfolded behind him.

"Oh, my," Jezebel said. "What are you?"

"I'm a puck."

"Puck? As in hockey?"

"As in nature sprite. We used to be known as fairies, but that term took on a different connotation and we haven't reclaimed it despite some solid efforts to try. My name is Robin Goodfellow."

"I'm Jezebel."

"I know. Jack called ahead, said you were coming."

"Jack the cute waiter?"

"Jack is really a mischievous forest imp who disguises himself as a waiter."

"To blend in? Is it to lure women to this magical land?"

"No. It's for the tips. On a good night he can pull in three hundred dollars. But whenever he meets a sexy woman, he gives her magic beans to bring her here."

"But why?"

"For Pan."

"Pan? As in cooking?"

"As in the prince of this realm. He's kind of a letch. He loves horny, unfulfilled ladies such as yourself. And he throws the best parties. He is the Hugh Hefner of our land."

"What land is this?" Jezzy asked, looking around. "It's beautiful."

"Have you heard of Oz?"

"Of course."

"How about Never-Never Land? Narnia? Wonderland?"

"Yes. Which one is this?"

"None of them. We don't want to get involved in any copyright infringement lawsuits. So we call this magical kingdom Phlegm."

"Phlegm? As in mucus?"

Robin frowned. "I know. It's a terrible name. But we don't have to worry about anyone suing us."

"I don't expect many merchandizing opportunities for you, either."

"Sadly, no. But we do have our own language here."

"You do?"

"Have you ever heard of Phlegmish?"

More proof that puns weren't funny.

"I assume you want to go to the party at the castle tonight?" Robin asked.

Jezzy clasped her hands together in excitement. She very much wanted to go to a party, especially since this was supposed to be erotica, and she hadn't gotten laid yet.

"A party sounds wonderful."

"It shall be wonderful. But Prince Pan requires all attendees to be horny when they arrive."

"I'm very horny right now."

"Are you sure?"

Jezebel nodded.

"I'll have to check."

Robin pressed his palm against her breast, rubbing it over her erect nipple, making her squirm. He caught it between his fingers and rolled them slightly, and then his other hand was suddenly between Jezzy's legs, pushing into her.

She whimpered and he slowly worked two fingers in an out of her. "You are, indeed, very wet. But Pan requires his guests to be even more excited."

"I can't get much more excited. I'm going to come all over your hand. Please... please don't..."

Robin abruptly stopped, taking both hands away.

Jezebel cried out in protest. She was really starting to hate the Magical Kingdom of Phlegm.

"I think, to put you in the proper mood, a love apple is required."

"Or you could just fuck me," she said, slutty as she could manage.

"Perhaps. But first, the apple."

Robin's wings flapped, lifting him off the ground.

Jezzy watched in astonishment as he flew to a tree laden with the largest, most lush apples she had ever seen. They were a rich, deep purple, and seemed to throb and pulse on their branches. Robin reached up and plucked the darkest, juiciest-looking fruit from the tree.

"I can be a good friend to you, Jezebel. All I ask is that you give me something in return, as a token of your friendship. I am rather self-absorbed and like my friends to make me feel important to them. Do you think you can manage that?"

Jezzy's mouth watered. "Oh, yes. Friendship should be reciprocal. It's only fair."

Robin flew to her and held out the shiny, crimson apple. "Then please, eat this for me."

When the apple touched Jezebel's fingers, it began to shimmer and vibrate. Jezzy stared at the succulent fruit, enamored by its beauty, luxuriating in the way it made her whole body flush.

"Go ahead, Jezebel."

Jezzy brought the apple to her mouth and took a dainty bite. The apple was so delicious that her tongue began to tingle. "Mmmm."

"Isn't that the best apple you've ever bitten into?"

"Ooooh yes." Jezzy chewed, enraptured by the preternaturally wonderful taste of the apple. The juices slid over her tongue and down her throat, tingling all the way.

"Take another bite, Jezebel." Robin grinned at her. His fly was open, and he was sliding a long, tapered hand over his large, erect manhood.

Jezebel felt the tingling move down her throat, over her breasts and deep within her nipples.

"Ooooh," Jezzy breathed. "I think I like love apples."

Robin's hand stroked his engorged member quickly, as his eyes devoured Jezebel. With his other hand, he flicked his fingers, and Jezzy felt her skirt being tugged down. She hadn't even felt the zipper opening.

"Lift your arms, Jezebel," Robin said, breathless.

Jezebel did as she was told, gripping the apple tightly, she lifted her arms high, and her peasant blouse slid over them and dropped onto a nearby orange tree.

"Can I pick a bunch of these to take home?" she asked, the wetness dripping down her thighs. "They'd make an amazing pie."

"May I kiss you?" His voice was so soft and gentle, that its vibrations went right through her.

"Yes," she said, panting lightly. The tingles had made their way to her sweet spot, and she teetered on the edge of orgasm. The pleasure was so intense that she reached out for Robin, whimpering.

Her lips parted and met his, the tip of his tongue teasing her, making her groan. His hands roamed her neck, her shoulders, her belly, her chest. He wrapped his fingers in her hair, holding her head firmly, and whispered, "May I kiss you between your legs?"

"Yes."

Dropping to his knees, Robin licked her belly button, then lower, as his wings folded around her and the feathers stroked the small of her back.

When his tongue touched her clitoris, it was as if an electrical shock went through her body, and an involuntary scream wrenched itself from Jezebel's throat.

"Such sweet music," he murmured, burying his face in her.

He began to lick, and Jezebel grabbed his head, pressing against him, so close, so close...

And then he was standing, his arms tight around her, his magnificent ebony wings extended and flapping, and they were up, up, up, sailing above the trees.

Jezzy moved her hips forward, trying to rub her womanhood against Robin's considerable, steely length.

"Wrap your legs around me, Jezebel," he whispered, his tongue flicking her earlobe.

Jezzy brought her legs up and locked them around Robin's waist, trying to lift high enough to slide over his manhood.

"Do you want me inside of you, Jezebel?"

"Yes... please," she begged. The world spun beneath them, her body rising and falling and spinning.

"Not yet," Robin said, his tone playful. He held her slightly away, so that her most sensitive spot couldn't reach him.

Jezzy pushed her hips forward, yearning for contact. "Oh, please, Robin. Please."

"Please, what?"

"Please slide inside of me."

"I thought you promised yourself you would only make love if you felt mutual affection."

"I—" Jezzy's mind was foggy and befuddled. She was dizzy and horny and if she didn't have an orgasm soon she was afraid her mind would snap.

"You what?"

"I like you, Robin. I really *really* like you. Please."

Robin threw his head back and laughed. "Ok, Jezebel. If you say so." He brought Jezzy closer to him, close enough so that her hot, swollen nub just barely touched his length, which was standing straight up.

"Ooooooh," Jezzy sighed, as intense little shivers of pleasure shot through her womanhood. Her tunnel began to clench in the beginnings of a sublime orgasm.

But then Robin moved her away again.

"No!" Jezzy shouted. "Please, Robin! Please let me come."

"But the affection must be mutual, Jezebel. Perhaps I don't like you at all. Perhaps I'm just using you."

"I'm okay with that. I swear. Please."

"I do like you, Jezebel."

"Thank god! Now fuck me!"

"But I think you may rush into things. Your need to be liked, to be loved, leads you to many unfulfilling experiences. You need to learn to savor and enjoy. Let me teach you."

Jezzy wanted to scream, frustration winding with arousal, and a tear slipped down her cheek. The pressure in her clitoris almost beyond bearing. But she said, "Okay. Teach me."

Robin leaned his head down and lowered his lips to Jezzy's breast, taking her nipple between his lips. He sucked lightly while flicking his tongue across the sensitive orb. She cried out, the walls of her honeyed cave clenching with need.

"Ooooooh," she murmured, rocking her pelvis forward, brushing her hot spot against him. Little electric bursts shot through her loins, moving through to her belly and breasts, making her head loll back and her mouth drop open. Jezzy was nearly insane with need.

Robin nibbled lightly, sending tiny shock waves of delight through her.

"Aaaaah," she moaned.

"Do you like that?" Robin asked her.

"Oh, yes," she whispered, biting her lip.

Robin brought her closer, moving his stiff, velvety rod against her moist pussy. His breath was hot on her nipple.

"Would you like me to slide inside you?" He moved more quickly, using feather strokes across her clitoris.

"Yes! Yes, please," she replied, the sensations his teeth on her nipple created making her crazy. Her clit ached for release, the pressure building to an impossible level. She felt her orgasm rushing up within her.

Robin pulled away.

"No! Please, Robin! Please fill me with your manhood!" Her hips were thrusting forward of their own accord.

"Pretty please?" Robin grinned, nipping at her bottom lip with his teeth.

"P-pretty p-please," she managed, her teeth gritted.

"Pretty please with a cherry on top?" He smiled.

"Oh, fuck you!"

"As you wish." And with that, he lifted her effortlessly and lowered her onto his member, sliding deep within her sugared cave.

Jezzy gasped and cried out, the pleasure so intense, it was almost painful. "Oh, God!"

"The name is Robin, Jezebel, and you'll not ever forget it," he said, smiling at her as he thrust deep inside of her, using his hands to plunge her downward.

Each plunge downward was heavenly and excruciating in intensity, her need was magnified tenfold, and she moved her hips forward, allowing Robin's velvety, slick rod to caress her g-spot. Jezzy moved forward, kissing Robin hotly. His lips were soft as he slipped his tongue over hers. She sucked his tongue, then rolled her tongue around his, exploring his mouth. Kissing him sent her over the edge, and for a moment her entire body went numb. Then tension uncoiled and she began to come.

"Ooooh Robin!" She screamed, ripples of delight thrilling through her, then blasting her body and senses into oblivion. Her entire body shuddered in a bliss Jezzy had never known. Her walls squeezed again and again, as pleasure peaked and crested, fading and flashing through her once more.

Robin shouted, stiffening and thrusting into her deeply, reaching the very core of her being. Jezzy felt his hot seed shooting into her. The heat of his juices leaving her tingling and warm. He thrust deeply into her again and again, his orgasm going on and on.

Jezzy felt like she was flying ... which, actually, she was.

Her pleasure ebbed as Robin slowed. He rested his head on her shoulder and sighed against her skin.

"That was magnificent," Robin breathed against her shoulder.

"Yes, it certainly was," Jezzy replied. "Thank you, Robin. I've never had an orgasm that intense. It was mind bending."

"That is what happens when you take the time to savor your arousal," Robin said. "You just need to learn control, and for that you need practice."

"Practice?" Jezzy said. "Will you practice with me?"

Robin chuckled. "I'd be glad to, Jezebel. But you should also practice with other lovers, to get really good at it."

"Other lovers?" But whom?

Robin's wings gently lowered them both to the ground. They wrapped around her, soothing and caressing her down from her body bliss. He released her, stepping back and assessing her. "Nice. Very nice."

Jezzy looked down at herself. She now wore a dress of midnight black feathers. The areas around both breasts were free of feathers, as well as her special place. "Wow. This is gorgeous, Robin. But it doesn't quite cover my private areas. I'm not sure this is entirely appropriate for a ball."

"Oh, it's appropriate for this ball. The feathers move with you. They do not restrict you. You can move and do anything you like while wearing them, which, as you'll soon discover, is a must at Pan's balls." Robin broke out laughing. "Pan's balls! Ha! I'm so clever!"

"Right." Truthfully, Jezzy had forgotten all about the ball, and all she wanted to do was go to sleep. "Can I take a short nap, first? Would you like to nap with me?"

"Uh... I kind of have a date," Robin said.

"W-what?" Jezzy said, flabbergasted. "You made love to me just before your date? What kind of guy are you?"

"I'm a puck, Jezzy. We are notoriously fickle and promiscuous. Surely you didn't think we're in love."

"Well, no, but, I really do like you."

"And I like you. But I also happen to like anything with two tits and a pulse. I'm not boyfriend material. So I suggest you change your criteria, Jezebel. Instead of just seeking mutual affection, you should also seek mutual appreciation. A player like me will only appreciate you as long as the sex lasts. You deserve someone better."

"I do?"

"Yes, you do. You're a wonderful, beautiful, smart woman, and you need someone who appreciates that, and not only while getting laid. Just one more thing." Robin reached out and gently moved a hand across her eyes. He then looked at her face and nodded his approval. "Perfect."

"What is?"

"You have a mask of black feathers across your eyes. It's a masquerade ball. You'll need a mask."

Jezzy reached up and gently touched the mask of feathers, which were silky and soft. It felt like she had no mask at all. "Wow. This is so neat."

"You look sexy as hell, and believe me, I would know."
He winked. "Off you go, now, Jezebel." He patted her bottom.
"Follow the path to the castle. Do not stray off the path. You
have no time left for sexual excursions. You will miss the ball."

"Oh—okay." Jezebel was still a little confused by what
had just happened.

"Have fun, Jezebel." And with that, Robin lifted his wings
and flew up over the trees and away, vanishing into the night.

Jezebel Sleeps with the Fishes

The castle was much farther than it looked. Jezzy walked for the better part of an hour, and the sun had long since sunk into the earth, replaced by a round, fat, silvery moon. Stars had come out to look over Jezzy, blinking their greeting, and Jezzy smiled up at them, happy for the company. It was all so goddamn Disneyesque. If the moon began to sing, Jezzy wouldn't have been surprised.

She was filled with excitement and anticipation at the prospect of attending a ball at all, much less one thrown by an actual prince. She'd read about the Pan in a mythology book she'd gotten from the school library. The pictures depicted him as rather fearsome, with narrow yellow eyes and goat horns, and legs covered with hair. His feet were hooves, and he usually had his Syrinx with him—a musical instrument he used to arouse people and make them dance.

From the way he looked in those pictures, he was downright creepy.

Still, she wasn't planning on bedding him, though that might've been what Jack the forest imp and Robin the puck expected. Goat legs were just a little too freaky. But she did want to go to the ball. Perhaps she'd meet someone who liked and appreciated her there. Someone who didn't look like a goat. And she hadn't danced in ages. She loved dancing!

Jezzy looked down at her feet, now clad in leather shoes that looked like sandals, with black straps which wove in intricate webbing all the way up her legs, to her upper thighs, almost like fishnet stockings. They were the coolest pair of shoes she'd ever had, and the sexiest. They were also comfortable, as they were made to accommodate dancing. Robin had certainly dressed her for the occasion.

Finally Jezzy made it to the drawbridge leading to the castle. She looked into the water as she crossed over, watching fish jump playfully under the light of the moon. A woman's giggle startled her and made her pause, and Jezzy looked over the railing to look at the source of the sound. She peered into the dim light. "Is someone there?"

"Sssssh," she heard someone whisper. "She heard you."

Jezzy frowned. There was definitely someone down there, in the water. "Hello? Who is there?"

"Hello," came the reply. A female voice. "Who is there?"

Jezzy frowned. Was that her echo? Or someone pretending to be her echo? "I asked you first."

"Who's on first?"

"I know there's someone down there," Jezzy called out. "You can't fool me."

"That's not what we've heard," replied the voice. "It's all around the land that you gave it up to Robin the puck. Another notch in his belt. He's running out of room."

"He'll need a new belt," came another voice.

"Does he cut a new notch if he boffs someone he's boffed before?" the first voice queried.

"I don't know. How many times have we shagged him?"

"I've lost count."

"Excuse me!" Jezzy called.

The first voice answered. "We can hear you. No need to yell."

"Who is we?"

Gentle splashing sounds approached, and Jezzy leaned down a little further to see who was in the water. Two shapes slowly emerged, almost directly beneath her. They were beautiful young women, pale as the moon. One with long, midnight black hair and the other a glimmering, silvery blonde; their hair floating around their shoulders in the water. Large, mirthful eyes regarded Jezzy with amusement.

They appeared to be college age, and looked fit enough to be swimsuit models, minus the swim suits. Two sets of small, perky breasts bobbed on the surface of the water, nipples bare.

"Hello," the dark haired one said.

"What are you doing down there? Skinny dipping?" Jezzy asked.

"Skinny dipping?" The blonde girl queried. "What is that?"

Things sure were different in this place. "Swimming naked."

"Yes," the blonde replied. "We are swimming naked."

"Would you like to join us?" asked the dark-haired beauty.

Normally, Jezzy would have been shocked by the offer. But after banging a puck while soaring over a magical floating kingdom, she was finding herself a little more adventurous.

"I would actually love to, but I'm late for a costume party at the castle."

The girls smiled at each other, then looked back at Jezzy.

"We shall come with you," the dark haired girl said. "We always enjoy Pan's parties, and we can visit our sister, Syrinx. Pan keeps her there."

"Keeps her? In a dungeon?"

For some reason, Jezebel found the thought of a dungeon to be terrifically hot.

"No. He put a spell on her," the blonde answered. "Syrinx was a terrible tease, and she would dance for Pan and get him very aroused, and then leave before he climaxed."

"She was pretty mean to him," the brunette agreed. "And he warned her he would curse her if she kept it up, and she didn't listen. So he turned her into a musical flute made of reeds."

"That sounds horrible," Jezebel said.

"It depends on your definition of horrible," the blonde said. "He blows into her, using his tongue and lips to make her sing. His mouth is all over her. The musical sound she makes is her moaning and coming. And he plays her *all the time.*"

"Mmmmmm," purred the brunette. "I don't think I could handle it. I'd go *insane.*"

The blonde shrugged. "A taste of her own medicine. She was a cocktease, and wouldn't let Pan come. Now he makes her come constantly."

"Can the curse be broken?" Jezzy asked.

"Not until he finds someone he fancies more. Then he'll release Syrinx, and turn her back into a mermaid. So far it hasn't happened. Anyway, we should get ready for the party."

And with that, both girls dipped down into the water, and two fish tails surfaced and waved at Jezebel.

"Heavens!" Jezzy cried, when the girls breached the water at a ladder leading up the bridge. "Did you see those two fish? They were enormous! You need to be careful in that water! You might get eaten!"

The girls both giggled, their laughter like the tinkling of bells.

"Those were our tails! We're mermaids! I'm Peony," said the blonde. "This is my sister Nerah."

Jezzy's face scrunched up. "So your upper bodies are girl, and your lower bodies are fish?"

They nodded.

"But you said you shagged Prince Pan. So how exactly... um... I mean to say how can you... with no... uh... you can't spread your... you know..."

"How can we fuck him? Nerah asked.

Jezebel nodded, feeling embarrassed.

"Well, if we're in the water, we use our mouths," Peony said.

Nerah nodded. "Prince Pan loves that."

"So how do you... I mean... do you have... do you enjoy..." Jezzy's voice trailed off.

"How do we come?" Peony said.

Jezzy nodded, blushing. On cue, both mermaids began to tug and twist their nipples. Their moans began as deep, throaty rumblings, and quickly escalated into whimpers and screams. It only took a few moments for them both to quake with obvious orgasms.

"Mermaids have clits for nipples," Peony said, catching her breath.

"Also," Peony began to heave herself out of the water using the ladder, "the moon kindly offers us the magic to change our tails into legs in the night time."

As she'd explained, as she climbed the ladder, there was a brief flash of light and legs appeared.

"Legs, and a pussy," Nerah said, following her sister up the ladder. "Want to take a look at ours?"

Not wanting to be rude, Jezzy said sure. Besides, when would she ever get another chance to see a mermaid's womanhood?

Both Nerah and Peony laid down on their bridge and opened their legs, raising and holding their knees.

"Get down close," Peony said. "Don't be shy."

Jezzy knelt down, putting her face between Peony's legs. She'd never seen a woman this up close before, and it felt both embarrassing and thrilling. Peony had delicate, tiny, pink labia, delicate and perfect.

"Spread me open, Jezebel."

"Are you sure?"

"Yes. Please."

Jezzy reached up slowly, as if about to stick her hand into an electrical socket. When she touched Peony, the mermaid began to wiggle and moan.

But that didn't make any sense. If a mermaid had clits in her nipples, why would it feel good when she was touched down there?

Jezzy slid her finger up and down the length of Peony's slick feminitinity, and then used her fingers to lightly part—

"Oh, my," Jezzy said.

Peony had a clitoris down there as well. In fact, she had three of them, stacked on top of each other like peas in a pod. Transfixed, Jezebel began to stroke them, up and down, marveling as they stiffened under her touch.

"Do all mermaids have three clits down there?" she asked and Peony squirmed and panted.

"No. Nerah has four, the lucky bitch."

"Come and look, Jezebel," Nerah said.

Jezebel switched over to Nerah, who was holding her dark brown labia open for Jezzy to see.

"It would feel so wonderful if you ran your tongue across them," Nerah said.

Jezebel had never done anything like that. She'd messed around with a girl years ago, in college, at a Def Leppard concert after drinking too many coolers, and that had been the extent of her lesbian experience. But she couldn't deny that stroking Peony and listening to her moan had turned Jezzy on. So she lowered her face and gave Nerah a soft, lazy lick.

She tasted like salt water taffy. Delicious.

Jezzy settled in, doing what she liked men to do to her. First fast and hard, then slow and soft. Then she pulled away, forced Nerah to lift her hips to meet her mouth.

As Nerah's cries grew louder, Jezzy felt herself become so turned on she was beginning to dry hump the air. Then, suddenly, she was penetrated.

She turned, startled and groaning, and saw Peony was kneeling behind her, working her fingers in and out of Jezzy.

"You poor thing," Peony said. "Only one clitoris." She stroked Jezzy's clit with one hand as the other continued to probe deeper and deeper. "I don't see how you can manage."

"I... can... manage..." Jezzy said, squeezing her eyes closed and feeling an orgasm welling up within her.

"Please don't stop," Nerah panted.

Jezebel had become so caught up in what Peony was doing to her, she'd stopped licking Nerah. So she lowered her head again, and also worked a finger inside of Nerah as Peony was doing with her.

It was almost too much to keep track of, giving pleasure to Nerah while receiving pleasure from Peony, but when Nerah began to come it was such a turn-on that Jezzy began to come as well. And so, apparently, did Peony, who had bent down over Jezzy and was rubbing her breasts against Jezebel's feather outfit.

Their three voices mingled into a long, drawn out, musical crescendo, and when Jezzy stopped shaking she collapsed atop Nerah, exhausted.

"Maybe one clitoris is enough," Peony said. "You gushed all over me."

Jezebel blushed. "I'm... I'm sorry. I..."

Peony smiled, then licked one of her glistening fingers. "Nothing to be sorry about. You're as succulent as a love apple. Maybe I'll get a chance to taste you at Pan's party."

"I'd like that," Jezebel said. "But I must confess, I don't normally have sex with..."

"With mermaids?" said Nerah.

"With women."

Nerah laughed. "Neither do we. But sleeping with women is sometimes easier."

"There isn't all the baggage that comes with men," Peony agreed. "They're so urgent. So demanding. And the poor dears can only come a few times a day."

"Plus, many men don't appreciate women," Nerah said. "They don't understand our needs, and don't care about trying to."

"That's what I'm looking for," Jezebel said. "A man who likes me, and appreciates me."

"Well, perhaps you'll find someone at the ball." Peony licked another finger, then stood up. "We should be going. Pan doesn't like anyone to arrive late."

Pan's Masquerade Ball

The three of them headed up the gently curved road toward the castle. Jezzy was thankful for the flat sandal type shoes she wore. She looked down at the feet of the mermaids. "Aren't your feet sore?"

"We're used to being barefoot. Our feet are tougher than yours. Besides, Pan loves bare feet," said Nerah. "He likes to suck our toes. He has a bit of a foot fetish."

"Pan has a bit of an *everything* fetish," Peony added.

When they arrived at the castle, the entrance was flanked by two large men, all sinewy muscle. They wore nothing but red masks over their eyes. Shimmery, sandalwood scented oil covered their bodies with a lovely sheen. Their lengthy members were engorged, and pierced with rings and studs.

"Those two are Michael and Lance. They're twin brothers," said Peony. "Hello, you two. Nice to see you again."

"Always a pleasure, Peony," said Michael, the brother to the left of the entrance. His brother smiled and nodded.

"Who is your pretty friend?" asked Michael.

"This is Jezebel," Nerah said.

"Very nice to meet you, Jezebel." Michael's eyes moved over Jezzy and he licked his lips. "I hope to get to know you inside."

"Nice to meet you, too," Jezzy said. She squirmed under his gaze, becoming aware of a warming in her nipples, and the familiar heat between her legs. A fantasy appeared, full blown, in her head, of the two brothers touching and pawing at her, one studded cock in her mouth and the other filling her up.

Maybe the Magical Kingdom of Phlegm had some sort of aphrodisiac in the air, which made Jezzy so much hornier than normal. Or maybe the love apple's effects lingered.

Or maybe, as she suspected, this was all a dream.

Lance handed a silver mask to Peony and a gold one to Nerah. There were several bottles of liquid behind him, and he chose one, pouring the fluid into his large hand.

"Lavender, my favorite," Peony said. "You know me so well, Lance."

Lance grinned, then rubbed his hands together, then using long, luxurious strokes, moved his hands over first one of Peony's legs, then the other. Her body gleamed where he rubbed her. Scented oil. Jezzy could smell the intoxicating fragrance from where she stood.

Lance took his time, and Peony's eyes closed as she sighed.

"Your hands are the loveliest in all the land," she murmured, her voice just above a whisper.

Jezebel loved a good hot oil massage, and secretly hoped she'd get the same treatment.

"May I pick an oil for you, Jezebel?" Lance asked.

"I was so hoping you would."

He chose an ornate, diamond cut bottle and poured oil onto one large palm, then rubbed his hands together, coming toward Jezzy. He slowly dropped to one knee. His face was inches from her special place, and tension pooled there, making her heart speed up and her breaths come more quickly.

Lance massaged the musky, vanilla scented oil onto one leg, bringing his hands ever higher, moving up her feather dress. He massaged her inner thigh moving closer to her pussy, while the other caressed her bottom. Lance's hands moved away, leaving Jezzy chilled from the absence of this warmth. She opened her eyes, startled that she'd closed them. She watched as he poured more oil onto his palm, shivering with anticipation as he rubbed his hands together.

Again, Jezzy closed her eyes and almost swooned when Lance's hands touched her other leg. They encircled her calves, moving sensually over them, higher and higher until they were sliding over her upper thighs. Jezzy burned with embarrassment as a trickle of her excitement dribbled down her inner thigh.

She gasped lightly as one hand slid over her swollen folds, finding her hidden jewel and feathering over it ever so softly. "Oooh."

"You smell sweet already, Jezebel You don't really need scented oil here. Would you like me to skip this spot?"

Jezzy heard similar little moans coming from beside her, but didn't know if they came from Peony or Nerah. She felt far away. "No, please. Don't stop."

Lance's hand moved away and Jezzy almost cried, feeling the loss of its heat on her most sensitive part. She was weak in the knees, dizzy with need, and her legs wobbled a little as she waited for Lance to touch her again.

Finally, after what seemed an eternity, Lance again began to stroke, the scented oil mingling with her own juices. Her lips had plumped as pleasure sailed through her, and her hips jutted forward involuntarily, gyrating and inviting him to enter her.

Lance slid his fingers into her slick folds, lightly swirling them over her sensitive pearl, sending electric currents of pleasure through her. "Oooh my," she moaned, swooning forward. "Oooh, yeeeessss."

Tension pooled into her sweet spot, and she felt her orgasm teetering on the edge, about to soar through her, when Lance's fingers vanished from between her legs, moving gingerly up and over her hips. She cried out in frustration.

"I'm sorry, Jezebel, but your orgasm belongs to Pan. You are a new guest, and he always gives new guests their first orgasm at the ball." Lance massaged oil over her belly, then slowly over her breasts.

Jezzy tingled all over, sexual excitement making her walls contract with need.

Lance pulled her close, crushing her breasts against his hard chest as he rubbed oil over her back. Jezzy moved her face up to his, standing on tip-toe. She brushed her lips over his. He kissed her back, long and dreamy, probing her mouth with his tongue.

"Mmmmm," she murmured.

Lance pulled again, gently pushing her back. "That is all I'm allowed to give you. My job is merely to arouse you so that you're properly prepared for the ball."

"But—but I won' tell," she sputtered. "I promise."

Lance chuckled. "Worry, not, pretty one. Your pleasure awaits you inside."

He moved aside and motioned with a sweep of his hand toward the entrance.

Reluctantly, Jezzy walked over the threshold and into the castle.

"They are delicious, aren't they?" Peony asked Jezzy. Her eyes were glazed and a soft blush covered her face, neck and the tops of her perky breasts.

"Sinfully delicious," Nerah agreed. She was sporting the same rosy glow, her eyes just as glazed as Peony's.

Jezzy was certain that she looked much the same, if not more so.

"But to bring someone so close to orgasm and then just leave them hanging is cruel," Jezzy said, feeling her bottom lip actually jutting out into a little pout.

"Perhaps we can learn Pan's curse, and turn the twins into flutes," Peony said.

"Flutes?" said Nerah. "How about trumpets. Something long and hard we can blow."

The women all shared a laugh.

As they moved further into the castle, music sounding like tribal drums and flutes floated on the air, making Jezzy feel even more aroused. She was so turned on, it was becoming uncomfortable.

"I've never felt like this before," Jezzy said. "Is there a ladies room? I think I need to—"

"To take care of yourself?" Peony asked.

Jezzy nodded, blushing.

"Pan wouldn't like that. It's his party. You can come only if he allows it."

"That's mean."

"It's called teasing, Jezebel. When someone teases you enough to bring you close to orgasm but doesn't allow you to release, the orgasm is magnificent when it actually comes," Peony said. "Just wait. You'll see."

They had come to an enormous room filled with people dancing and gyrating to the beat of the drums and the high notes of the flute. Many of the people were engaged in sexual acts. Jezzy's mouth dropped open as her gaze wandered over the naked bodies on what looked like a huge dance floor.

There were women's heads bobbing up and down or back and forth, their mouths full with erect manhood. She saw men pleasuring men that way too, and men pleasuring women, their tongues flicking over the mounds of their partners. Women also pleasured women, long, tapered fingers moving in and out of slick nether regions, the legs of their partners spread wide. There were men thrusting behind men, men thrusting behind women, on top of women, women on top of men, plunging up and down and rotating their hips. There were cries of passion and pleasure.

But Jezzy's shocked gaze was drawn to a stage, to a figure which sat on a golden throne above the spectacle of animal passion before him. A man with a head of coppery red curls catching the light from the flames of an enormous fire in the hearth behind him.

He held an instrument to his lips, which looked like several flutes placed together, each flute shorter than the last. He looked up and caught Jezzy's stare, lowering the musical instrument. The dancing and sexual movements ceased. Everything seemed to be suspended in time as this magnificent creature regarded her with a mixture of interest and amusement.

His features looked as if they were cut from stone; strong, square jaw, high cheekbones and a noble nose. Horns curled backward on his head, almost the same color as his hair. His lips were full and sensuous, and they smiled as his narrow yellow eyes burned into hers.

Finally he stood, his fine, muscled chest gleaming in the firelight. He reached a chiseled arm toward her, beckoning to her.

Jezzy blinked, staring at his lower legs, which were covered in dark red, curly fur. His feet were cloven. "Heavens", she breathed.

"Heavenly," Peony said.

"Delicious," Nerah said.

"Who is *that*?" Jezzy asked, her breath having all but left her.

Both mermaids sighed and at the same time said, "Prince Pan."

Peony gave Jezzy a nudge. "What are you waiting for? He's summoning you. Go!"

"Is that a good thing?" Jezzy asked, watching as the prince held her gaze and continued to beckon her. She'd made love to a guy with wings, and gone down on a mermaid, but goat legs—that was just a little too weird.

"It's an honor," Nerah said. "Hurry, before he changes his mind."

The prince smiled at Jezzy, lowering his head and bringing the instrument toward his mouth. A slow, sensuous tune came from it, rich, gorgeous notes lifting on the air, and making Jezzy feel dizzy and lightheaded.

"He's playing the Syrinx, just for you. He likes you."

"The Syrinx?" Jezzy asked, sounding far away to herself.

"The musical instrument he is playing. Our sister. Her name was Syrinx. He is playing her for you alone."

While it was no doubt music of the medieval variety, the instrument did indeed sound like a woman in the throes of unbearable passion, each note a different, wailing sigh.

Jezzy felt her hips swaying, and her feet began moving forward. She realized distantly that she was dancing toward the stage where the prince stood. Vaguely she was aware that the people who were on the floor parted, making a walkway for her.

Jezebel's body twirled, then her hips rotated, and her legs moved forward in dance steps she had never performed in her life. She knew in her heart that this was an ancient dance, a special one that was performed for Pan only.

Jezzy heard herself giggle, and her heart become light. Heat swept over her and her head buzzed as sexual desire made her nipples ache and sent little electric currents to lick at her loins. She moaned, as the vibrations of the music went through her, each note like a lover's kiss.

Soon Jezzy reached the stage, and she felt hands around her legs and waist, lifting her up. Through hazy eyes she saw two sets of arms reaching for her—Michael and Lance—and then she was lifted and standing, quivering before the prince.

He continued playing the Syrinx, and Jezzy's body moved and gyrated, stepped and twirled for him. With her body, she told an age-old story of passion and desire, the meaning of which she sensed on a primitive level, but wouldn't have been able to verbalize.

Also, there was much twerking.

As she swayed before him, her hands came up and caressed her fragrant breasts. Her fingers plucked at her nipples, making them peak, aching to be kissed and sucked.

One hand slid down over the feathers of her dress, to her slick mound. Her fingers found her most secret, sensitive spot, swirled over it, making tiny sizzling circles of pleasure.

"Oooooh," she cried, feeling an orgasm racing from deep within her. "Ooooh, God."

Yes. My name is Pan. Say it. His voice was in her head, deep, dark and sweet.

"Pan," she breathed. "Pan…"

The prince continued playing, the music wrapping around her, licking and kissing her everywhere, her hands accompanying, as if Pan was using her hands to do his bidding.

Jezzy's mouth opened as the first spark of her orgasm alighted within her.

Pan lifted his mouth from the Syrinx and lowered it to his lap.

Jezzy whimpered. "Please don't stop."

Pan's lips curved into a devilish smile.

Jezzy's body continued to sway gently before him, awaiting his command. "Tell me what you want me to do. I'll do it. Just please, don't stop playing."

Pan's smile widened. "Pan says touch your toes!"

The crowd around her groaned. "Not again," someone said.

"We just did this!" Another yelled.

A cacophony of good-natured complaints filled the air around Jezebel.

"Enough!" Pan shouted.

The crowd went silent.

He said, patiently, as if speaking to a class of kindergarteners, "Pan says, touch your toes."

"W-what?" Jezzy sputtered. "I don't understand."

She looked around, baffled, staring into the crowd. Everyone behind her was touching their toes, naked bottoms lifted into the air. Beneath her, next to the stage, was Lance, the twin who had oiled her.

"Psssst!" he said.

"What is going on?" Jezzy whispered..

"Just touch your toes. Pan is like a spoiled kid. He has too much power and time on his hands, and he just loves to fuck with us. But if you don't do as he says, he'll send you out of the castle. It's just like Simon Says. Just do whatever he tells you to do."

Pan watched her, waiting, tapping a cloven foot and strumming his fingers on his long, erect manhood. "Well?"

Jezebel reluctantly bent down and touched her toes.

"Very good!" Pan shouted. "So far, everyone can stay. Everyone up!"

Jezzy was about to move upward but Lance once again whispered, "He didn't say *Pan says*."

"Oh! Thank you!" Jezzy remained down, looking between her legs at him.

Lance grinned. "Think nothing of it. I'm quite enjoying this view."

Pan's laughter bounced off the castle walls. "Excellent! Now, Pan says…"

There was a hushed silence in the room. Everyone waited.

"Bounce on one foot!" Pan roared.

Everyone stood straight and began hopping on one foot. A couple of people lost their balance.

"Out!" Pan shouted. "Everyone who fell, Pan says get out of my castle!"

Several people hung their heads in disappointment, heading for the doors.

Pan let out a gleeful, childish laugh, then lowered a hand to his lengthy, engorged manhood, and began slow, rhythmic movements. He spread his legs and his amber gaze penetrated Jezzy as he pleasured himself. "Pan says... do the Macarena!"

Somewhere from the back of the stage, Macarena music swelled into the air.

Thank goodness Jezzy had just been at a wedding where they played the Macarena song every twenty minutes. Every drunken idiot there had requested it. She went through the movements of the Macarena dance, careful not to look at anyone else, as someone was sure to throw her off.

"You! You! YOU! And YOU! BUSTED!" Pan's finger pointed again to the unfortunates who had messed up the dance. Pan threw his head back and laughed. "OUT!" He bellowed. "Get the hell out of my castle! And don't come back! Until tomorrow night!" He shook his head. "I love that dance." He chuckled. "It's good to be a prince."

Jezzy closed her eyes and continued doing the Macarena. This was truly bizarre! But at least he wasn't demanding that they do the Hokey Pokey.

"Everyone do the Hokey Pokey!" Pan bellowed.

Jezzy almost did, then remembered, he hadn't said, 'Pan says'. But a few people began dancing the Hokey Pokey.

Once again, Pan screamed and pointed and threw people out. He then giggled and wiped his eyes. "This is way too much fun!"

His eyes scanned the crowd, then he said, "Pan says... watch me pleasure myself."

Jezzy's eyes moved over Pan's rippling torso, to his strong arm moving up and down as he stroked his member, little grunts coming from deep in his throat.

Erotic, supernatural energy rushed through Jezzy as she watched the massive prince bringing himself closer and closer to releasing. His pleasure becoming her pleasure. She had never known such a connection, such a desire to want to please someone else. Realization wrapped with her own desire. Jezzy realized with a kind of surprise, that stepping outside of herself and delighting in the pleasure of others was a turn-on.

Mutual affection was one thing. Mutual appreciation was something even nicer.

"Very good," Pan said, his arm moving more swiftly. His golden eyes continued to bore through her, seeming to see straight into her. "Pan says, pleasure yourself."

Jezzy had forgotten about the people behind her. She gazed, hypnotized, into the Prince's eyes, and slid a finger over her swollen, needy pearl.

"Yes," Pan said, stroking himself faster.

A tiny prickle of heat began deep within her walls, swelling into excruciating pleasure.

"Pan says... don't come."

Jezzy let out a small cry. She'd almost let go! She lifted her finger from her delicate bud, quivering with the need to release.

"Very, very good."

Just then, a few orgasmic cries sounded in the room.

Pan tilted his head, looking disappointed. "You know the drill. Out!"

Barely finished with their orgasms, several men and women headed for the door.

"Now, only Jezebel," the Prince said. "Pan says, continue to pleasure yourself. Place a finger on your sweet spot and make little circles for me."

Jezzy did as she was told. She once again slid her finger over her clit and began making little circles.

"Pan says, gently twirl your nipple with the other hand. But remember—Pan says don't come yet." Pan lifted his pelvis slightly, as if preparing to come himself.

This aroused Jezebel greatly, and when she moved her fingers to her nipple and began to twirl the sensitive, rosy nub, she felt that she couldn't hold off much longer. She was certain to be tossed from the castle.

She watched Pan's eyes narrow with arousal as he watched her, tugging at his privates faster and faster.

Watching him was making her even more excited. She wasn't going to be able to stop herself. And she didn't want to be kicked out of the castle.

No one had said there were rules about talking, so she said to the prince, "Oh, please. Let me come."

"Pan says no."

"Prince, I can't stop myself. I... I... can't..."

Jezzy closed her eyes and tried to disconnect from her body, to think unsexy thoughts. But all that came into her head was an image of Pan, stroking himself.

"I'm... going to come," she whimpered.

"Pan says not yet."

"Then please, I beg you, let me stop touching myself."

"Pan says not yet."

Jezebel began to scream. Not in pleasure, but in frustration. Her body was betraying her. She had completely lost control. And much as she wanted to stay at this lovely party, there was no way she could stop herself now. She opened her eyes, her mouth forming an O, her breath coming out in ragged gasps as the biggest orgasm of her life was about to overtake her.

"Pan says come," he grunted, spilling his seed over his rapidly moving hand. He threw his head back and bellowed, bucking his hips upward.

Jezzy's inner walls contracted as her orgasm pulsed through her. She screamed, a tidal wave of pleasure rushing over her, only vaguely aware that invisible hands held her in place. Jezzy cried out again and again, watching as bursts of light exploded before her eyes. She was sent to a place in ecstasy she had never been. She felt her eyelids squeezing in time with her spasms, going on and on and on until she couldn't tell if it was multiple or just one, long, delicious, never-ending orgasm.

"Pan says stop touching yourself."

Relieved, Jezebel let her hands drop off her body. She let out a deep breath, feeling so weak that she could have gone to sleep right there on stage. Then a roar came from the crowd, and Jezebel realized it was people cheering and applauding.

"Give it to her!"

"Fuck her hard, Pan!"

"Give us a good show!"

Jezzy felt herself being lifted by the twins and lowered over Pan's lap. She was shocked that he hadn't lost his erection. If anything, his manhood seemed even harder.

The head of his enormous, steely length touched the opening of her quivering pussy. The anticipation was too much. Her delighted clit peeked out from beneath her folds, hungry for more stimulation. Her womanhood begged to be filled. She wanted to be impaled upon Pan, fucked long and hard, even as she wondered if she could take all of him inside.

Pan lifted Jezzy and effortlessly turned her around, so that she was facing the crowd. Everyone stood watching her, as she sat, legs spread over each of Pan's tree trunk thighs. Pan positioned her so that her steamy mound lay against his waiting member. Her clit pushed toward it, wanting attention. Jezzy's lips parted and her lids closed half-way as the prince pushed her hips forward and began a slow, erotic gyration of his hips, moving himself against her clit.

She moaned as Pan's movements created a glorious friction, which sent shivery little jolts of pleasure against her sweet spot. Any thought of controlling the show of her arousal in front of the crowd was gone.

As the crowd watched her, they began seeking pleasure of their own. Several openly stroked themselves, groaning and grunting their passion. Women dropped to their knees, spreading the labia of waiting, eager females whose hips were pushed forward in anticipation of enthusiastic tongues.

Men sucked the raging erections of other men, or pumped hips into their jutting bottoms. Women sat atop moaning men, bobbing up and down in an increasingly frenzied pace as they watched Jezzy's mounting arousal.

Jezzy watched the tangle of various sexual positions. Heat raced up her body and tension balled in her loins. She ached to have Pan's stiff, enormous rod sliding inside. She heard herself whimper from far away, and tightened her thighs against Pan's.

"As you wish, pretty Jezebel," he said, slowly penetrating her.

Jezzy gasped, his manhood filling her completely, stretching her and resting up against the mouth of her cervix. She felt herself quiver and fresh heat washed over her. The prince lifted her slowly until his tip was barely inside, then pushed her gently back down, filling her, moving his hips in a divinely slow pace.

He adjusted his hips, and his rigid member curved and pressed up against a spot so sensitive, deep inside, that her eyes rolled back in ecstasy. Pan's hips made small, gentle thrusts, massaging that spot, and Jezzy cried out again and again, the sensations swirling through her.

Pan snapped his fingers. Startled, Jezzy's eyes shot open. But he did not cease his relentless movements. Through a fog of desire, Jezzy saw Nerah and Peony being lifted onto the stage. Pan's hands moved from Jezzy's hips and she saw them, large and strong, gesture to her breasts.

Nerah and Peony knelt on either side of them and each began kissing and licking Jezzy's breasts, nibbling and sucking her nipples. She felt a delicate finger slide over her soft, honeyed folds, and find her most sensitive spot. The finger moved, making quick, soft little circles over her protruding, swollen bud, and Jezzy tried to move her hips forward to move against it.

Jezzy rode Pan's magnificent manhood, ever more urgent. Her walls trembled, and she felt another orgasm bulleting forward, her need for release reaching a fever pitch. Then Pan thrust upward and forward, the sensation so sublimely exquisite, that Jezebel's orgasm crashed through her with the violence of a tsunami.

As she let go, Pan thrust upward and pulled her hips down, so that he was impossibly deep within her. The last contractions of her orgasm rippled over his pulsing cock, and he roared into the sex charged air, the sound unearthly.

Jezzy was lifted from Pan and placed on a red, velvet sofa, which seemed made especially for sex. It sat higher off the ground than an average sofa, as high as a table, making it the perfect height for most men to reach with their hips.

"I understand that you are in search of someone who appreciates you, pretty Jezebel," Pan's voice melted over her, making her skin prickle with new, awakening arousal. "Let us see who does."

Jezzy lay back on the sofa, turning her head to see the masked figure of a man climbing onto the stage. As he approached, Jezzy observed with interest the considerable height of the man. He was long and lean, his muscles defined and sinewy. The sandalwood scented oil on his body shone in the flickering firelight. His penis was short and thick, and jutted upward, toward his belly.

Jezzy awaited his entry into her hot, wet cavern, but the man didn't stop. Instead, he walked past her and stood over her head, as if waiting for something.

"Blindfold her," Pan said. "We shall see if she knows true appreciation by feel."

Nerah walked over to the man, a red blindfold in her hand, and smiled at Jezzy. She handed the blindfold to him and kneeled next to her. Peony appeared on her other side. She leaned in and whispered in Jezzy's ear. "This will be fun."

"With your eyes covered, your other senses will become more acute," Pan said. "Would you like to be restrained also? Some especially enjoy the restraints."

"Oooh, yes," Nerah cooed. "Accept the restraints. They make it so much more delicious. You have no choice but to focus on the sensations. It's perfectly lovely."

"I love the restraints," Peony agreed.

"Yes," Jezzy replied. "I'd like the restraints, please."

"Very well," Pan responded.

The blindfold was placed over Jezzy's eyes, and then her hips were pulled toward the edge of the sofa. Her feet were placed in stirrups, which spread her legs wide. Her hands were tied with what felt like velvet straps, fastening them tightly to the sofa. Another strap was buckled across her belly, making all but her smallest movements impossible.

"Oh, my."

"Don't worry," Nerah said, flicking her tongue over Jezzy's earlobe as she whispered. "You'll love it."

"O-okay."

"Let the test begin," Pan bellowed.

Moments later, Jezzy felt Nerah and Peony's lips around each of her nipples, and their playful sucking and nibbling renewed the fire within her. She felt fresh wetness between her legs, and her lips opened as she tried in vain to move her hips forward, searching for something to touch her.

Then something warm was pushing against the mouth of her womanly cave.

"Oh, yes," Jezzy murmured. "Please."

The eager thing slid into her, and Jezzy lifted her pelvis to accept it.

"Yes, yes," she whispered.

The mystery man plunged into her, using long, determined strokes, his pubic bone hitting her hungry clit with each one. His slippery cock hit her g-spot expertly, and continued thrusting into her, his hands on her hips.

Jezzy heard his grunting, and the sound impassioned her further, making her moan and whimper. She didn't know what he looked like, but he felt heavenly inside of her. He moved faster, back and forth, in and out, making Jezzy moan louder and louder as her desire built. Her nipples sang where Peony and Nerah sucked and licked them, nibbling and then flicking their tongues over them again and again.

The hard, swollen member inside of her grew bigger and harder, and Jezzy's head whipped deliriously from side to side as her pleasure hovered, suspended for what seemed an eternity.

"Enough," Pan's voice said. "Next."

Jezzy almost cried as she felt the unsatisfied rod being withdrawn.

She whimpered, "No, please! Don't stop! You haven't come!"

"Someone else will bring him to release," Pan said.

"Was I not good enough?" Jezzy said, her voice growing thick in her tightening throat. She was surprised to find that she was genuinely disappointed that the man hadn't had an orgasm with her.

"You were," Pan replied. "You are. But there are other eager men, waiting to have their turn with you. You are changing, transforming. Do you feel it, Jezebel?"

"Feel what?" she breathed.

"You're becoming unselfish."

It was such a strange observation, especially when she was so turned on. But it hit Jezebel right in the core of her being. She *was* selfish. It was always about what men could do for her, not what she could do in return. But she had really wanted to make that last man come, to reward him for the pleasure he'd given her.

She had appreciated him.

"I understand," she said. "Where is the next man?"

Pan's laughter shook through her. "Perhaps you need a little more practice."

"Yes. I want to… to please someone else."

Within moments another hard member was pressing at her opening, and then sliding up into her wetness. Jezzy moved her hips forward, her sizzling pussy eager for it, but her soul also eager to satisfy another person.

Her walls clenched over the long, slender manhood inside of her, grasping, unwilling to let it go. As the unseen man plunged into her, he moaned, sending shivers of delight through Jezzy's entire body. Her tingling bud responded, swelling and aching, but she focused on using her muscles to stroke him, milk him, make him feel good.

"You *do* understand," Pan said.

Jezzy felt the hair fall over her belly and hot mound. Then soft, sensuous lips were around her clit, sucking lightly. Jezzy's body quivered, as a deft tongue licked and flicked over her sweet spot with feather light movements.

The rigid shaft pushed deeper and deeper inside of her, and her bare nipple suddenly felt another mouth upon it, and another tongue swirling around it, making Jezzy arch her back and lift her chest as far as her restraints would let her. The man's cries grew loud, and Jezzy felt a wave of heat as her orgasm built once again.

"Please, please let him come," she moaned. "Please... let... me... "

"Stop," Pan's voice called out. "Next suitor, approach."

"No! Please!" Jezzy cried, and she felt her blindfold grow damp with her tears. She pulled against the restraints. She screamed out in anger and frustration.

"Now, now, Jezebel. Have you quite finished your tantrum?" Pan's voice cooed, syrupy against her ears.

Jezzy's bottom lip protruded in a pout. "Yes."

"Excellent. Then let's continue, shall we?" His voice was light with amusement.

Jezzy lay on the sofa, panting, her breaths ragged from her outburst. "But why won't you let me make the man come?"

A cry of pleasure erupted behind her.

"He just got a blowjob," Nerah's voice said from just over her pussy, and Jezzy felt her own juices dripping from what must've been Nerah's chin, onto her belly. "So did the last guy. He's just quieter when he climaxes."

"Uuuggghhh!" Jezzy yelled.

But then another engorged, considerable dick was gliding into her opening and pushing deep. Jezzy sighed, the feeling so wonderful that she seemed to be floating. The mouths on her nipples continued their work, and Nerah's mouth and tongue resumed her playful assault on Jezzy's most sensitive place.

Each stroke of the man's hips sent bursts of electric pleasure through Jezzy. Tension balled in her loins, and her walls squeezed around the mystery man's relentless thrusts. His hard shaft pushed her further and further toward oblivion. A prickle of burning heat began deep in her wet channel, and within seconds her pussy ignited and clutched at his driving thrusts. Her orgasm teetered on the brink, all it would take is one more stroke, one more lick, one more nibble—

"Stop!" cried Pan. "Enough!"

"No! Not enough!" Jezzy insisted.

But no one else was called forward to pleasure her. Even the mouths of the mermaids were gone. Jezzy was left in the dark, behind the blindfold.

"You've been an excellent student, Jezebel. But you've some learning left to do."

Jezzy lay on the table, still restrained, still blindfolded. Her entire body quivered with unreleased need and frustration.

Suddenly the blindfold was removed, and she blinked her eyes against the firelight. The twins, Michael and Lance, released her restraints. Jezzy was disappointed. She felt slightly abandoned. She sat up, her head hanging, looking at the floor.

"Now, now. Don't be so downhearted," said Pan. "I have much to show you." With that, he clapped his hands. "Bring me the golden hen."

Chapter 5

Jezebel Makes a Promise

A tall, lean woman with long, shining chestnut hair was lifted to the stage holding a cage. Within the cage was a hen, golden from head to toe. Jezzy had never seen any creature like it. The hen blinked at Jezzy, unimpressed.

"Thank you, Kiki," Pan said.

The lean woman nodded.

"What is that?" Jezzy asked. "I don't care who you are, or how much learning I need to do, or how big of a penis that thing has. I will not have sex with a bird."

Pan shook his head, chuckling. "Now you're just being silly."

"About not having sex with the bird?" Jezzy said. "Because I won't."

"The very idea of it." Pan waved his hand, dismissing the line of conversation. "Let's move on."

"How big of a penis does that bird have?" Jezzy asked.

"It doesn't. It's a female. Can you stop talking about sex with the bird, please? It's making me uncomfortable." Pan turned to Kiki. "You may step down."

Kiki exited the stage with the help of the twins. Then the three of them began to make out.

Jezzy looked on with jealousy. She wanted just ten minutes with those two. Even five minutes, with just one.

"Focus, Jezebel." Pan gestured to the bird in the cage. "This is a golden hen, which lays golden eggs."

"I hope I can use them to pay someone to satisfy me, because I'm becoming very cranky." Jezzy crossed her arms.

"No, but you can use the eggs to satisfy you."

Jezzy stared at Pan. "I don't even know what to say to that."

"Nerah, would you demonstrate, please, on Jezebel?"

"With pleasure," Nerah said. She opened the cage and gently lifted the golden hen. "Ooooh my pretty Lenny. That's my sweet girl," she cooed, petting the hen's head.

The bird made a cooing sound back, rubbing her head under her palm.

Lenny? Jezzy thought. She sighed. *Just go with it. When in Phlegm...*

Nerah reached under Lenny's belly and rubbed her tummy. "You like that, don't you Lenny? Rub the belly? Who's a good bird? Hmm? Are you a good bird? Are you my gorgeous birdy?" She placed her palm under the bird's bottom area.

Suddenly Lenny squawked and laid a perfect golden egg into Nerah's waiting hand.

Jezzy felt her brows come together. This was the strangest thing she'd ever seen.

Nerah smiled at the egg in her hand, and brought her other hand beneath it to cup it. "Oh my. This one is certainly a jumpy one."

Jezzy stared at the egg in Nerah's hand as she approached. "Oh!" she cried, when she noticed that the egg was jumping and vibrating in Nerah's hands. "What kind of egg is that?"

"It's a magic pleasure egg," Pan replied. "This one is for you."

Cries came from the crowd below the stage.

"Yes!"

"Show her the egg!"

"Give her the egg!"

"Oooh, I want the egg!"

"Pleasure egg?" Jezzy asked.

"Yes. Nerah, show her how it works," Pan said.

"Lie back", Nerah said. Peony joined her.

"No, let her stand. Allow the audience to view her better," Pan said, his voice growing as thick as his enormous rod. He started to stroke. "Stand facing the audience, Jezebel."

Jezzy did as she was told. She stood up on shaky legs and walked to the middle of the stage, facing the crowd. "Like this?"

"Yes," he grunted.

"Spread your legs, Jezebel," Peony whispered into Jezzy's ear, her lips capturing her earlobe and sucking lightly. "You will like this."

"I'm not sure…" Jezzy was feeling nervous and exposed. Even though everyone in the room was basically naked, they were all focused on her. Some stroked themselves. Some licked their lips. Some stroked their neighbor and licked their own lips. Some … well, you get the idea.

And the egg was pretty bizarre, too.

"You've learned to appreciate your lovers," Pan said. "But you still need practice trusting them."

"Trust is essential," Peony said.

The crowd waited, silently, for Jezzy to make her decision.

"Okay," she said. "I'll trust you."

"Wonderful," breathed Peony, her hand sliding down Jezzy's belly and lightly playing over Jezzy's still slippery pleasure pearl. Desire ignited and surged through her body. She moaned softly, and she moved her legs further apart on the stage floor, her hips hitching forward to accept Peony's fingers.

Jezzy watched the crowd through half-lidded eyes. She felt their arousal heightening, an electric charge crackling in the air. She felt as if they were touching her too, with their gazes, their energy, their wanton desire.

The sensation of Nerah placing something warm and hard up against her slick opening blended with the rest, the object undulating and vibrating, sending delicious sensations trilling through her.

The magic golden egg.

"Aaaahh," Jezzy groaned. She no longer cared what the object was. Just that it was placed inside of her. Her need had grown so strong that she only wanted release.

The egg vibrated and jumped as Nerah slid it high into her hot, swollen cave. The egg drilled at her walls, and wiggled and vibrated higher, then lower again, finding her G-spot as if it knew exactly where it was.

But then, it must. It was magic, after all.

Jezzy rocked her hips, feeling the magic egg pulsing and jittering deep inside. Peony's fingers made gentle swirls over her slick nub, creating delectable ripples of bliss.

"Ooooh, my," Jezzy murmured, her voice husky with heat.

Peony moved aside, her fingers leaving Jezzy's needy clit and her mouth abandoning her nipple. Jezzy felt the absence of her touch as a loss, and felt her lip quiver, even as her arousal built. "Where are you going?"

Peony was holding out her hand, and Nerah, who still gripped the chicken, passed another, slightly smaller golden egg to her sister.

"Now turn around, Jezebel," Pan said.

"For what?"

"We're placing this one in your bottom."

Jezzy had never done anything related to anal before. She thought it was kind of gross and dirty.

"I don't want to," she said, shaking her head.

"You'll love it," said Peony.

"I've got one in me right now," said Nerah.

"I don't know…"

"Watch," Peony said. She bent over in front of Jezzy, then placed the tip of the egg against her own bottom. She slowly slipped it inside her, stretching herself open until the egg disappeared. Peony grunted, then moaned, as she stood up again. The look on her face was one of obvious arousal.

"Does it… does it hurt?" Jezzy asked. Her knees felt liquid, the buzzing against her G-spot making it hard to remain standing.

Peony shook her head, then closed her eyes. Her body began to shake, and Jezzy realized the mermaid was having an orgasm.

Or maybe it was an assgasm?

"You have to trust us, Jezebel," Nerah said. She was holding another golden egg. "Trust means trying new things. Breaking boundaries while understanding that you're safe."

Jezebel glanced at Pan, who was stroking himself even faster.

"It will feel good, Jezebel," Pan said. "It will also turn me on."

The egg in her pussy was making it impossible to think clearly, but she knew, deep down, that trust was even more important than mutual affection and appreciation.

"I'll try it. But if I don't like it…"

"Then we'll remove it immediately," Pan said. "If you don't like it, just say so."

Jezebel nodded nervously, then bent over, so far she could see Peony approach between her legs. From her upside-down view, she saw Peony had the egg, which twitched and vibrated with a low humming sound.

"You have to relax your muscles," Peony said.

Jezzy did the opposite, squeezing tight. But when she tensed up her rear muscles, she also tensed her pelvic muscles, which increased the already-intense vibrations of the egg nuzzling her G-spot. Jezzy began to tremble from pleasure, and

then she had four strong hands on her legs and buttocks, stroking and massaging. The bodybuilder twins, rubbing in more
oil.

"You need plenty of lube," Michael said, as he rubbed
her gently between her legs, starting at her pussy and moving
backward until his large finger tickled her *there*.

And it felt okay.

Actually, it felt good.

And as Michael continued to massage oil on her, it began
to feel *really really* good. She hadn't ever realized how many
nerve endings there were in that particular area, and when they
were being tickled and stroked, it was an entirely new sensation for her.

Jezzy relaxed, luxuriating in his touch, welcoming it.
Lance moved from her legs to her breasts, rolling her nipples
in his strong, oily fingers.

"Can I slip my finger inside you?" Michael asked.

"Sure, of course you... oh!" Jezzy gasped.

She'd assumed Michael had meant inside her pussy, but
he'd taken the other entrance. It felt very odd, but it didn't hurt
at all.

"Is that okay?" he asked.

"I... yes. It's okay."

"Is it more than okay?" Pan was leering at her, continuing
to stroke himself.

"Well... I... I suppose it is."

"Can I move my finger in and out?" Michael asked.

Jezzy placed her hands on the floor for support, and nodded. Michael's thick finger began to move, and the thought of
such a large guy being so gentle with her, so obviously concerned, was as much of a turn-on as the sensations he was
creating.

"When you're ready, Peony has lubed up the egg," Michael said. "But only when you're ready."

Jezzy nodded, closing her eyes, feeling him slowly slide in and out of her. That motion, combined with her nipples being lightly pinched, and the egg inside of her, were all blending together in a marvelous way, like different sections of an orchestra.

"I'm ready," Jezebel surprised herself by saying. "I trust you."

She opened her eyes and watched Peony approach. When Michael removed his finger, Jezebel felt empty, and she missed it. But then the tip of the egg pressed against her, warm and buzzing, and began to slowly stretch her open.

"I'm… I'm going to come…" she wailed.

"Not yet," Pan said. "Wait until it's in all the way."

Jezebel felt herself being stretched wider, and wider, until it was almost uncomfortable.

"It's in!" Pan said, clapping his hands.

"Stand up, Jezebel. Just concentrate on the pleasure you're feeling." Peony's voice was sweet and encouraging.

Within seconds, Jezzy couldn't concentrate on anything else. She closed her eyes. She'd almost forgotten the crowd, but now she listened to the moans and cries of mounting pleasure and release in their moans and murmurs. And as she did so, the undulations of the magic eggs seemed to grow in intensity. She'd never felt so *full*. Tiny flames licked at her wet walls and burned against her G-spot. And the other egg—the one she'd been worried about—made the ecstasy even more intense. It was so intense she began to cry out, her voice rising with each passing moment.

Her knees began to buckle as her pleasure crescendoed.

"No, stand up, Jezebel. You are so beautiful to watch," Pan said, his voice strained, his own release imminent. "Let them watch you."

Lance and Michael appeared at her sides and lifted her, helping her stand.

The orgasm began deep and high; a tiny prick, twisting and igniting and bursting. Her insides squeezed and clenched, and her orgasm spread, spasms clenching every muscle as Jezzy screamed. The orgasm went on and on, and she barely noticed the two men holding her up for the audience as she came and came.

And came and came and came.

Finally, as her orgasm faded, she opened her eyes to the crowd, who were at various stages of any number of mind-bending acts. Jezzy blinked her eyes, and tried to stand. Her body was spent.

For the moment.

As she was held by the twins, the eggs inside her stopped vibrating, as if they knew she was sated. A second later, waiters carried out platters of food and refreshments and set them on a long, seemingly endless banquet table. Pitchers of wine, water and juice arrived, along with several different cheeses, fruits and crackers. There were also sweet treats. Cakes and cookies, and chocolates.

Lots of chocolates.

Jezzy realized she was famished.

"Yes, Jezebel. Eat," Pan said. "You'll need your energy." His smile was positively wicked.

Jezzy reclined on a black, silky love-seat and allowed a stocky, sun-burnished man to feed her grapes. He stopped, filled her goblet with wine, and held it to her lips.

"You were outstanding. I've never seen anything like you. You're exquisite, Jezebel."

"Thank you," Jezzy said, and was awed to find that she was blushing. She'd just had sex with several men and two women in front of countless people, and a mere compliment was making her blush. "What is your name?"

"Don't you remember? From the restaurant."

Jezzy blinked and realized who it was. The facial features where the same, but she hadn't recognized him because he wasn't wearing his waiter outfit. Instead, he was naked, his muscular body looked like it had been cut from marble, his impressive manhood stiff, with a slight upturn.

"Jack!" Jezzy squealed. "You gave me the beans!"

"Indeed I did."

"Thank you so much for that."

"You're very welcome."

"Did my miserable blind date, Chet, give you a good tip?"

"I don't know. I think he's still there, talking as if you hadn't left. Something about *Love in the Time of Cholera*."

Jezzy laughed. Chet had moved on from Russian literature to Columbian.

"Well, perhaps I can tip you later," Jezzy said, and winked. The wine, which she was drinking rather quickly, was making her feel warm and floaty. "Does Pan give every new person lessons?"

"Not every new person. I think he likes you. I know he thinks that you're special."

Jezzy smiled. She wanted to feel special. It's what she'd always wanted. Perhaps that was the cause of her selfishness in the first place. It was like a craving for her, the need to feel special. Wasn't every girl like that?

Jack fed her little chunks of cheese on small, herbed wafers. The food was delicious. Jezzy was beginning to feel like she never wanted to leave the castle.

"Does anyone live here with Pan?"

"Just his servants."

"Maybe I could be a servant. I like it here."

Jack threw his head back and laughed, his dark, wavy ringlets fell away from his forehead. "You'll never be one of Pan's servants."

"Why not?" Jezzy prickled, feeling suddenly blustery.

"Because you're too extraordinary. He likes you front and center. In the limelight. Not scurrying quietly about, trying not to be seen. That will never be you."

Jezzy considered this as she watched Jack pick up a pine-apple chunk from a fruit plate.

"Do you find adequate sex partners at every one of Pan's parties? Partners who satisfy you?"

"I'm satisfied by satisfying my partners. But I can't come."

Jezzy was stunned. "You don't come? You don't want to have an orgasm?"

"I'd love to be able to orgasm. However, a terrible, wicked witch named Lucinda put a curse on me. I can get an erection, but I cannot orgasm. I can't feel any pleasure at all down there."

"Oh, no!" Jezzy whispered, mortified. Her heart went out to Jack. "That must be horrible. Whatever did you do to deserve such a punishment?"

"I made love to her daughters." Jack grinned. "All three of them. They were triplets. Absolutely adorable. I simply had to have them."

Jezzy giggled. Her head buzzing pleasantly. Then she frowned. "Still, that's quite a curse for what seems to be a very minor infraction. The witch was that protective of her girls?"

"No. She was that jealous." He smiled at her, his skin taking on a reddish hue. "I was supposed to take her on a date. When I arrived at her house, she wasn't home. But her daughters were, and when she finally arrived it got ugly."

"I'm sorry about that, Jack."

"It's my burden." He shrugged. "At least I can still get it up. But enough about me. How about you? You seem to be enjoying your stay in Phlegm."

"I am. I've had a very good time, and I've also learned a lot."

"About what?"

"About affection, and appreciation, and trust. I'm also discovering, while I'm here, that I'm rather selfish. I've been on so many terrible dates, but part of the blame is mine. No one can please me. It's a terrible affliction." She made her expression as serious as possible. "I don't know if I can be fixed."

"I don't know if I can fix you, Jezebel, but I know that I could please you."

"You are pleasing me right now," Jezzy said, leaning forward. "Maybe I could please you. Maybe, if the right woman were to come along…"

Jack looked suddenly sad. "No, my sweet. It's nothing to do with you. You're beautiful and sexy in every way. But this curse, it's unbreakable."

Jezzy frowned. "Nothing is unbreakable. There must be a way."

"If there is a way, I haven't yet found it," Jack said. "I've fucked for days straight. I've tried every position, every type of sex. Pills, potions, toys. I can stay hard as a rock, but I don't feel anything. No one can help me, I'm afraid."

"Did you apologize to the witch?"

"Of course. Candy. Flowers. Greeting cards. I even wrote her a poem."

"Really?" Jezebel loved poetry. "Can I hear it?"

Jack cleared his throat, then recited:

"I'm really, very sorry.
Let's have sex tomorry."

Jezzy frowned. "I can see why that didn't work."

"Actually it did. We made love the next day for fifteen straight hours. But she still didn't lift the curse."

"You sure she's a witch?" Jezzy asked. "Sounds more like a bitch."

"I suggested she go to counseling. That probably didn't help matters."

"No, probably not."

"So I wrote her another poem."

Jezzy opened her mouth to stop him, but he was already reciting.

"You're really hot, Lucinda,

I spy on you through the winda."

"Just ... no."

He heaved a great sigh. Even his erection might have drooped a millimeter or so. "She's never going to lift this curse, and I'm afraid there isn't anything anyone can do about it."

Jezzy narrowed her eyes. One thing she couldn't bear was to be told she couldn't do something.

"May I at least try?"

"It will just frustrate us both. But I'd be happy to make love to you. I'd enjoy that, even if I have no feeling down there. I really do enjoy making women come."

Jezebel almost agreed, but the thought of her having multiple orgasms and Jack feeling nothing at all seemed incredibly selfish. Instead, she lowered her head and took his erect member into her mouth.

She sucked.

She licked.

She stroked.

He stood there, stoic, not making a sound. Jezebel realized it was very frustrating to be trying your best and getting no reaction.

Jack patted her head. "Don't blame yourself, Jezebel. I can tell you're very good. But the curse…"

She'd never seen an erect man so sad before.

"I, my dear friend Jack, will find a way to break this curse. This, I pledge to you," she said, buoyed by her resolve. "Now tell me where I can find this witch."

～❦ Chapter 6 ❦～

Jezebel Begins Her Quest

After bidding goodbye to Pan and her new friends (and promising she'd return as soon as she could), Jezebel left the castle and headed west for the much-feared Ghastlibad Forest.

"Is it called Ghastlibad because it is both ghastly and bad?" Jezzy had asked him.

"No. It was named after an ogre," Jack had said. "Artemis Forest."

Ghastlibad Forest turned out to be rather pleasant, with plenty of colorful trees all shaped like large cocks, and beds of small, bulbous mushrooms shaped like small cocks, and curved bushes shaped like Wilfred Brimley's mustache.

There were also other bushes, shaped like cocks.

Jack had wanted to go with her, but Jezzy had insisted on going alone. She didn't want any help, because she wanted this to be a fully unselfish act. Jezebel was going to break Jack's curse, no matter how many orgasms she had to have to do so.

Eventually she came upon a lovely stone bridge spanning a creek, and as she began to cross she heard the most beautiful singing voice. A tenor, lifting high above the trees. It was a song of happiness and of loss, of the celebration of the rising sun and of sorrow when it set, of the yearning in the hearts of those who dare, and the pity for those who never try. All sung to the tune of *Ram It Up* by the thrash metal band Stormtroopers of Death.

Jezzy stood on the bridge, and when the song ended she applauded politely, even though she had no idea who or where the singer was. In this magic kingdom it could have been the trees singing, or some strange invisible creature, or even the bridge itself.

"Who is applauding?" the voice said.

"My name is Jezebel. Where are you?"

"I'm under the bridge."

Jezzy leaned over the side, looking to the ravine below. "What are you doing under there?"

"I'm talking to you. Duh."

"I mean why are you under the bridge at all? Are you a troll?"

"Why would you say something mean like that?"

"I'm sorry… I'm new to this land, and from where I come from, I've heard stories about trolls who live under bridges."

"That's a prejudiced stereotype. There are all manner of creatures who live under bridges."

"Which manner of creature are you?"

"I'm a troll."

Jezebel frowned. "So you start flame wars on website forums to cause trouble?"

"That's an Internet troll. I'm a real troll. With warts and boils and covered with patches of hair. That's why I live under the bridge. I'm far too hideous to lay eyes on, so I hide here. My name is Eden."

"I've heard that trolls eat maidens. Is that true, Eden?"

"That's another stereotype. It's bad enough being ugly and having to live under a bridge, but when people continue to perpetrate bigotry like that, it hurts."

Jezebel felt her heart break. "I'm so sorry, Eden."

"Ever since I was turned into a troll by the wicked witch, Lucinda, I've been so very lonely."

"You were cursed by Lucinda, too? I'm looking for her."

"Why? She's most disagreeable."

"She cursed a friend of mine."

"She curses a lot of people. She is a witch, after all."

"Why did she turn you into a troll, Eden?"

"Because I wouldn't bed her. And now I'm condemned to live under this bridge until some fair maiden makes love to me."

It had been several pages since Jezebel had been in a sex scene, plus she was working on being less selfish, so she boldly stated, "I'll make love to you, Eden."

She heard the troll sigh. "You aren't the first maiden to say that. But they can never go through with it. I'm too terrible-looking."

"I can close my eyes. Or use a blindfold." Jezzy had enjoyed the blindfold at Pan's castle.

"That won't work. For the curse to be lifted, the woman has to respect me. That means keeping her eyes open, and not sleeping with me out of pity."

Jezebel had pity sex in the past. More times than she'd publicly admit. Bad blind dates that ended up with a sympathy blowjob. Unattractive men who had crushes on her in college. A beer too many at a party which led to quick and unfeeling sex in the coat room. Jezzy hadn't respected any of those men. And afterward, she hadn't respected herself. It hadn't been the noble self-sacrifice she'd hoped it to be, and while her partners had gotten off, Jezebel didn't feel they'd respected her, either. They'd gotten what they wanted and didn't care that she'd gone unsatisfied.

"Maybe if we get to know each other for a bit," Jezebel said. "We can learn how to respect each other. I really enjoyed your singing."

"So did other maidens. But my signing isn't enough. Once they see me, they no longer find me worthy. If I have no dignity, how can I expect anyone to respect me? Which is why I eat women."

Jezzy gasped. "You *do* eat women!"

"Sometimes, for hours," Eden said.

"That's atrocious!"

"I'll lick and suck and nibble on them, and I can even make some of them come. But they still don't respect me."

Jezzy blew out a breath. "So that's what you mean. I thought you meant really eat, like a snack."

Eden laughed, and it was musical. "That's ridiculous! And disgusting!"

"I'm so pleased to hear that."

"Everyone knows that trolls eat live goats."

Jezebel made a face.

"Kidding!" Eden quickly said. "Mostly we eat porridge. I have a pot of porridge, if you're hungry. It's nine days old, but some like it that way."

"Thank you, but I just ate. I think you should come out, so I can see you."

"I'd rather not."

"If you want me to respect you, you have to respect yourself, Eden. Be confident. Women love confidence."

"It's difficult to be confident when you look like a toad covered in dried vomit."

"Talk like that isn't making me want to sleep with you."

Another heavy sigh. "Very well, then."

Jezebel looked to the other side of the bridge, and a lumbering figure scaled the bank and stood before her.

Ugh. He *did* look like a toad covered in dried vomit. Boils and scabs and warts and other assorted bumps were everywhere, and he had more hair sprouting from his ears than most men had on their entire head.

But Jezebel was determined to see past that. Beauty was more than skin deep. If this was going to be more than just pity sex, she needed to respect Eden. That meant finding something about him she admired, rather than pitied.

"Wow," he said. "You're so beautiful, Jezebel. May I eat you?"

Jezebel almost winced, but held it in. The idea of that ugly face between her legs didn't turn her on one bit.

"Not right now, thank you," she said. His sad face became sadder. "But there is something I would like, if you don't mind."

"Of course, maiden Jezebel." He performed a theatrical bow. "I'm at your service."

"Can you sing me another song? You have such a beautiful voice."

"Certainly. I can sing about you if you'd like."

"About me?"

"Sure. I got mad freestyling skills."

Eden began to sing, a cross between the forlorn poetry of Jim Morrison and the electric intensity of Meatloaf. He sang of Jezzy's kindness, and selflessness, and beauty, and it hit her like an axe to her heart. For the first time ever, she understood why girls swooned over boy bands, and why groupies banged rock stars. It was such an intimate, intense, and arousing experience to be serenaded, that midway into the song, Jezebel got down on her knees and reached for Eden's pants, undoing the rope he used as a belt, pushing his tattered pants down to his ankles.

Happily, his cock wasn't covered with boils or warts like the rest of him was. In fact, it was quite nice. Long and heavy, it had a fat glans that she really wanted to swirl her tongue over.

Patience.

Jezzy started with her fingertips, skimming up the insides of his legs, from knee to thigh to hip.

Goosebumps broke out over his skin. He flexed, growing a little fatter, a little longer.

His voice changed, growing deeper and picking up an Isaac Hayes vibe.

Heat kindled between Jezzy's legs. Extending two fingers, she swiped the bottom of his sack, then up his underside, lifting his shaft, bringing her face close. His skin was velvety smooth to the touch, and before she reached the head, she curled her fingers around him, his thickness growing and pulsing with life.

"And now she's got her hand on my cock," he sang, voice deep and soulful, "and has made me hard as a rock."

When she reached his ridge, she stopped, then let each finger fall on the underside as if she was playing a piano. Tat-tat-tat-tat. Tat-tat-tat-tat. Soft and slow, in time with his singing.

He kept growing, kept hardening under her touch. As ugly as the rest of his body might be, his erection was beautiful. Strong. Thick. Responsive. And pointing straight up to the sky.

"Oh, my," Jezebel cooed, her exclamations sounding like the stylings of a backup singer.

She brought her face closer. For a troll who lived under a bridge, he smelled quite nice. Earthy and musky. But with a touch of something else. She breathed deeply.

"It's Axe body spray for trolls," he said, reading her mind. "Woodland Sexventure. I like it more than Funky Swampass."

"Keep singing."

"She's a dirty little whore," he continued, "who makes me beg for more."

Jezebel loved being sung to, but even more than that, she got really turned on when men talked dirty to her. It was somewhat shameful and embarrassing, but maybe that was part of the allure. Being called a slut and a naughty girl, and told in explicit detail how hot they thought she was and what they wanted to do to her, could really get Jezzy off when she was in the mood for it.

And she was *definitely* in the mood.

Jezzy grasped him at the root and stroked all the way to his tip. Then she licked her hand and stroked him, making his shaft slick, friction warming it up by several degrees as she pumped up and down.

"Sing *dirty* to me," she said.

He complied. He sang he wanted to lick her slit, suck her clit.

That she was a filthy skank, giving his cock a yank.

That she knows how to lick it, and he knew where to stick it.

That she needed to be fucked fast and hard, from behind.

That line didn't rhyme, but it was still a turn-on.

Jezebel stroked him faster, and then she gasped. Her whole body had begun to vibrate. The magic golden eggs still inside her apparently could sense she was heating up, and they began to buzz.

She ran her tongue along his length, just the tip, flicking and teasing, wanting to be the dirty girl he sang about, wanting to make him come all over her face and tits. She put her lips on his head, lightly raking her teeth across his foreskin.

"Please oh please oh please suck it…" he crooned.

Jezebel opened her mouth and took him inside, loving the feeling of his manhood, loving how his singing suddenly went up an octave, wanting to suck him deep into her throat.

Eden sang that her mouth was liquid silk, that he was ready to blow his load, that she was such a good little cocksucker.

Then she withdrew, her lips moving against the head of his erection, nibbling, slipping in a little swipe of her tongue.

"Beg for more." She blew lightly over him, taking tiny licks at the little slit in its center. He tasted salty, a hint of what was to come.

"Please. I'm begging you. You're a goddess. You make me feel so good. I'm going to spurt. You're going to make me spurt."

When he'd groveled enough, and she was so hot she couldn't bear to tease him any longer, she slipped him inside her mouth and took him deep into her throat. Then, his length glistening, she fitted him between her breasts, cupping them close, capturing his cock between her two surging mounds.

Rising on her knees, she stroked upwards, the feathers of her party dress skimming against his sensitive skin. Her nipples tingled, hardening to points, and rasped against his rough belly, the sensation deliciously painful and pleasurable at the same time. His tip sank between her tits, then she moved down his length, and broke from her flesh, surging free.

All this sinking and surging was really getting Jezzy hot. Not only was she wet (really, when was she *not* wet in this story?) she was empty and aching and she didn't know why.

Actually, she did.

"Do you want me to sit on your face?"

"Yes, please, oh god…"

She looked up at him, his troll features contorted in ecstasy, and Jezzy didn't find him hideous at all.

She found him dirty. A filthy man whore. An uncontrollable animal. The realization that she was about to get eaten out by a dirty, filthy troll was so hot that she practically came just thinking about it.

Suddenly she was being lifted up, her legs spread over the troll's wicked face.

She bent forward in a sixty-nine, her lips devouring his hard length. She moved her mouth up and down Eden's rod, using her tongue to torture him with long, luxurious licks. Then she tugged on his balls with one hand, while gripping his shaft with the other. She moved her lips up and down over the head of his cock, sucking and licking, his cries urging her on.

"Are you a dirty troll?" she asked.

"Yes."

"Does the dirty troll like getting sucked?"

"Yes. He also likes eating pussy."

Eden began with feather light licks to her hot, swollen bud, which strained forward, seeking his tongue. He then brought his mouth up and sucked her clit between his lips, between his teeth, and nibbled gently.

Jezebel moaned over his member, bobbing her head faster, and rocking her hips against his face. She made little pleasure sounds deep in her throat as she sucked on him, "mmmmph, mmmmph, mmmmph."

Eden pumped his hips upward, thrusting his manhood into her mouth. Jezzy relaxed her throat muscles and took him in deeper, swallowing him and releasing, swallowing and releasing.

"Oooooh Jezebel!"

"Mmmmmph," she replied, pumping her own hips downward more urgently. "Mmmmmph!"

Jezebel screamed in her throat, her mouth moving faster than ever over his dick as she came. Her body quivering and quaking in a glorious explosion of pleasure.

Eden thrust twice more and his own orgasm spilled into her mouth. Jezzy swallowed his hot seed, sucking even harder, seeking out every last drop as her own orgasm began to wane.

Eden lay on his back, his hands on her hips, gasping as if he'd just run a marathon. "Sweet Jupiter," he breathed. "That was simply magnificent. Thank you, Jezebel."

Jezzy rolled over onto the grass beside him, her breaths coming raggedly as she came down from her own release. "Outstanding, indeed. Thank you. I quite enjoyed that."

After a few moments of staring at the sky to collect herself, Jezzy glanced at Eden.

But the troll was gone.

Instead she was looking at a handsome young man with blonde hair and nary a blemish on his nearly perfect body. "Eden, you ... you've changed."

Eden stared at his hairless, wartless hands, then touched his strong jaw, chiseled cheekbones, and flowing hair. His eyes widened. "You did it, Jezebel! You broke the curse!"

"I respected and admired your singing," she said. "And dirty talk really gets me going. Oh, and your cock is way hot."

"So it wasn't pity sex. It was genuine."

"It sure was."

"What about you, lovely Jezebel? Still plan to go to the abode of the wicked witch Lucinda?"

"I do. I promised a friend that I'd do whatever it took to break the curse on him."

"Is this your boyfriend?" Eden asked.

"No, just a friend."

"Wow. What a selfless act," Eden said. "You're a very unselfish woman, Jezzy."

"Believe me, it's new. I'm not sure if it'll stick."

"Well, because you helped to break the curse Lucinda put on me, I owe you a favor. I'll help you obtain the potion that undoes curses."

"There is a potion?"

"Yes, of course. For every curse, there is a potion to cure it."

"Why didn't you take a potion to cure yourself?" Jezebel asked, incredulous.

"What's the fun in that?" Eden said. "That sixty-nine we just did was a lot better than a potion, wasn't it?"

"It was nice. But you seemed so sad and miserable as a troll."

"Being a troll wasn't so bad, really. I could eat porridge all day and never gain a pound. People avoided me, so I didn't have to endure boring social events. And, this may sound strange, but I kind of liked all those scabs. Maybe I could get Lucinda to curse me again."

"That doesn't sound wise," Jezebel said. "The man I'm helping, he can get hard but has no feeling in his penis and can't come."

"Sounds awful. But there's worse. I saw one fellow turned into a parrot. Horrible!"

"Why was he turned into a parrot?" Jezebel asked.

"Because Lucinda caught him peeking in her windows while yanking on himself. Now he must watch her have sex or pleasure herself from his cage."

"Why didn't he just ask her out? Knock on the door?"

"That's not his kink. He's a voyeur. So I suppose he got what he wanted. I wonder what it feels like to molt."

"Are you sure you want to take this risk, helping me?"

He reached over and caressed her cheek. "Of course."

Jezebel's eyes misted over. "Thank you, Eden."

He stood and pulled his pants up his long, muscular legs. Then he cinched the rope belt around his tight abs. "Let's get on our way. It will be dark soon, and we don't want to be in Ghastlibad Forest at night."

Chapter 7

Jezebel Meets Ollie and Lucinda

As they drew deeper and deeper into the woods, the sky seemed to grow darker. Jezebel had the creepy feeling that they were being watched.

"How far is this place?" she asked Eden. "It seems like we've been on this twisty path forever."

Suddenly a flapping of wings sounded above them. Eden and Jezzy looked up, then fell backwards onto their butts.

Robin Goodfellow, the puck, flew down in front of them.

"Not you again," Eden said. "Haven't you done enough?"

"Not nearly, apparently," Robin said, crossing his arms over his chest. "Jezebel, what are you doing with this troll?"

"He's not a troll anymore. Besides, the only reason he ever was one in the first place was that wicked witch. She turned him into a troll because he spurned her advances."

Robin snorted and eyed Eden. "Is that what he said?"

"Yes." Jezzy eyed Eden. "You told me the truth, right?"

"Mostly," Eden said, his face scrunching up.

Robin rolled his eyes. "He and the witch have a thing for each other. He was turned into a troll for spurning her advances, that is true. But only because he had sex with all three of her daughters first, and he was too tired to get it up."

Jezzy looked at Eden aghast. "Is there a man around the beanstalk world who hasn't had sex with the witch's daughters?"

"Not likely," Robin said. "They are quite frisky. Dirty, dirty girls." His lips spread in a lecherous grin.

"And how would you know that?" Jezebel asked him, lifting her chin.

"I paid a visit to Lucinda's daughters. We had a pleasant ménage."

"Why hasn't she turned you into a parrot or a troll?" Jezebel asked.

"Because then I took one for the team and nailed Lucinda as well. In gratitude, she turned me into a puck. I quite like this form. I do get far more than my fair share of ass, I must say."

Jezzy sighed. "And I've had far more than my fair share of bullshit for one day, from the two of you. Enough. Are you going to help me get what I need to break my friend Jack's curse, or not?" Jezzy said, hands on feathered hips.

"Jack?" Robin said. "You are actually risking yourself for that dweeb?"

"He most certainly is not a dweeb. He's a very sweet, kind man, which is more than I can say about either of you two," Jezzy said. "On second thought, I don't need your help, either of you. I'll face the wicked witch on my own."

"Good luck with that," Robin said, and with a sweep of his hand, Jezzy's feather dress and mask were gone, and she was entirely naked. All that remained were the tie up shoes. "You can keep the shoes. I really love those on you. Now I have to go. I have another date."

"Ugh! It's a good thing this is a fairytale, or I'd be seriously worried about my health after having had sex with you, you man-whore!" Jezzy heaved a disgusted sigh and continued up the winding path. Robin's laughter following.

Before long, Eden caught up with her. "Wait. You really can't go there alone, Jezzy. It is dangerous."

"What do you care? You deceived me to get me to blow you!"

"Oh, come on. All guys do that."

Jezzy hesitated. "Good point. Okay, you can help me. But no more lies, fibs, tall tales or untruths."

"Those are all pretty much the same thing, but okay."

After a little while, the witch's cabin came into view. Dark, gnarled trees hung over the house, and a black cat lay on the front porch. Another, smaller cabin sat behind the first.

"Whose house in that one?" Jezebel asked.

"The triplets'. It's like a guest house. They are very comfortable there. Pretty decked out."

The smell of wood smoke filled the air, and smoke from a recent fire still billowed from Lucinda's chimney. Several bats flew out of the chimney and into the sky.

They approached Lucinda's abode and peeked through the windows. The rooms were dark with the ever gathering night, and they could see nothing but silhouettes of furniture.

"We're in luck. The witch and her daughters aren't back from gathering herbs for her potions. If she was here, we'd see her, dressed in a corset and wearing spike heeled boots. Sometimes she even likes to carry a whip."

She sounded kind of frightening, yet the way Eden described her, he seemed kind of excited.

"What does she do with the whip?" Jezzy asked.

"Ohh," he said, his eyes bright. "What *doesn't* she do with the whip!" He stared into the mist, and if she wasn't mistaken, his bulge seemed to be growing in his tattered pants.

"Ahh, okay," Jezzy said. "How do we get in?"

"Who goes there?" a deep voice intoned.

Jezebel started. "Oh my! Who is that?" she whispered to Eden.

"It's the door knob." Eden said, climbing the stairs.

"The what?"

"The door knob, silly." He took her hand and led her to the door. "Look."

A face made of wood regarded them with a stern look, the knob itself forming the face's nose. "Who goes there?"

Jezzy stared, dumbfounded. "I—I—"

"Eden. The witch's favorite troll. Please allow us entry, you knob, for we have brought herbs for her potions."

"I see no herbs."

Eden leaned over and whispered into Jezzy's ear. "He's onto us. You might have to do him."

"Do him?" Could he be saying what she thought he was saying? "You want me to have sex with a door knob?"

"He's the right height. Think of him as a glory hole."

"A glory hole?"

"A hole in a wall where a guy sticks his … never mind. Just bend over and back into him."

Jezebel frowned. This land of Phlegm was truly ridiculous. But since she'd promised to help Jack, and since she was still pretty wet from her tryst with Eden, she might as well give it a try.

She turned around, bent over, her breasts swaying, and pushed her bottom against the doorknob. "Is this really necessary?"

Eden laughed. "No. The door is unlocked."

"Eden!" she gave him a smack on the arm.

"It was hot. Keep going. I'd love to see you take him inside."

"That would be awesome," the doorknob agreed.

"Well, it isn't going to happen," Jezzy said. She stood up, trying to look annoyed, but she had to admit, the cool brass had felt pretty good.

Phlegm must be getting to her.

"How about a blowjob?" said the doorknob. "Think you could get your mouth around me?"

"She probably could," Eden said. "I speak from experience."

"Eden!" another smack.

"I've got a cousin who is a trailer hitch," the doorknob said. "You'd be surprised how often some bimbo sucks the chrome off of him. But me? Nothing."

"Don't people have their hands on you all day, twisting and tugging?" Jezzy asked.

"Oh, yeessssss." The knob shuddered. "It's wonderful."

Jezebel placed her hand on him and gave him a few twists while he moaned. Just for good measure, she rubbed her breasts against him, the cold making her nipples peak, and then they entered the witch's dark abode.

"We need light," Eden said. "Stay here."

He found wood next to the fireplace and placed two pieces on the dying embers. Within moments the flames came to life. The fire threw just enough light to see into the kitchen.

Jezzy waited next to the door, shivering. Outside, the door knob's chill had felt good. Now she was growing downright chilly. It was kind of fun being totally naked again, but she wished she still had her feather dress to keep her warm. She longed to stand next to a fire and warm herself.

"Dirty bitch!" A shrill voice shrieked within the room.

Jezebel jumped. "Heavens!"

"Dirty bitch!" The voice cried again.

Being called a dirty bitch was quite a turn on when she was already aroused. But when she was cold and uncomfortable, it was simply offensive.

"Look," Jezebel said into the dimly lit room. "I don't know who you are, but you're exceedingly rude."

"Yes, he is," Eden said, coming up beside her and rubbing his hands together. "That is Ollie. Lucinda's parrot. The one I told you about earlier."

"He just called me a dirty bitch," Jezebel said, indignant.

"He wants you to come closer, so he can get a good look at you. He's a voyeur, remember?" Eden walked to a corner of the room, where a large cage sat on a tall pole.

Jezzy followed, suddenly very conscious of the parrot watching the way her breasts swayed when she walked, the hardness of her nipples in the chill, the wetness glistening between her legs. She reached the parrot, his beady eyes devouring every inch of her.

"You are a very dirty bird." Jezzy said.

"Dirty bird!" Ollie shrieked, and bobbed his little blonde head up and down. "Dirty bird!"

Jezebel turned and scanned the room. "So tell me, dirty bird. Where does the witch keep her potions?"

"I'll break my parrot dick off in your ass!" Ollie cried.

Jezebel placed a hand on her forehead. "WTF?"

"Yes, he is a pervert. And not a lot of help. Just try to ignore him," Eden said to the right of her in the gloom. "I found some bottles."

"Shake those tits for me, baby!" Ollie screamed. "Let's see those puppies swing!"

"Oh, my God. Seriously?" Jezebel said. At first, the voyeurism was kind of hot. Now, with all these stupid comments, it was just ridiculous. "Why does she keep this thing?"

"Because she likes being watched," Eden said.

"If she likes being watched, why did she turn him into a parrot to begin with? Why not just let him watch through the window?"

"She likes foul birds," Eden said. "But then, all birds are foul. Get it? Like fowl spelled f-o-u-l?"

"Show Ollie the pink!" the parrot croaked. "Show Ollie the pink!"

"Maybe if you show him he'll shut up," Eden suggested.

"I'm not exposing myself to a bird. It's degrading."

"You're already kind of exposed."

She glanced down at her bare breasts. "I suppose you're right."

"Besides, your body is so hot."

And although Jezzy was still kind of annoyed with Eden for not telling her the whole truth about his experience with the witch, having this gorgeous man calling her hot was helping make up for the rude parrot.

"Bend over, tootsie! I got a dollar!"

Ollie, indeed, did have some cash in his beak.

"If I bend over, will you shut up?"

Ollie did that nodding thing that parrots do, his head bobbing up and down.

Jezzy sighed and bent over.

"Spread them wide! Spread them wide!"

"This is turning me on," Eden said.

Jezzy had heard of bird watching, but never of a bird who watched. She gave her hips a little wiggle, sending her breasts bouncing, and felt something drop onto her back.

The money. Ollie had tipped her.

"Change for a five! Change for a five!"

"I hate this bird," Jezzy said. "Let's get back to business."

Eden sighed.

Jezzie scanned through the assortment of bottles. "Okay. Let's see. What might cure not being unable to come?"

"Can't come? Eat a plum!" Ollie screamed. "Can't come? Eat a plum!"

"Would you stop that idiotic babbling, Ollie!" Eden shouted at the bird.

"Wait!" Jezzy said, spotting a bowl of huge, dark purple plums. They were the largest plums she had ever seen. "Ollie, do you mean these plums?"

"Dirty bitch!"

"Come on, Ollie, just tell me," Jezzy said.

"Only one way to find out," Eden said. He took a small bite of a plum. "Mmmmm."

"What are you doing?" Jezebel cried. "What if they're poisoned?"

"They're delicious! Try one!" Eden took a larger bite, and juice dribbled down his chin. "Mmmmm. Most scrumptious plum I've ever tasted. She must inject potion into these. What does Lucinda put in these, Ollie?"

"Can't miss with cat piss!" Ollie shrieked. "Can't miss with cat piss!"

Jezzy shook her head. "Sometimes, you just don't want to know."

Eden licked his lips and took another bite. "I don't care what's in them. They are sweet and succulent. She must add honey and slow cook them or something."

Jezebel looked down at Eden's member, hard and straining at the fly of his tattered pants. "Oh, my."

Eden grinned. "Come here, Jezzy."

She had to admit, she was tempted. Except for a brief brush with a doorknob, she hadn't had sex in quite some time. But the thought of the lecherous bird watching wasn't quite what she had in mind. Why couldn't the damn thing say something sexy?

The thud of footsteps sounded on the porch. Jezzy gasped. "The witch! She's here! Hide!" She scrambled under the table and crouched behind a chair.

The door opened, but Eden didn't move. Well, most of him didn't. His hand was moving just fine, stroking his member through his pants.

A woman with black, shaggy hair stepped into the house and froze. She wore a leather corset that hugged her narrow waist and lifted her generous, and very bare, breasts. Taking in Eden, her mouth dropped open. Her gaze fell to his hand, and a grin crossed her darkly gorgeous face. Then she turned and called out the door. "Go back to your own house, girls. I'm tired."

Footsteps on the stairs, and the girl's voices and mischievous giggles sound through the air, then faded as they moved away from the house.

Jezebel held her breath.

"Well, what do we have here?" Lucinda said, an obscene smile crossing her strawberry lips. "It's my old friend, Eden. And no longer a hideous troll."

Eden didn't say anything, but a moan breached his lips.

"You look so delicious, Eden. I've missed you. However did you manage to break the spell?"

Jezebel quaked in fear beneath the table. If Lucinda saw her under there, she would definitely be cursed. Perhaps turned into a parrot, or a troll, or a doorknob, or who knew what? Her mind spun dizzily, trying to find a way to get out from under the table, steal a plum, and then escape the wicked witch's cabin.

"How did you turn back into this gorgeous piece of man-meat, hmm?" she asked again.

Jezzy strained her ears to hear how Eden would answer.

"Love," he said.

"Love?"

"I... love you, Lucinda. I think I always have."

The witch cackled. "You don't love me. You're just afraid of me."

"Not true! The first thing I thought of when I realized that your curse was broken, lovely Lucinda, was that you're the one I want to make love to. Your wild hair. Your spikey nipples. Your vicious whip. You're the one I've always wanted. And now I want you more than ever!"

Yes! Jezzy smiled. *Keep going.*

"Really?"

"I've been a naughty, naughty boy. Just look at how turned-on I am," he said.

Jezebel watched in horror as Lucinda's spiked heeled boots approached the table.

"I've always been fond of this table, Eden. I've fantasized about you taking me on it, many times."

"Dirty bitch!" Jezzy heard Ollie squawk. "Under the table!"

Jezzy's heart drilled against her ribcage. *Shut up you idiot bird!*

"No, Ollie. Not under the table. You won't be able to see us. I want Eden to give it to me on top of the table."

Jezebel clenched her teeth and prayed that Lucinda wouldn't find her. That blasted bird kept screeching, "Dirty Bitch! Under the table!"

"Oh, shut up, you nitwit! I'm busy." Lucinda leaned a hip on the edge of the table, her long legs spread. Looking up from her hiding place, Jezzy could see the witch wore no panties. And that she was neatly shaved and very wet.

"Come here, you bad boy."

Eden slowly approached.

"What are you afraid of, hotsuff? That I'll curse you again if you don't perform to my satisfaction?"

"It has crossed my mind," he said.

"Well, then. You'd better perform to my satisfaction. Lift me onto the table."

"Yes, Mistress." Eden did as she said, his powerful legs and straining fly right in front of Jezzie.

Lucinda's delicate hands came into view and untied the rope holding up Eden's pants. The tattered garment fell to the floor, revealing his erection. Then suddenly he cried out, and milky liquid spurted on the floor in front of Jezebel.

"That wasn't good, Eden. Not good at all." Lucinda's voice was edged with rage.

"Forgive me, lovely Lucinda. You are so beautiful, I couldn't help it!"

"Come here."

Eden moved closer to Lucinda, his pants around his knees. His limp member simply hung, as if asleep.

Now they'd be found out for sure!

Jezzy bit her bottom lip, thinking of what she could possibly do.

"Lucinda," Eden said. "Let me pleasure you, first. You are so beautiful, I'm certain that your taste will arouse me again. I'm overwhelmed and… Intimated by your loveliness."

"Excellent idea, Eden. But then, you'd better be ready. Or I'll be forced to turn you into a Porta-Potty."

"A Porta-Potty?"

"No pressure," the witch said, cackling.

Eden knelt so that his face was between Lucinda's legs, and close enough to see Jezebel hiding in the shadows beneath the table. "I'm sorry," he mouthed to her. His eyes were round with fear.

Wait!

Jezzy had an idea! An inspired idea! An inspired and pretty damn hot idea!

She quietly crawled forward. Gesturing with her hand for Eden to begin his work on Lucinda, she leaned in and took Eden into her mouth.

He responded immediately, hardening, growing. A moan of desire came from his throat as Jezebel moved her mouth over his shaft, taking him deep down into her throat and coming back up, sucking the head of his manhood, then circling it with her tongue.

"Mmmmmmm," Eden murmured. "Mmmmmmm."

"Suck it! Suck it!" Ollie opined.

"Ooooh yes," Lucinda moaned. "You obviously like my taste, Eden. I'm pleased." Her voice was throaty with arousal.

Jezebel continued, licking, sucking, now fingering his balls, gently kneading as she worked his steely length. Her body flushed with erotic excitement, and her abdomen tightened with tension. Jezzy felt herself grow wet, and she moved one finger over her sweet spot, swirling her finger as tiny bursts of pleasure shot through her belly. Almost cried out, then remembered Lucinda, who was moaning loudly on the table above her.

She wanted Eden inside of her so badly! She ached for it. Perhaps just for a minute. She was sure it wouldn't take her longer, so aroused was she. She felt like she could come any second.

She pulled her mouth away, and felt Eden's manhood thrust against her lips, chasing her mouth. Turning around, she positioned herself on all fours and backed into him as she'd done to the doorknob. Only this time, she tilted her hips up, opening herself, pushing at his stiff rod.

Still working Lucinda with his mouth, Eden thrust his hips forward, sheathing himself in Jezzy.

She tightened around him, feeling him slide to the hilt. She was so excited, so wet.

Eden began a slow thrust, and Jezzy used her elbows to prop herself up, matching him stroke for stroke as she moved her hips in time with his. She arched her back, her nipples grazing the floor. His balls slapped her with each hard thrust. The position made the magic eggs go into overdrive, and Jezzy felt herself quivering with the beginnings of an orgasm. Eden's manhood rubbed over it, and he shuddered and hardened inside of her.

"Oh!" Eden moaned, his words muffled. "Oh that's fantastic!"

"Yes! I am fantastic!" Lucinda's cries became louder. "I want you inside me!"

Oh no! Jezzy moved her hips faster, focusing on the sensations and feeling her hot, slick channel tightening with the first orgasmic contraction. The pleasure was blinding, and she bit her lip to keep from screaming. Spasms moved through her and her body flushed with heat.

"Now, Eden!" Lucinda cried. "Or I swear you'll be the newest toilet at Lollapalooza!"

Eden pulled out of Jezzy, who was still enjoying the last pulsations of her pleasure. She watched from underneath as he stood, his erection long and swinging and glistening with her juices. He grasped Lucinda's hips and shoved his full length into her. Lucinda's legs encircled his waist and her cries became one long scream.

Now! Grab the plum and get out of here before they finish! Jezzy thought. She moved to the other side of the table, then crept out from beneath it.

The bowl of plums was right next to Lucinda's head.

Eden watched her with panicked eyes. He reached out and grasped Lucinda's hands and yanked her into a sitting position.

"Hey!" she yelled. "I was really close, you dimwit!"

"I want to see your beautiful face up close as you release, Lucinda."

"Ooooh. Well, then. That's just fine."

Eden gestured urgently at Jezzy from behind Lucidna's back.

Jezzy wasted no time. She snatched a plum, then ducked beneath the table.

"On second thought," she heard Eden say. "I want to see your gorgeous back. I want to take you from behind, like an animal." He let out a growl.

Lucinda giggled. "Eden, you are a wild, dirty dog!"

"Dirty dog! Dirty dog!" yelled Ollie.

Jezzy waited as Lucinda's feet came down upon the floor and faced her. Eden's feet came around Lucinda's and his legs bent as he slipped into place and jammed his shaft home.

"Ooooh yeeeessss!" Lucinda cried. "Yeeeesss!"

Jezzy snuck out from beneath the table once more, passing Lucinda and Eden's legs. Gripping the plum in her hand and hoping that Lucinda wouldn't turn around, she quietly tip-toed to the door.

She turned back toward Eden, who nodded at her, his expression ecstatic.

"Did you like being a troll?" Lucinda said.

"Yes, Lucinda."

"Call me Mistress."

"Yes, Mistress!"

"When we're done I'm going to turn you into a goat. A horny goat."

"Thank you, Mistress."

"Do you really love me?"

"I love you, Mistress."

Jezebel studied his face, his excitement at sex with Lucinda plain as day, and realized he might actually be telling the truth.

And why wouldn't he be? How many wrong guys had Jezzy fallen in love with? Apparently Eden and Lucida had some sort of S/m thing going on. Maybe this was a game they'd been playing for a long time.

She thought about that for a moment. All her life Jezzy had been searching for love. And she had loved men. But it hadn't been enough. Love alone didn't make for a good relationship.

But if there was more than love, if there was also mutual affection and appreciation and trust and respect, and if she could stop being so selfish, so needy, and instead find fulfillment meeting the needs of another, and trust him to do the same for her, then maybe she could find her happy ever after.

It was certainly something to think about.

Jezebel crept out the door to the sound of Ollie shrieking "Give it to her! Give it to her!"

As Jezzy made her way past the cottage, she noticed three young women, identical to one another, heading down a path toward a stream. Each was shaped like an hourglass, with pumpkin orange ringlets framing apple cheeks and beatific smiles. Robin Goodfellow was lounging on an old, fallen tree, stroking his enormous manhood, wearing nothing but a grin. The girls giggled as they approached him, their dimpled bottoms jiggling merrily.

Robin spotted her and winked, beckoning her to join them.

Jezzy smiled and shook her head and continued into the trees. She'd had enough excitement for a little while. But Jack was right. The triplets were adorable!

Chapter 8

Back at Pan's Castle

Jezzy was certain that she was lost. She'd doubled back the way she'd come, following the twisty vine back through the woods, but she was terrible with direction, and when she'd come to a three pronged fork in the road, she'd chosen the one to the furthest right. On the corner of that road sat a sign which said, "Shortcut to Pan's castle."

"Well, that certainly makes things easier," she said. "Thank goodness."

Jezzy followed the path over the moat and to the steps in front of the castle. Lance and Michael were back at their posts on either side of the door, grinning happily.

"Jezebel," Michael said. "Pan awaits. You flew out of the castle so quickly, he wondered if you would be returning."

"There was something I needed to do," Jezzy replied.

"Go on in, Lance said. Pan will be thrilled that you're back. He's been on the verge of tears since you left."

Jezzy blinked. "Really? Wow."

"Everyone has missed you. Including my brother and me."

Michael nodded. "But you look different, Jezebel."

"Robin took back his feather dress. He's kind of a dick."

"I meant you look more confident. More at ease," Michael said.

Lance nodded. "Like you've found a sense of purpose."

"Well, I suppose I have. You can really tell?"

The twins nodded. "You were beautiful before. But now you're absolutely radiant. Please, come inside."

They opened the door and Jezebel stepped into the castle. A soaring, delightful sound was coming from Pan's Syrinx, and as she entered the ball room, Jezebel was greeted with the welcoming sight of an orgy in progress.

When Pan's amber gaze caught sight of Jezebel, he smiled and called out to her.

"Jezebel! Welcome back!"

Jezebel was pleased to see him again, but she also anxiously began to scan the crowd for Jack.

"Come here, dear girl. You are positively glowing. Where were you?"

"I needed to go to witch Lucinda's house to get the antidote to break the curse on Jack. You know about his... condition, I assume?"

The great Prince lowered his horned head. "I do. And were you successful in your quest?"

"I was," Jezebel responded.

"Ah. I'm impressed, Jezebel. You ventured to the wicked witch's house, putting aside your fears and throwing yourself into danger for the sake of someone else. You've shown that you are an unselfish person and lover."

Jezebel smiled. "Thank you. It's been enlightening."

"Well, this is a fairytale, so why don't you beat the readers over the head with the moral of the story?"

"I'm afraid I don't have one yet. I've learned that I mustn't be so selfish, and that a good relationship requires mutual understanding and patience. Both partners must be loving, trusting, and caring, and they must appreciate and respect one another."

"Wow," Pan said. "And you found all of that out in just seventy pages, in between all of those lengthy smut scenes?"

Jezzy nodded.

"But you said you haven't found the moral yet."

Much as she liked talking to Pan, and being in his company (even though at that moment it was a bit placating), she really needed to keep her promise and help Jack.

"Well, the story isn't quite over," Pan said when she didn't respond. "So until then, I grant you one wish. Anything you like. Do you have a wish?"

"I do," Jezebel answered.

Pan tilted his head to the side. "And what is that, pretty Jezebel?"

"I want for you to turn Syrinx back into a mermaid so that she can go back to the moat, where she belongs."

Pan's eyes widened in surprise, and his mouth dropped open. "But my Syrinx, it's what I use to bring people happiness and arousal."

"You can do that with any instrument. Happiness and arousal comes from within. You've taught me that yourself, Pan. You know this to be true. You need to let go of your self-ishness and release Syrinx back to her sisters."

Pan lowered his horned head and thought for a long moment. "Very well." He snapped his fingers and the Syrinx vanished, replaced by a lovely, red haired mermaid sitting on his lap.

"Syrinx, you are beautiful," Pan said, a tear slipping from his eye.

She slapped Pan's face, hard. "You are a very naughty prince!"

He nodded. "Indeed I am."

A sly smile crossed the lips of the mermaid. She gently caressed the prince's cheek where she'd slapped him. "But I like it. I have needs that I demand you see to."

Pan grinned. "Of course."

"Allow me to blow you for a while, my prince."

She immediately began to devour Pan's engorged member.

Jezebel turned toward the crowd and searched for Jack, and then found him at the back of the room, a gentle smile on his face.

Jezebel felt her heart swell. It was a feeling unlike anything she'd ever known before. It was more than affection or trust or respect or even love.

It's need. I need him.

She turned around, lifting her arms into the air, and fell backwards into the crowd. A multitude of hands and arms broke her fall, and began moving her from the stage toward Jack.

When she finally reached Jack, the hands set her down in front of him. She held out the plum before Jack and said, "I just want you to know that if this plum doesn't work, I'll still keep my promise. I'm not going to give up on you, ever."

"No one has ever gone to such lengths for me, Jezebel." His eyes became glassy. "I love you."

"But do you need me?" she said, hopeful.

Because that was indeed the moral of the story. Two people could like each other, respect each other, trust each other, and love each other. But it was only when they needed each other that the relationship could truly work.

"Yes, I do, Jezebel. I need you."

"Oh, Jack."

"I need you like the trees need the sunshine, and fish need water, and deer need salt licks, and—"

"Just shut up and take a bite," Jezebel said.

She held the plum to his lips, and Jack scowled. "Smells like cat piss."

"But it works!" Jezzy said. "Now take a bite!"

Jack hesitated, then plugged his nose with one hand and brought the plum to his mouth with the other. He took a large bite.

"Mmmmm," he said, juice dribbling down his chin. "It's delicious!"

Jezebel watched as his erection grew.

"It's working!" he said. "I can feel again!"

Jack threw the plum aside and pushed Jezebel up against a wall, lifting her bottom high as she wrapped her legs around his waist. "Ooooh. Jack!"

She cried out as he entered her, sliding in deep. "Oooh my!"

Jack hiked Jezzy higher up on the wall, and ground against her mound as he thrust into her. He moved painfully slowly, pausing to grind erotic, delicious circles onto her wet pussy, and then moving up and down, dipping his pelvis upward with fast, bullet-like movements.

Jezebel felt like she was in heaven, and she looked deep into Jack's eyes and captured his lips in a long, dreamy kiss. His tongue explored her mouth as he gazed back at her, locking her in the moment with him. She moved her hands over his back as he thrust into her, then slowed and pressed his pubic bone against her clit, his cock dancing inside her.

She locked her ankles more tightly together and squeezed her eyes shut as the climax began shivering within her.

"Look at me, Jezebel," he grunted. "What do you see?"

Jezzy searched Jack's eyes. "I see a man who loves me."

"Yes," he whispered. "And do you know what I see?"

"What," Jezzy heard herself say, as if from far away. The sensations were taking over, and it was hard for her to hold off much longer. "What do you see?"

"I see a woman who loves herself," Jack said, and smiled.

Realization dawned on Jezzy just as her orgasm began taking over her body. Yes! That had been it along. She loved herself enough to be able to love others, and allow others to actually love her back.

Selfishness was not self-love. It was blindness.

Now she could see! For the first time in her life, she felt love and felt loved.

And boy, did she love feeling loved. Her body shuddered and she quivered against Jack as a blinding orgasm sang through her. Every cell came alive, and she felt as if she were bursting. As she rode the climax, she saw Jerry, the mischievous forest imp, thrusting into Peony on the stage. She was on all fours, her head bobbing on Robin, who stood before her. Nerah was restrained on the velvet sofa, enjoying one in a line of suitors awaiting their turn.

In fact, everyone was engaged in some kind of sexual play.

Except for Pan, who sat back on his throne, finally looking utterly and completely spent, his erection at half-mast.

"I'm not done with you yet, Pan!" Syrinx said, standing on his arm rests and grinding her pelvis into his face. "Play me!"

He did, and Syrinx began to moan, eerily similar to when she was a flute. It enraptured the crowd.

As Jack plunged upward, his body stiffening as he screamed out, Jezzy felt another orgasm sweep over her. They held each other tightly, and Jezzy felt as if she were melting into Jack. He pushed deeper and deeper into her as he moaned into her mouth. Jezzy's climax was long and sweet, and so intense that for a moment she forgot her own name.

When they finally fell against each other, Jack still holding Jezebel up against the wall, she felt him smile against her shoulder. "That," he gasped, "was absolutely outstanding."

"Yes," Jezebel said. "But I think it's time to go."

Jack pulled away from her shoulder and his face was stricken when he looked at her. "You're leaving?"

"Yes," Jezebel said. "You're coming with me, right?"

Jack's face broke into a smile. "Of course. So what next? Moving in? Getting a joint bank account? Registering a China pattern at Macy's?"

"Let's play it by ear," Jezebel said.

Jack held her hand and they were walking to the exit when a booming voice bellowed, "PAN SAYS...!"

Jezzy and Jack stopped and looked at each other. Both grinned.

"Well, I suppose we can stay a little a while longer," Jezebel said. "After all, when in Phlegm..."

Part 2

Fifty Shades of Puss in Boots

Chapter 1

Little Jack Horner Isn't so Little Anymore...

J ack?" Jezebel stared open mouthed at her ex-boyfriend. When she'd hustled to the appointment this morning, Jezzy never dreamed she'd run into him. If she'd had even an inkling, she would have...

Would have what?

Lost ten pounds?

Bleached her hair blond?

Worn something sexier?

Jez was dressed in a mini skirt, but it matched her jacket and qualified as more professional than provocative. Her heels weren't as high as she remembered Jack liked, and her blouse fit loosely, not showing her ample breasts to their best advantage.

Had she known, Jezzy would have done *something* to gird her confidence. As it was, she was caught completely off guard. "What are you... I mean... you're my client?"

"The Bean King. Yeah." He gave her a smile. Same as ever with his strong chin, twinkling eyes, and perpetually amused expression, Jack looked good. Better than good. In fact, the outline of strong shoulders and tight abs under his white button-down was enough to make Jezzy's knees feel a little rubbery.

"I go by the name John for business," Jack continued, "which is probably why you didn't realize it was me. Although John Horner is pretty similar to Jack Horner."

"I thought the name was John Homer. I really need to talk to my assistant about his handwriting. I had no idea today's client was you."

"And I had no idea you're the force behind Playing With Matches. So you did it, huh? Started your own business? That's awesome, Jez."

His words felt good, but she was far too shocked to appreciate the praise fully. Jack had been the most attractive, most exciting, and most fun guy Jezzy had ever dated. For a while, she'd imagined they'd get married. But with her ambitious, entrepreneurial dreams and his laid-back happy-go-lucky charm, she'd felt they'd grown apart. After two years of hot romance interspersed with bitter fights, she'd called it quits.

"So you aren't waiting tables anymore, I see."

Jack laughed. "I've been lucky."

Jezzy glanced around his office. As big as her entire apartment, it was all leather and mahogany and soft, plush carpet. Luxury upon luxury. "Lucky? You're a millionaire!"

"Billionaire, actually. Millionaires are so 1980s."

"A billionaire. And that's nothing compared to putting an end to world hunger with those amazing giant beans of yours."

Jack beamed. "I have a new variety that will feed a family for a month. I'm also making a fortune with my side business; Whole House Air Fresheners. Six people under one roof eating nothing but beans can put a strain on the closest families."

Here the lazy boyfriend she'd believed wouldn't amount to anything was a huge success, and Jez was still struggling to get her matchmaking business off the ground. She felt inadequate, and she didn't like that feeling one bit.

"I guess you have everything you could possibly want."

"Not everything. That's why I called Playing With Matches. I have money. I have my philanthropy. I'm changing the world for the better. But I don't have anyone to share that world with. I want to find someone special, Jezzy. A wife. And the extra, uh, sexual guarantees your service makes really aroused my curiosity."

"You want your wife to also be your sexual soulmate."

"Just like your company's motto."

"Yes. *We'll find your sexual soulmate, so you won't have to masturbate.*"

"Cute. And it rhymes."

"We had another verse, with loner and boner, but it wasn't as catchy."

Jack leaned forward. "You can really do that? Find my sexual soulmate, I mean?"

"I can. Playing With Matches is a unique combination of dating service and sex therapy. Sometimes it takes a few tries, but my specially designed compatibility algorithm combined with my extensive, hands-on approach to sexual therapy qualifies me to—"

"Hands-on?" He arched his brows.

"I facilitate things between a couple. Make sure sexual communication is present from the very beginning of their relationship."

"You always were amazing in bed. Not that we were actually *in bed* very much." He grinned. "I'm sure you're really good at this job."

Jezzy could feel a flush moving up her neck. "Thank you."

"Which is why I'm sorry I can't use your service."

What?

For a moment, Jezzy just stared. He wasn't hiring her? "But isn't Big Cock Billionaire Magazine doing a cover story on your wife hunt?"

Big Cock Billionaire Magazine, as any reasonable person immersed in pop culture could expect, was the biggest publication in the world.

"Yes, a cover story. It will be part of the Prince Charming's Balls issue. The one featuring the big parties his father throws for him, and the prince's intimate grooming tips. There's a big one coming up, you know. A party, that is."

Jezzy knew all about the ball. She'd even received an invitation. Unfortunately she hadn't landed the job of finding Prince Charming a wife, his father instead insisting on inviting all eligible females to the ball and marrying his son off that night. A little backward, to be sure, but that kind of courtship was common in the land of fairytales. Love at first sight and rushed weddings led to happily ever after in these parts. It was the perfect place to be a matchmaker.

"I was really hoping to have found my wife before the ball. I know time is tight, seeing that the ball is tonight, but I'll just have to find another matchmaking service. Any recommendations?"

"Recommendations?"

He was kidding, wasn't he? Prince Charming was big in fairytale world, but Jack was the Bean King. And whoever landed the Bean King as a client would have not only exposure in Big Cock Billionaire Magazine, but probably television spots, a book deal, opportunities money couldn't buy. Playing With Matches would be a huge success overnight. Jezzy needed this job. And besides, Jack finding a mate without her input just felt wrong.

"You have to hire me, Jack."

Jack shook his head. "I don't think it will work. I'm afraid we have too much of a history."

"Too much of a—" Jezzy couldn't believe this. Everything hinged on her landing this client, and here her history with Jack was precisely the thing that would sink her? "Our history is an advantage. After all, who knows your sexual tastes better than I do?"

Jack stroked his chin, the sexy light stubble making a rasping sound against his fingertips. "I don't know, Jez. I have reservations."

"Tell me what they are. I'm sure I can waylay any worries you have. I'm great at this job, Jack. It's my calling. I will find you the woman of your dreams. I will make sure she knows how to kiss you, how to swirl her tongue around you, how to take you deep inside, and even do things you've never even dreamed about."

"Uh, I meant I have reservations for lunch. If you want to argue your case, you can dine with me."

The restaurant was within walking distance, a very up-scale place with linen table cloths, flowers, snooty waiters, and the crème-de-la-crème of society as guests. Jezzy allowed the waiter to swoop the white napkin across her lap, grateful she'd decided to wear a classy skirt and conservative blouse for the potential client interview instead of some of the more risqué outfits she saved for later sessions, just in case a little facilita-tion was needed.

After a waiter took their orders and brought them wine, Jezzy looked Jack straight in the eye, trying to think of him as just another client she was trying to help.

"How can I convince you our history won't get in the way of finding your perfect match?"

Jack took a slow sip of wine, studying her over the rim of his glass. "Show that I don't still turn you on."

"What?"

"Convince me you can control yourself in a stimulating situation, and I'll give you a chance to find me the perfect wife."

Jezzy fought to keep from rolling her eyes. "I can control myself, Jack. I'm a trained professional."

"Then prove it." He motioned to the waiter, and the man brought him a white box tied with a pink bow. Jack handed it to Jezzy. "Open it."

Curiosity growing, she slipped off the lid. Inside was a hunk of translucent pink rubber and shaped like a butterfly with four straps stretching from its wings. Only instead of six legs dotting its underside, this butterfly had a four inch rubber penis thrusting from its center.

Jezzy stared at the rubber butterfly. There was only one thing it could be. "A vibrator?"

"A remote controlled vibrator," Jack said, holding up something that resembled a key fob for his car.

Jezzy glanced around the posh restaurant. The older couple to their right whispered politely as they ate their soup with not even the hint of a slurp. The table of four, grayed businessmen drank martinis and discussed the stock market. A dowager and her daughter ate in silence behind them, the proper amount of disdain in their expressions. "And you want me to wear this? Here?"

"Yes. If you can remain professional throughout our lunch, I'll hire you to find me a wife."

Jez blushed. That scoundrel! Did he hope he could embarrass her? Was this payback for her breaking up with him? Well, maybe Jack had forgotten, but she was not one to back away from a challenge. And with the success of her business on the line, Jezzy would do whatever it took to make him her client.

"Piece of cake." She picked up the box, excused herself, and found the ladies' room. The bathroom attendant smiled at her and held the door open, glancing down at the box in her hand.

"Thanks," Jezzy squeaked, trying her best to hide the bright pink butterfly. Once safely inside the privacy of a stall, she lowered her silk thong, hiked up her skirt, and took the butterfly from the box.

The straps were easy enough to figure out, fitting around her hips and buttocks like a harness, and the vibrator itself...

She spread her thighs and fitted the dildo portion between her folds, swirling it around a little to moisten it with her juices. Then she slid it home.

The rubber shaft wasn't long, but it was thick enough to make her feel deliciously full, and the butterfly's head and antenna nuzzled her sensitive bud. She tightened the straps to keep it in place, then pulled up her thong, smoothed down her skirt, tipped the curious attendant, and returned to the dining room.

Jack watched her approach the table and sit, a sly grin spreading over his lips, the mischief in his eyes almost undoing her right there. "Ready to continue?"

"Ready," she said, not sure in the least.

It had been a while since her last orgasm. While it was her business to make sure that clients found fulfillment, sexual and otherwise, she'd had little time for her own. In other words, Jez was brimming with horniness, and Jack hadn't even turned on the vibrator.

Already off to a bad start.

He set the remote on the table, and Jezzy glanced at it nervously, then made eye contact with him. She let out a long, slow breath, then settled into work mode. She was a professional. She could do this.

"Okay, you say our history will help you do your job. So tell me, Jez, what kind of woman do you think would be my sexual soulmate?"

As she opened her mouth to reply, Jack pressed the button on the remote and turned the dial.

A low buzz quivered against her most sensitive place, sending little shivers of pleasure through her. The vibration tickled over her and delved into her, the sensations feeding off each other. Jez tried not to gasp. She crossed her legs. Realizing the position only increased the butterfly's contact, she uncrossed them.

"So what do you have for me, Jez?" Jack prompted, those damn eyes twinkling with such mischief.

Jezzy tensed her thighs, forcing herself to remain still.

"Um, you need someone who is adventurous. Who isn't afraid of trying new things."

"Good. Yes, that's important to me." Jack turned the dial up and the vibrations intensified. "What else?"

Jezebel bit the inside of her cheek to offset the tendrils of delight dancing between her legs. She'd grown wet very quickly, and she could smell her musky arousal. She hoped Jack couldn't.

She took a deep breath, focusing on Jack's question. "What else? Uh, someone who is intuitive. Who can read what you want. From your body language, the sounds you make, your facial expressions... your eyes."

Jezebel looked into those eyes now. Jack's chocolate brown gaze seemed to be melting into hers. She suddenly had vivid memories of seeing those eyes watching her as she sat on top of him, her breasts bouncing, nipples stabbing the air. Even now, she could feel his thick, hard length thrusting upward inside of her, filling her with need, vibrating...

She tore her focus away from him. She needed to get a hold of herself, before she lost it and screamed out her building pleasure in front of the whole restaurant.

"Are you okay, Jezebel?" he asked.

Jezzy felt her panties grow even wetter. They were nearly soaked. "I'm fine, Mr. Horner."

"Oh, Mr. Horner. Nice professional touch."

"Like that?"

"As much as watching your beautiful face while you're fighting an orgasm? Not quite."

"I thought you wanted to hear about what kind of woman I think you need."

"I'm listening."

He put the dial up to the next setting. The vibration became unbearable, and loud enough that the people sitting at surrounding tables must be able to hear. Jezzy squealed a little. She'd begun to buck and squirm against the butterfly, involuntarily, and she knew that she wouldn't be able to hold out much longer.

"She doesn't have to be beautiful, but that wouldn't hurt. She needs to like to laugh, to have fun. She must love to suck cock."

The last sentence came out a touch too loud, and the table of businessmen all turned to stare. Several smiled her way, as if they could see her arousal or were imagining her sucking their cocks.

"That is indeed important," Jack said. "I remember you used to actually come when you were sucking my cock. Do you remember that too, Jez? What it was like to have my cock in your mouth?"

Jezzy's lips parted. She imagined his manhood dangling in front of her, and wanted nothing more than to take him deep into her throat. But admitting so would be admitting defeat.

"This isn't about me, Mr. Horner. But I certainly can find a wife for you who will enjoy it. Or one I could teach to enjoy it."

"Excellent answer. What else, Jez?" He twisted the dial to the next setting.

Jezebel held her breath for a moment, fighting off the un-bearable pleasure. This was cruel and unusual torture. Why couldn't he just trust her for heaven's sake? Must she really endure this terrible little test?

Her frustration level mounted, and strangely, her anger was only serving to make her arousal more unbearable. Je-zebel tried to remember the silly fights she and Jack had during their relationship. Only, she couldn't really remember what the fights had been about, but what she did remember was the in-credible make-up sex. The wild, animalistic...

She bit her bottom lip and squeezed her eyes closed, forc-ing her pelvis to stop rocking. Her skin was burning up. Her breasts felt heavy, heaving, her nipples tight. She sensed that not only the businessmen were watching now, but the older couple, too. *Please don't let me come now. Please, oh please.*

"You were saying?"

"They have to enjoy coming, having you lick them, penetrate them in all different positions, experiment with toys and other kinky fun. And they can't be ashamed to be naked and aroused, even in public." Jezzy wanted to be naked now, to have all these respectable diners in the restaurant see her distended nipples, the wetness soaking her thong, watching her breasts bounce as she plunged up and down on Jack's—

"Jezzy, that's a terrific observation. You're not ashamed to be aroused in public, are you?"

"No."

"So you wouldn't be embarrassed if I asked you to hike up your skirt and spread your legs so I can have a better look."

Jez set her jaw, and then did what Jack asked. Not only did he look, but almost everyone in the restaurant was staring.

"It's a job interview," Jack told them. "She isn't allowed to come, even though I'm controlling the vibrator in her panties. See?"

He turned it up higher. Jezzy refused to move, even though a scarlet blush covered her entire body.

"For the remainder of the interview, Jezebel, would you mind putting your hands inside your shirt and pinching your nipples? You know, since this is strictly professional?"

Through clenched teeth she answered, "Of course, Mr. Horner."

She slipped her hands inside her silk blouse and into the cups of her barely-there bra. Her fingers quickly found her taut nipples and tugged on them, intensifying the ache between her legs. Her orgasm was so close she was ready to scream.

"Jezebel?"

Jack's voice brought her back from the edge. She forced her mind to her business, to the spread in Big Cock Billionaire Magazine, to anything other than Jack and the heat and the hungry throb between her legs. "I've already started your profile and have a few suitable candidates in mind. I can find your perfect match, Jack. Trust me."

"And you don't want me for your own anymore?"

Jez shifted her hips, trying to keep herself from bearing down against the tremors. "No. I just want to do my job."

"Sweet Buddha on a cinnamon roll!" One of the ogling businessmen had soaked the front of his own pants and was wiping himself with a napkin. The old couple nearby were holding hands, the woman's eyes closed, the man with his hand down her pants.

"Watching you is making me hard, Jez. Really hard. We could go into the bathroom. You could suck my cock. I could fuck you. You could come, be as loud as you want."

Did she want to? She *needed* to. What she wouldn't give to feel him thrusting up into her, bringing her sweet release. "I just want to do... my job. Find you... wife."

"But we've had so many good times, since that night that you took the beans off my erection. Remember?"

Of course, she remembered. She could feel his soft tip now, taste...

No, no, no...

"That's... behind us, Jack. It didn't work out."

"But maybe it could..."

Her skirt was around her waist now, and she could see diners craning their necks to get a glimpse between her legs. She glanced down and spotted the pink butterfly emerging from the confines of her skimpy thong, in full view of half the restaurant. Without prompting from Jack, she'd begun to pinch her nipples harder, surrendering to the pleasure.

"We could put on a show right now for all of them," Jack said, his voice soft, teasing, tempting. "Just think how good that would feel, how right..."

Jezzy's orgasm hovered, just within reach, drawing her, powerful as Jack's entreaties.

No. She couldn't give in. She'd worked so hard. She had to prove herself. She couldn't fail. Forcing her face to relax, she said, "It's over Jack. But I can help you find true happiness."

Jack stared at her for a long moment, then once again, he raised the device.

Oh, please! No more, please! I can't take it. Please don't turn this infernal device on higher. Jezebel felt close to tears. She couldn't believe she'd lasted this long, her whole body was pulsing, and if Jack turned the device one notch higher, she would explode into screaming orgasm. There would be no more holding back.

Jack's finger pressed down...

And turned the device off.

Thank heavens! Jezebel blew out a sigh of relief.

"I'm impressed Jezebel. You really remained professional. You stayed in control."

"Thank you, Mr. Horner."

"I guess whatever was between us has no power over you now, and you are in the perfect position to find me a wife."

Jezzy nodded, her whole body buzzing too hard for her to form thoughts, or words, or unintelligible sound.

"There's one more thing." Jack motioned to the waiter, and he brought another box to the table. White and tied with a big pink ribbon as the last had been, this one was two feet long and one foot wide.

Jezebel swallowed. Her pussy throbbed with need, clenching, and somewhere deep inside, she hoped the package contained a dildo as big as the box itself. "What is this?"

"Something to help you service me. I mean, provide this matchmaking service for me. I think they will help you do your job."

"They?"

"Open it."

Jezebel untied the pink ribbon and lifted the box's lid. Inside was a pair of black, leather boots. Not regular boots, but sexy ones with spike heels that stretched to mid-thigh.

"I'd love it if you'd wear them, Jezzy."

She tore her attention from the sexy footwear and focused on Jack. "I thought things were over between the two of us."

"They are. You just proved it."

"Then I don't understand why you want me to wear these."

"This isn't about you and me. I want you to show my future wife what turns me on," Jack said, staring down at her bunched up skirt, drenched thong, and the moisture glistening on her inner thighs. "And I'd appreciate it if you'd skip the panties, too. There's nothing sexier than a bare puss and boots."

Chapter 2

Snow White Isn't as Pure as She Looks...

An hour later, wearing the sexy boots and nothing under her skirt, Jezebel emerged from the restaurant's restroom, the remote-control vibrator stashed inside her purse next to the tablet computer she used to run her dating algorithms.

Unfortunately, after eating lunch and then freshening up, she hadn't had time to satisfy herself, and her sensitive areas were so aroused, Jez felt as if the butterfly was still in place.

"Ready with my first match?" Jack asked, holding the door open.

Jezzy walked out into the sun, cool air swirling up under her skirt and inspiring chills to race over her skin. "We're meeting her at the Brothers Grimm Country Club."

"Is that a private club?"

"No. The Brothers Grimm are in the public domain."

"Hmm. That sounds promising." Jack's gaze skimmed up Jezzy's legs and over her skirt, pausing on her prim, professional blouse.

A flush of heat followed Jack's roaming eyes, and Jezzy's nipples hardened in response.

"I've heard rumors that there's a new all-nudity rule at the country club," he said with a little smile.

Jezzy swallowed into a dry throat. In her haste to set up the meeting, she'd forgotten the club's new rules. Not that it mattered. Jack was there to look for a sexual soulmate. Nudity was bound to happen in that kind of search.

At least if you were doing it right.

"A group of eccentrics who made their fortune in diamond mining bought the place," Jezzy mused. "They have an interesting vision."

Jack focused on her erect nipples, poking out through the conservative attire. He grinned. "So it's true? No one is allowed to wear clothes?"

"It's true. The atmosphere might help you get to know your future wife as quickly as possible."

"Strip away our defenses? Bare our, uh, souls? Good idea."

"I told you I know my job. I'll find you a wife who is the perfect sexual fit for you. You're not going to regret hiring me for this, Jack."

"I'm sure I won't. And I can't wait to start the process. Now come with me. We'll take my motorcycle."

He led her to a beautiful bike parked in front of the Bean King offices. All gleaming chrome and powerful twin engines, the motorcycle wasn't a model Jez had ever seen before.

"It's beautiful."

"Thanks. I figure it will give my future wife a reason to grab me and hold on. Shall we?"

"Uh, we? You want me to ride with you?" Jez glanced down at her skirt, painfully aware of her nudity underneath.

"We need to get to the country club, right? You know, transportation? Is there a problem?"

"No, no, of course not." If he hadn't remembered she was no longer wearing panties, Jez wasn't going to bring it up. She'd just have to find a way to make it work.

Jack gave her a neon pink helmet, pulled on his own slick, silver model, and hopped on the bike. Jez hiked up her skirt as much as she dared and slung a leg over, settling behind him. She was relieved to find the black leather seat curved upward in the back enough to hide her bottom. Of course, it also cradled her between the legs and tilted her forward, her nipples brushing Jack's back.

I'm here to do a job, she told herself. *Not to get off. And not to get back together with my ex. I'm a pro. I can handle anything.*

Jack started the bike's engine, and it growled to life, making things so much worse. Jezzy's seat cupped her mound like a warm vibrating hand, threatening to send her over the edge. She tightened her grip around Jack's waist and bit her lip in an attempt to stamp down her rocketing arousal.

"Ooooh," she moaned.

"All right back there?" Jack turned his head toward her.

"I, uh, have just never been on a motorcycle like this one before."

"I had it custom made to massage your most sensitive areas. I mean, a woman's most sensitive areas. Not you in particular. But do you like it?"

"It's quite comfortable, yes." Although *comfortable* wasn't the right word. More like exquisite torture. The remote control vibrator test might be over, but that didn't mean Jezzy could give up her professional demeanor. Grabbing hold of a client and screaming out endless orgasms was not generally acceptable behavior while trying to find him a wife.

Jack started the bike, and they were off, the twin engines roaring loud enough to mask Jezzy's involuntary moans. Each tiny bump and dip in the road shot through her like a lightning bolt, and moisture had begun to trickle down her thighs.

Jack didn't seem to notice, even though he did kind of rev the engine more than necessary, and sort of went out of his way to hit pot holes.

At a red light, when Jezebel was about ready to scream, Jack turned his head and said, "So, tell me about the woman who might become my wife."

"She's... um... renowned for her beauty. Skin as white as snow, lips as red as rubies. Hair as black as night. A pussy so tight she can crack walnuts. Seriously, people from miles around visit her when they have jars they can't open. Her muscle control is extraordinary."

"And she's... adventurous?"

"Of course. My algorithm rates her ninety-six-percent compatible with you."

"Is that good?"

"I designed the system when we were still dating, and you and I are only fifty-five-percent compatible. So you see? Trust me, and I'll find you a mate who's perfect for you."

"I trust you, Jez."

The shiver that peppered her skin had nothing to do with the vibrations from the bike. And thinking back to when they were together, Jez had to admit that he'd always been supportive of her fantasies, whether they were sexual or ambitious, even when he'd had few ambitions of his own.

When they finally arrived at the nudist commune, Jezebel was thankful to finally climb off the motorcycle. Her pussy throbbed and ached for release. The continuous stimulation had her clinging to the edge, and she was grateful for a moment to compose herself before they entered the huge, wrought iron country club gates.

That moment never materialized.

"Mr. Horner! Ms. Jezebel! Welcome to the Brothers Grimm Country Club."

A small fellow with a big smile stepped out of the guard house flanking the gates. A beard draped over his belly, brushing his large, uncircumcised manhood.

"I'm Rumpleforeskin, at your service."

With a wave of his hand, the barrier swung open, and Jez and Jack stepped inside.

Green lawns rolled, surging over hills and plunging into valleys, smooth as a woman's curves. Boxwood dotted the path leading to the golf course, their plush evergreen foliage sculpted into phallic shapes and famous nudes. David here. A three-dimensional Birth of Aphrodite there. A Mona Lisa, topless with nipple clamps (maybe that's what she'd been smiling about these past five hundred years.) Birds sang glorious tunes, but old ones that didn't require licensing fees. The scent of roses perfumed the air. Everywhere Jezzy looked, there was beauty and a feast for the senses.

It was quite an improvement from the old county club, which was modeled after a sewage treatment plant, and had a staff that slapped guests and called them rude names, like "Sir Sucks-At-Life" and "Miss FartArse". How that place had ever found investors, Jez couldn't imagine.

"What you've done with the country club, it's beautiful," Jezzy told Rumpleforeskin.

"Agreed," said Jack. "They used to call me 'Mr. Jack-Off-In-A-Corner.' How did they ever find investors?"

"Well, we're under new management." Rumpleforeskin winked at Jez. "And once you take off your clothes, you'll only enhance the beauty, Ms. Jezebel. But leave the boots on. They're super hot." He sniffed, his nose zoning into her nether regions. "It's not my business to pry, but you seem incredibly aroused. Do you and your husband need to take care of business? You can use my office."

"Oh, he isn't my husband," Jezzy quickly said.

"Well, you seem to be on the very verge of orgasm. Would you like me to lick you? Shouldn't take more than one or two strokes."

She shivered. "Thank you for the offer, but I'm here on Mr. Horner's time."

The dwarf nodded, then sniffed at Jack's crotch. "You also seem uncomfortably aroused. I can offer you the same service I offered the young lady. I happen to be gifted in that area."

Rumpleforeskin stuck out his tongue and touched it to the tip of his nose. Then he licked his own eyebrows. Then he parted his hair and tucked it behind his ears.

"Very impressive," Jack said, "but I'm afraid we are in a bit of a rush."

"I understand. Another time, perhaps."

Rumpleforeskin showed them to an undressing area next to the guard house and left them to remove their clothing.

Jezebel had never minded being nude. Truth be told, she loved it, often thinking she should take a vacation at an all-nude resort once Playing With Matches got off the ground. But as she started to unbutton her blouse, she felt a little quiver in her belly.

She glanced at Jack, who hadn't even started to undress. "Something wrong?"

"Not at all. Just enjoying the view."

He motioned at the landscaping outside the little changing hut, but Jezzy got the idea he wasn't really referring to boxwood and green lawn. "Go ahead," he said.

She turned her attention back to her blouse. The buttons pulled free, lower and lower, until the fabric parted, exposing her sheer, black bra, her nipples dark shadows poking out against the white curve of her breasts.

"Here, let me." Jack circled behind her. His fingers caressed her back, and then he slipped the hooks free, and slid the bra off her arms.

Cool air swirled over her soft mounds and teased her nipples to lurid peaks.

"Do you need help with the skirt?" Jack asked, his voice carrying a huskiness it hadn't moments before.

Jezzy swallowed hard. "I've got it. You focus on stripping off your own clothes."

Bare breasts swaying, she unhooked the waistband of her skirt with shaking fingers. Soon she would be entirely exposed to Jack's eyes. What's more, he would be naked as well. And instead of imagining his strong, surging member, as she had in the restaurant, she would see it right in front of her, close enough to reach out and touch.

She faced away from Jack, unclasped the skirt and lowered it over her hips, down her thighs, over her boots, then when it was pooled on the floor, she stepped free. She bent at the waist to retrieve the garment.

Behind her, Jack groaned.

She turned around. He had taken off his shirt and tie and ditched his pants, wearing nothing now but a pair of tight boxer briefs that stretched to cover his bulge. His eyes ran over her heavy breasts and tingling nipples, then ran down her belly and focused on the shaved spot between her legs.

"You look good, Jez. That first view from behind almost undid me."

Her already nervous stomach jumped a little. "I thought... I mean you and I..."

"Are finished. Yes, I got that." Jack pushed the briefs down his legs, and his magnificent erection sprang free. He looked down at its stiffness. "I'm sure this isn't about you, exactly. I'm just, uh... excited to meet Snow White."

"I can see that," Jezebel said, unable to pull her eyes away from his manhood. His shaft was long and thick and corded with veins. And while a light dusting of hair sprinkled his chest and led like a trail over his belly and to his groin, his root was smooth-shaven, making him look even larger, his balls swinging heavy underneath. But the thing that drove her most insane about Jack's cock was the prominent ridge and large head, so fun to circle with her tongue and take deep into her throat.

Her legs felt like rubber. She licked her lips, her mouth dry. "We should find Snow White. I'm sure she's eager to meet you."

Jack nodded. "Right. I can't wait."

They emerged from the changing hut and found Rumple-foreskin (although after a few seconds of staring at Jezebel's nudity, his foreskin wasn't so rumpled) and he led them up the path toward the golf course, trees and lovely exotic flowers on either side.

Jezebel remembered the flowers that had called to her after she'd climbed up the beanstalk in her last adventure. Robin the Puck had told her that the flowers would ravage her and make her come over and over again with no respite. She'd met Jack on that adventure. And before she could catch herself, her eyes slid to him.

He'd been working out a lot and his muscles rippled beneath his skin as he walked. And that stiff rod was calling to her. If only she could slide on top of it...

She snapped her gaze away. *Stop it! You're working for Jack now. And thinking about his big, thick, long, hard cock is only going to make you hornier. You are not here for yourself. You're here to find Jack a suitable wife. You're a professional.*

Jez wondered how many more times she'd have to remind herself of that. Lots, probably. Then she willed herself to focus again on the flowers, wishing they were like Robin the Puck's. If she was going to keep her composure around Jack, she needed to come, and soon.

Finally they came to the seventh hole, where a group played golf. Well, if having all manner of sex with one another could be considered playing golf. There were some naked elves, a centaur who was hung like a horse, a horse who was hung like a larger horse, a larger horse who was hung upside-down from a tree, a guy named Hung whose name was hung around his neck, and several Pacific Islanders. An elf who was receiving a blow job from another elf noticed them watching and gave them a wide, toothy grin. He giggled, hips thrusting like a jack hammer, his beard flopping against his round belly.

Others were experimenting with golf balls and clubs. Jezzy recognized the four businessmen from the restaurant teaching four women how to drive, only there didn't seem to be a ball on the tee at all. Or clubs in the women's hands, either. In fact, instead of driving, they seemed to be getting ready to tee off a mini-orgy.

One of them motioned for her to join in.

And the strangest thing about the scene was that all of them, man, woman, and fairytale creature, no matter what they were engaged in, were singing (or humming) a merry tune.

> *My next door neighbor, Dawn*
> *Was sunbathing on the lawn*
> *She took off her swimsuit*
> *And I saw the crack of Dawn.*

"Climb in the golf cart," Rumpleforeskin said, motioning to a golf cart Jezebel had been too distracted to notice. "Snow White is waiting at the water hazard."

They climbed in, Jack offering Jezebel the seat beside Rumpleforeskin and jumping in back.

Jezzy glanced down at the cart's controls and noticed the dwarf feeding his member into a tube that jutted up from the vehicle's floor.

He smiled up at her. "We've switched the whole country club over to renewable energy. This cart is all about suction."

"Suction?"

"Yeah, it sucks my cock."

"And how does that work?"

"Well, I fit the head in here, just like this, and…"

"I mean, how does that power the cart?"

"The cart? It doesn't. The cart runs on gasoline. But being sucked like this sure renews my energy!"

Jez frowned. "Are we going to have to put up with many more stupid jokes like that?"

"Probably. For the remainder of the book, I'm guessing. That's how we distinguish ourselves from all the other erotica out there. We're funny."

"*Funny* is stretching it a bit."

"This tube is stretching it a bit, too."

"Not funny."

"Hmmph. I'd tell you to blow me, but that's already being taken care of."

"Hey!" Jack said, confronting the dwarf. "Be polite. There's no reason to be short with her."

Rumpleforeskin chuckled. Jezebel rolled her eyes.

Great. Two comedians, one golf cart.

Rumpleforeskin shifted into gear, and they bounced up the hill, the dwarf leering at Jezzy's bouncing breasts while thrusting in and out of the sucking attachment. His smart-assed comments were replaced by moans, and Jez wasn't sure if that was an improvement because it only reminded her that she was still horny. By the time they reached the water hazard, Jez was so tired of seeing others gain pleasure, she was tempted to jump on the gearshift.

But when Rumpleforeskin stopped the cart, Jezzy's attention was captured by a lovely female voice humming. She forgot all about manual transmissions and turned toward the sound.

There, between the trees, she could see the sun sparkling off the water hazard. But Snow White wasn't on the banks playing golf, as Jez had hoped. She was in the water, and not playing golf at all. Instead, she appeared to be taking a bath.

Jezebel looked at Jack, who was beaming at Snow White. "See? I told you she was beautiful."

"And you didn't exaggerate." Jack's engorged member twitched at the sight.

Snow White lifted her lovely, dark head and looked up at them. She swirled soap over her breasts, giving her taut nipples a particularly good scrub.

"You must be Jack and Jezebel. So pleased to meet you. I apologize for not being ready yet. Being the fairest of them all takes a whole lot of washing. If I even get a bit of dirt under a fingernail, the magic mirror on the wall drops me down a dozen places. I haven't had spaghetti in ages. Too messy."

"Messy," Jack said. "Indeed. Spaghetti is very messy. They should blend it into a smoothie so you can drink it with a straw, then it wouldn't be messy. Heh heh heh."

Jezebel had never before witnessed the loopy grin Jack wore. Her heart sank a little, but she lifted her chin and gave Snow White a bright smile.

"No apologies needed. We're a little early, I'm afraid. Please, finish your bath, and we'll wait for you here on the bank."

Snow White plunged into the water, and when she emerged, her snow white skin glistened. Her lovely pink nipples jutted out, water dripping off their sharp peaks. Her long, coltish legs met at a trimmed pussy, a thin line of glossy black hair pointing the way to her tight little nub.

And when Snow strode out of the hazard and walked toward them, her breasts jiggling with each stride, her naked beauty was enough to make Jezebel feel a little dizzy.

"Impressive bounce," Jack said.

"Thanks." Snow White glanced from Jez to Jack. "Sounds like you're in the mood for a game of golf, Jack. It's great fun the way we play it here."

"How about a threesome?" Jack asked, as a wolfish smile spread across his face.

"I don't know a thing about golf," Jezzy said, not sure she was up to remaining professional in light of what she'd already seen at the country club. "Besides, the point is for you two to get to know each other."

"No," Snow corrected. Slowly, she bent forward and poked a tee into the grass, exposing her shapely posterior and soft pink folds. "The point is to get a hole in one."

"Fore!" Jack declared, stepping up behind her.

Jezzy faded back from the couple, her facilitation skills obviously not required. She should be pleased that Jack and Snow were hitting it off so well. They really were a perfect match, and the exposure in Big Cock Billionaire Magazine was just what Playing With Matches needed. What Jezzy needed.

So why do I feel so…

Jealous?

Am I actually jealous?

Of course not. I'm over Jack. Besides, I don't get jealous.

"You look jealous," Rumpleforeskin said.

"I'm certainly not."

"I'm enjoying the tube, but if you want I could throw you one."

"Throw me one?"

"A little slap and tickle. A quick poke and stroke. Give you a good slogging. You're quite a bit taller, but my brother gave me a pair of stilts."

"Let me guess," she deadpanned. "His name Rumpelstiltskin."

"No. His name is Steve. He's an accountant. Do you know why ladies love accountants?"

"Because they're good with figures."

"What? No, because they can get their taxes done for free. Ladies hate doing taxes. Want me to get the stilts?"

Jez watched as Jack reached out and caressed a hand over Snow White's buttocks, then slid his fingers between her legs.

He moved them up and down, his hand shiny with her juices, then slipped two digits deep inside. "Gotta say I love a woman with an open stance."

Snow wiggled back against him, spreading her legs wider, and he continued to plunder her with his fingers, his member jabbing her backside as if desperate to join the fun.

Despite herself, Jezzy found herself moving, too, her hips thrusting, matching the rhythm of Jack's hand. She threw a desperate glance at Rumpleforeskin, and he shrugged.

"Too late. I came while watching them. They're one hot couple, aren't they?"

"Yes," Jezzy said, struggling to maintain a prim demeanor. "Very hot."

"I could lick you if you'd like." Rumpleforeskin stuck out his tongue and cleaned out some wax from his left ear.

"That's nice of you, but I'm here in a supervisory capacity."

"Supervisory? You're wetter than a tadpole in a Florida swamp."

"Just mind your own business, please."

"Just trying to be helpful," the dwarf said.

After what seemed like an eternity, Snow White finally finished placing the tee and straightened. She sidled up to Jack and peered down at his manhood. "You seem to be ready to play."

"I don't have a club," he said.

Snow White took his hard length in her hand, stroking down to his tip then back up to his root. She lowered herself to her knees, his cock right at mouth level. "What do you mean? Your wood is right here."

"Oh, yes," Jack murmured. As if on cue, his cock flexed under Snow White's hand.

Jezebel clapped a hand over her mouth to hold in a groan.

"But how about golf balls? Don't we need some of those?"

"You have a couple of balls right here. And they have the cutest little dimples."

Snow lifted his stiff shaft, his scrotum hanging heavy beneath, and lathed long, fat licks along Jack's quivering sack. Then she took it fully into her mouth.

Jezzy squirmed, imagining the weight of Jack's testicles on her tongue, feeling them tighten as his arousal intensified.

She was going to lose it for sure.

"I could stick my thumb up your ass," Rumpleforeskin said to Jez. "If you want."

She ignored the little man.

"So maybe it's time to play golf?" Jezebel called to Jack and Snow, her voice sounding a little more irritated than she intended.

Snow let Jack's balls fall from her lips and looked up at Jezzy. "We are playing golf. I told you the way we play it is fun. Wait until later, when we're playing the back nine. That's when the divots will start to fly. We might even have to pull out the sand wedge."

Jezzy made a face, not quite sure what all that meant but too afraid to ask.

Jack was beaming. "I like this game, Jez. Snow White is an amazing ball-washer."

"Thanks, Jack." Snow winked up at him. "I can't wait to check out your backswing."

And that should be the last of the stupid golf puns, Jez hoped.

Jack wiggled his brows. "Sure you can't join us, Jez?"

Jezzy shook her head. She didn't want to be a third wheel, and yet she wished she hadn't dismissed the game so quickly. She'd really never imagined golf could be so exciting. Where she came from, balls and clubs were... well, balls and clubs. The antics involved in the game at this particular country club were unlike anything she'd ever seen before. It would have been fun to join in.

But this game wasn't for her. Jezzy's focus had to be on Jack and his future wife.

Not on fun.

And not on herself.

Snow White was lucky. Jack was handsome and ripped, and he made King Midas look like a pauper.

And he used to be mine.

Jezebel pulled her eyes away and sighed wistfully. The sexual chemistry between Snow and Jack was palpable. Proof the Playing With Matches algorithms were dead on.

I should be happy.

"Let's get on with the game," cooed Snow White. "I can't wait to show you my ten-finger grip."

Ugh. More golf innuendo.

Before Jezzy had a chance to grimace, Snow wrapped both hands around the base of Jack's cock. Twisting her hands in opposite directions on his shaft, she moved them closer and closer to his tip. At the same time, she swirled her tongue over his head. Reaching the end, she started twisting back down, her mouth taking in each inch her hands vacated.

Jack groaned deep in his throat.

After several minutes of this, up and down, up and down, Snow ran her tongue along the underside of his shaft. When she reached his balls, she gave them a few more kisses, then started moving back up his length. When she reached his head, she parted her ruby red lips.

"Oh, yes," Jack moaned, pushing himself inside.

Hot need licked at Jezzy as she watched Snow take Jack deep into her throat.

Just like I imagined doing at the restaurant.

"I love the way you choke down on the shaft," Jack moaned. "You really know your way around a club."

She grabbed his butt, one cheek in each palm. Her cheeks grew hollow as she sucked hard on the head and Jack's hips began to thrust.

"Oor slii a il oooo a eft," Snow said, her mouth full of wood.

"I beg your pardon?" Jack asked her.

"She said you're slicing a little to the left," Jezzy offered. Jezzy had always loved that about Jack's driver. It hit her right every time.

Oh, dammit. Now I'm doing the dumb puns.

As she watched, Jez felt warmth trickle down her inner thighs like liquid honey. She squeezed her legs together, the aching in her core almost too much to bear. Her folds felt like they were swelling, her walls clenching with desire.

"Well, it seems like you two are getting along smashingly already," Jezebel smiled, gritting her teeth and stamping down a spike of envy. She wanted to be the one who was being putted. Or birdied. Or bogied. Or anything at this point, no matter how stupid the golf joke was, as long as it was pleasurable.

But even more, she needed to be successful at finding Jack a wife. The ball was tonight, and she'd have to be a success by then.

Being the reason for Jack's happy new engagement will certainly give my business unheard-of credibility. No matter how hard it is to watch Jack have sex with the lovely Snow, I can do this.

Jack guided Snow White onto her back in the grass. He knelt over her, and a shiver went through Jezzy as she watched his tongue gently, then firmly flick one of Snow White's nipples, then the other. He began slowly, sensuously sucking each nub, taking his time.

Jezebel braced herself. Watching Jack pleasure Snow might be too much for her to handle. Her clit pulsed steadily with unreleased need, and her nipples stretched straight out, announcing their desire for all to see. Her entire body felt unbearably hot and she was becoming hornier by the second. So horny that she was considering taking Rumpleforeskin up on his many offers. But when she turned to look at the dwarf, she found him asleep on the front seat, snoring softly.

Jack's fingers reached the V between Snow's legs and his middle finger slid between her folds, slowly moving back and forth, then in little circles over her little pink clit. Jack lifted his gaze to watch Snow White's face as he pleasured her. His eyes were shining with desire and it made Jezebel think of all the times he had looked at her like that.

Jezzy's breaths came short and quick, her heartbeat like the fluttering of bird wings in her ribcage. Her mounting passion was equal to her rising envy, and the confusion was making her head spin.

And when Jack brought his mouth between Snow White's snow white thighs, Jezzy could feel the clenches of either an orgasm or tears or maybe both hover just out of reach. She tried to stay her wiggling bottom, pretending that she couldn't imagine exactly how Jack was licking Snow, thrusting his tongue into her, sucking and nipping her sensitive bud.

Snow's moans were almost too much.

Her screams were worse.

And finally when Snow was sated and Jack looked back up at Jezzy, his glistening smile was the worst of all.

Memories flooded Jezebel, followed by questions.

What had happened to her and Jack?

Why had they broken up?

Jezzy shook her head, scolding herself inwardly for feeling nostalgia about a relationship that was clearly over.

"Take a swing," Snow White moaned. "I think you're ready to sink that hole in one."

Jack positioned himself between Snow White's milky thighs and she wrapped her legs around his waist.

Jezzy watched as Jack slid his enormous manhood into her. He began a slow, steady thrust, bracing himself with his arms. Plunging, thrusting, and all the while, keeping his eyes glued to Jezzy's face.

Oh my god, I can feel his stroke just as if he's doing it to me.

The breeze picked up just then and the most delicious shiver moved over her as it kissed her taut nipples. She felt her lips part, and let out a soft sigh.

Jack continued staring at Jez, his thrusts into Snow White becoming more frantic and urgent. Suddenly he slowed and made several short, close little jabs into her.

Jezzy knew what he was doing. He was probing Snow's center of pleasure, as he'd done to Jez many times.

The effect was instant. Both for Jezebel and for Snow.

A scream broke from Snow White's lips. Jack's grunts could barely be heard over Snow White's cries. He gripped Snow's creamy white bottom and began a punishing thrust, driving deeply into her.

Jezzy's pussy now throbbed and ached terribly. She couldn't help remembering all the times Jack had used that well-grooved swing of his to bring her to ecstasy. The way his rock hard cock felt plunging deep inside of her, filling her, demanding orgasm after orgasm.

And then Jack's intense gaze penetrated Jezebel, staring straight into her soul.

He's making love to her, but staring at me.

She wondered what Jack was thinking. To punish her? To show Jez what she was missing since she dumped him? Or was he watching to make sure that she wasn't getting turned on? He'd fire her in a second if she was, Jez was sure. But by the looks of it, he was pretty pleased with Snow White. Maybe didn't even need Jezzy's services any longer.

Good. Then I've succeeded.

But...

If only I hadn't failed him in our relationship.

If only—

"Jezebel!" Jack's voice tore from his throat. He gripped Snow's hips and plunged deep, holding on as his own orgasm rocked his body.

He called my name! Jezebel thought.

Why did he call my name?

When Jack's trembling climax finally ended, his face became slack.

"Yes, Jack?" Snow said. "You want something?"

"Wha... What?" he said, as if dazed.

"You called for Jezebel."

"I did?"

"Yes, but she's all the way over there, and I'm right here. Since I'm the one who is going to be your wife, I would think you'd call for me if you needed something. Now what is it?"

Jack appeared to be at a total loss. He looked at Jezzy, his eyes searching hers. Jez kept her face neutral.

"I'm sure it was nothing," Jezebel said. She was so flushed, and so horny, and so confused, she just wanted to get away.

"No, no, wait." Jack held up a hand. "Um, uh, Jez, would you show Snow White how I like to be kissed?" He turned to Snow. "Not that I didn't enjoy your kisses, Snow. But this is pretty interesting. I think you might like it."

"I'm always ready to learn something new. Especially if it means our wedding kiss will be extra special."

Jezzy froze. She wasn't sure what Jack was up to, but kissing him would be just...

Would be just...

Dreamy.

No, no, too much. Kissing him would be way too much, when his heart and cock clearly belonged to Snow White. When Jezzy was far too close to losing control as it was.

"Just a few pointers, if you will," Jack said. He no longer looked like the suave billionaire who had it all together. Instead, he looked like the boy she used to love.

"I— I—" Jezebel sputtered. She felt herself flush. Her feet were rooted to the ground. She couldn't move. Couldn't breathe.

She felt like a deer in the headlights.

She felt like a fraud.

Tears pricked the corners of her eyes. A large lump rose in her throat.

"Jez?" Jack's face crinkled.

"I'm... I'm sorry. Please excuse me." She whirled and ran for the gate.

Jezebel ran behind a grove of apple trees not far from the green. She swiped at her eyes, angry at the tears that had sprung from them. Angry with herself.

"Great, Jez. You just blew the whole job," she muttered.

What's wrong with me?

She heard a giggle and peeked from around the apple tree she hid behind. Snow White was still smiling as Jack leaned in and whispered something in her ear.

And then Jezzy knew.

This had nothing to do with Snow White.

It had nothing to do with matchmaking at all.

Jezebel still cared for Jack. She'd made a big mistake breaking up with him, and now there was nothing to do except to watch him marry someone else.

New tears filled her eyes and Jezebel ran. She ran until she came to the gate. She quickly retrieved her clothes and her tablet computer, and then she urgently punched the buzzer. "Rumpleforeskin! I need to be let out, please!"

But Rumpleforeskin didn't answer.

"Rumpleforeskin!" Jezzy shouted, annoyance raising her tone.

"What? Who is this?" came the little man's voice from the intercom.

"It's Jezebel."

"It can't be Jezebel. She's in the back of my golf cart."

"No, I'm not. I'm at the gate."

"But how did… Witch! You command the damned powers of teleportation! Cursed you shall be to the flames of hell!"

"You fell asleep. I walked."

"I didn't fall asleep. I recall every single moment. Jack Horner and Snow White, having sex. The two-headed dragon with diamonds for eyes who gave me a magic milkshake."

"That was a dream."

"But the milkshake seemed so real. I don't want to live in a world without magic milkshakes. They're so magical."

"Are you letting me out or what?'

"Give me five minutes."

"Jezebel!" Jack shouted from behind her. Breathless, he caught up with her. "What's wrong?"

"N-nothing." Jezebel took a breath and straightened, composing herself. Still, she had trouble looking into his eyes.

Jack gently touched her arm. "Jez, I hired you for your comprehensive service, including the sexual portion. If there's something getting in the way of that, please let me know." He paused. "Is there something getting in the way of you working for me?"

Jezebel lifted her gaze to Jack's concerned face. His eyes questioned hers. For a moment she imagined that they held a note of hope. Of desire. Of feelings.

For her.

Of course, any hint of feelings were only in her head. She was seeing what she wanted to see. Why would Jack hire her to find him a wife if he wanted her back?

"Your eyes are red and watery, Jezebel. You've been crying. Tell me what has you so upset."

She gave her head a mental shake and took a deep, shaky breath. "Allergies. I'm allergic to peonies."

"Allergy" Jack titled his head, a skeptical look on his face. "There aren't any peonies around here."

"Not true. I just saw your peonies plunge into Snow White."

Nice recovery. Hide your feelings with a joke. Now finish this. It's your job. Be a pro.

Jezebel took a deep breath and let it out. It was done between her and Jack. Over. She was the one who had dumped him, and now he was moving on. She would go to the ball tonight, watch him announce his engagement to Snow White, and smile even though her heart was shattering into a million pieces.

"Yeah," he said, face drooping. "About that. I... I don't think she's the one, Jez."

Jezebel was shocked by the pronouncement. "What? Why? You two seemed to be hitting it off fabulously."

Jack waved a dismissive hand. "I don't want a country club wife, Jez. Right after we finished she had to immediately go take another bath. So stuck on being the fairest of them all. That's not for me."

Jezebel wasn't sure how to react. Any personal satisfaction she felt was negated by her professional disappointment.

"But you were ninety-six percent compatible."

"Nice lady. Good looking. Great sex. But I can't be with someone who will never eat spaghetti because she might get messy."

"What about your spaghetti smoothie solution?"

"That's idiotic. I just said that to get laid."

Jez smiled a little. That sounded more like the old, poor Jack, not the Bean King.

"Okay. Snow White is off the list."

"So who is next?"

Jezzy's smiled waned, but she pulled out her tablet computer and looked up the next candidate. "I have just the woman for you, and my algorithm shows that she's ninety-seven percent compatible."

"And who is this mystery woman?"

"Let's just say that where there's a wool, there's a way."

Jack cracked a smile. "Oh. I get it. You're setting me up with Little Bo-Peep. I've heard of her."

"Is that why you have that sheepish grin?"

"Looks like we're going from golf jokes to sheep jokes."

"You're paying me well, Mr. Horner. I certainly wouldn't want to fleece you out of your money."

"Let's see, I can go with a *seen not herd* joke, or talk about *going on the lamb*, or we could just *flock* to Bo-Peep's right now."

"That would be best. I'm getting tired of these puns."

"Me, too. When's the next sex scene?"

"Hopefully very soon." Jezebel winked. "Ewe just have to be patient."

Chapter 3

A Visit to Little Bo-Peep

By the time they reached the home of Little Bo-Peep, Jezebel's emotions were under control, and her mind was focused back where it should be—on finding Jack a wife—despite the motorcycle's delicious vibrations still tickling her nether regions.

The house was a lovely pink cottage, complete with a white picket fence and tiny blue flowers dotting the front.

"Lovely place," Jezzy observed.

"It's a little tame, for my taste." Jack looked at the house, doubt in his face.

"Just give it a chance," Jezzy said. "Sometimes people will surprise you."

Jezebel rang the doorbell. Bo-Peep came to the door in a pink ruffled dress with puffy sleeves. She wore white boots, and tawny curls tumbled out from beneath a blue bonnet. In one hand she carried a white shepherd's crook.

"Well, hello. You must be Jezebel and Jack. I'm Bo-Peep. My friends just call me Bo. Please, come in."

Jack stared at Bo for a moment, then slid a side long look to Jezebel. Covertly he shot her an eyeroll followed by an exaggerated yawn. He looked like he wanted to bolt.

"Thank you," Jezebel said. She grabbed Jack by the sleeve and tugged him through the doorway with her.

Bo's puffy dress made swishing sounds as she walked, her boot heels clicking on the floor.

"I thought we could get to know each other a little better in the activity room."

"I bet she's going to offer us milk and cookies." Jack whispered. "And I feel like tossing my cookies. Right now."

"Do you trust me or not?"

Jack's gaze was so intense it made her knees feel bendy. "I trust you. I've always trusted you."

"Then give her a chance."

Jez also suspected Bo was a bad match. The shepherdess was sweet, no doubt too tame for Jack's tastes. For the life of her, Jez didn't know what went wrong. Her computer had shown the match to be very strong.

Bad data? Faulty programming? Or had someone just pulled the wool over the computer's eyes?

*That's the last sheep joke. We swear.

Still, Jezzy had to let this play out. Jack wasn't her only client. Bo was one, too. And first impressions don't always matter. The heart tends to find its own level. All it takes is getting to know someone.

Dropping back to whisper in Jack's ear, she said, "Play nice. If it's not working out, I'll make sure this is short."

Bo stopped and glanced behind her. "The activity room? Does that sound okay?"

Jez plastered a smile to her lips. "It sounds lovely, Bo."

Bo led Jack and Jezebel down a red spiral stair case. Then down a corridor with several doors along each wall. She stopped in front of one door and turned, smiling beatifically at Jack and Jezzy. "Are you ready?"

"Um, sure," Jack said.

"Yes," Jezzy said.

"Then I have just one question for you," Bo said.

"Chocolate chip," Jack answered.

Jezebel elbowed Jack and offered Bo a smile. "What's the question, Bo?"

The sweet young woman opened the door and stood in front of the doorway. "My question is, have you been naughty?"

She stepped aside. A nude man stood just inside the doorway, looking meek.

"I've been waiting, Mistress Bo."

Bo-Peep reared her foot back, and then kicked the man square between the legs.

The man screamed, dropped to his knees, and cupped his privates.

"What the—?" Jack said, taking a step back.

"Just wait for it," Bo said.

The man moaned and groaned, and then wept. "Thank you, Mistress!"

Jezebel lifted her brows.

"Would you like another?" Bo asked the man.

The man groaned, then removed his hands from his manhood. Bo gave his goods a harsh stomp.

"Thank you, Mistress!" he howled.

The man crawled past Jezebel and Jack, moaning in apparent agony.

"I forgot about that appointment. Good thing he's easy to take care of. Pays me a mint, too," Bo winked. "Please, come in."

Jack and Jezebel glanced at each other but didn't move.

"Are you coming or not?" prodded Bo.

Jezebel stepped through the door first, Jack following. The floor beneath her boots was spongey, padded with something akin to wrestling mats. There was an X shaped frame along one wall, a pillory straight from the 1400s, and various tables and machines that Jezebel could only imagine the uses for.

There were also other devices. Handcuffs and shackles by the dozens. Chains, whips, and paddles. Dildos of all sizes and colors, as well as blindfolds and gags and feathers and candles.

"I wasn't aware you run a sex toy shop, Bo."

A sudden, loud ripping sound made both Jack and Jezebel jump and turn toward Bo.

She'd ripped her dress open, which clearly had hidden Velcro openings, and the sweet, fluffy concoction was now puddled on the floor. Bo stood before them, lean and sinewy in a black leather corset, which lifted her bare breasts up and thrust them forward. Her nipples jutted straight out; each pierced and decorated with hoops.

Bo's caramel hair curled in wild, cork screw ringlets all around her head. She wore open-crotch leather boy shorts, showcasing her shaved pussy, and the glinting silver barbell through the hood of her clit.

"This is my playroom. And these are my play clothes." She did a twirl, spinning on the white boots, which were laced in a crisscross pattern all up the backs of her legs.

Jack gazed at Bo, his mouth hanging open.

Jezebel found her voice. "You didn't mention this in your Playing With Matches online application."

"Sure I did. I said I was into role-playing games."

"I thought that meant Dungeons & Dragons."

"I don't know about dragons. But I am into dungeons. And bondage. And discipline. And sadism. And masochism. And dominance. And submission. Among other things. Right now we're role-playing. I'm the mistress, and you'll address me as such. You're my slaves."

Bo pushed Jack down on a leather chaise lounge that was shaped like a rollercoaster.

"You're not going to kick me in the nuts, are you?" Jack asked her.

"That's a highly specialized service that I provide at an extremely high price, although I'm sure you can afford it. Would you like to try?"

Jack cupped his hands over his crotch. "No, thanks. Not today."

"Maybe another time, then." She stood before him, almost straddling the odd chair and jutting her pelvis forward, her crotch inches from his face. "There are other games we can play."

Jack seemed uncharacteristically nervous, but the bulge in his pants told a different story.

"What kind of games are we talking about?"

"Are you sure you both want to explore this?" Jezzy asked. She'd never discussed this type of sex play with Jack, and somehow her algorithm hadn't detected this propensity in Bo.

Bo turned her shepherd's crook upside down and used the curved end to gently tap at Jack's erection. "It looks to me like Jack would like to stay. Wouldn't you, Jack?"

"Oh, yes," Jack murmured, looking at Bo's pussy and licking his lips.

"Yes, what?"

"Yes, Mistress."

Bo smiled, her bowtie lips parting to reveal startlingly white teeth. "Good. Then we'll begin." She swished her cane over their heads. "Time for you to undress."

Jack lost no time unbuttoning his shirt.

"You too, Jezebel," Bo said, the tone in her voice reminding Jezzy of a patient preschool teacher correcting recalcitrant children. "We all need to wear our play clothes in the playroom."

"But we don't have any play clothes with us," Jezzy pointed out.

"If Jack didn't bring play clothes, he'll just have to be naked."

Jezzy turned to Jack and found he'd already stripped down to his boxer briefs, his hard-on stretching the fabric to its limit.

"And me?" Jezzy asked.

"You can keep those boots on."

Although there seemed to be no real reason for Jezzy to undress if her facilitation services weren't needed, Bo seemed to have a strong idea of how she wanted to proceed. So giving a shrug, Jez started unbuttoning her blouse and stripping off her skirt, all the while watching Jack ditch the underwear, his cock surging free.

Eyeing Jack's endowment as well, Bo gave an appreciative moan, her crimson mouth stretching into a devilish smile. "Bippity! Boppity!"

Two enormous men walked through a hidden door in the velvet-covered wall, each so tall he had to bend low to fit through. They wore nothing except black leather masks and several strategic piercings, and they were both so muscular they had to be professional body builders.

In unison, they said, "Yes, Mistress?"

"Bippity, chain Jack's wrists to the ceiling, above his head."

"Yes, Mistress," Bippity said.

He led Jack under the support beam and shackled his wrists above him.

"Now a spreader bar for his legs."

Bippity chose a steel bar from the wall, roughly a meter long with a shackle on each end. He put one on each of Jack's ankles and forced his legs apart so Jack stood spread-eagled, his member poking straight out. The center of the bar was then fixed to the floor with another chain.

"Bobbity, outfit Jezebel with my special nipple clamps."

"Oh," Jezzy said, her nipples peaking at the delicious thought. She had been aching to be touched for what seemed like forever. "Thank you, Mistress."

"Please take a seat on the sex chair." She motioned to the rollercoaster inspired chaise lounge.

Jezzy took a seat. Now that she knew it was a sex chair, her imagination immediately began conjuring up uses for the contours of furniture such as this.

Boppity gathered the clamps, then knelt beside her. He covered her breasts with his big mitts, fondling and caressing, cupping and pinching.

It all felt marvelous, but Jezzy wasn't sure his actions had anything to do with applying nipple clamps.

"Boppity?" Bo reprimanded. "Quit feeling up our guest. If you do a good job, maybe you can have your way with her later."

Jezzy gave the masked Boppity a little smile. She didn't mind the thought of this man mountain plunging into her, if that was what this meeting required.

All part of the job, right?

She looked back at Jack. Smiling as if he'd just won the lottery, he watched Jezzy, as if drinking in her nudity with his eyes.

A shiver seated itself between her legs. When she felt the weight of the clamps pinch one nipple then the other, she gasped. Tight as clothespins, but not so tight they ached. Then they began to vibrate, sending delicious sensations through her breasts, tendrils of delight shivering over her skin.

"Oh, this is lovely, Bo."

Bo glanced from Jez to Jack. "When I address either of you, you say 'yes, Mistress'. Is that clear?"

"Yes, Mistress." Jack wore a goofy smile. He looked at Jezzy. His cock twitched.

"Yes, Mistress," Jezzy said.

Role-playing, huh? Maybe there was something to this.

Bo tapped Jack's erection with her shepherd's crook.

Jack jumped, then moaned.

"Did you like that, you dirty boy?" Bo cooed at him.

"Yes. Wow, I really—"

Bo Peep swung out, lightning fast, and smacked Jack again, this time harder.

"OUCH!" Strung up and helpless, he stared at her in shock. "What the hell?"

"What do you say?"

"Oh. I'm sorry, Mistress. Yes, Mistress."

Jezebel watched, wide-eyed, and despite her better judgment, a little aroused. The scene before her was strange and frightening, and yet along with the pleasant buzz and weight of the nipple clamps, she was getting very turned on.

And judging from the exuberance of Jack's erection, it was obvious he was enjoying himself as well.

Jezzy and Jack had dabbled in a few of these games before. A paddle here, some fur-lined handcuffs there, but they'd never taken it very far. Still she knew Jack liked a good smack on his backside. She opened her mouth to inform Bo of this then bit back the urge. Better to see how things went first. Bo seemed to like being in control, and if Jezzy wasn't careful, she'd end up cuffed and paddled herself.

Surprised, she realized the thought excited her. In fact, she felt heat pooling in her nether region and powerful stirrings of arousal deep inside.

Bo pulled at the handle of her shepherd's crook and what emerged was a long, black whip.

"What's that?" Jack asked her, his face alarmed.

"It's a whip, my dear Jack." Bo gave the whip a practice crack in the air then snapped it at Jack's thigh.

Jack jumped. "Ow! What was that for?"

"You forgot to call me Mistress. Twice." Bo snapped the whip down again, quick and sharp.

"Mistress! Mistress!" Jack bawled.

Bo smiled, walking around to look in Jack's face, her bustier creaking. "That's better."

Jack appeared momentarily fearful then his hard root bounced and twitched before Bo. A loopy smile spread over his face.

"It is true. I've been a bad, bad boy."

Bo used the whip's handle to toy with Jack. She pushed his member down, and it bobbed back up eagerly. "You've been a bad, bad boy, what?"

"Mistress!"

Jezebel imagined herself in front of Jack with the whip. All of that power. Her skin broke out in gooseflesh, and she felt her eyes droop lustily. Her pussy was slippery with her juices and she could smell her own musk.

Snapping her fingers, Bo said, "Lower him."

Bippity flicked a switch and the overhead chains began to unwind. Jack's weight pulled him downward until he was leaning back at a fifteen degree angle, most of his weight on his wrists, staring up at the ceiling. When the top of his head was level with the bare V between her legs, Bo snapped her fingers.

Bippity flipped the switch to stop the chains. Stepping forward so that Jack's mouth was between her thighs, Bo jutted her hips forward. "Lick me."

Jack's tongue snaked out and he flicked it quickly over Bo's pink nub.

Jezebel couldn't look away. Warm, slippery nectar was dampening her inner thighs as she squeezed her legs tightly together. Her breasts felt heavy with the clips, her nipples pulsing. She felt a warm flush move over her skin.

She glanced around the playroom, growing frustrated. This sitting here, watching Jack again as she had at the country club, was driving her crazy. Professional or not, she yearned to be part of what was going on. Since Jack was busy with Bo, maybe she could locate Boppity again. Or Bippity. Or both of them at once.

"Slower and harder," Bo said, her voice husky.

Jack gave a moan as he sucked her pleasure nub between his lips. His face moved in little circles as he played.

Jezebel could see Jack's chin become slick with Bo's juices, and her clit twitched. She wanted release more than anything and closed her eyes, wishing that she were the one standing over his mouth.

Bo grabbed Jack's face and ground her pussy into him. "Harder, naughty boy!"

Jack's face pressed firmly into Bo's crotch, and she rode his face. His hips started moving, humping the air below him, and his cock strained forward toward his belly. His abs rippled with tension, and a thin sheen of perspiration beaded his body.

Jezebel found herself panting lightly. Her cheeks heated with what she was certain was a furious blush. She was so wet now that she was sure she would come if she watched much more of this. Her hungry pussy quavered and her nipples sang. Tension balled deep in her lower abdomen.

"Yes!" Bo shuddered and quaked, and screamed with pleasure. Her orgasm seemed to go on and on, and by the time her vocalizations ended, Jezebel was so envious of her release, she almost walked over and tried out Jack herself.

If only...

Recovering from her multiple pleasures, Bo snapped her fingers. "Hot wax."

"Waaamph?" Jack said with a mouth full of pussy.

"It hurts. But you'll like it. I promise," Bo said.

Boppity brought a tall, scarlet, burning candle to Bo, who lowered the candle over Jack's chest and tipped it slightly so that a single drop fell onto his nipple.

Jack yelped, his hips thrusting upward. He whimpered, but it was a whimper of desire. Jezebel had heard it before, when she had teased him relentlessly one night with an hour long blow job, getting him close but not letting him come. She remembered it well, every second, and if she closed her eyes, Jezzy could almost feel Jack's length against her tongue.

Moving her hand over slightly, Bo tipped the candle again and another drop fell, this time onto Jack's other nipple.

Again he yelped, then plunged his hips upward, "Oh, Mistress! I'm going to come!"

"No, you may not!" Bo brought the whip down on Jack's legs.

Jack groaned. But he didn't come.

Pretty neat trick, Jez thought. *Pain to temper the pleasure.*

Bo released his face and stepped back. "You are a terribly naughty boy. A dirty boy. And now, it's time for your next punishment."

"Oh, yes Mistress," Jack said.

"Time for a paddling."

Jezzy almost groaned. Jack enjoyed a spanking, and Jez had to admit she did as well. She had no idea how she'd get through this without giving in and touching herself.

Bo called to her henchmen. "Lift him up again."

Bippity flicked a switch and there was a loud hum as Jack's body was righted and he was once again vertical.

Jezzy shivered. Closing her eyes, she imagined what was coming next, yet instead of Bo holding the whip, she pictured herself in the Domme's place, smacking him with a paddle, the way she'd done when they were dating. Watching him moan and grow unbearably hot and hard because of her.

"Time out!" Jack called.

Jezebel's eyes snapped open.

"Excuse me?" Bo propped one hand on her hip. With the other, she raised her whip, ready to strike. "Time out, what?"

"Mistress! I beg your mercy, Mistress. I'm enjoying this greatly, but since this is kind of my search for the perfect wife, I'd like my matchmaker's professional input here."

Jezebel lifted her brows. *What in hell was he doing?*

"Very well," Bo said.

Jack shot her one of his mischievous smiles. "Jezzy, show Mistress Bo how you paddled me in Paris."

Jezebel's heart gave a little jump. It was just what she'd been thinking about, just what she'd been wishing for. Now was her chance. Perhaps her last chance. She may never get to paddle Jack again.

"May I, Mistress?" she asked Bo, expectant.

"You may."

Jez stood on shaky legs and approached.

"Choose from the wall. There are many paddles, and other devices to play with," Bo's eyes were practically glittering.

Jezebel chose a long, oval paddle from the wall, similar to the one they'd used before.

"Spit on the paddle, Jezebel. The moisture makes the pain more intense."

Jezzy did as instructed and then approached Jack. She swung, but pulled back a little at the last second, and the paddle hit with a light smack.

"That's how Jack liked to be paddled in Paris?" Bo threw her head back and laughed. "That was so light, it was barely worth doing."

Jezebel flushed with embarrassment. "I... I was just warming up."

"You can do it, Jez," Jack called.

Not about to be laughed at by a client, Jezebel drew back and swung hard. The paddle went *CRACK!* against Jack's ass, sending vibrations up Jezzy's arm and a thrill through her whole body. She was so excited she could hardly stand up straight.

This time Jack groaned.

"Ask her for another," Bo commanded.

"Please, Jezebel, may I have another?"

Taking a cue from Bo's nod, Jez smacked him again. Jack groaned even louder.

Bo circled around to Jack's front. She brought the handle of her whip to his face.

"Suck it, slave."

Jack opened his mouth and took the whip handle between his lips. When Bo nodded, Jezebel landed another blow on his bottom, and he moved his mouth forward onto the handle.

"So, you say that you've been a naughty boy?"

Bo thrust the handle in and out of Jack's mouth. At the same time, she tugged roughly on his erection.

"Mmmmph," Jack replied.

"Good." Bo pulled the handle out of his mouth, then wrapped the whip's thong around his stiff shaft and yanked it taut.

Jack moaned. His pelvis thrust forward, pulled by Bo.

Jezebel didn't want to be outdone. If this was her last chance to paddle Jack, she wanted to enjoy every last second, and Bo was stealing her thunder with her infernal whip.

Well, Jezebel would show her! She brought her hand back and swung it toward Jack's ass as hard as she could, then followed up with a series of quick, bold smacks.

"Oooooh yes!" Jack bucked his hips forward.

Encouraged, Jezzy landed several more smacks to his reddening ass cheeks, fast and furious.

Jack moaned again. "Oh, hells, yes!"

Jezebel's inner walls clenched with want, and she was now so wet she could feel her warm nectar dripping down her legs. Her breasts swayed, heavy with the vibrating clamps. Her blood thrummed in her ears, as loud as Jack's grunts.

This Domme stuff was fun. But the pulsing of her pussy was maddening. The spanking seemed to be making matters worse rather than better. Jezebel had never seen Jack's manhood so hard. The erection looked painful, reaching upward, bobbing back and forth. The head was almost purple.

"Go ahead, Jezebel. Try something else," Bo said. "I'm sure this slave will enjoy whatever you dish out."

Jezebel walked over to the wall and perused a section of oddly shaped light bulbs.

"What are these?"

Bo smiled, looked at the objects with lusty eyes. "Those are violet wands. They emit a small electrical charge. A shock, like when you touch something metal after rubbing your feet on the carpeting. They can be quite stimulating."

Jezebel chose a wand with a large ball on the end. "This one looks like fun."

"It's one of my favorites," Bo said.

Jezzy walked over and stood in front of Jack, flicking the button on the wand's handle. It glowed purple. Jack seemed both enthused and worried at the same time.

"How much is this going to hurt?" he asked.

"Show him," Bo ordered.

Jez reached out and touched the wand to Jack's belly. There was a spark and a snapping sound.

"Uuhh!" Jack flinched away from the shock.

A thrill coursed through Jezzy's whole body, and her pussy spasmed.

She held the wand to his chest, a little longer than she had with his belly. It buzzed and sparked.

"Aaaaaaah!" Jack cried, humping his hips once again.

"You like that?" Jezzy cooed. "Bad boy?"

Jack's face seemed panicked, but at the same time his hips strained toward her.

"Touch it to his prick," Bo said.

"Is that what you'd like, Jack?" Jezebel moved her face next to his, close enough to kiss him. "Should I shock your cock?"

Jack's face contorted. In pain? In desire? In desperation?

"Answer her, slave," Bo ordered, releasing the whip from his manhood and cracking it against his backside.

Jack cried out. Then he whispered, "Yes."

Jezebel reached the violet wand downward and gave Jack's rock hard rod a small *zap*.

Jack yelped, then shuddered. His breath came in gasps. He looked up at Jezzy, his face filled with longing.

"Oh, Mistress, please let me come."

Jezzy forgot that they were role playing. Looking into his eyes, seeing his need, she immediately reached for his member and began to stroke. "Yes. I will let—"

Bo snatched the violet wand from Jezebel.

"That is enough! How dare you take over and allow him to call you Mistress? I am the Mistress! You are merely a guest!" She snapped her fingers. "Bippity! Boppity! Lock this naughty girl in the pillory. I believe she needs to learn her place!"

Panic shot through Jezebel. Her heart batted against her ribcage like a butterfly in a jar.

"Wait! I'm sorry, Mistress! This isn't about me, it's about finding Jack a wife!"

Bo laughed. "You were quite enjoying your participation just a moment ago. There is no turning back for you, Jezebel. So suck it up, buttercup."

Bippity and Boppity each took Jezebel by an arm and led her to the pillory; a wooden framework with holes cut into it for locking head and hands.

The contraption was barbaric!

It was positively medieval!

This whole scenario had spun out of control!

So why aren't I stopping it right now?

Shock and dread ripped through Jezebel, while at the same time, her body hummed with new excitement. She'd be completely and utterly helpless in the pillory stock. Bippity and Boppity could have their way with her, and she would be powerless to stop them.

Bo could spank her and whip her and shock her, and she would be powerless to stop her.

Jack could...

Jack could do whatever he wants to me.

Oh, my.

Bo's brutes bent Jez forward, placing her neck and hands into the holes, and then they lowered the top and locked it into place.

The wood felt hard and cold against her throat and wrists. Jezebel tried moving, but only succeeded in limited wiggles. Because she was leaning forward, her bottom and pussy were completely exposed to Bippity and Boppity behind her. Shame reddened her face.

It was just as she'd imagined. They could do anything they wanted, she couldn't even see behind her. She was completely helpless.

"Perfect!" Bo said, her voice dripping with malicious intent. "Now to select a paddle."

Even though she'd been spanked before and enjoyed it, Jezzy was seized by a very real fear of the pain to come. She tensed her butt, closed her eyes, waiting for the blows to rain down.

Instead something moved lightly over her folds, then settled on her clit and pressed. Jezebel gasped, the sensation was so pleasurable she almost begged for it never to stop. She realized it was the handle of a paddle.

Bippity? Boppity? Bo? Jezzy couldn't tell.

"Just look at you, naughty girl," Bo's voice said behind her. "You're so swollen and wet, I bet you'd beg for any man to fuck you right now. Isn't that right?"

Jezebel squeezed her eyes shut, the idea of a cock filling her, driving into her while she was helplessly detained was exciting beyond words.

"Y-yes."

"Or maybe something other than a man."

The paddle handle slid into her, and Jezzy's breath caught in her throat. Slick with her juices, it moved deeper, poking in little downward movements, right against Jezzy's g-spot.

A tremble of need claimed her. "Oh!"

She tilted her hips upward, trying to open herself wider, to take the handle deeper inside. But as soon as she did, the paddle withdrew.

Jezzy let out a whimper and bit her lip, not wanting to beg and humiliate herself further in front of Jack.

I'm in such a pickle.

Hell, right now I'd be happy to be fucked by a pickle.

Anything would do.

Friction of any kind.

A tongue.

A hand.

A strong breeze.

Anything!

"You look so hot right now, Jez," Jack said. "All I can think about is having my way with you, making you scream with pleasure."

Although Jezebel could not see Jack, the rough passion in his voice sent shivers of need quavering through her. She could picture his face, filled with passion, and his steely, jerking cock reaching for her.

In fact, she was so caught up in Jack that she'd forgotten that she was to be paddled as well. So when the first smack came, it was a surprise.

Jezebel squeaked, shocked. The sting on her bottom felt hot, then warm, and her clit quivered.

Another smack with the paddle, harder than before.

Jezzy cried out, her face burning with humiliation. She'd never been in this kind of position before. Spanked in front of people. Locked helpless in a pillory. Her legs trembled, her pussy clenching.

The spanking came harder, faster. One. Two. Three. Jezebel yelped and squealed, her bottom searing, her nipples buzzing. Her sensitive breasts swung heavy, and each time her nipple clips clacked against the pillory, she felt an extra zing of pleasure.

She was so drenched now, she was certain that everyone could see her juices running down her legs, her opening spasming, eager to be filled.

"Boppity, release Jack. I want him to punish Jezebel." Bo's voice sounded far away.

From the corner of her eyes, Jezebel saw Jack being led, staggering, to stand in front of her. He took a moment to get his feet under him, then his lovely, thick cock was flexing right in front of her face.

Jezebel looked upward into his eyes, and what she saw there was such a turn on. Jack was not only having fun, but he was having the time of his life. He was, indeed, having the joyful, wonderful sexual escapade she'd promised. Jez had helped to bring him out of his comfort zone, show him something new, and he was loving it.

"Violate her mouth!" Bo shouted.

Jack moved forward, pressing his rigid manhood between Jezebel's lips.

Eagerly she took him inside, tasting the salty tang of pre-cum. He moved his hips, thrusting deeper, and she stroked her tongue along his underside.

Jack moaned, his hips moving faster.

Jezebel sucked, unable to get enough of him. Her entire existence in that moment was accepting Jack's cock deep into her mouth, into her throat, swallowing over it, wishing, wanting him to spill his juices into her. The paddle came down again, the sting entwining with pleasure, and a spasm of delight began deep inside.

"Enough!" Bo's harsh voice shrieked. "Jack, step back. Neither of you are allowed to come without my permission."

Jack withdrew from her mouth, and Jezzy almost cried.

Bo came into view before Jezebel. Her breasts jutted forward, nipples pink and protruding. She stopped with her legs slightly spread, her shaved pussy in front of Jezzy's face, silver hoop glinting.

"Bop!" Bo yelled. "Press a vibrator against her. Directly on her clitoris. We'll teach you a lesson yet, you scrappy little nympho."

Boppity knelt beside her, feeling her up again. Jezebel bit her lip. She was already so hot, she didn't know if she could hold off climaxing until Bo gave permission.

As if reading her mind, Bo said, "If you come, Jezebel, I'll keep you and Jack here all weekend."

"But the Prince's Ball!"

"You can forget about the ball. I'll make you stay here and mop my floors, and..." Bo trailed off. "Sorry, wrong fairy tale. But I'll think of something terrible."

Bo was still ruminating over fairy tale punishments when Bobbity pressed something firm against her clit. When the vibrations began, Jezebel cried out like she'd been thrown off a cliff.

"OH! MY! GOD!"

Bo leaned down beside her, her green eyes flashing with mischief. "No coming, Jezebel. There are a lot of fairy tales out there. I can punish you for days."

Jez thought about protesting, but knew anything other than complete obedience would anger Bo.

"Yes, Mistress. No... no coming."

"Jack, you will now violate her pussy."

A thrill seized Jezzy. She'd longed to feel Jack inside her all day. The thought that she was about to get her wish seized her whole body, and it was all she could do to prevent herself from having a big, screaming orgasm right there.

But Bo wasn't finished yet. "Bippity, I want you to take Jack's place in her mouth."

Dizzy with lust, Jezebel's mouth immediately opened. One man between her upper lips and another between her nether lips? The thought was intoxicating.

Bippity's muscular torso came into view, his member large and erect, and thighs gleaming with scented oil. His thick cock bobbed in Jezzy' face, and she parted her lips and took his length inside.

At the same time, she felt Jack grasp her hips, his manhood pressing against her wet opening.

I'm going to come.

No! I can't come!

Think of something unsexy, Jez.

War.

Poverty.

Disease.

Rotten tuna.

Jack fucking me.

Oh, my. Jack is about to fuck me.

Then he pushed himself inside. Immediately her inner walls gripped him, squeezing, not wanting to ever let him go.

Jack began moving into her, in and out, in and out. Slowly, as if lingering with each stroke.

"Harder, lover boy!" Bo screamed, and then there was the sound of a loud *CRACK!*

Jack grunted. He drove himself deeper, his cock impossibly hard, swelling into her slick space like never before.

Jezebel tilted her hips upward, giving him better access, her breath exploding from her lungs with his every thrust. She had never wanted to be fucked so badly. She'd never needed it so badly.

THWACK! THWACK! Then *SNAP!* The sound of Bo's merciless whip against Jack's skin. His cries soared, sounding like the howling of a wild animal.

Jezebel would've felt pity for him, but his cries sounded so lustful, so filled with pleasure, that they only served to make her hotter.

"Scream, slave! I want to hear it!" Bo rose above Jack's rising screams. "Punish her! Punish the naughty little vixen!"

His cock plunged into Jezebel again and again, filling her, moving against her g-spot, driving her wild with want. Every nerve inside her walls seemed to ignite.

She sucked Boppity in rhythm with Jack, fueled by the plunges from behind. With every one of Jack's thrusts, the whip snapped through the air. Jezebel heard Bo's ragged breaths, and the husky arousal in her commands. She listened to Jack's ecstatic bellows when the whip hit, feeling such happiness that he was enjoying himself so much. Feeling so proud that she'd had a hand in it. Soon he would be married to someone else, but at least she could please him right now. At least they had this. One last time together.

The vibrations surrounding her little nub were so insistent, so delicious, and the feel of Jack thrusting into her the way only he knew how to do, the way she liked it most, was so overpowering that Jezebel couldn't help it. Her entire body grew hot, and her muscles started to grip low in her belly.

"Faster!" Bo screamed. "Harder!"

Jack drove into her, over and over, drawing out every sensation. Her bottom stung with each forward motion he made. Her nipples buzzed with need, and her clit flashed with a searing, exquisite heat. She cried out, little flames licking at her most sensitive spot. She teetered on the edge of orgasm, her entire body beginning to convulse.

"Very good, naughty ones!" Bo cried. "Now come! Come now or endure more torture!"

A deep bellow erupted from the giant, Boppity, then a shudder, and his hot juice spurted into Jezebel's mouth as quickly as she could swallow it.

Jack gripped her hips harder. His thrusts came faster, slamming into Jezebel.

Faster.

Faster.

His cock jerked inside of her, and he emitted a wolf-like howl just as Jezebel's entire body seized around him.

Firecrackers burst inside of her. Stars exploded before her eyes. She peaked once, twice, maybe more, she couldn't tell, pleasure overtook her, blanking out conscious thought, and Jack's cries melded with her own became Jezebel's whole world.

It was one helluva good lay, that was for sure.

Chapter 3

Rapunzel, Rapunzel, Take off Your Clothes…

Bo Peep quickly Velcroed herself back into her pink dress and bonnet (so quickly it was almost eerie), and she escorted Jack and Jezebel to the door.

"Give me a call if either of you is feeling naughty and in need of punishment."

Jezebel frowned at the innocent-looking Domme. "I thought you were looking for a husband."

"Oh, I am."

"But not Jack?" Jez glanced at him, hoping he didn't feel hurt by Bo's rejection.

Jack just smiled, as if totally unfazed.

"I like Jack quite a bit, but the man I marry will only have his wrists and ankles in shackles, not his heart."

"I don't understand. What do you mean by—"

Jack grabbed Jezzy's arm and pulled her out the door. "Thanks, Bo! See ya!"

When they reached the gate, his steps slowed. Once outside the picket fence, he slipped an arm around Jezzy's shoulders and smiled down at her, looking exhausted but deliriously happy.

"You enjoyed yourself," she said.

"More than you know."

"But you didn't seem upset that Bo didn't want to marry you."

"I had fun, but I didn't want to marry her, either. Can you imagine being whipped like that on a daily basis?" He gently patted his butt. "I would never be able to sit down again. Remember little Jack Horner needs to sit in the corner now and then."

Jezzy bit her lip. Strike two. She'd failed to find him a wife for the second time. Not only was the Big Cock Billionaire Magazine piece in jeopardy, but Jack was certainly doubting her match-making skills. She could be fired. Her reputation could be ruined. The bad press could mean Jezebel might lose her business, her livelihood. Get kicked out of her home and onto the street, where she would only be able to survive by blowing filthy hobos for twenty-five cents a suck.

It never occurred to her that she'd wind up with Jack at the end of the story, like everyone reading this already knows. But this gaping flaw in her character, and her inability to see the blatantly obvious, meant there would be a few more sex scenes.

So Jez worried about her future, Jack patiently waited for her to get a clue, and more deviant erotica awaited. Probably bondage. The author seemed to have a thing for bondage.

When they reached the motorcycle, Jack stopped and turned to Jezebel. "Look Jez. You've really gone above and beyond to find me a wife. I really don't think—"

Oh no! He's going to fire me!

Jezebel lifted a hand, palm up, stopping him mid-sentence.

"I have just the woman for you. She's perfect. Softer than Bo, more carefree than Snow, and the algorithm ranks ninety-nine percent compatible."

Jack stared at her, something like disappointment in his eyes.

"Let me prove myself, Jack. Please don't let me go, yet."

"Let you go?"

"Please don't fire me." Jezzy was shaking even more than she had in Bo's pillory. She forced herself to take a breath and push the desperation out of her voice. "This next woman is wonderful. You will love her, Jack. Trust me."

"I do trust you, Jez. I hope you know that."

"So you'll give me another chance?"

"I've been aching to give you another chance."

"Great!" Jez said, oblivious to what anyone else would see as crystal clear. "Let me punch in the GPS coordinates."

Jezebel played with the touch screen on Jack's bike, and then she rode behind him to their next destination, her arms tight around his waist, feeling happier than she had since…

Well, since they'd broken up.

"So how do we get in?" Jack asked Jezzy when they arrived.

They parked beneath the window of the tallest tower of a very tall castle, but there were no doors anywhere.

"This is where Rapunzel lives."

"So we have to climb up her hair? Like, for real?"

Jezzy looked up at the window and shrugged. "That's how the fairy tale goes. If nothing else, we'd at least better stick as closely to that part of it as we can. I have a feeling nothing else about that particular fairy tale will look anything like the original. The happy endings in Brothers Grimm stories aren't the same as the happy endings in massage parlors."

Jack sighed. "Okay. Fine. I just hope she's not too pushy. I'm looking forward to having a little more control this time." He lifted his arms and shouted up to the window. "Rapunzel, Rapunzel, please let down your hair!"

Nobody appeared at the window.

Jack tried again. "Rapunzel, Rapunzel, please let down your hair!"

After a long moment, a blonde head appeared at the open window. "Sorry! I'm running a little late." She hefted an armful of gleaming golden hair into her arms and let it drop through the window.

Jack gestured to the shimmering rope. "Ladies first."

"You just want to look at my ass."

"So?"

Jezzy started up the golden tresses, remembering the first time Jack had watched her ass as she climbed. When she was about twenty feet off the ground, she peered down at Jack.

"What is it? You're smiling," he asked her.

Jezzy hadn't realized that she'd been smiling. "This puts me in mind of our last adventure, where I climbed up the enormous beanstalk. Well, minus the perverted, caressing leaves."

"Only this time you're wearing a skirt," Jack said, peering up at her. "And no panties."

Jezzy's face heated, and so did her nether regions. She had to admit, she liked having Jack ogle her. Not as much as having him plunge into her from behind or slide into her mouth, but it was right up there.

If only it didn't have to end with him marrying someone else.

Jezzy shook away the thought. She was a matchmaker. Jack's happiness should be all that mattered. Not jealously pining for an ex-boyfriend. A handsome, well hung, billionaire ex-boyfriend whom she still loved.

If only he loved me, too...

"Hurry up!" Rapunzel shouted down. "This hurts like hell!"

"We're on our way!" Jezebel gave Jack a smile and continued the climb up Rapunzel's hair, enjoying the thought of him watching her every move. After a few moments she reached the top and threw one leg over the window sill. Rapunzel helped her climb through.

Jack was right behind her, springing through the window all on his own. He was both nimble and quick, and had plenty of practice climbing, since he used to live at the top of a beanstalk.

Rapunzel tossed her head, sending a wave through her golden hair, and Jezebel realized that under her crowning glory, Rapunzel wore no clothing at all.

Who coulda guessed?

"I'm so excited to get to know you, Jack. I'm Rapunzel."

"Likewise," Jack said, eyeing Rapunzel's full breasts and prominent nipples as they peeked out from between shimmering strands. "Is it a little warm in here? I think it might be a little warm in here."

Rapunzel rustled to Jack's side (that much hair makes a lot of noise). "Let me help you get more comfortable."

She unbuttoned Jack's shirt then slid it from his shoulders. "Better?"

"A bit," Jack said. "But it's still a bit steamy."

Rapunzel unbuttoned and unzipped Jack's pants. He was already partially hard, and when a tendril of hair wrapped around him as if in a caress, his erection flexed upward.

Jack was right; it was getting a tad warm. If it weren't for Jezzy's insistence on professionalism, she would have stripped naked at that very moment.

"Your hair is amazing, Rapunzel," Jack said. "So soft and sexy."

"Thank you."

"I have an idea," he continued, fingering the silky strand. "A way for us to get acquainted, but I'll need Jezebel's help."

Jezzy glanced from the mischievous glint in Jack's eyes, to Rapunzel's hair, and then back. After the fun they'd had with Bo Peep, Jezzy thought she might be able to guess Jack's idea.

"Have you ever tried being tied up?" Jezzy asked Rapunzel.

"Tied up?" Rapunzel said. "You mean, with my hair? What a wonderful idea!"

Jack's grin grew almost as exuberantly as his erection. He looked at Jezebel. "You read my mind."

"Wouldn't be the first time." When she and Jack were together, they would often finish each other's sentences. And they always seemed to be able to sense what the other wanted in bed.

It was almost like they were meant to be together.

"Would you do the honors?" Jack said, gesturing to the beautiful, very naked, and very eager Rapunzel.

"Certainly." Pushing the wistful memories from her mind, Jezebel focused on her job.

Rapunzel's hair covered the entire room and all its contents. The floor was covered in hair. The furniture was covered in hair. The large, heart shaped bed was covered in hair. It might be kind of gross, except that every strand was glossy, glittering, and golden.

If Rapunzel ever lost a hair while cooking, Jez thought, *she'd no doubt die a horrible, choking death.*

Jezebel picked up a lock. There were already several rings secured into the ceiling and walls, and Jezebel couldn't help but wonder if Rapunzel was more familiar with being tied up than she was letting on.

She gathered a section of the long, silken tresses and looped it into one of rings imbedded in the tower wall. Then she fastened the end around Rapunzel's wrist, stretching her arm above her head.

"That's just what I was thinking," Jack said, grinning.

Rapunzel clapped her hands. "What a wonderful idea! I've never thought of doing that."

Jezebel frowned and motioned to the walls. "But you have all these hooks and rings. I assumed…"

"Oh, that! I like to suspend myself. Pretend I'm flying. I love zip-lining across the tower. It's great fun! Would you like to try it?"

"Maybe later," Jezebel said. Rapunzel was awfully sweet. And beautiful. And Jack clearly was attracted to her, as evidenced by his bobbing erection.

Yes, at ninety-nine percent compatible, Rapunzel will make Jack a lovely wife. Mission accomplished. I won't be forced to blow dirty transients in alleys for two bits.

So why aren't I happier?

Puzzled by her ambiguous feelings, Jezebel went to work binding the beautiful Rapunzel. Once she was finished with her dainty wrists, Jezzy wrapped a thick lock of golden hair tightly around Rapunzel's ankles, spreading her legs apart and looping the hair through the sliver hoops on the walls.

"Oooh! I like this already!" Rapunzel said.

"Me, too." Jack was tugging on his stiff manhood, lust on his face as he drank in the sight of the helpless and bound Rapunzel.

Jezebel sighed, her heart sinking. She remembered when he used to look at her that way. And despite her best efforts, she couldn't help but wish it was she who was tied up for Jack now.

Jezebel eyed the mountains of hair still heaped around the tower, plenty for her to climb down and leave the two lovebirds in peace. "Your lovely date awaits, Jack."

"And lovely she is," Jack said. "But we're not yet ready."

Confused, Jezebel looked back at Rapunzel. "We're not?"

"It's your turn, Jezzy," Jack said, a wicked grin on his face.

"M-my turn?" Jezebel managed. Her heart jumped, then began to race, then launched into a samba, finishing off with an uptempo rendition of *If I Had a Hammer*.

"Yes. I require the hands on, sexual portion of your service," Jack clarified.

"Oh," Jezebel said. Here she was hoping he'd tie her up and enjoy her as much as he enjoyed Rapunzel. She'd wanted him to touch her, tease her, make love to her. Obviously she'd gotten carried away.

I'll take whatever I can get in the short time I'm with him, even if it's only in a professional capacity. He never needs to know how much I miss him.

Jezzy nodded, regaining her self-control. "I'm happy to help. Would you like me to test Rapunzel's responsiveness while you watch?"

"Uh, sure," Jack said. "I'd be okay with that."

Jezebel dropped to her knees, her face between Rapunzel's open thighs. The blond hair still covered her nudity like a curtain. The woman smelled as lovely as she looked, perfumed, yet with a musky scent that made Jezzy curious to taste.

"Wait," Jack said. "This won't do at all."

Jezebel stopped, her fingers an inch from the tresses draped over Rapunzel's folds. "What is it?"

"You can't properly test her. Not this way."

"Why? What's wrong?" The thought that she'd made a mistake when this was supposed to be her specialty made Jezzy's cheeks heat.

"It would be a much better test if you were naked, too."

That didn't make much sense, but Jez nodded anyway.

"But leave the boots," Jack reminded. "Without them this story wouldn't resemble the Puss in Boots fairytale at all."

Jezebel took off the blouse, her bra, and her skirt, then stood in front of Jack, pussy in boots. "Is this better?"

"Oh, yes. But there's one more thing." Jack took hold of Jezebel's hands and wrapped a silky shank of golden hair around her wrists, binding them in front of her.

Excitement shivered over Jezebel's skin. As he tied, her arms pushed against the sides of her breasts, plumping them and tilting their tingling peaks upward.

"You like that, Jez?"

"I'm here to serve the client's needs," she said, ever the pro.

"Good." Jack moved close to Rapunzel and smoothed her long hair back to reveal one naked breast then the other. Her mounds were full and heavy, her areolas a delicate pink. "Now I want you to lick Rapunzel's nipples."

Wrists bound, Jezzy stepped close to the blond beauty. She circled a stiff peak with her tongue, and a shiver shook Rapunzel. The shiver somehow spread to Jez.

"Now the other," Jack said, his voice raspy. "Suck it into your mouth."

Jezebel did, playing with the tight nub with her tongue while she sucked.

Rapunzel arched her back for more and moaned.

"Now rub your tits against hers, Jez. Nipple against nipple."

Jezebel moved close. At the first touch of her sensitive peak to Rapunzel's, a sensation zipped through her like that of a delicious shock. She moved against the blonde's breasts, still slick from Jezzy's mouth.

"Oh, yes." Jack blew out a hard breath. "Now that's responsive."

Jezebel wanted to suggest that it would feel even better with his cock sliding between Rapunzel's breasts, but she wasn't sure it was her place.

Of course, that didn't stop her imagination. Jez could almost feel his head gliding between the slick mounds, watching as it poked in an out, and she almost let out a moan.

"Now lick her pussy, Jez. I want to see if she's as responsive to your tongue as I am."

Jezebel lowered herself to her knees, and Jack opened the drape of Rapunzel's hair to showcase...

"Whoa." Jack said. "That's one helluva bush."

Indeed, the curly mounds springing up from Rapunzel's loins were something out of a 1970s porno film. And the carpet did not match the curtains. Rather than golden silk, Rapunzel's pubes were dark and kinky.

It almost looked like she had Jimi Hendrix sprouting between her legs.

"Can you find her pussy in there?" Jack asked, his voice tinged with concern. "Do you need a hairbrush? Scissors? A spotlight? A search party with bloodhounds?"

Jezebel used her tied hands to part the gigantic mound—seriously, it was like going down on a Chia Pet—and finally she saw a glimmer of pink hidden deep within. Jezzy brought her mouth to the center of Rapunzel's thighs, the hair wisped against her in a caress.

She laid a fat lick along the seam of Rapunzel's pussy lips, and the woman gave a shiver that seemed to shake the room. But Jezebel had only just gotten started.

She delved deeper, taking the excited nub into her mouth, rolling it with her tongue, then sliding into her sensitive tunnel.

Rapunzel squirmed, raising her pelvis.

Jezebel eased up on the pressure.

The best oral sex was all about teasing, Jez knew. Teasing and coaxing and alternating firm pressure with a light touch.

Jezzy began a rhythm. Soft licks. Hard licks. Penetrating Rapunzel with her tongue. Avoiding her completely and licking her thighs and belly button.

"Make her beg for it, Jezzy," Jack huffed.

She cast a sideways glance at her billionaire ex-boyfriend and saw he was stroking himself furiously.

"Beg me to lick you," Jez said.

"Please!" Rapunzel gasped. "Please lick me harder."

"Keep teasing her," Jack said. "Don't let her come yet."

Jack's orders were turning on Jezebel in a big way, but they seemed to incense Rapunzel, who was bucking and moaning and cursing in a way that would make George Carlin blush.

Seriously. Jez had never been called an "ass-banging monkey fuck whore bitch rhino slut" before. And while the foul language didn't bother Jez, Jack seemed to really enjoy it. He was beating meat harder and faster than Rocky at the packing plant.

So Jez continued to tease, Rapunzel continued to gyrate and scream obscenities, and Jack continued to abuse himself so savagely Jez feared he might rub off his foreskin.

"All right!" Jack said, abruptly halting his self-gratification. "I've had enough!"

At first, Jezebel feared she'd done something wrong. "I'm sorry, Jack. Did I misunderstand what you—"

"Wanted? No. But now I want something else."

"Anything. Just tell me—"

"What it is? Well, I'll do that if you—"

"If I gave you the chance to finish?" Jezzy said.

"Yeah." He grinned at her. "I need to try something for myself."

Jack pulled Jezebel to her feet then fed the hair rope binding her hands through a hoop in the wall straight above her. As he stretched her hands above her head, the rough hairs of his chest ticked her breasts and nipples, making them tingle.

The feeling of the soft hair binding her wrists excited Jezebel, but having Jack stand so near to her, right in front of her, his face mere inches from hers, made her feel all melty and googly-eyed. Jez could sense her own heart beating in her wrists, in her neck, and thought she heard it above the blood now roaring through her ears.

Jack brought his hands down. He was so close, Jez could taste his breath in her open mouth. Her lips were parted, and her own breaths quickened, making her breasts rise and fall. Her nipples poked forward, craving Jack's mouth and tongue.

"Does that feel good?" he asked, his cocoa eyes penetrating hers.

"Yes," Jezebel breathed, trying to keep the excitement out of her voice, wanting him inside her again.

"Good." He leaned forward and brushed his lips over hers. "Very good."

Jezzy caught herself leaning forward for a kiss.

But Jack leaned back, grinning. He brought the lock of hair between and around her, in a crisscross fashion, so that her breasts lifted and jutted forward. He then kneeled down, taking one of her nipples between his lips. He moved his tongue over it, back and forth, back and forth, then nibbled ever so lightly.

Jezebel gasped in pleasure. She tried to arch her back, the hair restraining her movement. The heat of his mouth felt so amazing, Jez felt herself grow even more wet, hot honey slicking her folds.

Jack pulled back, watched her face with a smirk, then worked the lock of hair around one leg, winding it all the way down until he reached Jezzy's ankle, pulling her leg far away from the other. He fed the hair through the hoop, wrapped it around the other ankle, and spread her legs wide.

Jezzy felt deliciously helpless. Similar to the pillory, but even more sexy because she was at Jack's mercy, not Bo Peep's. Her body hummed with excitement and anticipation of what Jack might do to her. What she hoped that he would do to her.

All in the name of therapy and matchmaking, of course, she reminded herself.

"Hey, you fucking elephant douchebag shit-lickers, did you fucking forget about me?" Rapunzel shook her whole body viciously, as if to remind them of her presence.

Jack stepped forward, standing in front of both Jezzy and Rapunzel. "Have you ever experienced edging, Rapunzel?"

"Like in sewing?" She asked. "I don't wear clothes."

"No, like in the Fifty Shades of Alice in Wonderland series. Alice experiences edging and orgasm denial. It's a real turn-on."

"What a coincidence! Those books are on my Kindle," Rapunzel said. "I haven't yet read them, but now I can't wait!"

"Make sure you have a friend, real or battery-run, near you when you do." Jack stepped forward. "Let me demonstrate."

Jezebel gazed at Jack as he stepped in front of Rapunzel, brushed his lips lightly across hers, then trailed fevered kisses along her throat. He feathered his tongue over Rapunzel's creamy breast, alternating between light kisses and little licks.

Rapunzel sighed, arching her back. "Oooooh."

Jack sucked her nipple in between his lips, flicking his tongue over it, biting lightly down upon it and making Rapunzel cry out. She strained her hips forward, clearly wanting Jack to touch her most sensitive area.

Jack stepped back, smiling. His face was flushed, and his manhood stood straight out, twitching. His eyes roamed over Rapunzel's lovely, curvaceous body, as if he were drinking her in. He moved forward once again and lightly stroked the basketball afro of Rapunzel's mound.

He obviously finds her attractive. I always suspected he preferred blondes.

Jezebel felt her heart squeeze as she watched Jack enjoying Rapunzel's body. *But if she's the one for him, then I've done it. I've succeeded. And Jack's happiness is important to me.*

Jezzy watched, becoming wetter, as Jack lightly slid two fingers over Rapunzel's pussy. She moaned and pushed her pelvis forward stretching her restraints and sighing.

Jezebel could see how slick Rapunzel was becoming. Her juices were shining on Jack's fingers as he gently stroked her, wispy movements, ever so lightly, up and down, then round and round.

"I think I like edging," Rapunzel sighed.

Rapunzel tried to move her hips against Jack's hand, but her hair cinched tightly limited her movements. She moaned. "Please, Jack. Devour me."

"In good time," Jack murmured. "You're beautiful like this, Rapunzel. Helpless and pleading, and horny as hell. Not many visitors to this tower?"

"I have the occasional visitor, but they are very impatient. They just want to get in and out, for the most part."

"That's a shame. You deserve better." Jack pressed his palm against Rapunzel's sweet spot, making slow circles.

"Oh, my gosh!" Rapunzel cried, squeezing her eyes shut. "I think I'm going to… I'm going to…"

Jack withdrew his hand, now sliding it upward and cupping one of Rapunzel's breasts while grazing his thumb back and forth over the pink little nipple.

"Uuuugh!" Rapunzel cried. "You dog-blowing ass-biting hippo scrotum! You're teasing me worse than that fart-muncher Jezebel!"

"This is what edging is."

"Then edging sucks the turds out of herpes pigeons!"

"You'll thank me later." Jack smiled, taking her nipple between his teeth and lightly pulling back.

As she watched Jack with Rapunzel, Jezzy felt her own folds swell, her clit protruding, as if Jack were stroking her, teasing her, bringing her to the edge yet not letting her go over. Jack flicked his tongue back and forth over Rapunzel's nipple, then rolled his tongue over it as his fingers skimmed down her belly, gliding once again between her now shimmering folds. The slow up and down movements, and Rapunzel's cries became louder as she squirmed against his fingers.

"I will fucking kill you and your whole fucking family with an axe if you don't let me come, you dildo-breath son of a whore!"

Jack merely chuckled, moving to the other breast and sucking the nipple between his lips and his fingers pleasured Rapunzel's secret pearl.

Jezebel felt so aroused, imagining it were her in Rapunzel's place, that she was dangerously close to coming herself.

Need stung her hard little nub, and she felt her hips moving forward, searching even for a stray strand of Rapunzel's hair to caress her.

"Oh! Oh, my gosh! Oh, my gosh!" Rapunzel's voice became high with urgency.

Jack moved away from Rapunzel, grinning.

"Die you goat blowing thunder shit asshole!"

"Have you been treated for Tourette's?" Jack asked Rapunzel. "I think we've gone past regular old dirty talk."

"LET! ME! COME!"

"It's edging. I'm denying you orgasm. Trust me. When you do come, it will be spectacular."

"I'm going to take a chainsaw and stick it up your goddamn—"

Jack wrapped a lock of Rapunzel's hair over her mouth and tied it there, effectively gagging her. Then he stared at Jezebel and moved in front of her.

"Your turn, Jez. Still have that self-control you showed me at the restaurant during your interview?"

Jezzy's heartbeat quickened yet again as Jack stood so close to her. "Of course. I'm a professional."

Jack leaned in and took her earlobe lightly between his teeth. His tongue moved over it as his breath warmed her ear, as if he were going to tell her a secret. The feeling of his breath was so intimate that Jezebel's legs went weak.

He swept his tongue over her throat and the knelt before her, planting little licks and kisses over one breast, then the other, moving around the nipples.

Jezebel sighed, feeling his soft chest hair against her hot folds, tickling her sensitive, swollen clit. She gritted her teeth, trying not to show how aroused she already was.

"You can't fool me, Jez. I know how much you like this. I've done it before. I know how you love to have your breasts licked and kissed, and how much you like this..." He moved lower, blowing a little puff of air over her.

The feeling of his breath on her folds aroused her madly. Of their own accord, her hips rolled forward, tightening the restraints on her wrists and around her breasts, squeezing them further.

Jack sat back on his heels, then stood, granting Jezebel a brief, much needed reprieve. "Rapunzel, you spend a lot of time alone in this tower. I imagine you have some interesting toys?"

Rapunzel screamed something unintelligible into her hair-gag, but her eyes turned toward a large wooden trunk next to the bed.

"May I?" Jack asked, walking over it.

"Mmphhmmmphhgrrrrr!"

"Thank you kindly."

Jack opened the trunk and smiled widely. "Well, you certainly have a nice variety here. He pulled out a large penis-shaped dildo. "And it vibrates," he said, switching it on.

Jack approached Rapunzel. "Let's try the high setting."

Rapunzel moaned, nodding profusely, trying to squirm forward against the hair that bound her.

Jezebel licked her lips as she watched Jack hold the vibrator against one of Rapunzel's nipples. As she arched her back and squirmed, Jack skipped the vibrator over her belly and pressed it, ever so lightly, against Rapunzel's glistening pussy.

Rapunzel's breaths became ragged gasps, and she began to buck.

"I don't think so."

He moved the dildo away. Rapunzel screamed in obvious frustration.

"I am thoroughly enjoying teasing you, lovely Rapunzel. I could do this for hours."

Jezebel eyed Jack's incredibly hard and erect cock as he teased Rapunzel with the vibrator. He moved his manhood between her legs and rubbed it back and forth several times as he held the vibrator against her sweet spot.

Rapunzel's eyes rolled up and her lovely red lips parted as she cried out in pleasure.

Once again, Jack stepped back.

More high-decibel screaming. Jez wondered if there were any earplugs in the trunk.

"Do you want me to stop?" Jack asked her.

Rapunzel shook her head frantically.

Jack chuckled again. "That's what I thought."

Jezebel was now panting, imagining that Jack was holding the vibrating dildo against her and rubbing his manhood between her lips. Either pair. Desire sent tremors through her, and her legs began to quiver.

Jack leaned forward and kissed Rapunzel's lips—the upper pair gagged with hair (though the lower pair were also gagged with hair)—so softly and with such obvious affection that watching it went straight through Jezebel.

Jezebel felt an odd mixture of envy, sadness, and scorching arousal as she watched them together. The chemistry between them was nothing short of combustible.

Then Jack removed Rapunzel's hair gag and plowed his tongue into her mouth at the same moment he drove his manhood into her, the vibrator pressed firmly against her clit.

Rapunzel screamed into Jack's cheeks, bellowing them out, becoming so loud, it was clear that she was about to erupt into orgasm.

Jezzy expected Jack to step back once again, but this time, he didn't.

Rapunzel's cries went on and on, and by the time she finished, Jezzy almost felt as if she'd had multiple orgasms right along with her.

Almost.

When Jack's buttocks clenched with his climax and he emptied himself into Rapunzel, their hostess sagged against her restraints and finally STFU, obviously wrung out with exhaustion.

Jack climbed off, and then turned his hungry eyes upon Jezebel. He clenched the dildo tightly in his fist, as if it were a weapon.

"And now it's your turn."

Yes! Jezebel thought, ready to squee. *Oh, yes!*

"Hey, bitches," Rapunzel said, yawning wide. "I hate to break up the party, but I need a little nap if I'm to go to the ball tonight. If you wouldn't mind, the window is that way. You can use my hair and let yourself out."

Chapter 5

Balling Prince Charming...

Jezebel dressed, hiding her disappointment that she wasn't going to make love to Jack one final time before the wedding. Rapunzel and Jack had obviously hit it off. She was a perfect match for him. The algorithm had predicted correctly. Jack would ask Rapunzel to Prince Charming's fairytale ball, marry her, and be blissfully bound (literally and figuratively) for life.

"Well, Rapunzel, it's been fun." Jack pulled on his pants and zipped them up as he approached Rapunzel, who was still tied with the golden locks of her hair.

"It certainly has been," Rapunzel said, yawning. Her eyes were droopy with drowsiness. "Maybe I'll see you at the ball later."

"Yeah. Maybe."

Jezebel frowned.

"Wait a moment," Jezebel said as Jack freed Rapunzel from the hair bondage. "Aren't you going to the fairytale castle together? That's where you're supposed to announce your engagement."

Rapunzel shook her head. "She's adorable, but kind of dense," she said to Jack.

Jack stared at Jez. "I'm not taking Rapunzel to the ball."

"W-what?" Jezebel stopped walking and stared at Jack. "But you looked so happy in there with her. There was sexual chemistry between you two. She's your sexual soulmate. According to my program, you're ninety-nine compatible!"

"She's certainly a great lady, and a lot of fun."

"Fucking-A I am," Rapunzel agreed. "But there has to be more than chemistry. It's obvious Jack doesn't love me."

"Well, why not?" Jezebel was torn between feeling like she'd failed, once again, and being relieved that Jack wouldn't be marrying Rapunzel.

It was an irrational feeling, because she'd have to give him up soon. Especially since time was running out. It would be night time in a couple of short hours they would have to be at the castle for the ball.

"His body was certainly into it," Rapunzel said. "But his heart wasn't."

This couldn't be! She was supposed to be the one!

A lump rose in Jezzy's throat.

What about the interview with Big Cock Billionaire Magazine? If Jack didn't get married, her match-making business would be ruined. Jez would be left homeless, sucking off tramps for pocket change.

"What about the interview with Big Cock Billionaire Magazine?" she said. "If you aren't getting married, my match-making business will be ruined. I'll be left homeless, sucking off tramps for pocket change."

"Dense, and kind of a drama queen," Rapunzel said.

"Jezzy, you won't be homeless. And why are you talking about sucking off tramps? What does that have to do with anything? Not that I think your business will be ruined, but there aren't any other job opportunities open to you? It's either run your own company, or blow bums? There's no middle ground there? Maybe a management position? The medical field? Real estate?"

"I can't fail at this, Jack," Jezebel implored. "It's too important."

"Jezebel, I don't want to continue this—"

Oh no! He's going to give up on me! Then I'll be a total failure! Think fast!

"Wait a second." Jezebel pulled her tablet from her handbag. She did a few quick calculations, then smiled. "I have an idea. A single looking for a spouse who I almost missed."

"Jez, I don't need to—"

"Come on, Jack. Take one more chance on me, please?"

Jack frowned.

"You still like trying new things, don't you?"

He nodded, albeit reluctantly. "You and I've tried a lot of new things together."

"Exactly. And I don't know why I didn't think of this before. I've been seeing this whole search from the wrong angle."

"You have?"

"Yes. But now I understand."

His expression brightened. "You do?"

"Yes. So will you give me one last chance?"

Please let him say yes, please, please, please...

"Of course, Jez. That's what I've been trying to say all along."

Jezebel let out a breath of pure relief. "Great. Fantastic. Stupendous. Leave everything to me. We need to get to the castle! Rapunzel, let down your hair!"

"Going to sleep," she droned. "Do it yourself."

They did a quick rappel down, Jezebel wished she'd asked Rapunzel what kind of hair conditioner she used because it was *seriously amazing*—I mean, why didn't this woman have an endorsement deal yet?—and then Jez was once again punching coordinates into the GPS on Jack's bike.

In the United States, amusement parks were often found surrounding the resident castle. Fairytaleland was no different in this regard. But the amusements in the park *were* different. Quite different.

When they arrived, Jezebel reluctantly let go of Jack's waist as he killed the bike's engine. She swung her leg over the bike and gazed at the castle thrusting into the sky behind the amusement park. The tower was erect and formidable, a stark reminder of her upcoming interview with Big Cock Billionaire Magazine, among other things, and Jez was struck again by the fear that she was running out of time.

She needed to have Jack engaged by the time the clock struck twelve or his coach would turn back to a pumpkin.

Wait, wrong fairytale.

She needed to kill the ogre who owned the castle and convince the king it belonged to Jack.

Wait, correct fairytale, but an ogre didn't own this castle, and Jack was so rich he could buy it any time he pleased.

She needed to find his soulmate and maybe get one last lay in before he was married.

Sounded like a plan!

Jezebel focused on the amusement park. From here she could see the Ferris wheel slowly turning and a twisty rollercoaster bulleting through the air. The delighted shrieks of the passengers cut through the impending twilight. Not just shrieks of fear and delight, but also shrieks of passion.

"You like amusement parks, right Jack?"

Jack climbed off the motorcycle. "I remember going to amusement parks with you, Jez. We had fun, didn't we?"

Jezebel smiled a little sadly. "We did. And this one is special. Trust me."

Jack took her hand and interlaced his fingers with hers. "I trust you, Jez. Always have, always will."

Jezebel's heart fluttered. This might be the last time they held hands. Her stomach knotted, and she wasn't sure if it was due to the pressure of finding Jack a soulmate in time, or because she truly didn't want to let him go.

But whatever the answer, it was too late for regrets. She had a job to do.

"Hello, Jezebel!"

Jezzy glanced up and spotted the prince standing at the top of a water slide. He cut an impressive figure, six feet tall and all chiseled muscle, large, grey eyes and striking Nordic features. Rumor had it he had once looked like a frog, before he'd had work done.

But however his perfection had come about, the man was undeniably gorgeous. He was also undeniably naked.

He slid down the waterslide and sailed through the air, landing on both feet in front of Jack and Jezebel. "Jezebel, how lovely to see you."

He kissed her hand, then turned to Jack and dipped into an exaggerated bow, waving his arm with a flourish. "Prince Charming at your service. Pleased to make your acquaintance. I just got Jezebel's email saying the two of you were on your way here. Her idea is interesting, don't you think?"

Jack looked puzzled. "I always find Jezebel's ideas interesting."

The prince grinned. "Then let's begin! I have just the ride. I think you'll quite enjoy it. Follow me."

Jack shot a confused glance at Jezzy, and she answered with a smile. Then Prince Charming motioned for them to follow, and he started off through the amusement park.

They passed several rides, including a giant rocket that shot into a dark cave, a giant drill that sank into a deep hole, a monorail that raced back and forth through a tight tunnel, and a giant cock that thrust repeatedly into a huge vagina.

Finally the prince stopped at a trampoline platform. A structure of poles surrounded it, and from each a harness dangled from bungee cords. Several naked couples already occupied the ride, bouncing while enjoying all manners of intercourse.

Vaginal intercourse.

Oral intercourse.

Anal intercourse.

Philosophical intercourse.

Political intercourse.

And every other kind of intercourse Jezzy could imagine (except bestial intercourse and incest, since Amazon doesn't allow them).

The whole scene was crazy and arousing and made Jezebel keenly aware it had been at least a long time since her last orgasm.

"It looks like fun!" Jack watched with a grin on his face, looking like a kid at Christmas.

The prince watched Jack with a gleam in his eye. "Would you like to try it?"

"Absolutely!"

"Excellent! You will need to remove your knickers, Jack," Charming said.

Jack dropped his pants faster than Jezebel had ever seen him remove them before. Of course, he *had* practiced a lot today.

"Come on, Jez."

Trying to ignore the tingle in her nipples and nether region, Jezebel shook her head. Time was ticking away, and this was her last chance. She had to put Jack's future happiness over her own needs. "It looks very enjoyable, but I think I'll sit this one out."

Jack looked at the platform of bungee bouncers. Everyone had a sexual partner and there were no stragglers. "But who will I bounce with?"

Charming chuckled. "Why, with me, you silly dilly."

"W-what?" Jack's mouth dropped open.

"Prince Charming is your date," Jezebel said. "I don't know why I never thought of including men in the search, before. But according to my algorithm, you two are one hundred percent compatible! Not only do you have all of the same likes, dislikes, kinks, turn-ons, hobbies, and affectations for the same sports teams—"

"Go Packers!" both Charming and Jack said, pumping their fists in unison.

"—but you're also the same size, which means you can exchange wardrobes. You can wear each other's Nikes."

"Guys don't really trade shoes, Jez," Jack said.

"But if you decide you want to, you can! This match is perfect!"

Jack shrugged. "He seems like a cool dude, but I don't know about this, Jez."

"Oh, don't be a pansy," Charming said. "You're going to love this. I promise."

"Have you tried this ride with a man?" Jack asked Charming.

"Well, I've tried it many times with women, and once with a man after eating some magical mushrooms. I'm pretty sure I enjoyed it. I was found wandering the outside of the castle dressed in only a fireman's hat and singing YMCA."

Jack considered, eyeing Charming's erection suspiciously. Then that impish grin broke over his lips.

"Okay, we'll give it a shot. But I think we need a little facilitation. Jezebel, would you start us off by showing Charming how you blew me in Bangkok last summer?"

Just the memory of their time in Bangkok sent stirrings deep in her loins. The thought of taking Jack into her mouth again turned her on so much that Jez immediately felt warmth gather between her legs.

The prince stepped forward, holding a harness for Jack. "Here, Jack, put on your harness while Jezebel gets undressed."

"Thanks," Jack said, and both men grinned at her.

Jezzy shrugged. If her clients needed her help, who was she to argue? Especially since it might be the last time she took Jack into her mouth. She stripped down to her sexy boots, and when she turned back to the men, they were both bouncing in their harnesses, their stiff erections bouncing with them.

She stood in front of Jack. "Now let's see. How did I blow you in Bangkok?"

"Very well."

Since Jezzy and Jack had split up, she'd tried not to think too much about Bangkok, but now she couldn't help but indulge. That time was one of the happiest in her life, back when she'd still been struggling coming up with tuition for school, and Jack seemed to have even less ambition than he did money.

She might not be able to go back to that time, but she would enjoy Jack while she still could, and then after he'd married and moved on with his life, she could add this memory to her collection of hot and happy thoughts.

Jezzy bent at the waist, Jack's beautiful, fat cock bobbing before her face, and a *whoosh* of arousal moved over her. She blew on his engorged tip then licked the ridge slowly, swirling her tongue around his circumference. Her walls tightened, then clenched. Before she realized it, she had let out a soft moan.

"I think you're enjoying this as much as Jack is, Jezebel."

Glancing behind, Jezzy could see Charming had taken his own manhood, which was astoundingly large and thick, into one hand.

He brought his other between her legs, caressing. "Jezebel, your lips are unbelievably sexy."

Jezzy wasn't certain which lips he was talking about, but either worked for her. She felt unbelievably sexy as she moved her mouth over Jack's cock and began to slowly slide it back and forth, her bare breasts swaying with the rocking movement. She massaged his underside with her tongue, taking him more deeply into her mouth each time she moved forward. He seemed to grow harder with every stroke she made.

She placed her hands on Jack's harnessed ass and he glided forward easily, aided by the suspension by the bungee cords. She focused on the little divot on the tip of the bulbous head, flicking her tongue back and forth, back and forth, then once again twirling around him. Warmth dripped between her thighs, slippery under Charming's fingers. Her nipples brushed Jack's legs, the friction sending a zing of pleasure through her.

Moaning, Jack began to thrust his hips.

Behind her, the prince slipped a finger inside her.

Then two.

Then three.

Jez spread her thighs wide. She was so wet, so hungry, and as Jack swung against her, she pushed back against Charming, wanting his fingers to penetrate deeper.

"You are so incredible, Jez," Jack said. "Just like Bangkok."

Pleasure flushed over her, and Jezzy took him fully into her mouth, feeling the head push against the back of her throat, then brought her lips all the way back again. She tasted a drop of his salty nectar on her tongue and the taste made her pussy quiver.

Jack bounced gently up into her mouth, then came down, almost all the way out. He groaned, then grunted. "I might need to get one of these contraptions, Charming."

"Yes, it's quite delightful." Grunting, Charming grasped Jezzy's hips and bounced into her, his manhood pushing against her opening from behind then sliding inside.

"Oh," she said around Jack's cock, then sucked him deep into her throat.

"Oh," Jack echoed.

"Miss Jezebel feels quite delightful, too." Charming's next thrust came harder, sending the three of them bouncing into the air, Jezzy bridged between Jack's cock and Charming's.

Jack let out a long groan. "I'm going to come."

Jezzy let him slide from her mouth. "Not yet."

"But Jez..."

"You two have to get to know each other. That's why we're here!"

"Absolutely right." Charming pulled himself out of Jezzy. "Well, then. Let's see if I'm as talented with my mouth."

Charming did a somersault into the air and turned upside down. "Catch me, Jack!"

Using his quick reflexes, Jack caught Charming's hips, holding him suspended upside down.

"Fabulous! We could take this act on the road!" Charming said, his mouth less than an inch from Jack's glistening manhood.

Jezebel noticed that the sun was sinking on the horizon. "You're stalling, Charming."

Charming sighed, looking at her upside down. "So I am. I need to confess. I'm a little insecure. Not sure what to do."

"Just do what you like done to you. Suck the way you like being sucked. Use the same techniques. I use a lot of tongue," Jezebel said.

"I'm losing wood here, Charms," Jack said.

Charming wrapped his arms around Jack's hips and pulled himself downward toward him, taking the tip into his mouth.

He twirled his tongue around the head, then around the ridge, then bounced Jack lightly up and down in the harness to aid in the sucking.

Jack moaned, his eyes squinting with arousal. "Amazing."

Jezzy watched Charming suck Jack, his own shaft bobbing with each bounce. She squeezed her thighs together, trying to stay the throb in her pussy. She wished she could jump on Jack and bounce away to her heart's content, take Charming in her mouth, all of them tangled in a hot, erotic embrace. She pinched her nipples, caressed her swollen sweet spot, anything to squelch her maddening desire to join the fray.

"Why don't you try the same thing with me?" Charming asked. His considerable rod jerked up and down before Jack's face, as if agreeing. "As you can see, the cords make us virtually weightless. You can pull and push me up and down as you like."

Jack looked at Charming's bobbing dick dubiously, then let out a moan of pleasure as Charming continued sucking on his erection.

"Oh, please suck me, Jack. This boner I have, combined with the blood currently rushing to my head, is making me feel faint."

But apparently not terribly so, Jezzy thought, because he resumed sucking and licking.

"Okay. But I really... don't know what I'm... doing."

"Neither did Charming," Jezzy pointed out, "and he's doing a fantastic job, isn't he?"

"Oh, yes." Taking a deep breath, Jack grasped Charming's hips and licked the head of his engorged member.

Charming moaned, and began sucking and licking faster.

Jack answered, then took Charming into his mouth. At first he moved slowly, but as Charming became more and more aroused, moaning in his throat and humping Jack's mouth, Jack became more enthusiastic.

Jack groaned, pulling and pushing Charming up and down into his mouth, apparently forgetting his doubts and really getting into the vertical 69. He did a gentle bounce up and down, moving in unison with Charming's mouth.

It was a lovely cycle of horniness and debauchery, as were the antics all over the amusement park.

Jezebel watched as Jack and Charming pushed each other up and down, sucking and licking, weightless in the bungee cords, and the stirrings in her walls became unbearable. Her nipples had tightened hard and were throbbing something fierce.

The prince's long, elegant fingers squeezed the cheeks of Jack's ass. Then he pushed a finger into Jack's bottom.

Jack's eyes snapped open, but then rolled heavenward as Charming sucked the head of his cock, thrusting his finger in and out.

Seeing these two sexy men so aroused made Jezebel so horny that her clit throbbed and her pussy walls clenched. Man on man was *hot!*

The prince let Jack fall from his lips. "Don't come just yet, big boy. I have plans for you."

Jack pulled his mouth from Charming's glistening cock, looking more than a little disappointed that the 69 was being cut short. "What plans?"

"Something different." Charming did a back flip back onto the floor of the trampoline, and bounced for a few minutes, waving his arms in little circles in the air.

Jack began bouncing as well. "But I was so enjoying the outstanding 69 we were having."

"I did too." The prince let his bouncing slow until he was just gently bobbing on the trampoline in front of Jack. "But now it's time for you to sit on my pecker."

"What?" Jack looked both shocked and puzzled.

"And the sexy Jezebel will blow you at the same time."

A big smile spread across Jack's face. "Well, that might work nicely."

Jezebel felt drunk with need. She was on the edge of orgasm, and knew that if this continued she'd come again without anyone even touching her. But now? Now she could do it while her lips were wrapped around Jack.

"I second the idea," Jezzy said.

Charming patted the head of his incredibly hard cock. "Come and sit, Jack. Or should I say, sit and come?"

"I've never done this before," Jack said.

"You'd never given a blowjob before, and that was fun, right?"

"True. Okay." Jack stood up in his harness and turned so he was facing away from the prince.

"Jezebel," Charming said. "Come over here and grab a harness, hot stuff."

Jezebel did as he said, then knelt in front of Jack. She was so excited about the idea of sucking Jack's manhood again that a shiver moved over her and a light sweat beaded over her skin. She hoped the sheen looked sexy to Jack as she took his member into her mouth and massaged the smooth skin with her tongue. She began with light sucking, and Jack responded with a passionate moan, moving his hips up and down.

"Jezebel, play with his balls," Charming said, "I'm going to get him ready."

Jezebel slipped a hand beneath Jack's cock and took his sack into her hand, lightly palpating with her fingers as Charming lightly massaged his passage with a sweet-smelling lube that hung from a nearby bungee.

"Aaaaaah," Jack responded. He moved his hips faster and faster, jackhammering (no pun intended. Okay, it actually was intended.) Jezebel's mouth and throat with his cock.

"You like my finger in your ass, Jack?" Charming asked him.

"Oh, yes. Yes!" Jack moaned.

Jezebel licked and sucked, devouring Jack like she'd been starving and he was her first meal in days. She focused on the head, sucking hard, then soft, feathering her tongue along the tip, then lathing fat licks over the head. Her nipples moved against Jack's thighs, and she lost herself to sensation.

"Are you sufficiently horny, Jack?" Charming said.

"Yes! Oh, yes!" Jack looked like he was ready to try anything right then.

"Fabulous!" Charming's words were once again clear. "Now slowly lower your sweet buns. I'm still wet from your luscious mouth, but I've just added some tingling lubricant. I call it *jiffy lube*. I carry it around for when little Elvis's muscle gets sore. You know, from all the shows we do. He positively adores it. My dink will feel sensational in your ass."

"Don't use the word 'dink', Charming. It harshes my mojo," Jack said.

"Okay, then. Lower your sweet buns onto my fuck-stick. Or do you prefer 'bat'? I'm well enough endowed to call my cock a bat, aren't I? How about my *love bat?*"

"That's too vampire-ish. Like being nailed by Count Dracula."

"Staked by Count Dracula?"

"Can you just stop it with the nicknames?"

"Okay. My cock."

"That works," Jack said, beginning to lower himself onto Charming's cock.

Jezebel continued licking and sucking Jack as he settled on Charming's lap.

"Whoa," Jack said. "It hurts... a little... but you're hitting a spot..."

"That's your prostate gland. AKA the p-spot."

"Jez has hit it before... with her finger... but this is more... *intense.*"

"Well little Elvis the vampire love bat is a bit bigger than a finger, dear heart."

"Charms..."

"Fine. My cock. My cock is bigger than a finger."

"It sure is. I'm not sure how long I can hold out."

"Just take it easy there, Jack," Charming said. "Jezebel? Keep it up."

Jezebel made love to Jack with her mouth, delighting in his taste, his hardness, the scent of his arousal. In the past, there had been days when they'd gotten lost in each other, just like this. Spending hour upon hour pleasuring one another before collapsing exhausted, then waking to do it again.

"I think I'm going to come," Jack grunted.

Wanting to see the action, Jezzy let him slide from her mouth, and then squeezed her breasts around his manhood, gliding her mounds up and down his slick shaft. He felt so good. So hot. An orgasm built, her muscles clenching and spasming.

"Oh, god!" Jack lifted his hips. "Oh, god!"

"Jezebel," Charming grunted, looking over Jack's shoulder, his voice hoarse with lust. "That is so hot. I want to see Jack come all over your luscious tits."

Charming used his knees to bounce, letting suspension and gravity do much of the work for him, as his cock went deeply in, then came almost all of the way out of Jack's bottom.

Jack thrust himself fiercely between Jezebel's breasts and Charming assaulted him from behind. Then Jack's face contorted in ecstasy, something Jez knew so well.

"I'm going to come!"

Charming humped faster. "Me, too!" he said through gritted teeth.

Their dual orgasms felt like they shook the whole amusement park.

The sight was so incredibly sexy and erotic that Jezebel felt her own climax bloom. Her walls clenched, squeezed, and released over and over as she held on to Jack, shaking and quivering as his essence squirted over her nipples.

Best. Ride. Ever.

Chapter 6

And Jezebel Still Doesn't Get It...

ack and Charming removed their harnesses and Jezzy cleaned herself up with a tissue that hung from a bungee cord. That probably doesn't make much sense, but has any of this so far?

As she did, Jack stretched out his hand and clasped the prince's.

"Well, Charming, you certainly stretched my boundaries. Not to mention my bottom. But as fun as it was, I don't think I'm as attracted to men as I am to women."

Charming nodded. "It was great fun, Jack. Anytime you'd like to take a ride, please drop by."

"I will."

"Well, I'll see you both on the red carpet."

The Prince waved and marched off, and Jezebel threw the tissue into a garbage can (which hung on a bungee cord). She was teetering on the verge of despair. The ball was in an hour, and she hadn't found Jack's soulmate. The sinking feeling in her stomach made her want to throw up. There was no getting around it. She'd failed.

"Jack, I'm so sorry, but—"

"Jezebel, you keep apologizing all the time."

"I know, and—"

"You don't have to keep apologizing."

"I'm sorry, but I—"

"You just apologized again."

Jezebel felt like her whole world was crumbling, but she stayed strong. "Look, I know you had faith in me, Jack. And I really do appreciate it."

Jack's face turned solemn. "I still have faith in you, Jez. But the reason I hired you in the first place is—"

"Hi, Jezebel!" a female voice called out.

Jezzy turned around, grateful for the interruption. No doubt Jack was about to fire her—she was sure of it—but she'd been given a momentary reprieve. There, near the red carpet entrance to the castle, perched on a silver throne on the top of a carnival-style shooting game, was...

Well, it was the sweetest, most beautiful, and nicest woman Jezebel had ever known.

"It's my friend, Alice!" Jezzy said to Jack. "I haven't seen her since college!"

"Alice? The actress from Alice's Sexual Piercing Adventure?"

Jezebel had almost forgotten that Alice was Jack's favorite adult film star. "She must be in Fairytaleland to ball the prince... I mean for Prince Charming's Ball. Would you like to meet her?"

"Would I!"

"Then follow me."

They wound through the crowd gathered around the game. As Jezzy drew closer, she could see that Alice wasn't merely watching the game, she was part of it.

A big part of it.

Half bursting out of a barely-there blue dress, Alice sat with the flouncy skirt hiked up, legs spread, and no panties.

Her privates were exposed for all to see, a gleam of sliver twinkling from the hood of her engorged clit.

Just below Alice's spread thighs was a duplicate of Prince Charming's head, mouth open, out of which protruded a large, rubber tongue. The game booth's banner read Jerk and Shoot.

A man below the pedestal stared up at Alice, stroking himself. A line formed behind him.

"Come one, come all!" A carnival barker wearing a top hat called to the crowd. "Test your power to make this famous movie star beg!"

A man in a rabbit suit stood at the front of the line taking tickets. As Jezzy and Jack drew closer, she noticed the bunny suit only covered his top half, leaving him naked from the waist down. His erect shaft curved upward in such a charming way.

"Jerk off into the clown's mouth, and watch Alice come!" The rabbit announced. "It's for a great cause, and everyone wins!"

As if on cue, the man pleasuring himself shuddered, cried out, and came, shooting his seed into the open mouth of a clown's head positioned a few inches away.

A bell sounded, *Ding! Ding! Ding!*

"We have a winner!" The man in the hat announced.

The rubber tongue belonging to the giant prince's head began to flap up and down, up and down between Alice's open thighs.

"Oooh! Oooh, yes!" Alice cried. She writhed in her throne, the dress slipping off one shoulder and exposing an erect nipple. "Ooooh it feels so good!"

But the tongue stopped after only a few seconds.

"No! Please! I was so close!"

Alice squirmed and pouted and panted, wiggling her perfect body and oozing sexuality.

"Isn't she fabulous?" asked the man in the rabbit suit.

"Isn't she stupendous?" asked the man in the hat.

"She sure is," Jezebel heard Jack whisper.

And Jack was correct. Alice—who Jezebel had practically worshipped in college because she was so smart and confident and pretty and sexy and adventurous and fun—seemed to have gotten even more fabulous and stupendous. Alice was absolutely perfect in absolutely every way. Seeing her again after so many years made Jezebel happy. But it also brought back some shameful feelings of insecurity. And a little envy. In school, Alice was always the most popular. The most beloved. On more than one occasion, Jez wished she *was* Alice.

The rabbit man continued his patter. "Hurry, Hurry, Hurry! Come one, come all! Try your hand at Jerk and Shoot. It's for a great cause!"

The next man in line stepped up to the rabbit. "What do I win?"

"Everyone's a winner!" The bunny man said. "Guaranteed! Or we aren't The Hare and the Hatter!"

"The Hatter and the Hare!" yelled the one in the hat.

"Well, yeah. I get that. You keep saying it again and again. But what do I win?" The man asked again.

"You get to jerk off! Into a plastic clown's mouth!" Hare said.

The man looked dubious.

"It's all for charity. Probably."

"What charity?"

"Who cares? Someone will get your money, and you get to jerk off!" Hatter shouted. "Come on! You'll be... amazed and astounded!"

"At coming in a plastic clown's mouth?" the man said.

"What does the clown have to do with anything?" another asked. "What's the difference between this and a peep show?"

"This is no mere peep show, my good sir. Peep shows don't have a plastic clown."

The first man rubbed his chin. "Your argument is pretty persuasive. I'll do it."

"Great!" Alice said, scooching down a little more, apparently readying herself for the tongue. "Go for it!"

The man freed willy and began tugging on himself, moaning and groaning, but nothing happened.

"Can she take off her dress and play with her nipples? For, uh, inspiration?"

"What a great idea!" said Hare.

"Why didn't we think of that?" asked Hatter.

Alice began to tug on her nipple rings and moan.

Next to Jez, Jack moaned. His cock, which was limp only moments ago, started to stir. "No wonder she's a star. She's inspiring."

"Inspiring..." Jezebel repeated. Truer words had never been spoken.

Apparently the man playing the game thought so, too. Within a moment he was shuddering and crying out, spurting into the clown's mouth. Alice writhed on the wiggling tongue, coming loudly for the crowd as her hips rolled and breasts bounced. Five more men lined up.

One of those men was Jack.

"You really like her?" Jezebel asked him.

"She's... uh... okay, I guess."

"You got into line to jerk off while watching her."

"Yeah. But it's for charity. Probably."

Alice raised an eyebrow. "So you're doing this for charity?"

"Well, sure. Plus, I've never wanked into a plastic clown's mouth before. I mean, who doesn't want to try that at least once?"

But Jezebel saw through Jack's lame excuse. Like all the other men here, Jack wanted Alice.

Which gave her a brilliant idea.

"Let me check something..." Jezebel fished her tablet from the pile of their discarded clothing. A few taps of the screen, and "Yes! You and Alice are 105% compatible!"

Jack frowned. "Jez, you know 105% is impossible. You can't have 105% of something."

"But the algorithms don't lie!"

"Jezzy...I think..."

"Don't think, Jack. Feel. This is it. Alice is your sexual soul mate. I just know it. You said yourself that she's stupendous."

"Yeah, she is. But..."

"I knew it."

When Alice had finished what had to be her eighth orgasm, Jezzy butted into line and waved at her.

"Oh my gosh, Jezebel! It's been so long since I've seen you!" she turned to her pitchmen. "Hatter. Hare. Take five."

"Five what?" asked Hatter.

"Five dollars?" asked Hare.

"Five steps forward?"

"Five Viagra?"

"The Jackson Five?"

"Hawaii Five-O?"

"The Hobbit: Battle of the Five Armies?"

"Slaughterhouse Five?"

"The Five Fingers of Death?"

"Now that's an obscure reference," Hare said, looking at Hatter.

"It's an old kung-fu movie."

"Fu Manchu?

"Egg foo young?"

"Do these guys have an off button?" Jack said, loud enough for them to hear.

"Take a five minute break," Alice told the irritating duo.

"Break dance?"

"Breakfast?

"Breaking Away?"

"Breakin' 2: Electric Boogaloo?"

"You're both fired," Alice said.

Hatter and Hare beat a hasty retreat. Hopefully to go find some ADD medication.

Alice walked over to Jezzy and enfolded her in a hug, their bare breasts rubbing together, nipple massaging nipple.

She heard Jack groan. A sexual groan.

Yes. Alice and Jack will be the perfect couple.

Jezebel felt a sad little smile move over her lips. She should be happy. She'd done her job. Fulfilled her contract. Earned the glowing review she was sure to get from Big Cock Billionaire Magazine. And yet all she could think about was that it was over. Jack wouldn't need her to facilitate with Alice. They would be fine without her.

Dusk was turning into night, and the castle seemed to glow under the moonlight. Fireworks burst in the night sky beyond the mighty tower, calling the party goers to the ball.

Jezebel took a deep breath.

It was time for her greatest triumph.

And to say goodbye.

"Alice, I'd like you to meet Jack."

"Jack Horner, the Bean King?"

"Guilty as charged."

They shook hands, the touch lingering. To Jezebel's horror, tears filled her eyes, turning the sky into a watery mosaic of color.

"Are you crying, Jezebel?" Alice asked, touching her arm in a gesture of sincere concern.

"Crying?"

"You are," Jack said. "That's what it's called when tears are running down your cheeks. What's wrong?"

Jezzy shook her head. "Nothing's wrong. I'm just... I'm just so happy for you both."

"For us both?" Alice asked. "Why?"

"Big Cock Billionaire Magazine here!"

Jezebel turned toward the voice and came eye-to-eye with the two carnival barkers from the Jerk and Shoot booth. The man with the hat held a microphone in front of her. The one wearing half a rabbit suit snapped a photo.

"Hatter? Hare?" said Alice. "You're working for Big Cock Billionaire Magazine?"

"We had to find new jobs since you fired us," said Hatter.

"And we can't resist taking pictures of your lovely nakedness wherever it may turn up," said the Hare.

"By the way, this one ain't too shabby, either." Hatter crooked a thumb at Jezzy. "I wouldn't mind having a little tea party with her, if you know what I mean."

"He means sex," Hare said.

"I want to put my penis in your body," Hatter said. "Anywhere at all."

"He'd even do an armpit."

"I've done armpits before."

"How was it?"

Hatter shrugged. "It was the pits."

Jezebel blinked back her tears and focused on the pair. They looked much the same as they had at the game booth, only this time, the Hatter was also sans pants, and his manhood rivaled the size of his microphone.

Jezebel tried to comfort herself with the fact that Big Cock Billionaire Magazine would be covering Jack and Alice's wedding, but she knew that her tears weren't happy ones.

Jezzy realized, finally, 28,000 words into this story, that she still had it bad for Jack.

And now?

Now it was too late.

"Why don't we get a few pictures before we start the interview?" Hare said.

Jezzy turned away from the camera, doing her best to wipe the tears from her eyes.

"Certainly. Why don't you start with the happy couple, Jack the Bean King and his lovely bride-to-be, Alice."

"Bride-to-be?" echoed Alice.

"Bride-to-be?" echoed Jack.

"The two of you are perfect together," Jezebel said, not wanting to pretend any longer. "I can see it. The whole of Fairytaleland can see it."

"I can see it," said Hatter.

"I can see it," said Hare.

"I can see it," said Hatter.

"You said that already."

"The first time was for my left eye, the second time for my right eye."

Hare nodded. "I can see it."

"Jack is no doubt quite attractive," Alice said. "But I'm already married."

Jezebel's face pinched. "You're already married?"

"Sure. Remember Lewis from college?"

Jezzy thought back. "The guy who liked to wear your panties?"

"That's him!" Alice pointed in the direction of the castle. Paparazzi crowded the red carpet, snapping photos of celebrities arriving for the ball. And sure enough there was Alice's boyfriend from college dressed for the ball in a bow tie and lacy pink panties that only half covered his manhood. "Isn't he cute?"

Jezzy was stunned. "Ah, cute. Sure."

"You're not judging his sexual proclivities, are you Jezzy? We shouldn't judge what others like, as long as it is consensual and among adults. That seems so unlike you."

Jezebel stared, her head buzzing. "No, of course I'm not, Alice. I'm so glad you've found someone to make you happy."

"We are happy. I love him dearly." And with that, Alice scampered to the red carpet and jumped into her husband's arms.

"Ahh, it's so lovely to witness true love," Jack said. "Don't you think, Jez?"

"Uh, yes." And it was. "There's only one problem."

"Problem?"

Jezebel tore her gaze from Jack's handsome face and looked at Hatter and Hare, standing there with their microphone and camera and erections, er, expectations.

"I promised to find your sexual soulmate, Jack. I promised to find you a bride. And..." She paused, her throat dry. "And I failed."

"Failed?" echoed the Hatter.

"Failed?" echoed the Hare.

"I'm sorry," Jezzy told them. "There will be no wedding for The Bean King. I'm afraid I have let him down."

She turned around to apologize to Jack, but he wasn't there. It took her a second to spot him kneeling on the ground at her feet. "Jack, wha—"

"You didn't fail, Jez. You succeeded."

"What? How?"

"I already found my sexual soulmate, climbing that beanstalk years ago. In fact, I set up this whole bride search and interview with Big Cock Billionaire Magazine to find out if you could ever feel the same way about me."

Jezzy felt dizzy, as if she'd just had multiple orgasms and was now hopelessly disoriented.

Jack opened a jewelry box and held it up to her. The biggest, most garish diamond ring sparkled from its black velvet cushion, so big that a crowd started to gather and paparazzi snapped pictures.

"So how about it, Jez? Could you ever feel that way about me? Will you be my bride?"

"But, but... the algorithms..."

"I don't care about the algorithms."

"But I'm not Alice..."

"No, you're not. You're Jezebel. And you're who I want. You've been who I wanted all along."

Jezebel's chest constricted, making it hard to breathe. "We aren't a perfect match. What if it doesn't work out?"

"I love you, Jez. And I know getting married is a risk, like jumping over a cliff. But the only one I want to take that leap with is you. Will you jump with me?"

Tears streamed down Jezzy's face. Her heart raced, and her whole body trembled. "Oh, Jack. I'm so sorry!"

His face fell. "You won't marry me?"

"No, no... I mean, yes, yes. I will marry you. I'm just so sorry I ever broke up with you in the first place."

"No, no, I'm sorry it took me so long to become someone you could love."

"No, no, no, I'm sorry I ever thought ambition was more important than love."

"No, no, no, no—"

"Can you both please stop being sorry!" Hatter shouted. He was now wearing a Stetson. "Are you two gettin' hitched or what?"

Jezebel looked down at her sweet Jack, and her heart filled with a happiness that she'd never before known. She'd succeeded after all. She'd found Jack a wife. She'd just never dared to hope his bride would be her.

"Yes, Jack. I'd love to marry you."

And the night was lit with the flash of a dozen cameras.

Part 3

Fifty Shades of Goldilocks

Marrying a Billionaire

S o what do you think? I just signed the closing papers this morning. Perfect, isn't it?"

Jezebel peered up at the thrusting tower of the castle's keep. The place was beautiful, massive, luxurious, maybe even nicer than the castle owned by Prince Charming himself.

"It makes me feel sort of small."

"That's only because it's so big. Wait until you see inside."

Jezebel's husband-to-be, Jack Horner, grabbed her by the hand and led her across the drawbridge and into the courtyard. Jack made his fortune by genetically engineering beans, which grew to gigantic proportions and could feed entire villages (though you didn't want to be downwind of the village after they ate.) She'd dated Jack years ago, after an adventure they'd had involving a beanstalk, but had left him because he'd lacked ambition.

It turned out that was the kick in the pants Jack had needed to start his own business, which led him to becoming one of the richest men in the world, and to eventually asking Jez to marry him. You can read the first two books in the series if you want all the hot details. But that's not necessary, because there is a sex scene coming up in just a few short paragraphs.

Their home-to-be was amazing from outside the castle walls. The inside blew Jezzy away. All cobblestone and flowers, the courtyard was larger than the biggest ballroom, and the air smelled like roses.

"The band will be over there," Jack said, gesturing to a stone platform. "And the dance floor here. And we have to have tables for dinner. You're planning a sit-down dinner, right?"

"Jack, this is all a little overwhelming…"

"That's the point, isn't it? Wait until you see this!"

Placing his hand on the small of her back, he guided her around the side of the keep to a private cove, green and white and fragrant with flowering honeysuckle. A flower arch stood at one end, a blue pond flanking one side. And best of all, a fountain erupted from the middle of the crystalline water and filled the air with its soothing music.

Jezzy clapped her hands to her chest. "It's exquisite, Jack."

"This is where you'll become my wife, and I'll become your husband. I can't wait, Jez!"

Jezebel took in the setting, just right for a wedding. Twirling the diamond ring weighing down her finger, she turned to face her future husband. But when she opened her mouth, no sound came.

She should be happy. She *was* happy.

"What's wrong?"

"Nothing."

"I know you, Jez. Something's up."

Jezzy gave Jack a smile. He'd worked so hard finding the perfect venue for their wedding, spent oodles of his oodles of money on this place, and there was no denying it was the most gorgeous and grand venue she'd ever seen.

So why wasn't she ecstatic?

"This place is perfect, Jack. But it feels so big, so grand… I just don't feel like I can measure up."

"What do you mean? You'll be the most beautiful bride ever."

She nodded, wanting to believe him.

"You will be. We're going to be so happy." Jack cradled her head in his hands and kissed her. His lips were tender at first, as if she was the most precious, delicate thing in the world. He teased her, nipping her bottom lip, dipping his tongue into her mouth, withdrawing. Then he gathered her into his arms.

As their bodies pressed tight, Jez could feel his manhood surge against her, his arousal growing. She spread her legs, letting him nestle between. Being held by him always made her feel precious. Exciting him made her feel powerful. Jezzy could have the worst day in the world, and Jack could make her forget all about it. His want for her. His need for her. The way his body responded, just as it was responding now.

"I have an idea," she said between kisses.

"Idea? What?"

Still kissing him, she unbuttoned her blouse and slipped it off her arms. A quick flick of the hooks, and her bra came next. Cool air caressed her naked breasts.

Her nipples were already peaking, and he leaned back to admire them, taking the weight of her mounds in his hands.

"You are so hot. Jezzy."

Jezebel smiled, again wanting to hear more, to lose herself in his words. But the niggle of doubt lingered. She'd always felt hot before. But in the past few months, she'd been so busy running her matchmaking business and planning their wedding, she hadn't had time to exercise. A few pounds later, and she wasn't feeling as sexy as she used to.

In fact, she was feeling downright frumpy.

"We can't do this, you know," Jack said.

Jezebel stared at him. "Why not?"

"What do you mean, why not? We planned we'd wait until our wedding night. Make things special. Romantic."

Now Jack and Jezebel had enjoyed sex before. In fact, they'd enjoyed *a lot* of sex *a lot* of times before with *a lot* of different people, not to mention mythical beings. And since this was Fairytaleland—a fantasy world where the sex was always safe and consensual and frequently out in the open—their lifestyle was shared by most of the residents. But one week, two days, five hours, twelve minutes, and fourteen seconds ago, Jack had proposed a wonderfully romantic idea to Jezebel. And since Jezebel had been half out of her mind at the time from a mind-bending series of multiple orgasms, she'd agreed.

They would abstain from sex until their wedding night.

She unbuttoned her jeans and pushed them down her legs, standing before Jack in only a silk thong.

"I need you, Jack. I just don't feel as if I belong in this beautiful, important, grand place."

"Of course you belong here. You're twice as beautiful, important, and grand as any castle."

"Then why don't you... don't you want me?"

"Of course I want you. Look." Jack pointed at his crotch. Sure enough, there was a major bulge growing in his pants. "You're an amazing woman, Jez. I'm sure all of them want you, too."

Jezzy followed his gesture with her gaze. Standing at the top of the castle wall, a dozen workmen leered at her. And, as could be expected, they were all jerking off.

Jezebel, like any resident of Fairytaleland, usually found it very exciting to have a bunch of strange men peering down at her nakedness. But with the extra pounds she'd put on and the stress she felt over the wedding, she wasn't sure what to feel. Right then she wanted reassurance, not to be so... on display.

"Jez? Are you all right?"

"I feel... fat."

"You look great." Jack eyeballed the workers. "Isn't she hot?"

"We're construction workers," one of them said. "We think anyone with a pulse is hot."

"A pulse is optional," another said.

"I once cat-called a garbage can rolling down the sidewalk," added a third. "I yelled, *Nice can!*"

"We're basically pigs," the first one said again.

There were general nods of agreement all around.

"But isn't Jezebel especially hot?" Jack persisted.

"Though the depictions of our profession in popular culture do tend to be on point when it comes to our vocal appreciation of the female form, there is more to women than their looks," said one of the men, who was beating off particularly fast.

The others nodded in agreement.

"She seems nice, but what's really important is her heart."

"And her mind. Smart, independent women are what does it for me."

"Relationships based on appearances never last. You need to have some common interests and goals."

"I'd have to get to know her as a person. I don't think objectification is cool."

"Her big tits make my dick hard."

"That's the answer I was looking for," Jack said, pointing to the rude one. "They all want to have sex with you, Jez. You can see that, right?"

"That's the general impression I'm getting."

"Do you like them looking at you?"

Even now, as inadequate as she felt about marrying Jack in this luxurious castle, she could feel her nipples harden in front of all those probing eyes. "Yes."

"Do you like knowing they want you?"

"Yes."

"Does it make you feel beautiful? Important? Grand?"

"Right now they're imagining kissing your tits. Like this."

Jack massaged her breasts then lowered his lips to them, focusing his talents on one then the other.

A groan came from the men, and Jezebel felt a little charge of excitement as several of them took themselves in hand and started to stroke.

"They're wondering what it would feel like to suck on your nipples."

Jack pulled one into his mouth, flicking with his tongue and nipping lightly with his teeth.

"Oh," said Jezzy on a breath. She arched her back, watching as the rest of the men shucked their pants and gripped their hard lengths.

Jack littered kisses over her belly, dropping to his knees in front of her.

"And they all want to taste your pussy."

He brought his mouth between her legs, circling and teasing, plundering and grinding.

Spreading her thighs, Jezebel rode Jack's mouth, her naked breasts bouncing, her nipples still glistening from his kisses. Moans echoed from all around her, punctuated by the gentle slaps of flesh on flesh.

Jack reached around her, his hands cupping her bottom, fingers kneading.

She rode him harder, faster, forgetting about the men above, forgetting everything but Jack. Pressure built, starting in her core and tightening until she let out a scream. Jezzy's body seized, and a roar rushed her ears. Legs weak, she sagged against Jack.

He held her up, grinding harder, keeping the orgasm going... forever... forever... then before she could catch her breath, his tongue brought on a second climax with the thundering blast of a freight train.

Her legs gave out, and Jack cradled her, holding her close. When her mind finally cleared and she could breathe normally again, she realized Jack was staring at her, smiling.

"Good way to break the place in, huh? Make you feel more comfortable?"

"It did relieve a bit of tension."

With all the pressures she'd been feeling lately, Jezzy was still sure of three things. She adored Jack. He loved her. And he was the perfect match. And yet...

"Can't you just fuck me, Jack? Maybe that's what I'm missing."

"I'm missing it, too. That's why it's such a good idea to wait. We'll be crazy for each other on our wedding night." He gave her a light kiss, then motioned over his shoulder. "Feel like taking on some of your admirers? I'd love to watch."

Jezzy glanced up at the wall. Several men were still stroking themselves, others already spent. But as exciting as the idea was, Jez just didn't feel up to it.

She let out a sigh.

"Something *is* wrong, isn't it?" Jack said, all traces of lust gone. "Tell me what it is, Jez. Please."

"I don't know." Tears welled in her eyes.

"Is it the wedding? Cold feet?"

"No," she said emphatically, although as the word crossed her lips, she realized she wasn't sure.

"Do you still want to get married, Jez? Do you want to marry me?"

"Yes. Of that I am sure."

"Then why do you seem so unsure?"

She paused a moment, wanting to be honest with Jack, yet not really knowing the cause herself. "I guess it's..."

"Yes?"

"Maybe a little..."

"What?"

"I don't know, Jack. I just feel nervous."

"I hear that's natural. We're getting married, after all."

"It's not that. I want to be your wife. More than anything."

"Then what is it?"

"I don't know."

Jack's face brightened. He took her by the hand. "I have something to show you that might help. A surprise."

As Jack led her into the castle, a few of the construction workers protested.

"Hey! Not done yet!"

"What are we supposed to look at now? Each other?"

"Sorry, fellas, the show is over," Jack said. "To make it up to you, I'll give you all a raise."

"She already gave me a raise," said the rude guy as he pointed to the tent in his pants. "That's the problem."

"Don't you men have smart phones?" Jack said. "I heard there's this new thing on the Internet. It's called pornography."

The men all whipped out their cells. Jack scooped Jez up and carried her into the keep and up the winding stairs. When he reached the door at the top of the tower, he shoved it open with one hip.

Crystal chandeliers hung from the ceiling. An enormous canopy bed angled from one corner, its coverings lacy and gauzy and divine. Next to it sat an ornate dressing table, covered with a magnificent arrangement of white roses. Fancy paintings of kings and queens spotted the walls, along with a particularly fetching one of dogs playing cards.

All in all, the space was breathtaking. Which was too bad, since the air smelled of (obviously) roses.

But the most incredible piece, better than all the paintings, better than all the flowers, better than even that soft, frothy, inviting bed, was the antique mirror in the room's center. It looked like something straight out of a fairytale.

Go fig.

"This is the Lords and Ladies chamber," Jack said, placing Jezzy on her feet. "It's the grandest room in the place, and I've set it up for you. It's where you and your matron of honor can get ready for the wedding."

"It's lovely, Jack."

"And this," he said with a flourish, stepping to the mirror, "is my wedding present for you."

It was a lovely mirror, with a beautifully ornate frame, but Jezebel wondered if this wasn't some not-so-subtle jab at her vanity, or that Jack was only interested in her looks, which would be superficial.

"Let me say, Jez, this isn't some not-so-subtle jab at your vanity, or that I'm only interested in your looks, which would be superficial."

"I never would have thought that," Jez said. "It's a very nice mirror, Jack."

"It's more than just a nice mirror. It's magic." He stood in front of it, angling so he could view himself from behind. "I had trouble pulling myself away from it earlier. Makes my ass look awesome, doesn't it?"

"Your ass always looks awesome, Jack."

"As does yours. But this mirror shows us our ideal selves. You see yourself as I see you; absolutely perfect."

Jezzy eyed her reflection. But despite the fact that she was still buzzing from her exhibitionism in the courtyard, and despite the fact that she loved the thoughtful gift, she didn't feel perfect at all.

She frowned. And then to her horror, her eyes misted with tears.

Jack looked stricken. "Seriously, Jezzy. Are you having doubts about marrying me?"

"No! Of course not."

"Then what is it?"

"I just feel... I don't know... fat."

"So you said." Jack stared at her. "Is this one of those trick questions that no man can answer correctly?"

"No."

"Because other guys have warned me about those."

"No, it's just that—"

"They say once you get married those questions start."

"No, Jack, it's not that. My problem is—"

"If I say that you don't look fat, you'll accuse me of lying to spare your feelings. And if I agree… well, to do that I'd have to be crazy, not to mention suicidal. And if I say—"

"It's not one of those questions, Jack."

"Look at yourself in the magic mirror, Jez. You're radiant."

"But the mirror is magic. That's not the real me. You said so yourself."

Jezebel began to cry again. Jack wrapped his arms around her.

"What can I do to make you happy, Jezzy?"

"I just think about our wedding and how perfect the plans are and how perfect this place is and how much I want to be your wife, and…"

"And?"

"And I worry that I'm not perfect enough for it all."

"Jez…"

She held up a hand. "Nothing you can say is going to help."

"How about those guys outside? They certainly think you're as beautiful as I do."

"Nothing they can say will help, either."

"Or do?"

"As much as it gives any woman a thrill to be objectified by construction workers, I don't think that's the pick-me-up I need right now."

"How about going to the spa? Isn't that what brides do before their wedding day?"

Jezebel wasn't sure what brides did, but the spa sounded promising. "Maybe."

"I'll set up a spa appointment. You can have whatever treatments you like. Whatever you need to help you feel as lovely as you are. How does that sound?"

"It sounds really nice." Jezebel gave him a sheepish smile. "I'm sorry for being so silly."

"Silly? Nah. Sexy? And how." He gave her a wink. "Now which spa would you like to visit?"

"Uh, I don't know."

"How about the one Alice was talking about Saturday night?"

Jezzy had run into her old friend from college on the day Jack had proposed, and they'd been best friends since. Sometimes the girlfriends would grab lunch. Sometimes they would have a foursome with Jack and Alice's husband, Lewis.

Yeah, *that* kind of foursome. Fairytaleland, remember?

Jezebel searched her memory. "You mean the spa that's part of the Hellfire Club?"

"Alice and Lewis made it sound pretty terrific."

Jezzy had to agree. Luxurious. Decadent. And very relaxing. "Will you go with me?"

"Can't. I have to attend the Bean Summit. And then it's the wedding. But you should go, Jez. The bride and groom aren't supposed to see each other before the wedding, right?"

"I guess."

"So spend the day at the spa, stay overnight, and the next morning, Alice can meet you for all that pre-wedding stuff."

Jezebel smiled. "Pre-wedding stuff?"

"I don't know. Like hair and makeup and general pampering. You deserve it, Jez. I want you to feel beautiful on our special day. From what Alice said, that spa is just the ticket."

Alice was beautiful. And every time Jezebel saw her, she felt a little tweak of envy. "You think the spa can make me look like Alice?"

Jack laughed. "You don't need to look like Alice. I love you just the way you are."

Jezzy knew Jack had a weakness for blondes. She'd seen it first hand in an encounter they'd shared with the fetching Rapunzel and again when he'd met Alice for the first time. The idea of dying her hair had hovered in the back of her mind ever since. "But you'd love me more if I looked like Alice, wouldn't you?"

"I love you just the way you are. I mean it, Jez."

"So you'd hate it if I was a blonde?"

"Of course not. If it's what you want, go for it."

Jezzy eyed herself in the mirror. If she had blonder hair, a tighter body, and a smoother complexion, she would surely feel the magic. And then she would be as perfect as the rest of her wedding day.

"But what about our agreement?" Jez asked. "The Hell-fire Spa is a sex spa, isn't it?"

"For what they charge, it had better be."

"But we've been saving ourselves for our wedding night. No sex, remember?"

"Having orgasms at the spa doesn't count."

Jez knitted her brows. "I know neither of us is the least bit jealous. But maybe you should tell me what is allowed."

"You can have whatever you want, as long as it isn't my cock."

But that was what Jezebel wanted most of all.

She smiled, false bravado, for Jack's sake. "Then hi-ho, hi-ho, it's off to the spa I go."

The Spa at the Hellfire Club

ezzy stood in the reception area of the Hellfire Club, mouth open and eyes rounded. The place was every bit as luxurious as Alice had said; marble floors, brass accents, velvet draperies hanging at the windows, and butter-soft leather furniture.

It reminded Jezebel of an expensive bordello.

Or at least, how she imagined one would look. The only bordellos Jez had been in were middle class. Nice enough, but just as there was a difference between pub grub at the local tavern and a five star restaurant with Chez in the name, Jez assumed the Hellfire Club Spa would be a bit more decadent than Murray's Bathhouse, where a guy named Murray exfoliated you with his old wool socks.

A tall, willowy woman with long, red tresses smiled a welcome, and Jezzy couldn't help but notice the woman was nude (that is something you tend to notice, after all). Like the décor, this woman was stunning.

"You must be Jezebel. I'm Bare."

"Indeed, you are," said Jezzy, her eyes skipping over the woman's lush breasts, curvy hips, and perfectly smooth nether place.

The woman giggled. "That's my name. Bare Bottoms. I'm a member of your transformation team."

"Transformation team?"

"Yes. A transformation team is made up of many professionals who guide you through your spa experience. I am directing your experience, but it takes a village to provide all the pleasure a woman deserves."

"Didn't Hillary Clinton write a book about that?"

"I believe she did." Bare looked Jezebel up and down, and then took Jezzy's hands in her own. "Don't worry about anything during your stay here. Your transformation team knows just what you need."

"You do?"

"Your fiancé has booked you for the deluxe package."

"So when I leave the spa, will I be as perfect-looking as you?"

"You'll be as perfect as you feel."

Not sure if that was a promise or an avoidance of the question, Jezzy just nodded and smiled.

"You'll love it, Jezebel," Bare said. "We were voted the best spa in Fairytaleland by people who vote for things like that. Not only do you leave looking like a million bucks, we make you feel heavenly. By the time you walk out, you won't even recognize yourself!"

"Good." Jezzy said. "I want a change. A big change."

"Then come along with me. We'll get started." Bare led Jezzy into a small dressing room and gestured to a kimono hanging from a hook on the wall. "You'll need to remove your clothing and put on this robe."

Jezzy did as she was told, feeling a little silly to be clothed while Bare was totally, uh, bare. But when the silk garment wisped gently against her skin, she decided a little silliness was worth it.

Way worth it.

She joined Bare in the corridor, and the woman led her to a glass door and ushered Jezzy inside. "This is where the transformation begins."

Jezzy stepped into a large room filled with large reclining chairs filled with people. Both women and men occupied the area, all in different stages of being robed or disrobed and all being waxed and massaged, manicured and pedicured, cut, colored, and styled. But one thing they all had in common was the glazed look on their faces... oh, and the moaning, sighing, groaning, and crying out in obvious ecstasy.

The staff is sexually pleasuring them.

There were so many hands working on each person that Jezzy had missed it at first glance. But now that she really looked, she could see that some of the hands were massaging nether regions and using special tools in special places.

Jezebel felt a twinge of arousal between her legs and smiled.

"We'll start with your hair." Bare led Jezzy to a styling chair. "Just sit down and make yourself comfortable."

Jezebel sunk into the soft leather. Bare pushed a button, reclining the chair, and then placed her fingertips on Jezzy's forehead. She started with little circles at the hairline, massaging away the tension in Jezebel's face and scalp.

Jezzy closed her eyes and felt her entire body begin to relax.

"Oh, what have we here?" A husky, seductive voice said.

Jezzy opened her eyes and focused on a big blonde wearing a pink satin negligee. The woman jutted a hip out and nodded approvingly.

"Well, aren't you a doll face?"

"Thank you," Jezebel said.

"Jezebel, this is Titania." Bare said, still massaging Jezzy's scalp.

"Titania?" Jezzy said. "I don't get the fairytale reference."

Titania vogued. "Shakespeare, girlfriend. Queen of the Fairies. But I'm not actually a queen. I'm definitely a 'he' under this pink babydoll. I just like dressing up in women's clothes. But trust me, beneath my lace panties, I'm all man, sugar."

"Bare Bottoms is also from Shakespeare," Bare offered. "I was in King Lear."

"I don't remember you," Jez said.

Bare smiled. "Who do you think the king was leering at?"

Titania tilted to the side and whispered to Jez, "That rascal Billy edited out her scene, but she's in the uncut version. Personally, I think King Lear is much better with some lesbian spanking, but what isn't?"

"Pleased to meet you, Titania," Jezebel said.

"It's so mutual."

"You are rocking that negligee, Titania," Bare said. "But I'm glad you put the fishnets away. They're kind of tacky."

"Don't you dis my fishnets, girl. I get lots of compliments on those." Titania pulled up a chair and began running his hands over Jezzy's feet, then calves, then thighs. "You have lovely legs, Jezebel."

"I do?" Jezzy said, genuinely surprised.

"Yes. Fantastic muscles. Are you a runner?" Titania ran one strong hand over the back of one of her thighs.

"I was. I've let it slip recently." Jezzy felt a flush of shame at having let her physical fitness lapse. She'd just been so busy. "I've let everything slip, and now I'm getting married."

"Congratulations, sugar! You'll be a stunning bride."

"I hope so."

"I know so." Titania gave her a wink. "You need to relax, girl. And I'm here to help you do that."

Jezebel closed her eyes again, the feeling of Titania's large, male hands kneading her legs was heavenly. The soothing, sensual movements had always turned her on. Even more than a kiss. It was just so intimate. Combined with Bare's scalp massage, Jezzy wasn't sure if she was going to fall asleep or have an orgasm.

"So being a masseur here at the spa and Queen of the Fairies must keep you awfully busy." Jezzy was now so relaxed that her voice sounded far away.

"Nah. I'm no masseur. I just like feeling girls up," Titania said.

"He's an excellent groper," Bare agreed. "One of the best. He's in high demand, even though he doesn't really work here."

"So you're not part of my transformation team?"

"Officially? No. I just like to keep my hands busy."

Speaking of Titania's hands, they were moving high on her inner thighs, skirting the edge of her robe, gently caressing the muscles there. The motions were so sublime that Jezebel heard herself moan again, and heat gathered between her legs.

"Mmmhmm," Titania said. "You've got that right."

Jezebel's breathing quickened. She spread her legs and pushed her hips forward, wanting his fingers on the center of her desire.

Titania complied, moving two fingers in little circles over Jezzy's most sensitive spot, mimicking Bare's scalp massage.

"Oooh. Oooh…" Jezzy moaned.

"Oh, yes," Titania purred. "And don't you forget it."

"I'm not likely to," Jezzy murmured. The sensations were so pleasurable, she found herself moving against Titania's fingers, seeking more and more. She couldn't remember the last time she felt so turned on.

Well, actually she was this turned on an hour or so earlier, but that was with Jack. She was always turned on with Jack. Titania was a perfect stranger.

"You're so damned pretty, and your body is so lush, I can't help touching you, Jezebel," Titania breathed. "I'm so glad your fiancé requested me."

"Jack asked for you?"

"He said he wanted the best for you. And of course, I'm the best." Titania dipped a finger deep inside her, and Jezzy caught her breath.

"I'll say." She eyed the pink negligee, wondering if Titania was as talented with other parts as he was with his fingers.

"It's time to get the swatches," Bare said.

"Swatches?" Jezzy echoed. "You don't mean those plastic watches from the eighties, do you?"

"Heavens, no. I'll be right back."

Jezzy closed her eyes, losing herself in the amazing talent of Titania's hands and imagining what kind of wonderful hedonistic device a swatch might be.

"Okay, here they are, Jezebel. Tell me what you think."

Jezzy opened her eyes and focused on the large, white demonstration board Bare held in front of her. Peppering the display were little bunches of strands salons used to showcase the variety of hair color offered. "Ohhh, you meant a swatch… for color."

"You thought I was referring to something else?"

Jezzy shook her head, a little embarrassed. "I thought it was something that would give me pleasure."

"Oh you just wait, sugar," Titania cooed. "You think I'm talented with my hands?"

"But first," Bare said, "you must pick a tint. We have fifty shades to cover the grey. Or in your case, we have fifty shades to spruce up the brunette."

Jezzy took a deep breath. "I want to be a blonde."

"Lovely choice!" Bare plucked a swatch of strands from the board. "What do you think of this color? It's called Innocent Buttercup."

"Pretty, but too soft," Jezzy answered.

Bare held up another swatch, this one almost white. "And this? This one is called Platinum Tramp."

"Hmm, I think that one is too hard for my complexion."

Titania gave a tone of approval. "I think you're right, baby cakes. Although there's nothing wrong with hard."

"All right," Bare selected a third.

"Ohhh, girl, wait until you see this one," Titania said, giving her clit a little shimmy.

Teetering on the edge of an orgasm, Jezzy looked at the newest swatch of hair. "What is this one called?"

"This? It's Dirty Slut Blond."

Just then, Titania did the most amazing figure eight with one finger while penetrating with another and pirouetting with a third.

"Oh, that is JUST RIGHT!" Jezebel screamed.

And she liked the hair color, too.

"Dirty Slut Blond it is!" Bare said and handed the swatch to Titania. But instead of mixing up the color, Titania fanned the little bunch of hair over Jezzy's mound then circled the outside edge of her nether lips.

Chills raced over Jezebel's skin, followed by shivers. Her nipples poked upward under the silk robe. "Oh my, that's delicious."

"Isn't it though?" Titania said, continuing to move his fingers while he swirled the swatch. "Dirty Slut is amazing, and it will really bring out your eyes."

"I love it already," Jezzy managed between moans. She tilted her hips, trying to open her thighs wider. Where the light tickle of the hair had first been delectable, she was now starting to crave more. Titania's tongue along with his fingers would be nice right about now.

Bare moved back to the head of the chair and resumed playing with Jezebel's hair, this time brushing color from roots to ends. But like everything Jezzy had experienced so far at the Hellfire Club Spa, this was no ordinary color. A cool tingle stole over her scalp, raising goosebumps down her arms. In fact, between Bare and Titania, Jezebel felt shiverfabulous from head to toe.

"Look how hard your nipples are, sweetums," Titania said.

Jezebel looked, marveling at the hard peaks. Feeling excited and a little naughty, she loosened the robe's belt and let the silk slide to either side, exposing her bare breasts.

Titania didn't miss a beat with the Dirty Slut swatch. He circled one nipple then the other, his fingers still dancing over the sensitive pearl between her legs.

Jezzy arched her back. She squirmed. She moaned. And finally the pressure built and the walls of her pussy started to clench. "I'm going to come."

Titania immediately stopped all the scrumptious things he was doing.

"No, no, no! Don't stop!"

"We have to Jezebel," Titania said. "Your hair has reached the perfect shade."

"That was fast."

"Oh honey, Dirty Sluts are fast."

"But, but…"

"Don't worry," Bare said in a soothing voice. "We have more work to do. Just relax."

Jezebel tried her best, focusing on the promise of delights ahead. And while the ache of desire deep inside wouldn't let her relax, exactly, it didn't prevent her from enjoying the feeling of Bare rinsing her hair with warm water and lathering it with jasmine scented shampoo. It was followed by a rich conditioner.

"For the next part, I'm afraid you'll have to be restrained," Bare said when she was finished.

"Restrained?" Jezzy's shiver of delight turned to a shiver of fear. "Why?"

"Oh, you'll see." Titania wiggled his brows. "And you'll like."

Bare pushed a button, and soft leather cuffs popped out of the styling chair's arms and foot rest. Then switching positions,

Bare fitted the soft cuffs on Jezzy's ankles, while Titania secured her wrists.

Jezebel could wiggle her bottom and arch her back, but not much else. She was trapped. Her pulse began a triple beat in her throat, and her skin beaded with gooseflesh. Butterfly wings fluttered low in her belly.

Bare smiled. "I'll be doing your waxing today."

"And hair is my specialty," Titania said.

"I thought fondling was your specialty."

"No, that's my hobby."

"So you're a professional hair designer?"

"Well, no. I guess that's a hobby, too. Essentially, I like to fondle all parts of a woman. Feet, legs, pussy, tits, hair... But I don't like to cut all parts of a woman. I reserve that for hair, just so you know."

"Oh... good..." Jezzy suddenly felt a little more helpless than she was accustomed.

"Don't worry," Titania said. "I'm a cosmetology graduate of the School of Hard Cocks, and if I can make a gay man swoon over one of my cuts, I can please anyone."

Jezebel had to admit that the best haircuts she'd ever seen were all sported by gay men. "I'm sure you'll make me look divine."

"Girl? You said it!" Titania chuckled and began combing out Jezzy's long, now-blond hair, and then he got out his shears. "I'm going to bring your hair up to your shoulders, sugar. It's just too long right now."

"That's fine," Jezzy said. To tell the truth, her hair had been feeling rather heavy lately. Taking some of the length off would help make her feel freer. It was all part of her transformation.

And sure enough, with each snip, Jezzy felt more and more unshackled, despite the cuffs on her ankles and wrists.

While Titania worked, Bare applied hot wax strips to Jezzy's legs. The warm strips felt lovely, but Jezebel had been waxed before. And although she loved how smooth waxing left her, she wasn't crazy about the process itself. When the wax strips came off, they hurt. There was no way around it. And the thought of having to endure the pain while bound and defenseless freaked her out a little.

Well, a lot.

Jezebel watched Bare lift a silver bottle from a small appliance that looked like a warmer. The bottle had a divot on one end of the lip, which was clearly meant to make pouring easier. The shape of the bottle and the divot for pouring, reminded Jez a little bit of an erect penis.

"What is that?" Jezzy asked.

"It's another kind of wax. Here at the Hellfire Club Spa our waxing services are twice as thorough as anywhere else."

More pain. Great.

Jezzy did her best to smile.

"You look nervous," Bare said, her perfect brows pulling together.

"No, I'm... I'm okay."

"You're concerned about the discomfort, aren't you?"

"Well... a little."

"Oh, you don't have to worry about that here at the Hellfire Club Spa."

"Why not?"

"Because here, more than anywhere in the world, we know how to turn pain into pleasure." Bare winked then leaned down and flicked a switch on the side of the chair.

Jezebel heard a buzzing sound, then a humming sound. Soon she felt a plastic wedge move up from the seat of her chair and ease between her legs. "What the—"

"Wait for it," Titania said, combing and snipping. Snipping and combing.

Another buzz. Another whirl, then a nozzle peeked out of the wedge between her legs, and warm water started spraying on her delicate folds.

"Oh!"

Titania laughed. "Nice, mmmm-hmmm?"

"Mmmm-hmmm!" Jezzy said, moving what little she could to make the water stream hit her in her most eager places. The spraying attachment felt similar to the shower head she used at home, which had several adjustments. This attachment did as well, because what was a thin stream of warm water only a moment ago now felt like a hard, bulleting spray, stopping and starting every half second. "I like it!"

Now the bulleting spray turned into several soft streams, which rotated over her. It felt like velvety fingers moving over her folds, skipping maddeningly over her sensitive pearl, first firmly, then soft and gentle. Each automatically changing adjustment was a different kind of exquisite torture.

Just then, Bare tore off the first wax strip.

Jezzy sucked a breath between closed teeth. Sweat bloomed over her skin.

Bare reached down to the panel. "Let's turn it up a little. It will intensify the pleasure of the wax."

"Pleasure?" Jezzy asked, then she felt the spray between her legs press harder, and she couldn't speak. The water surged like the jets in a hot tub, while another stream circled her clit, never quite touching. Her abdomen tightened, arousal coiling deep within. Her hips rocked forward, trying to catch the rotating spray.

Bare ripped off the second strip.

Jezzy arched her back. Her skin burned, the heat spreading over her like wildfire, then centering in her core. Her whole body seized, the relentless and ever-changing shower between her legs winding pleasure and pain so tightly together, she couldn't pick one from the other.

Bare moved higher on Jezzy's thighs, applying and ripping, applying and ripping. By the time she reached the tender folds surrounding Jezebel's core, Jezzy's breath was coming in ragged pants, and she was so close to coming, she could think of nothing but the throbbing need between her legs.

Bare turned off the spray.

Jezebel tried her best not to whimper. "Please, can you—"

RIP!

Jezzy let out a scream, partly from the oh-so-intimate pain, but mostly from the oh-so-mindbending pleasure that chased it.

RIP!

Jezebel bucked in the chair, trying to raise her pelvis, to absorb the pain, to tip herself over the edge.

RIP!

The first grips of orgasm tightened, then ebbed.

RIP! RIP! RIP!

Bare hadn't touched Jezebel's clit, and yet Jezzy came anyway. She cried out, thrashing on the chair, needing more pressure, more intensity, just... more.

The spasm faded, but like an appetizer, instead of satisfying Jezzy, the taste only served to make her hungrier. She moaned, watching Bare through an erotic haze as she pinched one of Jezzy's nipples.

"Oooh," Jezzy murmured, arching her back. "Please, don't stop."

"I think you're ready for the second part of your waxing." Bare leaned down to turn the water jets back on, her full, naked breasts swinging gently. Then she slowly tipped the silver bottle so that a tiny bit of wax spilled onto Jezzy's stiff left nipple.

Jezzy startled, her body lifting from the chair, the cuffs holding her securely in place. The discomfort was unlike anything Jezzy had ever felt before. Heat seared through her nipple, a sharp sting, and then the pain spread through her breast, then over her belly and loins. She felt her walls tighten, preparing for release.

The powerful spray continued massaging, caressing, driving her out of her mind. Her hips bucked off the chair, wanting more, needing more.

"I'm thinking she likes her treatment so far," Titania said, brushing out Jezzy's hair.

"Uuuuh," Jezzy replied, unable to form intelligent words. The only thing she wanted was to come, and come hard.

"I beg your pardon?" Bare asked, grinning down at her.

"I think she wants you to turn off the chair," Titania said, his tone teasing.

"No! Please," Jezzy begged. "Turn it up!"

Bare leaned down and turned the dial.

The pressure of the teasing spray went right through Jezzy. She gritted her teeth, moaning. The smaller, massaging spray circling her hungry clitoris was sweet torture. She felt herself teetering on the edge once again.

Bare gently tipped the silver bottle and a single drop of melted wax dropped on to Jezzy's right nipple.

Again, Jezzy felt burning pain for only a split second, then the pain turned into a delightful agony which scorched through her, leaving her breathless. Her nipple hardened and tightened, then seemed to push forward for more. Her pussy squeezed with want, making her aching little bead pulse slightly in and out.

"You really like that don't you, Jezebel?" Bare asked her, her rosy nipples poking forward. Her lovely russet hair gleaming under the lights of the spa.

"I'm so close." Jezebel said on a moan.

Bare leaned down and switched off the chair.

"No! I want to come!"

Bare smiled down at her. "Oh, you'll come. Your package includes providing you with the best, most intense orgasms possible."

Jezebel didn't need the best orgasms. Right now, she just needed another orgasm... *any* orgasm. "Please!"

"Patience, girl!" Titania said.

Jezzy's body felt positively on fire. She closed her eyes for a moment. Her whole body locked in tension.

"Now look how tense you are. That will never do." Titania started massaging her shoulders, but though it felt divine, a simple, chaste massage was not what Jezzy had in mind.

"Please, I need more."

"More, huh?" Titania winked at Bare.

Bare nodded and selected another bottle from the countertop. She squirted a blue-tinged lotion into Titania's palm then into her own.

"What is that?" Jezebel asked.

"This? This is my favorite." Titania resumed his massage, this time working from her shoulders down over her naked breasts.

Bare started caressing Jezzy's legs, kneading her thighs.

Within seconds, all of the areas they touched started tingling with cold. Jezebel's nipples came alive, more sensitive than ever. "Oh my!"

Bare poured another drop of blue lotion onto her fingertip. With a devilish grin, she placed the drop onto Jezzy's aching little bud, and began slowly rubbing it in.

Jezebel's hips shot forward and she cried out. The bliss was so strong, she began bucking the air, her clit bursting.

She thrashed. She moaned. The lotion changed from cold to hot, hot to cold, then like a tsunami, Jezzy's climax rushed forward, crashing over her, and her entire body seized. She squeezed her eyes shut while colors burst behind her lids. Wave after wave came, so intense she forgot her own name, or why she was even at the spa.

When the orgasm finally ebbed, she looked up to see Titania smiling.

"It was worth the wait, wasn't it, sugar?"

Jezebel smiled back, feeling a little sheepish. "I'll say."

Bare clapped her hands together. "Wait until you see your new look."

"I think you look good enough to eat," Titania said. The chair whirred into an upright position, and he handed her a mirror. "What do you think?"

Body still tingling and hair blown out, Jezebel stared at the glamorous blonde in the mirror, turning her head this way and that, her golden locks shimmering in the salon lights. She didn't look like Alice, not exactly, but she certainly no longer looked like the old Jezebel. She almost didn't recognize herself.

"Well?" Titania raised his bushy brows.

"Jack will love it. I think I even look a little thinner."

Bare gave her an encouraging nod. "You've burned a lot of orgasm calories."

"I've seen fantastical stories of quick weight loss on TV infomercials and read them in email spam, but to visibly lose weight in the hour and a half I was in the styling chair? That's crazy."

"This is the Hellfire Club, sugar. Things happen magically here. At least anything having to do with orgasms." Titania helped her out of the chair and into her silken robe. "And if you liked the fat-burning here in the salon, you're going to love the next part of your spa package."

"What's the next part?"

Bare clapped her hands together, smiling brightly. "Sexercise!"

Chapter 3

And Now, As You Guessed... Sexercise!

Wow."

Jezebel looked around the exercise room, wide-eyed. The place was huge, the workout machines brand new and obviously state-of-the-art, but the real eye opener was that every man and woman working out was naked. Completely, utterly, totally naked. And not only that, they were either moaning and screaming in ecstasy, or grunting in what looked like satisfied release.

If Jez's gym had been like this, she would have gone more often. Providing people wiped the equipment off after they'd finished, of course.

"Don't you love exercise, Jezebel?" Bare asked.

Jezebel felt she needed to be honest. "I've never been a huge fan of exercise machines. I find them so boring. I prefer to run outside in nature. But these people seem to enjoy it."

Bare smiled. "Here at the Hellfire Club Spa, we make exercise pleasurable. Definitely not boring at all. People can't wait to get on our machines, and it's very hard to get them off. I mean, it's easy to get them off, as you can plainly see. But it's difficult to get them away from the workout machines once they're on them."

"No! Don't make me leave! Please!" A man screamed, tears running down his face. He was clutching the handles of an exercise bike as two large, muscular men (who clearly spent a lot of time on the machines as well) attempted to pry his hands from the handle bars, and another pulled him from behind.

Bare shook her head. "That happens a lot."

"What's so special about these machines?" Jezzy asked.

"Let me introduce you to the man who can show you." Bare took Jezebel by the hand and led her to one of the enormous, ripped men who had carried the screaming man away. Unlike the naked people working out, this man wore a red Speedo with the word TRAINER printed across the waistband.

"I'd like to you meet Hercules. Hercules is part of your transformation team."

Hercules looked like a mountain, standing well over six feet with muscles bulging everywhere. He wore his hair in a brush cut, which showcased chiseled features and deep brown eyes.

"Nice to meet you, Jezebel."

"It's my pleasure."

"It certainly will be," he winked. "The first step is to get into your workout gear."

"Workout gear?" Jezebel must have missed something. She glanced around for Bare, but the woman was gone. "I'm sorry, but I don't have any workout gear."

Hercules threw back his head and laughed. "Of course, you do. Look around you. You have just as much workout gear as anyone else here."

Jezzy glanced around. "I don't see any gear. They're all naked."

"The gear they are using, dear Jezebel, is their bodies. That's all that's required for a good workout, you know."

"Oh," she said, finally understanding. "So you want me to take off my robe?"

Hercules nodded. "Let me see what we have to work with."

"Okay." Jez untied the robe's belt, hyper conscious of Hercules's eyes on her. Her pulse picked up. A jitter seated deep in her chest.

Silly.

Here Jezebel had just been naked in the salon, Titania's and Bare's hands all over her. She'd been half naked in front of a dozen construction workers earlier. And in the past, she'd always found stranger's eyes on her nude body exciting. But now?

Now she could only think about how imperfect her body was.

"What's wrong, Jezebel?" Hercules asked.

"I can only think about how imperfect my body is."

"No one's body is perfect. You're only as perfect as you feel."

"That's what Bare said."

"And Bare is a beautiful woman who walks around naked all the time." Hercules eyed her expectantly, as if he'd just proven his point and was waiting for her to recognize it.

Jezzy did her best to smile and nod. She didn't understand any of it, really. But she'd come to the Hellfire Club Spa to be transformed into a beauty for her wedding day, and if she didn't comply with the program, that wasn't going to happen. So scooping in a deep breath, she opened the robe and let it slip off her shoulders.

Standing naked in a room of naked people shouldn't be a big deal, Jezzy supposed, but her nipples hardened and her nectar started to flow, and instead of thinking about exercise, she found herself holding her breath and searching Hercules's face for the verdict.

He looked Jezzy up and down, his gaze lingering on her heavy breasts, her tingling nipples, and the freshly waxed spot between her legs. "Nice bod, Jezebel."

Jezzy flushed a little, wanting to believe him. But when she checked out his skimpy shorts, she couldn't see much of a bulge. She stood a little straighter, arching her back and thrusting out her breasts, hoping that would help.

"But I think we need to tone you up."

Jezebel slumped. No wonder seeing her hadn't made Hercules's bulge grow. She was flabby and out-of-shape. Frumpy. Just as she'd felt. "Where do I start?"

"How about trying a spinning class?"

Jez wasn't crazy about spinning classes, but whatever it took to make her body more attractive, she would do it. "I've attended a few spinning classes."

"Not like this one. Not only do these bikes have special features to make the ride more enjoyable, but we have several different sizes." Hercules led Jezzy to a room lined with exercise bikes. "When you find one you like, we'll get the class started."

"Great." Jezebel walked over to a smaller bike. Swinging her leg over the seat, she put her feet on the pedals. She studied the bike, noticing a bright, round green button on the console. "What does this button do?"

"That's the jack-off feature. It's used by the men. A robotic hand emerges from the seat. It works quite nicely."

"Does it have a feature for women?"

Hercules grinned. "Begin pedaling and find out."

Jezebel started at a slow and easy pace. The seat began to vibrate, but she had to lean forward quite a bit to fit her mound on the leather. Something poked her slightly from the seat. "Ooo, what was that?"

"That is the vibrating seat and fucking feature for women. Some men like it, too. A dildo emerges from the seat to provide an extra penetrating workout."

"Nice. But I'm afraid this one is too short. It's barely entering me at all."

"Try that one over there," Hercules pointed to a bike with a blue seat. "You might find it more to your liking."

Jezebel dismounted the first bike and swung a leg over the seat of the second. Fitting her feet on the pedals, she started to pump. The seat came to life, and vibrated so strongly that the entire bike shook. Her breasts bounced. Jezebel had to grip the handlebars tightly to keep from falling off. Her sensitive little bud shrank into the safety of her folds.

"I feee-eeeel liii-iiike aaaaa miiii-iiilk shaaaaaaake!"

"Give it a chance," Hercules said. "Pedal harder."

Jezebel did as he suggested, the bike feeling as if it was locked in a high gear. Something moved up against her moist opening and pushed into her wet tunnel... and pushed... and pushed... deeper... deeper... deeper...

When the dildo pressed against her cervix with no sign of stopping, Jezzy leaped off the seat and stared at a rod that was at least three times the length of the last bike she'd tried.

"No, no, no... Too long!"

Hercules chuckled. "Yes, but certainly you've had large penises inside you before."

"That's not a penis. That's a shish kabob skewer!"

"All right. All right. We'll try another bike." Hercules pointed to a glittering purple exercise bike across the room. "How about this one?"

Jezebel crossed to the new bike, letting out a sigh of relief. She was actually feeling a little queasy from all the vibrating, and her breasts kind of hurt, as if she'd been jogging without a bra. She settled into the new bike's seat and started to pump the pedals.

The seat came to life, a delicious hum cupping her womanhood. The tremors awoke her hardening bud, and tension tightened in her abdomen. Within moments the dildo breached her opening and slid into her wetness. Then just as she was starting to feel very full, it drew back to ready itself for another thrust.

She let out a long sigh.

"Just a wild guess, Goldilocks, but I'm thinking that one is just right?" Hercules said.

"Oooh yes… " Jezebel murmured, her eyes closed. "Oh, oh, oh, OH!"

Jezebel pedaled faster as a sweet orgasm gripped her, clenching her muscles, moving through her, and leaving her breathless. It was over far too soon.

"Now you see what a difference the right bike can make." Hercules grinned.

"Yes. I certainly do." Jezebel panted, slowing her pedaling down to catch her breath.

"Good. So you're ready for the game then."

"The game?"

Before Hercules could explain, people started filing into the room; a couple of women, then a few men. Every one of them was naked, and they each seemed to know exactly which bike they wanted.

"These people have been here before, I guess," Jezzy observed.

"Yes. They love this game."

"What kind of game is this?"

"You'll see. Your last orgasm came far too quickly. I'm betting it wasn't exactly mind boggling."

Jezzy nodded in the affirmative. Once she'd mounted the perfect bike, she'd been so eager for completion, she'd rushed to achieve it. But she had to admit, it wasn't as mind-blowing as her experience in the salon, and the fact that Hercules had noticed, too, made her feel a little inadequate.

"This game will force you to postpone your gratification, and as a result, your orgasms will be bigger and more intense. It also involves some healthy competition."

Competition? Jezzy wasn't keen on competition. "Do we have to compete?"

"Afraid you'll lose?"

"Well, yes," Jezebel said honestly.

"And you don't like to lose."

"Does anyone?"

Hercules chuckled. "No, I suppose not. But that will just make you more motivated."

Jezzy frowned. "Isn't improving my body enough motivation? Do I have to risk losing, too?"

"There's nothing that builds confidence better than taking a risk." Hercules winked. "Now we play the game. Has everyone chosen their bikes?"

A cacophony of voices spoke in the affirmative, except for two men who simply stood there. One wore a large top hat with a tag that read 10/6. The other wore bunny ears.

It was Hatter and Hare. Jez met them when they were working for her friend, Alice, and now they worked for Big Cock Billionaire Magazine.

"Are you here for me?" Jezebel asked the duo. They'd previously done a story on her and Jack, and she guessed they'd followed her to get some kind of pre-wedding scoop.

"Who are you?" asked Hatter.

"Do we know you?" asked Hare.

Jez was confused. These two weren't mental giants. In fact, calling them intellectually deficient would be insulting to all of the stupid people in the world who wouldn't want to be drawn from the same well. Had they forgotten who she was? Or were they playing one of their silly games? Or were drugs somehow to blame? Hatter did have a tinge of bloodshot in his eyes to go along with his spaced-out look. And Hare was eating an entire roasted turkey. There was also a very faint smell of marijuana in the room.

Plus they were both smoking joints.

Jez was ready to rail into them, to tell them to mind their own business. She was finally loosening up, relaxing for the first time since the wedding announcement, and now they would no doubt bombard her with questions and take photos and refuse to let her complete whatever transformation the spa had in store for her.

But then she remembered her hair.

I'm a blonde now. And it's shorter.

They don't recognize me!

"I'm Goldilocks," she answered, following Hercules's lead.

"Goldilocks," said Hatter. "Is that like Master Locks?"

"Masturbate?" said Hare.

"Rebate?" said Hatter.

"Jason Bateman?" said Hare.

"I loved Jason Bateman on Growing Pains," said Hatter.

"That was Kirk Cameron," said Hare.

"Didn't he direct Avatar?" said Hatter.

"Was that the movie with the blue people?" said Hare.

"That's the Smurfs," said Hatter.

"Did you know Smurfette was a cubist painter?" said Hare.

"Of course. She's famous for her blue period," said Hatter.

"I heard that was only once a month," said Hare.

"It was, until she missed a period," said Hatter.

"That's why he's known as Papa Smurf," said Hare.

"No wonder they're blue. Unplanned pregnancies are serious business," said Hatter.

"Who the fuck are you guys?" said Hercules.

Hatter stuck out a thumb. "I'm Hatter. That's Hare. We're here for the spinning class."

They began to rapidly spin around, twirling like little tornadoes, so fast that Hare dropped his turkey. Soon after they were both tumbling, ass over teacups, out the door.

"Did you know those jokers, Jezebel?" Hercules asked her.

Jez shrugged noncommittally.

Hercules closed the door and faced the class. "Okay, the object of the game is simple. You pedal as fast and as long as you can, without coming. The winner gets free entry into the Healthful Food Orgy, available only to our most treasured VIP members."

Jezebel looked at the other contestants in the spinning class. They were all licking their lips, fierce competitiveness in their eyes.

Self-doubt needled her. She frowned at Hercules. "You could've warned me. I would've stuck with the first bike."

"But where is the sport in that?" He tipped his blocky head back and laughed. "Okay! On your marks!"

All contestants lifted their bottoms and leaned forward.

Jezebel did the same.

"Get set!" Hercules said.

All contestants sat on their seats.

"Go!"

And the pedaling began.

Jezebel started with a steady pump, not too fast, not to slow, pacing herself. Where the other contestants might become exhausted quicker, she hoped she'd have the energy and endurance to continue.

But much to her dismay the steady, firm vibrations of the seat cupping her was at once more pleasurable than she'd hoped. Her nub swelled and poked forward, responding to the stimulation.

The dildo thrust upward into her opening. The machine seemed to sense the location of her g-spot, and when it began a spinning movement right *there*, Jezebel caught her breath. Her nipples tightened and protruded shamelessly. Her breasts swayed and jiggled with each pump on the pedals, and she noticed some of the men glancing her way.

Unfortunately her swinging tits didn't distract her competition, but instead seemed to make them more determined. Their pedaling quickened, and although many were already moaning and sighing under their breaths as the robotic hand pumped their erections, all of their faces remained resolute.

Jezzy wanted to be that resolute.

But it was damn difficult. Jez's stomach and back bunched with tension. Her arousal level kept creeping up, no matter how much she tried to ignore it. Watching the other contestants was making her hornier with each passing moment. She closed her eyes, trying to focus on the burning muscles in her legs. But having her eyes closed only made her more aware of the growing need in her core.

"You're all doing very well," Hercules called out. "And you've all made it to the next level."

"What is the next level?" Jezebel asked, breathless.

"Nipple lickers! Theseus!" He bellowed. "I require assistance!"

The door opened and a guy came in. A muscular guy, not as massive as Hercules but just as cut.

"This is Theseus," Hercules said to Jez. "Another trainer here at the spa."

"Theseus?" Jez asked. "Why does that name sound familiar?'

"Mythology," Theseus said. "I was the founder-king of Athens. Son of Poseidon. Killed the Minotaur in the labyrinth. Ring any bells?"

Jez shrugged. "It's all Greek to me."

"Theseus and I will assist everyone in putting on their nipple buzzers. Everyone keep pedaling."

Jez kept a steady pace, trying to control her breathing. But it wasn't any use. Despite her best efforts, the bike, with its vibration and thrusting, was really turning her on. When it was her turn to have the nipple contraptions fitted, she arched her back and thrust out her breasts for Theseus.

"Give it to me," she said, boldly.

"I will later," Theseus winked. He pinched her right bud until it was stiff, then pulled a retractable cord from under the handlebars of her bike and attached it to her right nipple. He did the same with her left, teasing her to uncomfortable stiffness before placing the device. "You have lovely tits. Really, really scrumptious. I hope you win and make it to the Healthful Food Orgy."

"Thanks." Jezzy looked down at her breasts, each attached to an HR Gigeresque metal tube. "So what do these do?"

"They're nipple lickers," Theseus said. "They lick."

He pressed a button on her bike's control pad. Tiny flicks engulfed her nipples, as if small tongues were hungrily lapping. But they seemed to alternate hot and cold, wet and dry, tingly and pinching.

"Oh!"

"Yes, each nipple licker has the icy hot lotion inside to intensify the decadence. Do you like it?"

"Oh my gosh, yes," Jezzy's hips moved forward and she pressed herself against the seat. She was so stimulated, her clit so engorged and aching, that she felt on the verge of climaxing.

"Okay," Hercules shouted, clapping his hands together again. "The race is on!"

Jezebel's eyes flew open. She hadn't even been aware that she'd closed them. She drove down hard on the pedals, launching into a fast rhythm. The vibration vibrated. The nipple lickers licked. The dildo dildoed.

All around her, naked people moaned and groaned, sighed and panted. All inside her, eagerness crackled with the intensity of high tension wires.

Three of the contestants came at the same time, bellowing their release.

Jezzy pedaled and pedaled and pedaled and pedaled, all the while feeling the heavenly vibrations of the seat and the dildo plunging in and out of her steadily tightening tunnel, the friction against her g-spot, the maddening massage of her nipples.

Just a little while longer…

Jezebel heard scream after scream, and saw her competitors fall, one after the other, like a bunch of dominoes. As they did, their bikes stopped. It must have been some sort of automatic shut-off switch, which was a shame, because if Jez had to lose, she wanted to lose multiple times.

Finally, besides her, there was one spinner left. He glared at Jez from across the room, pedaling fast and gritting his teeth. Sweat trickled over his lean, sinewy body.

"Only Jezebel and the reigning champion, Studly Hungwell, remain," Hercules announced.

"Your name is Studly Hungwell?" she said to him.

"Stage name," he said. "My given name is Macho Dick. I'm the fourth Macho Dick in the family. I come from a long line of Dicks."

Jez frowned. Neither of those names had anything to do with fairytales or any other kind of literature. Instead of being part of this story, they seemed more like just a cheap joke.

"Will Jezebel dethrone Studly?" Hercules said, continuing his poor imitation of a sportscaster. "Or will he continue to reign supreme?"

"What?" Jezebel puffed. "He's never been beaten?"

"He's getting beaten right now," Theseus said, glancing at the mechanical hand jerking Studly off. "But he is undefeated."

Great.

Now the chance of winning this game seemed so slim, Jezebel wondered why she should even continue to try. Why not just give up right now? At least if she never really tried, she couldn't be a true loser, right? And the orgasm lurked just one sexy thought away.

But then Studly Hungwell smirked at her, as if reading her mind.

Loser. Loser. Loser.
Fat. Fat. Fat.
No. No. No.

Suddenly a new determination bloomed within Jezebel. Resolve fueled her, giving her strength she didn't know she had. Which led to a wicked idea.

If one sexy thought could do me in, might the same be said of Mr. Hungwell?

She felt herself smile back then run a long hungry gaze down his body and focused on the part of him being fondled by the robotic fist. It was time to knock the king from his throne... or bike, or whatever.

It was time to fight dirty.

Between ragged breaths, she called out to him. "You're... so big... I... want to... suck your... cock!"

He looked surprised, then a look of frank craving crossed his face.

"Imagine... it's me... sucking you now..." Jez continued. "Come... in my mouth! Come... for me!"

Studly's eyes clenched shut, his face contorting.

This was going to work! This was going to work!

Then Studly regained his composure and he smiled through gritted teeth. "Your tits... are... making... me so... hard."

Now all Jezzy could think about was the weight of her swaying breasts and the firmness of his manhood. From there, it was only a small skip and a jump to imagining the tip of his shaft sliding upward, protruding from her cleavage, a drop of pre-cum glistening on his—

This wasn't going to work! This wasn't going to work!

She'd misjudged both Studly and herself. Not only had he seen through her strategy, Jez had forgotten how much dirty talk turned her on.

She glanced back his way.

He stared at her as if transfixed. His lean body glistened with sweat, and with each push of a pedal, his hips thrust forward, as if he wasn't biking at all but instead driving into her.

As if he was as turned on as she was.

"It's a race!" Hercules shouted the obvious.

It was a race, all right. And Jezebel wasn't going to lose.

"I can... feel your cock... feel it sliding... between my tits... feel you coming... on my nipples..."

Studly moaned, his face flushed with exertion and lust. He clearly really did want to fuck her.

And the thought of him entering her nearly sent her over the edge. "Fuck... me! I'm... your... dirty little... slut! My pussy... aches... for... you!"

"I'm ... going ... to ... eat your ... hot ... wet ... pussy!"

"I want to ... suck your rod dry! Drink ... every ... last ... drop!"

Oh, fuck, I'm turning myself on.

Jezebel's body sang with desire. The little clamps vibrating on her nipples sent electric bursts of pleasure trilling through her. Her belly tightened.

Studly moaned, his skin flushed deep pink, then he grunted, "I want to fuck ... your tight ... ass!"

The thought of him sliding into her ass at that moment seemed wildly erotic. The dildo rotating against her g-spot was merciless, sending jolts through her body.

Jezzy heard herself whimpering, and Studly's eyes watching her with obvious lust made everything so much worse. Her pussy squeezed uncontrollably. She was on the verge of an enormous climax, and bit down on her bottom lip, concentrating for all she was worth.

No! Don't come first! No! NO!

Studly suddenly waggled his tongue at her, making quick little licking motions. And at that moment, the thought of his tongue swirling over her clit was simply too much.

Her body seized, the orgasm gripping her with such force it was all she could do to stay on the bike. But even as she was wracked with pleasure, she was also wracked with regret.

I lost!

I failed!

I suck!

And the thought of sucking made Jezebel come again.

Then, through her coital fog, she saw that Studly was also in the grip of ecstasy. He bucked forward and fell across the handlebars, bellowing out her name as his legs shot out to the sides.

The rest of the room (the losers) broke out into applause.

"Well," Hercules said. "We haven't had this happen before. A dead heat. Theseus, what do you think? Should both of them enjoy the Healthful Food Orgy? Or neither?"

Theseus tapped his chin in thought. "I think we should let them both in. I don't know about you, but both intrigue me."

Jezebel smiled. They had tied! She was so proud of herself for not losing to the reigning spinning king, that she felt positively euphoric. The self-confidence she felt at that moment was even more pleasurable than any orgasm she'd ever had. It was addictive. She wanted more of it.

And strangely, the confidence was causing faint stirrings deep inside of her loins again. Success and achievement were turning her on. Who'd have thought? Self-confidence is sexy! Not just to others who recognize it in a person, but for the person experiencing it.*

*This is the moral of the story. It will be repeated again and again so you don't forget it.

"Very well," Hercules said. "You have both earned a spot at the Healthful Food Orgy. Follow me."

Studly approached Jezebel and offered his hand. "Good game. My name is Hansel."

"Wait, I thought you were Macho Dick."

"That's my family name. But I didn't ever go by that. Believe it or not, I got teased a lot."

"And you didn't get teased for Studly Hungwell?"

"Studly Hungwell is my stage name. I work in the porn industry."

"Why didn't you stick with Macho Dick?"

"Believe it or not, it was already taken."

Jez could believe it. "So what's with Hansel?"

"That's my nickname."

"Why?"

"It means Little Hans."

Macho aka Studly aka Hansel held up his hands, which were indeed quite small.

"It's a blessing, really," Hansel said. He placed a tiny hand on his own spent cock and said, "Look how big my manhood seems now. And if I played with your boobs, they'd appear two cup sizes bigger."

"Impressive," Jez said, impressed. "And a good name for Fairytaleland. Fits right in with Gretel."

He rolled his eyes. "That's my sister."

"Are you *that* Hansel and Gretel?"

"That's us."

"I'm thrilled to meet you," Jez said, thrilled to meet him. Everyone knew the famous, thrilling story of Hansel and Gretel. It was a real thriller.

"Of course we've grown up since then." Hansel said. "Gretel and I don't go wandering around the woods anymore. Although I do enjoy visiting the wicked witch, Lucinda. She does, indeed, love to eat me. You should see how she gnaws on my bone."

"So it wasn't your finger you stuck through the cage bars that she checked for plumpness?"

"It was not. And we weren't children. We were both above the legal age of consent wherever this book is being read. Lucinda was something." His face grew wistful.

Jezebel remembered the witch Lucinda from her adventure up the beanstalk, although Jez's opinion wasn't as favorable. "Where is Gretel these days?"

"She's stripping down at Hot Tails. You wouldn't believe how many fairytale characters work there. Great for making a little cash on the side." He looked her up and down. "You should skip on over there and shake your booty. I bet you could rake it in."

"Um, no thank you," Jez said, although she supposed it was more flattering that Hansel found her hot enough to be a stripper than not.

"Come on, you two," Theseus said. "We don't want to be late."

"To the Healthful orgy we go!" Hercules sang out.

And with that, Jezebel headed to the orgy, her appetite whetted for more than just food.

Chapter 4

A Healthful Orgy of Delights

Jezebel stared, wide-eyed, at the long wooden table that was weighed down with an enormous variety of food. Berries of all sorts were set in dishes all along the table. Apples, pears, mangos, and a wide array of other fruits sat on decorated platters. Three different flavors of yogurt smoothies cascaded from curvy fountains. Nuts, seeds, and vegetables sat on rotating, tiered trays.

"This is incredible." Jezebel said. "It looks so healthy."

"Well, it was healthy once," Bare said. "Now it's healthful."

"I never understood the difference between the two."

"Allow me to explain," Theseus said, stepping into the room behind Jez.

"Please do. Nothing turns a girl on like proper grammar."

"Healthy means alive and fit. Healthful means it will help you stay alive and fit. If you ate healthy food, you ate something while it was still alive, which would probably result in it screaming."

"If you ate me, I'd scream," Jez said.

"Which is a healthy response."

"And would no doubt be healthful," Bare added. She stood in four inch white furry slides, which accentuated her lovely flared hips and long legs. "I'm glad that you made it to the orgy, Jezebel. I was so hoping that you would. This event will nourish you like nothing else."

Jezebel's stomach grumbled. This time, after leaving the gym, she hadn't bothered to put on the silk robe, but had walked in completely naked, the buzz of the competition and spectacular orgasms fueling each step. Now it felt a little strange to be thinking of feasting in the raw, but Jezzy supposed if Bare could do it, she could learn to do it, too.

Bare chose a large red strawberry and dipped it into a white, frothy cream. "This is whipped Greek yogurt. It's delicious."

"And healthy," Jez said. "Because yogurt contains lactobacillus, which is still alive when you eat it."

"Like bacon."

"And eggs."

Jezebel turned and saw Hatter and Hare had somehow gotten into the orgy. Hatter now wore an Easter bonnet, and Hare had a fluffy cotton tail sticking to his naked bottom.

At least Jezebel *hoped* it was a fluffy cotton tail sticking to his naked bottom; it could have been a whole bunny shoved up his ass.

"What are you two doing here?"

"We're eating," said Hatter, eating a melon.

"And having sex," said Hare, having sex with a melon. A different melon.

"Do you know that I know that you know the loveliest poem about fornicating with melon?" said Hatter.

"I do know that you know that I know it, you know," said Hare.

"I do know that you know that I know that you know that I know you know it," said Hatter.

"I know," said Hare.

"Do recite for us," said Hatter. "We need to fit at least one of these stupid poems into every story, for continuity's sake."

Hare cleared his throat, then stuck out his bare chest and assumed an oratory position.

"I had sex,
With a melon,
Now I'm wanted,
As a felon."

"It is true," said Hatter. "Sex with fruit is illegal in Fairytaleland."

"But he's got his penis in a melon right now!" Jezebel pointed.

Hare struck another pose.

"I wanted to be a physicist,
But I'm a fruit boinking recidivist."

"Did you write that one yourself?" said Hatter.

"No. That was the famous melon objectivist, Ayn Rind."

"How many readers do you think are getting these obtuse jokes?" said Hatter to a large, muscular, naked man who was holding up a giant globe of the earth.

The man shrugged.

"This is all becoming increasingly meta," Jezebel said. "And I really don't think you're allowed to attend this orgy without being invited."

Normally, Jezebel wasn't so rude. But she knew it was only a matter of time before these two discovered who she was. Then it would be pictures, and interviews, and harshing the mellow she'd been cultivating since her arrival.

"But we do have invitations," said Hatter.

He lifted up his bonnet and produced a piece of paper.

"Admit two," Jez read aloud.

"I once stole twenty-seven thousand dollars from a convenience store," admitted Hatter.

"I once stole twenty-seven thousand dollars from Hatter," admitted Hare.

"There we have it," said Hatter. "Two admissions."

"Hey, who are you guys?" Theseus said.

"I'm Hatter," said Hatter. "This is Hare. And I'm Hatter. I believe we've already met."

"Who are you?" said Hare.

"I'm Theseus."

"Theseus?" said Hatter. "You mean the one that has all the synonyms?"

"That's Thesaurus," Theseus said.

"Thesaurus is here?" said Hare, reaching up to fix his hair. "I love that guy. He's so smart."

"And clever," said Hatter.

"And intelligent," said Hare.

"And quick-witted," said Hatter.

"And astute," said Hare.

"And perceptive," said Hatter.

"Also, he's hung like a horse," said Hare.

"A stallion," said Hatter.

"A bronco," said Hare.

"A steed," said Hatter.

"A colt," said Hare.

"I heard he came from Pittsburgh," said Hatter.

"I believe you meant to say he came from filly," said Hare.

"Of horse he came from filly," said Hatter. "All horses do."

"Do you know what came straight from the horse's mouth?" said Hare.

"I think I do," said Hatter. "A bit."

While they went on with their irritating wordplay, Jezebel slunk to the other end of the table. Tomorrow she would be married. She needed to relax and improve her self-confidence, not listen to puns. Not that she wanted to think ill of anyone, but part of her hoped that Hatter and Hare were both violently murdered.

No. That's not nice. That's not nice at all.

Gently murdered.

That's much nicer.

"Would you like a strawberry, Jezebel?" Bare asked.

Jezzy turned to face her. "That sounds lovely, Bare."

Bare selected a piece of fruit and stepped close, one breast brushing against Jezebel's. She slipped the tip of the strawberry between Jezzy's teeth.

Jezebel took a bite, sweet juice filling her mouth. "Mmmm."

Bare moved closer, her skin soft, her stiff nipple playing against Jezebel's.

Jezzy smiled, an idea coming to mind. She plucked a strawberry from a nearby bowl and offered it to Bare, and after the lovely woman took a bite, Jezebel brought the remaining fruit to Bare's breast.

Bare's *bare* breast.

Jezzy swirled the strawberry around Bare's nipple, coating it with juice, teasing until it was taut. Then she slipped her hand under the soft mound and lifted, bringing the nipple up to her own lips.

Bare tasted as lovely as she looked, the strawberry tang mixing with the delicate flavor of her skin, the Jasmine scent of her hair. Her skin felt smooth against Jezzy's tongue, her lips, the texture soft as she nibbled. She moved to Bare's other breast, painting her with juice, suckling her clean. When Jezzy finally looked up, Bare was flushed, her breath coming fast.

"Let me."

Selecting a slice of papaya, Bare brought it to Jezebel, flicking her nipples with fruit until they glistened. A drop of sweet nectar wound its way into her cleavage. The juice was cool on Jezzy's skin, and when it was chased by the warmth of Bare's mouth, Jezzy couldn't hold back a moan.

Another moan echoed hers, and it took a moment for Jezebel to realize it hadn't come from her or from Bare.

"Here you two, try this." Hercules handed Bare a banana.

Bare smiled. Looking into Jezebel's eyes, she stripped the peel from the fruit. Then she brought the banana's tip to Jezzy's breast, toying with her nipple. She flicked it over one then the other, and then slipped the banana's length between Jezebel's breasts, sliding it up and down in the sweetness left by the papaya.

Theseus and Hansel joined Hercules. Of the three, only Hansel was naked, and as he watched the banana, his member flexed upward, as if straining to be noticed.

Bare smiled down at Hansel's cock, then gave Jezebel a wink. She slipped the banana free and dipped it into a nearby bowl of thick, creamy yogurt, then held it up to Jezzy's lips. "Take your time to really enjoy it."

Jezebel closed her eyes and swirled her tongue around the tip of the banana. The yogurt tasted tangy, a sweet hint of fruit underneath. She licked down the gentle curve, moving slowly, savoring. When she reached Bare's fingers, she gave them a little kiss, then moved back up the stiff length. This time, when she reached the tip, she took the whole fruit into her mouth, sucking the yogurt clean.

Groans erupted around her, and when she opened her eyes, she saw Hansel, Theseus, and Hercules gathered around. Theseus and Hercules still wore their Hellfire trainer shorts, but the polyester spandex blend did little to hide their excitement. Theseus looked as if he would burst free at any moment. Even Hercules sported a touch of bulge.

Apparently eating a banana was erotic. Who knew?

Bare handed the banana to Jezzy, and nodded, encouraging her to continue.

Jezebel glanced at the expectant faces. Her heartbeat accelerated. A flutter of nerves worked over her naked skin.

This is weird.

When I was nude in front of the construction workers, I felt safe because Jack was there.

Now he's gone. And everyone is watching me. They're expecting something.

It's scary.

It's intimidating.

I should stop.

But something inside Jezebel didn't want to stop. Something inside wanted to push her limits, take a greater risk, see what happened next.

She took a deep breath and pushed her fear aside.

If people like to watch, let them.

I'll even put on a little show.

Jezzy brought the banana back to her mouth, her hand shaking. She started slowly, nibbling the banana with her lips as if it was a cob of corn. Then she flicked it with her tongue.

Someone let out a low moan.

Heat flushed over Jezebel's skin, but the blush didn't come from embarrassment. She was getting excited herself. Turned on by all the eyes on her. The appreciative moans. The hungry expressions.

She focused on the men, not their bulges this time, but their faces in turn, meeting each man's eyes.

Hercules's were chocolate brown. And when she flicked at the banana's tip, they grew wide and round, and he released a low whimper.

Theseus's were hazel green. And when she revolved her tongue around the fruit, he stood up straight and mumbled to himself.

Hansel's were deep blue and dreamy. And when she opened her throat and sucked the banana deep, his mouth fell open a little and his body trembled.

Warmth pooled in Jezzy's core. Moisture glazed her inner thighs. It had been a long time since she'd done anything so blatantly exhibitionist. Not just being nude in front of construction workers or having sex with Jack in the occasional public place, but really preforming. And seeing how much she was turning these men on, how much she was turning Bare on, gave her a thrill.

Jez felt powerful. In control.

Confident.*

*There's that moral again. Told ya.

"Try this, too." Hatter reached out a hand, a whole kiwi balancing on his palm.

"You really need a pair." Hare thrust a second hairy fruit at her.

"Jezebel, would you like some more banana yogurt?" Hercules pushed his shorts down his thighs. Picking up the bowl, he poured a thick coating of yogurt over his erect length.

Knowing that Hercules was the son of Zeus, Jezebel was surprised by how little length there actually was. Herc, who was built like a Greek god (because he was a Greek god), had a cock that was small enough to get lost in Jezebel's fist.

In fact, it was practically small enough to get lost in Hansel's fist.

And here I assumed the lack of bulge in his shorts was due to my shortcomings!

Jez wondered if this was a steroid thing. She'd heard that juicing could shrink a man's manhood. Or perhaps his muscles were some sort of overcompensation. Maybe he'd always been small in the trouser tackle department, so he worked on getting the rest of himself huge.

She looked up at his face, a question on her lips, but saw no insecurity there. If anything, Hercules looked a little cocky.

A little cocky with a little cocky.

Well, if he can be cocky, so can I.

Jez turned to her group of voyeurs. "Should I have a little more banana yogurt?"

There were whoops and hollers, and noises like elephants trumpeting (which turned out to be coming from Hatter and Hare).

Jezebel lowered herself to her knees, her face precisely at the level of Hercules's groin.

The muscle man's lovely, little, straining member reached upward, toward his taut belly, and moved forward in little jerks, as if beckoning.

Jez peered up at the man mountain, then extended her tongue and began with a little lick along Hercules's glans.

His cock sprang upward, eager for more.

She gave him another swipe of her tongue, this time twirling around his circumference. The yogurt tasted rich and sweet. But it wasn't the taste that Jezebel found irresistible, it was his responsiveness.

Hercules groaned and ran his fingers through Jezebel's soft, newly blonde hair. He tilted his hips toward her, seemingly not with any design in mind, but just because he couldn't help it.

She took the head into her mouth, her nipples brushing against his muscled thighs, then accepted him deeper. Or at least as deep as he went. There was no need to relax her throat. No gagging. She could suck him right down to the base, fit him between her gum and cheek, and curl her tongue around his width.

"Oooh yeah, Jezebel. You're amazing."

"Lick him clean!" a voice cried from the crowd.

"Suck him dry!" another yelled above the cheering.

"She's a witch!" screamed a third. "Burn her!"

Hatter and Hare again, those assholes.

Hercules moaned and whimpered and thrust in and out of her mouth, his movements becoming frantic and urgent. "Oh, yes! Yes!"

"Theseus," Jezzy heard Bare say. "You take the peach yogurt. Hansel? Let's pour some strawberry preserves over you. We'll give Jezebel a real feast."

Out of the corner of her eye, Jezzy saw Theseus ditch his shorts. Hercules withdrew from her mouth, and there at the level of her eyes was the fattest cock she'd ever seen. Roughly the size of a soda can, Theseus's member was coated in yogurt, small bits of peaches flecking the prominent head.

"Wow," Jezebel said on a puff of breath.

"It's something, isn't it?" Theseus said, as cocky about his scale as Hercules had been about his.

Jezebel smiled. His dimensions might be a little intimidating, but like Hercules, his cocksure attitude inspired her to overlook the size issue.

She lowered her jaw, then stretched her mouth open wide. Her lips strained, burning a little at the corners, and even then, she could accommodate him only as far as his ridge. Unlike blowing Hercules, Jez couldn't swirl her tongue around him, or get much suction going. And deep-throating? Fahgettaboutit. But Theseus seemed pleased just the same, moaning and thrusting, his tight butt clenched, his generous sack plumping soft against her chin.

"Not many woman can do that, Jezebel," he said between grunts.

Jezebel pulled away, raising an eyebrow. "Are you saying I have a big mouth?"

Theseus began to answer, but stammered. Then Jezebel winked, and everyone, including Theseus, began to laugh.

"Me, next," Hansel said.

Jezebel did a double-take at Hansel's manhood, which looked like he'd been having carnal relations with a meat grinder. But what she first thought was blood turned out to be strawberry jam. She tasted his sweet tip, then slid his length into her mouth.

His cock skated over her tongue, filling her mouth, and reaching to the back of her throat. She pulled back, toying with the underside with her tongue, then relaxing her throat, she sucked him deep again.

Herc had been too small. Theseus too large. But Hansel was just right. (That's another Goldilocks joke, for those who didn't catch it at first.)

Jez alternated between the three men, flavors mingling on her tongue. Her tits felt full and tight, and her nipples burned with need. Not literally, of course; nipples on fire wouldn't be sexually arousing. But they were stiff and this was Fairy-taleland and Jezebel allowed herself to think in purple prose because it was suitable to the situation.

"May I try your tongue, Jezebel?"

Jezzy looked up to see Bare smiling down at her.

"I'd be honored, Bare."

Bare slathered Greek yogurt between her thighs and stepped in front of Jez.

Jezzy leaned forward, and tentatively began with tiny, slow circles around Bare's coated little gem. She moved first clockwise, then counterclockwise. She flicked the creamy nub then changed to slow, fat licks, the cream mixing with the tang of Bare's nectar.

"So good." Bare spread her thighs wider. She pressed her mound to Jezzy's mouth and ground against her rotating tongue. Then Bare arched her back, thrusting her breasts into the air, and as Theseus and Hansel each nibbled a nipple, she took their hard rods, one in each fist.

Jezebel's pussy was drenched and her thighs quivering. As much as she was enjoying her feast, she also wanted to climax herself. And like a deep itch she couldn't scratch, the need drove her hunger.

Bare shuddered and cried out, her entire body quaking as she came. Once. Twice. When her orgasms subsided, she sagged against Hansel.

"It's time to move on to the next course," she said on panting breaths.

"Wait!" called Hatter.

"Wait!" called Hare.

"It's time to clear the table," they said in unison.

A loud crash echoed through the room as fountains and platters, bowls and chafing dishes clattered to the floor.

Jezebel was about to ask what the hell they thought they were doing when Hercules lifted her from her knees, swooped her into his arms, and carried her to the cleared end of the table. He laid her on her back, and the rest gathered around.

At first, Jezzy felt exposed, vulnerable, with five men crowded around her, staring down at her naked breasts, her intimate folds, the glistening dampness between her thighs. Five cocks stretched over her, erect and ready, sacks hanging heavy underneath. Even Hatter and Hare didn't seem silly now, their shafts—one thick and corded with veins, the other curved charmingly upward—bobbing on either side of her head.

Jez remembered the construction workers, touching themselves as they watched her. But they'd been at a distance. Being watched up close was much more exciting. Her heart beat faster. Her breath came quicker. Her skin flushed with heat.

Jezebel spread her thighs, just a few inches at first, then a few more. She arched her back, thrusting her stiff nipples into the air. Then, feeling really bold, she leaned her head back, over the edge of the table, and discovered Hansel standing behind, his shaft hard and ready. Jez smiled up at him and opened her mouth. He slid inside, and she cupped her lips around him, protecting the tender skin of his glans from her teeth. Hansel moved slowly into her mouth, then eased out, cradling her head and neck with strong hands.

Jezebel gasped around his length as something cold dripped onto her sensitive folds. Her core tightened at the change in temperature.

"Just a little cream for your sweet pie," Theseus said in his deep voice. Then she could feel his mouth on her, heat chasing ice, tongue teasing clit, licking up every drop. He ground his lips into her and thrust his tongue inside.

Jez angled her hips, trying to take him deeper. "Domm dopp," she whimpered.

That was what *don't stop* sounded like with a dick in your mouth.

Theseus seemed to understand. He could apparently speak blowjob.

"Stop?" He laughed, the vibrations tickling. "I won't stop until I'm done eating."

Hatter, Hare, and Hercules moved their hands over her, whisper soft over her belly, harder on her breasts, kneading and pinching. She took hold of Hatter and Hare, one in each fist, not caring how ridiculous they were, not caring that they might recognize her, not caring about anything but the feel of their firm lengths in her hands and the way their balls rose and fell with each pump of her fists.

Hercules climbed onto the table. Straddling her body, he cupped her breasts and pushed them together, mounding them high. Something slipped into the channel of her cleavage, and even though she couldn't see it, she'd recognize the soft, firmness of an erect cock anywhere.

"Your tits are so luscious," Herc said as he slid between, kneading them with his hands and pinching her nipples. "So big and soft and beautif—Ahhhhh."

A splash of warmth bathed her breasts.

Hercules grunted and groaned, and then he was quiet. "Uh, sorry Jezebel. I didn't mean to come, but I just couldn't help it. You have the most beautiful tits I've ever seen."

Jezzy flushed at the compliment, wanting to wrap herself in his kind words.

"That reminds me," Bare said. "You haven't had a facial yet, have you Jezebel? A spa trip is nothing without a good facial."

"Mmmphmmmph," Jezzy said, her best shot at conveying the negative around Hansel's just right size.

"It's lovely, dear," Bare said. "And here at the Hellfire Club Spa, a facial isn't just for the face. We offer a special bukkake (she pronounced it boo-cock-ee) facial that covers the whole body."

Voices erupted around her.

"It's the most amazing thing."

"Makes your skin so soft."

"Tightens the pores, too."

"I love to come on tits!"

And as crude as whoever that last voice belonged to was (Hatter or Hare, anyone?), Jezebel had to admit she'd enjoyed having a man rub his cock against her breasts and climax on them, so much that she'd like to do it again. And having five—well, four, since Hercules was already spent—sounded fabulous.

She let Hansel fall from her lips, and shifted back on the table, this time wanting to see, to taste, as well as feel the warm slickness of their shafts against her skin. "Please, I'd like to try."

"Very well. Are you all ready?" Bare asked the men.

Hercules climbed down from the table and took Theseus's place between her thighs. His tongue was as strong as his muscular body, and he lathed her, teased her, and plunged it inside. Hatter and Hare climbed on the table, Hansel and Theseus on either side of her shoulders. All of the men focused on her, only her, their strong hands holding stiff, eager shafts.

The lust on their faces was almost too much. Jezzy felt hot and sexy and… powerful. She wanted them to come. She wanted to be bathed in their passion.

All around her, the men stroked, their motions growing more urgent, more frantic. Hips tipped forward, grunts and moans gaining volume. Hatter and Hare rubbed themselves over her nipples, sliding in the seed Hercules had left, slick skin against slick skin. Theseus and Hansel moved against her cheeks, and she turned her head this way and then that, licking one cock then the other.

And as Hercules's tongue kept up its exquisite torture, the first spasm of a climax clenched deep within her walls and her hips began to buck.

Jezebel cried out as the orgasm gripped her, but Hercules didn't stop. The men around her didn't stop. Wave after wave seized, letting go only to seize her again. And when the men finally added their voices to hers and the warmth of their essence coated her skin, Jezebel felt invincible.

Amid the splashing seed, Bare began stroking Jezebel's face with her fingertips. She started with Jezzy's forehead and cheeks then moved down over her neck, her chest, her breasts, massaging the fluid into Jezzy's skin. The men around them joined in, kneading her breasts, smoothing their hands over her belly, touching every intimate inch.

Jezebel closed her eyes. To have all those cocks worshipping her had been heady. To have all these hands, divine.

"That might be the hottest health food orgy we've ever had," Bare told her.

"It was so powerfully orgasmic, I feel the urge to recite poetry," said Hatter.

"Please control the urge," said Jezebel. "I beg you."

But Hatter, who now wore an oversized bowler hat, assumed the poetry position. The position involved standing up straight, chin out, chest thrusting forward, one foot slightly in front of the other. It looked as stupid as that description sounds.

Hatter cleared his throat, and began.

"I really love good teriyaki,
But even more, I love bukkake."

"Awful!" someone shouted.

"I'm going to be sick!" yelled another.

Someone else was sick, and the sound of retching ripped through the room.

Undaunted, Hare also assumed the position and began to recite.

"I really love my Kawasaki,
But even more, I love bukkake."

"Have mercy!" someone pleaded.

"Someone kill me," a woman cried. That woman may have been Jezebel.

Unperturbed, Hatter stepped in front of Hare, apparently not wanting to be outdone.

"I really love the movie Rocky,
But even more, I love bukkake."

"And you both are done," Hercules said, hoisting Hatter and Hare up by their necks.

"Wait, we have more rhymes!" cried Hatter.

"We haven't yet used disc jockey!" cried Hare.

"Or sukiyaki!" cried Hatter.

"Or field hockey!" cried Hatter.

"Or Nagasaki!" cried Hare.

"Don't use Nagasaki!" cried Hare. "That joke will bomb!"

"Too soon!" yelled someone in the crowd.

Jezebel wondered if seventy years really was too soon for nuclear genocide jokes, and decided it was, so she was pleased when Herc tossed the two reporters out of the room. Also, Jez knew, it was only a matter of time until they figured out who she was, and she was having such a lovely time she didn't want it ruined with unnecessary stress.

Plus, she really couldn't stand anymore bad poems. Who would let the author get away with such atrocities?

"My dear," Bare said, eyeing Jezebel. "You're so sticky you look like a glazed donut. We need to get you cleaned up."

So Jez went to get cleaned up.

Chapter 5

A Steamy Experience

Bare led Jezebel to the showers, where several VIPs were in the process of enjoying a sensual scrub-down by trainers with large, fluffy sponges. The shower stall formed a semi-circle of mirrors, and Jez watched herself as Bare poured some fragrant body wash onto a sponge and ran it over Jezzy's body, gently cleansing away the stickiness from the Healthful Food Orgy. The rich smell of the body wash—

sandalwood and brown sugar—along with the soothing strokes of the sponge, were so relaxing that Jezebel closed her eyes.

"Don't fall asleep, Jezebel. We have more in store."

After rinsing Jezzy under the warm spray, Bare took her hand and led her to a room with a large pool. Two broad-shouldered, handsome men lounged at one end, taking turns pouring honey onto their tongues from a small bottle shaped like a teddy bear.

"Mmmm," said one of the men.

"Mmm-hmmmm," said the other, dribbling honey over his chin.

Long russet locks curled on their heads. Matching hair sprinkled strapping chests before it tapered down into a sexy line that disappeared under the water.

So far, everyone Jezebel had seen at the Hellfire Club had been fairly hair-free, and she found the uncivilized, barbaric look of these two wildly exciting.

"Jezebel, I would like you to meet my twin brothers, Barry and Robare."

"Your brothers? How cool is that? Hey, wait a minute!" Jezzy clapped her hands to her breasts, finding this delightful. "I'm now a blonde, and you're the three bares!"

Bare's perfectly shaped eyebrows dipped low. "Bares? No, we're the three Bottomses."

"No, I just meant your names..."

"Our names?" One brother said.

"They all have bare in them."

The other brother shook his head. "Actually my name is spelled Robert. The pronunciation is French."

In another room, some unseen drummer played a rimshot.

"Robert," Jezebel said, not using the T. "Are you French?"

"No," Robert said, winking. "But I kiss that way."

"And I'm Barry," said his brother, "spelled B-A-R-R-Y. Like one of the Bee Gees."

"Is the G silent as well?" Jez asked him.

"Excuse me?"

"With Robert, the T is silent. And you said your name was spelled with a B and a G."

"No, it isn't spelled that way. Barry was one of the Bee Gees."

Jezebel was bored with the wordplay, and really didn't give a shit what their names were.

"I don't give a shit what your names are," she said.

"Don't you mean *Gibb a shit*?" Barry asked.

The brothers smiled and gave themselves a high five; one of those silly things boys did when they were pleased with something, but girls couldn't care less about.

Jez sighed dramatically. "Are you guys going to fuck me or what?"

"That's the plan," Barry said.

"This is an erotica book," Robert said.

"Thank goodness," Jezebel answered. "I was worried there would be more bad poetry."

"Barry and Robert are experts when it comes to sexual adventure therapy," Bare said.

"Sexual adventure therapy?" Jezzy echoed. "I've never heard of such a thing."

"It's cutting edge," Bare explained. "And your fiancé requested it specifically for you."

Jezebel grinned. Leave it to Jack. He of all people knew that adventure always made her feel like a new woman.

"By the time my brothers are done with you, you will have a whole new outlook on life. You won't even remember any of the bad poetry that came before."

Jezebel sighed. "Hopefully the poor readers won't be able to, either."

Barry and Robert climbed out of the pool, their impressive packages swinging heavy between their legs. At the sight of their long shafts and heavy sacks, Jezzy shivered with anticipation. Though she'd thought she'd been completely sated at the Healthful Food Orgy, she realized she was hungry again.

But not for food.

"We'll start with the steam room," Robert did declare. "It's most enjoyable."

"Indeed it is," Barry agreed.

The two men reminded Jezzy of big, cuddly bears. The coppery hair on their chests looked inviting. Jezebel found herself wanting to curl up on top of both of these men together, and rest her cheek against their soft chest hair. Among other things.

The two Bares led Jezebel to a room which was filled with thick, swirling steam.

"It's so nice and warm in here," Jezebel said, stating the obvious. The steam caressed her skin, making her entire body tingle.

Robert stood closely behind her, the soft hair of his chest tickling her shoulder blades, his lips lightly touching the back of her neck. He planted little kisses along the tops of her shoulders. "Do you fancy a sandwich, Jezebel?"

Jezebel felt a flush begin in her belly and sweep over her. A bit distracted, she murmured, "A sandwich? I'm sorry. I just came from the health food orgy, and I'm not *that* kind of hungry."

"This is not *that* kind of sandwich." Barry stepped in front of her, standing close. The soft, glossy hair of his body tickling over her quickly stiffening nipples.

"Oh." Jezzy's mind was buzzing now, and she was finding it hard to concentrate.

Robert's thick rod moved between the cheeks of her bottom and poked at her nether entrance.

Jezebel gasped. "What are you doing?"

Barry leaned down and captured a nipple between his lips, sucking firmly for a long moment.

Heat pooled between her legs, and she felt her bud swell. Her pussy became instantly wet. Hardly aware that she was doing it, she moved her hips forward, searching for friction. Tension balled in her loins, making her womanhood ache once again.

"The sandwich we are talking about," Barry said around her nipple. "Involves pleasure. Not food."

"Let us show you," Robert murmured against her shoulder, his lips tickling her skin.

"Well, if you must…"

Barry's fingers found her folds and made light little circles over her hard, needy clitoris.

Jezzy spread her legs wider, giving him access. She didn't care what happened, as long as he kept doing what he was doing. She heard the sound of a cap being flipped open.

"I've put some tingling lubricant on my cock, Jezebel. It'll make it feel really nice when I slide into your hot, lush little bottom."

"Wait... into my bottom?" Jezzy's eyes flew open. She twisted to stare at Robert's large erection. "But you're too big! Won't that hurt?"

"Not if it's done right," Robert said. "If you're properly aroused, it'll feel really good, Jezebel. And if you want me to stop at any time, I will."

"Are you aroused, Jezebel?" Barry asked her, his mouth was driving her wild, nibbling first on one nipple, then moving to the other, while his fingers moved back and forth over her slippery, swollen clit.

Jezebel's body prickled with need. She felt a deep flush move over her, and her mind grew hazy. "Oh, yes. But..."

Her face turned bright red, and Jezebel didn't want to reveal her true fear.

"Let me guess," Robert said. "You've never done anal before, and you're afraid you'll gorilla shit all over me."

"Or let loose with a bevy of thunderous tuba farts," Barry offered.

"That would be horribly embarrassing," Jezebel said.

"It won't happen." Robert stroked her back. "Trust me. When you feel pressure, just relax and push back against it, and then use your muscles to grip me."

"Besides," Barry said, "with Robert plugging you up, nothing can come out."

"Okay, if you both are sure..."

"I'm sure. I've butt-banged a lot of chicks, and none of them shit on my cock. So can I fuck your dirt trail or what?" Robert asked her, licking and nibbling her earlobe.

"Yes. You've won me over with your sweet talk. I want you all up in my ass. Please," she breathed. Doubts still needled the back of her mind, but she was caring less and less by the second.

Robert kneaded her bottom with strong fingers. The head of his cock moved against her nether opening, circling it lightly, trailing the tingling lubricant around it. Then his fingers dipped into her, working the lubricant inside.

The tingles felt cold, similar to the icy cream from the salon, but more tingly, and turned Jezebel on so much that her pussy squeezed several times in approval. "Oooooh."

"Is that nice?" Robert asked her.

"Yes."

Barry slipped a finger inside her other opening—the one meant for sex—and his palm massaged her hard little bud.

Jezzy's entire body seemed to ignite and come alive. Her nipples brushed steadily over the curling hairs of Barry's chest, creating a most pleasant friction. "Oh, yes."

"I'm going to put a finger in," Robert said, lightly pushing against the opening of her bottom.

"Please do," she gasped, barely able to form words.

Then she felt Robert's finger slowly slide inside, stretching her. The lubricant chilled, then made her so hot she pressed back against him. It felt foreign and strange at first. But then, as he began making slowly, short movements, she found the tingling and stretching growing more pleasurable by the second. The small thrusts awakened nerve endings within her bottom that she never knew existed, and Jezebel found herself wanting to take him deeper and deeper inside.

Barry's fingers teased her g-spot expertly, and his palm moved over her enflamed, needy clitoris, harder, then softer, then harder again. She found a rhythm and rocked back and forth, both Robert's finger and Barry's fingers moving in perfect harmony.

There was only one problem.

"Your fingers... inside me... they're... too small." Jezzy couldn't believe she was saying this, couldn't believe she'd ever feel this bold.

"You want me to thrust my cock inside you?" Barry asked.

"I want you both thrusting inside me," Jezebel managed to say.

"Get ready for your spa package!" Barry took himself in hand. Tilting his hips forward, he brought the fat head of his cock to her folds and swirled his tip in her nectar.

Jezzy watched, liking the sight of his thick, hairy length churning over her nub. Liking the feel of it even more. She was so wet, so ready, and although she had no idea how both brothers would fit inside, she wanted it. She craved it.

"My turn," Robert said behind her. "Knock knock, I'm at your back door. Can I come inside?"

She was still worried about the gorilla shits and thunderous tuba farts, because either would send her self-esteem hurtling into a stinky abyss. But Jezebel knew she needed to have some faith in herself, and going outside of her comfort zone would hopefully get her closer to understanding the moral of the story.

"Okay, but take it slow," Jezzy said.

"I shall. If it's too much, just let me know."

Robert moved into her and upward, breaching her rear entrance. His length stretched her, made Jez feel impossibly jam packed. Inside her she could swear she could feel Robert's and Barry's cocks almost touch, as if skewering her on a shish-kabob. Jezebel had never felt so full. This wasn't big-dinner full. Nor was it rich-desert full. This was none other than stretched-to-bursting packed in like sardines full.

And it felt just right!

Barry moved slowly and gently, in time with Robert. Barry's cock curved and stimulated her g-spot while his pubic bone moved steadily against her clit. The abundance in her bottom intensified the delight she was feeling in her tunnel. Jezzy felt so much pleasure at once that it was maddening. Heat rushed over her, more intense than the steam surrounding them.

"Ooooooh," she moaned, rocking back against Robert and forward with Barry. Her legs folded, weak, but the brothers held her upright with their hands and their steely members. Her sensitive nipples were crushed against Barry's chest hair, the friction much firmer than before, driving her wild. She kissed Barry, her tongue tangling with his.

She felt Robert's lips rake her shoulders as his thrusts became more urgent. His teeth nipped at her skin, adding just a little bit of pain.

"Th-this is the best ... sandwich I've ever had," she moaned.

"It's our favorite," Robert grunted against her shoulder.

"Uh huh," Barry agreed, looking into her eyes as he plunged harder and harder.

The first contractions began deep inside. Jezzy's body spasmed, her nether walls squeezing Robert just as her pussy claimed Barry. Her enflamed bud twitched against his pubic bone. Her entire body seized with a mind-blowing climax, the contractions going on and on and on. Jez screamed, so overwhelmed, she thought she might black out.

Robert and Barry rode her orgasm with her, their thrusts becoming frantic. Every plunge of their cocks made each of her contractions more intense. Finally both reached their peaks, first Robert, then Barry, roaring like bears.

After a moment they stepped away, disengaging with two audible *POPs*. Thankfully, nothing icky came out of her bowels.

"You are so sexy, Jezebel," Robert said once he'd caught his breath. He littered a trail of little kisses over her shoulders and back.

"So beautiful," Barry breathed against her lips. "Do you know how amazing you are, Jezebel?"

"I think I'm beginning to," Jezebel said. She had to admit, at this moment, she really was feeling kind of amazing. "And it's all thanks to you two, and this spa."

"No. No one is responsible for that but you." Robert said. "And we aren't finished with you yet."

"You aren't?" Jezebel asked, feeling so happy and satisfied, she couldn't imagine what else she might need at this moment.

"Indeed not," Barry said. "Next we take a dip in the pool."

Breath Play

The pool room was of ancient Roman style, complete with columns and various naked statues. Fragrant red and white rose petals floated in the steaming water, and as Jezebel sank into its soothing heat, she let out her deepest sigh all day. Along with one very tiny, ladylike fart.

Luckily, no one noticed.

"Nice, huh?" Barry said, he and Robert watching her from the deck.

Jezebel answered with a smile then swam to the other side of the pool, reveling in the scent of roses and the soothing caress of the water over her skin. When she reached the other side, she flipped onto her back and floated, allowing her breasts to break the surface. The water was so peaceful she felt as if she was being cradled by it. Her hair fanned out around her head. She watched as her nipples tightened, cool in the steamy air.

"There's nothing better than watching a gorgeous woman floating naked in a pool," said Barry.

"You think I'm gorgeous?" she asked the brothers, wanting to hear it again.

And again.

At least until she believed it.

"You look like a lovely mermaid," said Robert. "We know a couple. They come in here quite frequently."

"Ah yes," Barry looked wistful. "I do enjoy the mermaids. They're so cheeky. And I have a fish fetish."

Jezzy had met a couple of mermaids during her adventure up the beanstalk. She wondered if they were the same ones the brothers were referring to when she was distracted by two splashes. Jez glanced up to see the brothers swimming toward her. They stopped on either side, and each delicately squeezed a nipple with their fingers.

Jezebel took a sharp breath. She hadn't expected to feel energized for a while, but their fingers lightly playing with her nipples sent little shivers through her. "Ooooh."

"Your nipples are so lovely. May we taste them?" Robert asked her.

It was odd that he would ask so politely, considering he'd just shot his hot load up her ass. But it was very gentlemanly for him to do so. "Yes, please."

The brothers both sank lower into the water, steam floating all around them, and each captured a tender bud between their lips, then pulled back and blew a light stream of air onto her. The feeling was exquisite, the cool air chilling her nipples and making them tighten. Even in the water, she felt her folds become slippery. Her sighs echoed in the room, bouncing off the walls.

Barry skimmed a hand over her belly, and found her most sensitive spot, slipping his fingers gently over it, creating slow circles. Instantly, Jezebel felt heat pool between her legs, her abdomen tighten, and her little bud protrude, warming to the stimulation.

"You don't seem to believe us when we say you're beautiful, Jezebel," Barry said. "Why is that?"

"I-I don't know. I'm not too shabby, I guess. Hopefully the spa is improving my appearance a little."

Robert chuckled, gave her nipple a few flicks, then said, "it's not just about how you look, Jezebel. It's how you feel. It's who you are. You are physically lovely, without a doubt. But you are truly sexy on the inside as well. You are a strong, powerful woman who is bold and adventurous. Your beauty radiates from the inside out. That is what true beauty is."

"Yes," Barry said, now moving his palm over her throbbing bead. "You are more beautiful the longer you are here, because you are becoming more confident with each passing hour. When you feel beautiful on the inside, everyone sees it on the outside."

That sounded a lot like New Age psycho-pop bullshit to Jezebel. But she was finding it difficult to concentrate on what the brothers were saying. The sensations they induced in her were so distracting, and becoming stronger by the moment. Their voices were starting to sound like the adults in Charlie Brown cartoons. Mere garbled nonsensical murmurings (in case you never knew what Charlie Brown adults sounded like).

She closed her eyes and focused on the surges rippling over her. Much longer and she'd—

"Would you like to try something different, Jezebel?" Robert's voice broke through her sensual haze.

"Ah, okay." She heard the reluctance edging her tone. Truthfully, she was content as she was, with the two Bare brothers caressing and kissing her and repeating sweet words. She wasn't sure she was up for another challenge.

"You're not sure you're up for another challenge," Robert said.

"Can you read my mind?" Jez asked.

"No. I just read your interior monologue a few sentences ago."

"I was just thinking about my wedding," Jez said, ignoring the fourth wall Robert just broke. "I don't have much time left here at the spa. Instead of trying new adventures, shouldn't I be getting ready or relaxing or something?"

"There's plenty of time for that. Right now, you need to be stretching yourself, trying new things. That's the best way to boost your confidence."

Boosting her confidence sounded like just the thing Jezzy needed, but she wasn't sure this was the best way to do that. "If I look thin and beautiful, won't that make me feel confident?"

"You will feel as confident as you are."

That made as much sense as gills on a horse.

"How about a seahorse?" Robert said. When Jez looked at him funny, he shrugged. "I read your interior monologue again."

Jezebel forced a smile to her lips. "Well, if you think trying new things will make me more confident…"

Robert nodded. "We do."

"…then I guess I'll give it a try. What's the worst that can happen?"

"Drowning," Barry said.

"Excuse me?"

"It's called breath play," Barry explained. "It's a form of erotic asphyxiation. When you deprive your body of oxygen while coming, your orgasm is more intense."

"Deprive me of oxygen?" This didn't seem like a good adventure. Not at all.

"You won't die, lovely Jezebel," Robert said. "We would never let that happen."

"Probably," Barry said.

"And to everyone reading this chapter: don't try this at home," Robert said.

"You're not exactly selling me on this," Jez told them.

"Generally, it's one of the most dangerous games you can play," Barry admitted. "But we're professionals, Jezebel. Instead of cutting off your oxygen by choking you or putting a plastic bag over your head or any of that crazy stuff that no one should do, we're just going to ask you to hold your breath a few times while we dip you under water."

"And we'll be doing it in the shallow end." Robert pointed to the other end of the pool. "If you need to breathe, you just stand up."

Jezzy figured she could do that.

"And if you can't stand up for any reason," he continued, "we'll pull you up."

"Do you still trust us?" Barry asked.

"Yes. I guess I do."

"Would you like to try breath play, then?" Robert asked.

Jezebel thought of the sandwich. She hadn't been sure about taking Robert into her back entrance, and yet it ended up being one of the most pleasurable experiences of her life. This whole trip had been about trying new things, from hair color to spinning class to delicious smoothies poured over cocks.

"Okay. Let's do it. As long as we're sure I'm not going to die and wind up in the tabloids."

"You won't die, and the tabloids aren't anywhere within miles of us," Robert said.

Robert had failed to see Hatter and Hare, who worked for Big Cock Billionaire Magazine, peeking through the window and snapping pictures.

Barry swam between Jezebel's thighs. "I'm going to stimulate your gorgeous womanly parts while Robert teases your nipples. When you become very aroused, Robert will gently push your shoulders down so that your head is submerged. We will only keep you down there for a few seconds. If it's too long, stand up or lift your hand and Robert will bring you back up immediately. Let's try it, and if you don't like it, we'll stop. Okay?"

Jezebel really wasn't sure about this plan. Her heart thumped, and adrenaline spiked through her blood. It sounded scary. Allowing someone to submerge her and deprive her of air was so unnatural. But she did trust the brothers. After all, she'd known them for almost twenty minutes. Plus, one of them had been up her ass.

"Okay."

The brothers moved Jezebel to the shallow end, Barry between her thighs, hands beneath them, and Robert with his hands behind her shoulders. When they reached an area where Barry could slide into her without pulling her legs and hips too far downward, they stopped.

"Okay, Jezebel. Just relax and feel. We'll tell you when to take a breath and hold it." Robert smiled down at her from above her head.

Barry slowly pulled Jezebel's hips forward and took hold of his turgid length. Directing the position of her body with one hand, he used the other to tantalize her opening with the head of his cock. He slid it over her, dipping inside only to pull out and circle her engorged clit. His muscles rippled as he moved, and the line of hair that pointed to his thick rod was, at that moment, one of the sexiest sights Jezebel had ever seen. His touch was so light one minute, so firm the next, and so well placed, it made Jezebel gasp.

"Oh, that is just right!"

Within moments, she was rocking her hips upward, trying to position her pussy so she could take his manhood inside.

But Barry pulled away a little so that he wouldn't move into her. Instead, he continued the game, enticing her with his rod, adding little swipes and twirls with his fingers. At the same time, Robert pinched her nipples, twisting lightly this way and that, then flicking them with nimble fingers. His rigid length poked at her shoulder blade, and knowing that he was so excited turned her on even more. She heard herself moaning in frustration and desire, the sounds bouncing around the walls and columns of the room.

All she wanted was to feel Barry's hard erection inside of her, jamming into her, while his fingers played with her clit. "Please. Please fuck me."

Barry eased into her opening and Jezebel felt herself tighten around him. The feeling was divine, and she just wanted to stay like this... with Barry pumping into her and Robert pinching her nipples... forever.

Or at least until she came her brains out.

"Okay, Jezebel," Robert said from above, his tawny waves springing around his handsome face. "It's time to take a breath and hold it."

Jezebel filled her lungs.

"Ready?" Robert asked her.

Jezebel nodded.

Robert pushed her shoulders, and down she went. Warm water rushed over her face.

At first, Jezebel felt panic. But Barry continued thrusting into her, playing with her needy bead, and Robert's hands skated over her shoulders and once again found her nipples. They twisted and pinched, flicked and pulled, cupped and massaged.

Pleasure sang through her entire body. The longer she held her breath, the more intense it became. She wasn't sure how many seconds passed, but when her lungs began to burn, a bit of panic set in.

Strangely, that made the delicious agony more extreme.

Robert seemed to sense her growing need to breathe, and without Jez signaling him she was pulled back up to the surface. When her face popped out of the water, she let the breath go and took a few in.

All sexual stimulation ceased.

"Why are you stopping?" Jez tilted her hips upward, wanting Barry to continue. She tried arching her back, thrusting her nipples up toward Robert's fingers. But the brothers remained still, simply smiling at her.

"Are you very aroused, Jezebel?" Robert asked her.

"Yes! Dear heavens, yes! Please continue." She beseeched with her eyes, first Barry, then Robert. "Please."

"As you wish," Barry said. "Take a breath, Jezebel."

She took in a great gulp of air, nodded at Robert, and he pushed her under. Barry immediately began short little thrusts, the head of his cock massaging her g-spot. His fingers resumed their caress of her clit. Robert slowly twisted her nipples.

Jezebel wanted to moan, to gasp, but she couldn't while submerged. And her enforced silence seemed to make the pressure build.

Robert's fingers pinched Jezzy's tits more firmly, more roughly. Her pussy clamped over Barry's cock as it drove further and further into her. She could feel the orgasm poised to crash over her any minute. The buzz in her head—oxygen deprivation—made it almost unbearable. She was so close... so close...

Then she was lifted up again.

Frustration blossomed inside of Jezebel and she made a growling, annoyed sound when she reached the surface. "I think I'm ready to come, now."

"Soon, Jezebel." Barry grinned. He pulled out of her and released her legs.

Robert lifted her upward, so that she stood on her feet once again.

Jezebel looked from one Bare to the other, puzzled. "I haven't come yet. This can't be the end of the aquatic portion of my spa package."

"Of course not," Robert said. "That would be cruel."

"We're merely changing activities so that you can enjoy a different position," Barry said. "I think you'll find the next activity even more challenging."

"Okay," Jezebel said, her heart pounding and her whole body humming. "What's next?"

Barry placed his hands on her shoulders and gently turned her until she faced Robert. "How would you like to try giving an underwater blowjob?"

Jezebel looked into the water at Robert's thick, bobbing cock. It looked so lovely in the blue of the water. But she wasn't sure if she could hold her breath with a dick thrusting in and out of her mouth.

"I'm not sure I can—"

"I know," Robert said. "I can read. I'll pinch your nose closed. You'll be fine."

"And what will you be doing?" Jezzy asked Barry.

"Me?" Barry smiled. "I will enter your sweet pussy from behind. Are you ready?"

Jezebel's body buzzed. Her clit tingled as she gazed at Robert's thick length and beautiful bulbous head. So lickable. So suckable. And the thought of Barry plunging into her at the same time Robert filled her mouth made her wet.

Which, admittedly, was hard to gauge since she was waist-deep in water.

"Are you ready?" Barry asked.

"Yes."

"Excellent!" Barry grabbed Jezebel's hips and positioned himself directly below her bottom so that she was floating slightly above his lap, as if he were a chair under the water. Then once again he found her hungry opening and shoved his length inside.

Jezebel gasped with the sudden, sharp carnality of it. All of the sex she'd had already had made her incredibly sensitive, and now every movement seemed to bring her to the edge.

Barry pulled her hips and thrust, sinking deep inside. "Here we go, Jezebel. Take a breath and start sucking Robert's cock."

Jezebel took a breath and felt Barry duck down behind her, taking her down with him. She heard him suck in a breath as well, then the water moved over her face again. This time, she kept her eyes open, and her hands moved down Robert's taught six pack, helping Jezebel lead herself along the line of hair that pointed to his thick erection. She opened her mouth, excitement pulsing through her as she took Robert's head be-tween her lips.

At first it was tricky to move her mouth and tongue over him while he pinched her nostrils. But soon she got the hang of it and flicked her tongue around his ridge, using the pool water for suction and lubrication. When Jezebel got the rhythm down, that pleasurable head-buzz began to grow. She could faintly hear Robert's moans above the surface of the water, mingling with Barry's lusty grunts.

Barry drove into her, each stroke harder, deeper. His sack slapped against her nub with each thrust. His fingers gripped her hips, and the whole experience was so animalistic that she felt her pussy tighten and spasm around him, massaging him, urging him on.

Jezebel became dizzy, and began to thrash. Her entire body sang with passion and need. As if this was a dream. As if she was losing control of her whole being. As if she was about to come and come and never—

Robert slid from her mouth, and she was pulled to the surface.

"Don't... stop..." Jezebel tilted her hips, moving up and down on Barry's rock hard cock, straining to press her clit against his fingers. She was gasping for breath, and panting, her need to climax so strong that she couldn't think.

Barry removed his fingers and gripped her hips, lifting her almost all the way off of him. Only his head remained inside of her. "Easy, Jezebel. Slow down."

"I can't," she panted. "I can't."

"You can," Robert said to her, his face red, his eyes dark. "Be patient. When we all come, it'll be epic. You'll see."

When her breathing returned somewhat to normal, Barry slid back inside of her. "Are you ready, Jezebel?"

"Yes," she breathed.

"We don't want you to pass out completely." Barry's voice was husky, his breath cool on her neck. "I like you. Also,

I don't have any desire to bang a corpse. That's icky. And it would probably result in prison time."

"I'm not going to die," Jez promised, "but please don't let me up again until I give you the hand signal."

"What if, in the throes of passion, I don't see the hand signal?" Robert asked.

"Then I'll bite your dick off."

"I'll keep an eye out for that hand signal," Robert said.

Jezebel took a breath, and then she was descending into the water again. Rose petals floated past her eyes as she sank below the surface, and her hands eagerly walked down Robert's belly, leading her to his straining shaft.

He lifted his hips to meet her, and she took his head deep in her mouth, swirling her tongue around him. She pulled back, licking the length of his cock, and reached her hand between his legs, beneath his length, and gently massaged his sack. His cock jerked against her slightly open lips, urging her to let it in, and she did, licking and sucking as Barry made short, sharp thrusts into her.

Jezebel listened to the rising sound of the brothers' moaning and grunting as she worked her mouth over Robert's manhood. She licked the veins that ran along the length, and lightly ran her teeth along the skin. Then she used only her lips, massaging the head, fast at first, then slow and sensuous.

Robert's cock flexed against her tongue, and Jezzy took the head all the way to the back of her throat, caressing his balls with her palms. Her pussy contracted around Barry's member, and the first stirrings of her climax began deep inside. Her lungs burned, dizziness setting in, and that made her double her efforts on Robert's cock, her mouth sliding back and forth, slathering fat, luxurious licks along the head and length, her fingers found his sack and began massaging. She was determined that Robert would come, hard, into her mouth, and she wasn't stopping this time until he did.

Her determination must have showed, because Robert's cries sounded both urgent and helpless. His hands found her head and he gently held her face as he fucked her mouth, completely giving in to her demands.

Moving her ass backwards, she squeezed the muscles of her pussy, massaging Barry's cock as he jabbed into her. She wanted him to thrust deep and hard, and made her desires known with her movements. His cries and grunts joined Robert's and soon their lusty sounds mingled and she couldn't tell one from the other. His plunges became more frantic, and as her lungs began to scream, her body seized, and her walls began contracting over Barry's cock as blackness began to blur her vision.

At that moment, Robert spilled into her mouth, his salty flavor mingling with the taste of the pool water. She moved back, focusing and sucking on the head, milking each and every drop of his essence. Wave after wave of gratification claimed her as she sucked, her body shaking and quivering with each peak.

Then she was being lifted out of the water, into a more upright position, and Barry stabbed himself deeply into her from behind as she scooped in a breath of air, still quaking in climax. He gripped her, his body shuddering as he cried out. He shoved his steely rod deep, deep inside of her and her pussy quavered around him. Her orgasm faded as he slumped against her shoulder, panting.

"Jezebel," Barry said. "You are fan-fucking-tastic."

"Sen-fucking-sational," Robert agreed, leaning back against the wall of the pool, his face happy and satisfied.

"And no one died this time!" Barry said.

"No prison!" Robert said. "Yipee!"

Jezebel could find no words at all. She simply enjoyed the last pulses of her ebbing orgasm, feeling like the most powerful, most sexy, most alive woman in the world.

Hellfire Yoga

As Jack had arranged, Jezebel spent the night in a luxurious suite. But though the club offered plenty of evening social events of the stimulating variety, after the day Jezzy had enjoyed, she suspected she couldn't manage even one more orgasm. Tomorrow was her wedding day, and she needed her beauty rest. And although Jez was still a bit nervous about being the bride Jack deserved, her day had been so exhausting, she slept as deeply as if she'd pricked her finger on an enchanted spinning wheel.

The next morning was beautiful. The sun shone. The birds sang. And Jezebel's anxiety came back full force.

"It's my wedding day," she told the non-magic mirror in her room.

Being non-magic, it didn't reply and didn't show her to be as perfect as she wished.

Damn.

After a light breakfast in bed, she showered and dressed in a Hellfire Club Spa silk robe. Before she could wonder what to do next, a knock sounded on the door.

"Jezebel? Are you ready to begin your most special day?"

Quite the question.

Jezzy opened the door and came face-to-face with the perfect Bare, who was still... perfectly bare.

"You're so perfect," Jezebel said.

"Don't be silly. No one is perfect. For instance, I have this large mole on my back that looks like Abraham Lincoln."

She turned, and indeed had such a mole, almost fifteen centimeters long. And hair grew out of it exactly where Lincoln's beard was supposed to be.

"I don't know how I never noticed that before," Jezebel said. "Have you gotten that thing checked out?"

"Stage four malignant sarcoma," Bare said. "I have two months to live. But I'm still happy. See?"

Bare smiled wide to indicate how happy she was.

"Aren't you... bothered?"

"By my hideous carcinogenic mole and the impending death it represents? No, Jezebel. Because I have confidence in myself. And that's all that matters."

"I wish I had that much confidence."

"You have it inside you." Bare tossed her a wink. "In fact, I think that you'll be the loveliest bride in the castle."

"I'll be the only bride in the castle," Jezzy said.

"And you'll be lovely. But only if you relax. Here at the Hellfire Club Spa, we aim to give you an experience that's not too soft and not too hard, not too short and not too long, not too small and not too big, not too empty and not too full, not too light and not too firm, all so that on your wedding day, you'll feel just right."

"You're really hammering home the whole Goldilocks thing."

"Sometimes our clients aren't the sharpest knife in the drawer, so repetition is important."

"Hmm?"

"Repetition is important."

"Ahh. Good thinking," Jez said. "I just wish I could be as confident as you are."

"You will be."

"Hmm?"

"You will be confident."

"I wish."

Bare led her to a large room with mats on the floor and mirrors covering the walls. The air smelled distinctly of lavender and was hot enough to rival the steam room from yesterday.

A stunning blonde woman stood in the center of the room frozen in a yoga positon known as tree pose. She stood statue still, her eyes closed, her face peaceful, and her body very, very naked.

"Alice!"

Jezzy's matron of honor opened her blue eyes, and a bright smile crossed over her face. "Jez! Wow. The hair is great. Let me look at you!"

Jezebel obliged, untying her robe's belt and letting the silk slip from her shoulders. The lights in the yoga studio glowed on her bare breasts and the smoothness of her freshly-waxed pussy, the image reflected by every wall in the room.

"You look amazing."

"Not as amazing as you."

"Don't be silly, we're both amazingly amazing." Alice pulled her close for a hug. Their breasts pillowed into one another, nipple rubbing nipple. "I know I was scheduled to meet you for hair and makeup, but I just couldn't resist the idea of coming early and getting in a little yoga."

"That green guy from Star Wars?"

"Yoga, not Yoda. Wait until you try Hellfire yoga. It's hot."

"Everything at the Hellfire Spa is hot," Jez said.

"This is literally hot. A hundred and one degrees in the studio. That's thirty-eight Celsius for the readers outside the USA."

"We'll begin with some lovely essential oils," Bare said. She picked up a bottle from a cart near the studio's wall, the shape of the vessel reminding Jezebel of a penis, just like the bottles in the salon. She poured a dab of oil into Jezzy's palm then Alice's.

Jezzy took a deep breath, drawing in a scent that seemed to immediately loosen the tension in her muscles. "Mmm, lavender."

Alice rubbed her hands together, then brought them to Jezzy's breasts. She kneaded the soft mounds, running her fingers around Jezzy's nipples until they seemed to stand up, begging for more.

"That feels so good," Jezebel murmured. She smoothed her own palms to Alice's body. Starting at her rib cage, Jezzy smoothed the oil upward, lifting her luscious tits and cradling them, one then the other, while slathering the pink nipples with oil until they glistened.

"Ohhh," Alice moaned. "That smells and feels wonderful."

"Now that you're warmed up," Bare said in a soothing yoga voice, "raise your arms above your head, then keeping your chest up and back straight, we'll take a forward fold."

Being more experienced in yoga, Alice performed the pose first. She stretched upward, arching her back and thrusting her breasts forward, then she bent at the waist, bringing her head all the way down to her ankles, her legs remaining straight.

Forward fold.

And from where Jezzy stood, she had a clear view of Alice's more intimate folds.

"Jezebel?" Bare prompted.

Jezzy stretched then folded. The extension burned along her hamstrings.

"The crease is at the hip, Jezebel." Bare said, moving up between her and Alice. "Bend at the hip, then relax your back and neck..."

Jezzy felt something tickle her exposed labia. Glancing to the side, she saw Bare was standing close, smoothing oil over Alice's most intimate area, as well as Jezzy's.

"Relax," Bare repeated, still stroking.

Jezzy could feel the tension leave her muscles. Her back softened, the bend feeling more severe and more natural at the same time. The heat of the room, Bare's stroking fingers, Alice's sexy body, all of it combined to make her juices flow.

"Good, good. Now walk your hands forward, then stretch back into a downward dog. You first, Alice."

Alice walked forward on her hands, then tilting her bottom up in the air, she rested most of her weight back on her legs.

Jezzy had practiced this pose before, only not in a yoga studio. It was one of Jack's favorites, and Jezebel could almost imagine him behind her, driving his hard shaft inside her while his sack swung against her most sensitive spot.

She might be nervous about the wedding, but she was looking forward to the wedding night. It seemed like forever since Jack had been inside her.

When it was Jezebel's turn, she was wetter than ever. As she walked forward then stretched back, tilting her hips in the air, she couldn't help but wonder if Bare could see the moisture glistening at her opening.

"Perfect, both of you. Now I will begin with the backs of your legs." At that, Bare's hands began massaging, one on Jezebel's calves, the other on Alice's.

"You are so talented with your hands, Bare dear." Alice said. "And to do both of us at the same time? Simply amazing."

"Here at the Hellfire Club Spa, we aim to please."

Using slow and sensual movements, Bare moved up to Jezzy's knees, then over her thighs. She paused to pour more oil into her palms, then continued. Her fingers smoothed the oil higher, working it into her inner thigh, kneading the muscle, moving ever closer to Jezebel's quickly responding womanhood.

"Remember the breath, ladies. It's all about the breath. In through the nose, out through the mouth."

Jezzy tried her best to regulate her breathing, to slow her racing pulse.

Bare switched to the other calf, smoothing her hands over the muscles, working the heavenly oil into the skin, slowly, gently, then firmly.

Next to her, Alice moaned.

Jezebel squeezed her eyes shut. Bare's caresses combined with the luxurious scent of the oil was having a definite aphrodisiac effect. Jezzy's skin tingled, and her most sensitive area plumped in response. Despite her best efforts, her breathing quickened, and soon she felt the blood rushing in her ears as her pussy tightened with desire.

Then Bare's hands were massaging the cheeks of her bottom, lightly squeezing and kneading.

Jezebel let out a little gasp. Her nipples tightened and warmth gathered in her loins.

Bare paused again to pour more oil into her hands, then began working slowly over Jezebel's back, making slow, delicious circles with her palm.

"Your tits are so beautiful from this angle, Jezzy," Alice said. "Round and full. And your nipples... they're so distended and lurid. It's like they want to be sucked."

Jezzy glanced over at Alice's naked breasts and giggled. "Yours are so tender and pink. Like they're sweet and innocent and need a skilled tongue to bring them out of their shyness."

"Wouldn't it be fabulous if Lewis and Jack could see us right now?"

Jezzy imagined Alice's husband and her husband-to-be watching Bare pleasure them. Jack would be stroking his hard cock just at her telling the story. "A video sure would make a lovely wedding present."

Alice sighed. "I wish we'd thought of it. Lewis and my anniversary is coming up! Maybe we should call Hatter and Hare back in and ask them to record this."

"I'm sorry," Bare said. "But Hellfire yoga isn't about show. Performing for your husbands or those two buffoons violates the philosophy behind the practice."

"There's a philosophy behind the practice?" Jezzy asked. "I thought this scene was just about getting naked and bendy in a hot room with, you know, orgasms."

"Well, Hellfire yoga is about those things, too. Otherwise why would someone want to read this scene?" Bare smiled. "Buddha said, 'Be a lamp to yourself. Be your own confidence. Hold on to the truth within yourself as to the only truth.'"

"So Hellfire yoga is about exploring our own bodies? Not merely using them to give others enjoyment, but to enjoy ourselves?"

"That's very on the nose, Alice."

"Thank you, Bare. It will be such a shame when you die in two months."

"Actually, the doctor gave me seven weeks," Bare said.

"My goodness," said Jez. "Did you ask for a second opinion?"

"I did. He also said I had nice tits."

Jezebel marveled at Bare's and Alice's profound strength and wisdom. "So let's get to the enjoying ourselves part. This story is almost over, and that means the wedding will be here before we know it. I need to be perfect before then because right now I hate myself!"

Alice and Bare sighed, shook their heads, then turned their attention back to Hellfire yoga.

Bare's hands worked back over Jezzy's bottom, slipping between her legs, to the part that felt so exposed in this position.

And so, so, so hungry.

Bare lingered there, moving her fingers in little circles over Jezzy's protruding clit. Then she slipped a finger inside.

"Oh." The word puffed out of Jezebel on a breath of air.

"Oh," Alice echoed, and Jezebel knew her friend was feeling the same thing.

Bare pumped her finger several times before adding a second, then a third. Jezzy leaned into the stretch, tilting her bottom upward as much as possible to expose her entrance for deeper penetration. When Bare withdrew, Jezebel let out a whimper.

"Now breathe in and move into upward-facing dog, your weight shifting and lifting."

Reluctantly Jezzy lowered her hips and legs to the mat then arched her back until her arms were straight, her breasts poking into the air. Alice did the same.

Bare sat down in front of them, pouring more oil into her hands. She moved close to Jezebel and cupped a breast in each palm, then she resumed the massage.

If Alice had thought Jezzy's nipples were lurid before, they were positively garish now. They glistened with oil, and Bare rolled them between her fingertips and provoked them to hard, wanting peaks.

She moved her attentions to Alice, teasing her delicate, pink nubs, making her pale skin glow as if lit from within. Now Alice's nipples were lurid, too, and definitely no longer shy.

"You both have such beautiful breasts. I could fondle your nipples forever. Er... I mean I could fondle your nipples for seven weeks until the cancer kills me. Let's to do a bit more core work."

Jezzy was all for that. Her core was feeling very eager for work at the moment.

"Take a deep breath in. On the exhale, shift back into down dog."

Jezebel and Alice moved as one, rising back onto hands and feet, stretching their shoulders and legs, tipping their nether regions upward. Hot air caressed Jezzy's moist folds, and she had to admit she wished Hatter and Hare were still around. They were annoying, but Jez was sure they could help give her core the workout it deserved.

"Now walk your feet forward until you are back in a forward fold. Then keeping your back flat, return to mountain position."

She and Alice obeyed, and at the end of the maneuver, both were standing straight, their breasts pushed out, their shoulders back.

"Now take a long, cleansing breath." Bare stared at their naked breasts, now just a few inches from hers. "Beautiful."

Jezzy imagined rubbing her glistening chest over Bare's, over Alice's, feeling their nipples slide against hers, then taking them into her mouth...

Bare's voice cut through Jezebel's reverie. "We'll start with our bride. Jezebel, why don't you lie on the floor, knees bent?"

Jezebel did as she instructed. She looked up at the other two women, taking in the view of their breasts from below. Skimming her gaze down their bodies, she focused on the V between their legs, wondering if they were as excited as she was, if their tunnels were as wet.

"Jezebel," Bare continued. "Move into the bridge position."

Shoulders flat on the floor, Jezzy lifted her bottom from the mat, her knees bent and feet flat. She spread her legs wide enough to keep her balance, about a foot apart, her pussy open and exposed. Just the knowledge that Alice could see Jezzy's desire shining in her open folds made Jezzy's head feel light.

"Spread your legs wider," Bare said. "Hellfire yoga is also about giving and receiving equally."

"Do we get to touch you?" Jezzy asked. She'd so enjoyed licking Bare yesterday, devouring her, making her come. She'd be very happy to do it again.

"This is about you and your matron of honor getting ready for the wedding. I'd like to start by guiding you through touching each other."

Excitement trilled over Jezebel's skin, raising goose-bumps. Giving and receiving equally had always aroused her, and the thought of touching Alice made her feel hot all over.

That and the temperature of the studio. Obviously.

Alice moved close between Jezebel's open legs. So close Jezzy was sure her friend could smell her musk mingling with the lavender oil.

Alice smiled at Jezebel, her own face rosy, the tops of her breasts flushed a lovely shade of pink. She brought her hands to Jezzy's skin, working her newly oiled palms between Jezebel's inner thighs, stroking, massaging, caressing.

Lifting her pelvis higher, Jezebel heard herself make a frustrated little noise deep in her throat. Her hips rocked forward.

Alice brushed her palm over Jezebel's sweet spot.

Jezzy gasped. "Oooh."

Alice leaned closer, teasing Jez with her fingertips, and then adding her tongue to the mix. She started with a light flick over Jezzy's clit. As delicate as a whisper. Then she slathered Jez with hot, fat licks.

"Oh, my!" Jezzy said, her legs starting to shake with an oncoming orgasm.

"Wait," Bare interrupted. "Let's switch. Alice, it's your turn."

Jezebel almost cried. She wanted to come. Needed to. But since she also wanted to understand the secrets of Hellfire Yoga, she stifled her tears and rolled her spine down onto the mat.

Alice sat back on her heels, "Which position, Bare?"

"I think wide legged forward fold with your hands on your hips," Bare said. "Let's start with that one."

"Oh, one of my favorites." Alice turned her back to Jezzy and spread her legs, then keeping her back straight, she bent forward, nearly resting her head on the mat, her bottom high in the air. Her breasts plumped, gravity making it appear as if she was wearing an invisible push-up bra. And between Alice's wide-open thighs, her womanhood glistened.

Jezebel stood behind Alice. She had been enjoying Alice's wonderful caresses, but she was also excited to turn the tables.

Giving *and* receiving.

She held out her hands to Bare, and the auburn-haired beauty dribbled fragrant oil into her palms from the penis-like container. Jezzy rubbed her hands together, warm and slippery as her own nectar, and focused her attention on Alice.

Jezebel brought her palms to Alice and began massaging her shapely bottom. She couldn't take her eyes off Alice's shaved special place, her rigid nub, her glossy folds. Alice's core reminded her of a spring rose after a rain, fresh and pink with light dew shimmering over its petals. She breathed in the scent of lavender mingled with Alice's personal fragrance. The combination was intoxicating.

Heat beaded over Jezebel's skin. A pleasant tingling bloomed between her thighs. Kneading Alice's firm buttocks, she leaned forward and blew lightly across Alice's pussy.

Alice moaned, and her opening puckered inward.

Jezzy let out another stream of air, this time brushing Alice's nether lips with her fingers.

"Oooh," Alice said in response, and a little drop of honey escaped from her entrance.

"Good, Jezebel," Bare said. "I think you're getting the hang of our Hellfire Yoga program."

"It's a little different from the usual Bikram hot yoga, isn't it?" Alice said on an exhale.

"I'll say." Jezebel was proud of herself for being able to make Alice respond in such a positive manner. In fact, it felt rather addictive. She reached for the bottle of oil and dribbled it over Alice's now engorged folds. The oil moved in gleaming rivulets over her pussy, glazing it.

Alice rocked her bottom toward Jezebel and sighed. "Yes, don't stop, Jezzy. That feels so nice."

"Now both of you assume the constipated-elephant-with-a-boner-saluting-the-moon pose," Bare said.

They did. Quite easily, in fact.

Then Jezebel reached out and trailed a light finger over Alice's delicate flower, gliding it between the darkening petals and resting on her most sensitive spot. She daintily wisped a finger over it, then dipped inside. Wisp and dip. Wisp and dip.

Soon Alice's tunnel spasmed and tightened, and her hips began to rock rhythmically.

Jezzy licked her lips. Her face burned with a furious flush. She stroked the bottle of oil, marveling at the erect cock contours of it, then she rubbed its glistening tip over Alice, and penetrated her entrance.

Alice moaned as her opening stretched, fitting around the phallus. "Oh, yes..."

Jezebel pushed the bottle into Alice's tunnel, then pulled it back out. In and out. In and out.

Alice rocked her hips. "Yes, fuck me, Jezzy."

Continuing with the bottle, Jezebel leaned forward and feathered her tongue out over Alice's tight little bud.

"New stance," Bare ordered, "Crippled-hobo-eating-day-old-tacos-with-John-Tesh pose."

It was a trickier pose, but Alice and Jezebel fluidly stretched into it without breaking their oral connection.

Alice cried out. Her legs trembled.

Bare made a noise deep in her throat. She moved closer, just on the other side of Alice, watching Jezebel wield the bottle while her tongue toyed with Alice's nub. "You're doing very well, Jezebel."

Jezebel barely heard her, so caught up in the awesome feeling of power she had when Alice responded. She continued to swirl her tongue over Alice's nub, applying more pressure each time Alice's hips swayed back toward her. Jezzy's nipples brushed against Alice's thighs.

"Indeed, there are all sorts of muscles that need to be massaged and worked, tension eased and released." Bare's voice was thick and throaty.

Jezzy peeked over Alice's bottom to see Bare had slipped her long fingers between her own legs and they were now slowly moving back and forth.

This excited Jezebel even more, and a shiver of pure lust quivered over her. She resumed licking Alice, pumping the bottle harder and deeper, her friend's juices warm on her fingers and tongue.

Alice moaned loudly, rocking herself back, as if trying to take the bottle in deeper. Her muscles clenched, her tunnel contracting.

Jezebel applied more pressure with her tongue, licking then sucking. She thrust harder, in and out, in and out.

Soon Alice was gyrating, shuddering and screaming, bucking against Jezzy's hand and pulsating against her tongue. Jezebel heard herself moaning louder, her success at bringing Alice over the edge like a drug, a high that she never wanted to end.

"I think it's time for another position," Bare said. She was now squeezing both of her nipples, which were almost purple. She looked lovely with the rosy blush on her cheeks. She held out one hand for the bottle, and Jezzy withdrew it from Alice and handed it to Bare.

"Alice, ease into the Joan-of-Arc-burning-at-the-stake pose. Jezebel, stand in front of Alice and stretch upward into the Sasquatch-with-a-moral-dilemma stance, with your arms above your head."

Alice eased onto her hands and knees, with her face forward. Jezebel stood in front of her, her sex directly in front of Alice's face, and stretched her arms high above her head. The stretch did feel wonderful, but the pull in her lower abdomen only served to tighten the tension around her hungry clit, driving her mad with want. She was so horny, she didn't know if she could stand it. Frustration filled her, knotting her shoulder muscles.

"Easy, Jezzy. You're tensing up." Bare walked over and caressed Jezebel's shoulders, massaging the knots. "Remember to breathe. But don't breathe in the flames surrounding Joan of Arc. Then you'll die like she did."

Tough pose, Jez thought.

Jezzy drew in a deep, flameless breath, then let it out. She wanted to come. That would release the tension. But she needed to be patient. She could do this. She tried to relax her muscles. Then she felt a puff of air on her sweet spot. Her breath caught in her throat.

Alice grinned up at her with a mischievous look in her eye. "Giving *and* receiving is *just right.*"

Then Jezebel felt an ever-so-light touch wisp over her bead, and the ache tripled. She moaned, and her pelvis dipped forward, her pussy trying to move closer to Alice's mouth. She wanted to beg Alice to lick her. She felt slightly ashamed that she wanted it so badly.

Then Alice's tongue flicked over Jezzy's clit, and a lush thrill heated her thighs and made her legs tremble. "Yeah, just right."

Bare snuggled close behind Jezzy. Slipping her hands around either side, she cupped Jezzy's breasts and tweaked her nipples. She pressed her warm folds up against Jezebel's bottom, and Jezzy was surprised to feel Bare's moistness on her skin. The idea that she, Jezzy, had that effect on the lovely Bare was so exciting, she felt her own walls squeeze in response.

Alice made her tongue flatter and focused the top of it to administer slow, fat licks and sensuous circles over Jezebel's sensitive button. Tremors claimed Jezzy's legs and travelled up her belly. Her skin beaded in gooseflesh and her pussy quavered against Alice's tongue.

"Spread your legs, Jezebel." Bare's lips were close to Jezzy's ear, her breath tickling Jezzy's earlobe.

"Which pose?" Jez gasped.

"Woman-getting-eaten-out pose."

Bare's auburn hair brushed over Jezzy's skin, bringing the distinctive scent of jasmine.

Jezebel spread her legs further apart, careful not to dislodge Alice, as she seemed very intent on what she was doing. And who was Jezzy to argue? In fact, she could hardly think straight, Alice's licks felt so incredibly good.

Just then, Bare eased the cock-shaped bottle inside of Jezzy's opening from behind, thrusting and stretching, massaging Jezzy's g-spot expertly.

"Oh yes," Jezebel murmured.

"You are so sexy. Does it make you feel good that you're having this effect on us? Making us feel so turned on that we want to touch you? To fuck you?" Bare asked her, now driving the bottle deep.

"Yes!"

"Good. Now say, I'm a beautiful, confident, powerful woman." Bare quickened her thrusts.

Jezzy's mind was fuzzy with heat and desire. She was in a sexual haze, so it was difficult to string any words together, but she began, tension building so quickly that she knew that she was on the verge of exploding. "I ... am a ... beautiful ..."

"And confident." Bare drove into her.

"And... confi... confident..."

"And powerful," Bare urged, once again massaging Jezzy's g-spot.

"And powerful ... WOMAN!" Jezebel's orgasm rocketed through her, making her whole body shudder and shake.

"That's it, Jezebel. Give yourself to the cosmos. Breathe! Draw the whole universe into your body!"

The contractions took over. Jezzy's blissful clit pulsating against Alice's tongue. Her legs turned to rubber. A roar filled her ears, and her mind went blank. Wave after wave moved through her, taking her, lifting her. And when Jezebel's orgasm finally faded, she felt she might finally be starting to understand what Hellfire yoga was all about.

And she couldn't wait to get to the castle and marry her prince.

Er... Bean King.

Chapter 8

The Fairy Tale Wedding

Of course, Jezebel couldn't marry Jack right away. Not only was it still several hours before the wedding, but she and Alice had even more transforming to do before the walk down the aisle. But mani-pedi, hair styling, and artful makeup later, Jezebel and her matron of honor drove to the castle in a pumpkin pulled by mice (kidding, it was a Chrysler), and parked near the battlement, beside the parapet walk, next to the bartizan and chemise, under the postern, adjacent to the machicolation.

Castles were fucking complicated.

When they got out of the car, Jez was startled by two figures.

Hatter and Hare, replete with camera and microphone.

Oh no! thought Jezebel. *This is the absolute last thing in the world I need! I'm already worried about the wedding and the marriage! I don't need the paparazzi to grill me and make me feel even more unworthy! Why didn't I see this coming? All of the previous foreshadowing with Hatter and Hare has led up to this climactic crisis point where I'll be forced to overcome my fears or be doomed to utter failure!*

"Hey, chicks," said Hatter.

"Either of you seen the bride?" said Hare.

They still don't recognize me! I'm safe!

"Hatter! Hare!" Alice embraced them. "Why, Jezebel is right here! You didn't recognize her because she had a makeover."

Oh, darn it.

"Jezebel, is it true that you're marrying Jack Horner because you're pregnant?" asked Hatter.

"I'm not pregnant."

"You had an abortion?" asked Hare.

"I was never pregnant."

"Does Jack know you're barren?" asked Hatter.

"What? That's not true!"

"So he doesn't know your ovaries dried up and fell out?" asked Hare.

"Alice," Jez turned to her best friend, "tell them."

"This has nothing to do with being pregnant," Alice said.

"Thank you," Jez sighed.

"It has to do," Alice continued, "with Jezebel feeling she isn't good enough to marry Jack."

"Is it because you're fat?" asked Hatter.

"Is it because you're stupid?" asked Hare.

"Are you just a fat, stupid gold digger?" asked Hatter.

"A fat, stupid gold digger with no ovaries?" asked Hare.

Jezebel burst into tears. "How could you!" she screamed at the trio.

Then she turned to run away, but Hatter caught her arm.

"Before you run off sobbing, can we get a few pics of you topless?"

Jez posed topless for five minutes, but didn't enjoy it at all. When she and Alice finally got into the castle, Jezebel knew she had no choice but to call the wedding off.

"I have no choice but to call the wedding off," she told Alice.

"But why?" Alice asked.

"Haven't you read any of my internal monologue? Because the magazines are going to tell the world that I'm not good enough to marry Jack Horner. And they're right, Alice. I'm a loser. A fat, stupid loser."

"At least you still have ovaries," Alice said. "Don't you? That would suck if you didn't."

"Don't try to cheer me up, Alice. Tell Jack I can't go through with it. And give him a blowjob when you do. He really likes blowjobs..."

Jezebel burst into tears.

"Jez, stop being a drama queen. You havent' changed since college."

"You're my best friend!" Jez said. "You're supposed to try to cheer me up! When we were younger, you were always the confident, beautiful, popular one! I was so envious!"

Alice smiled and shook her head knowingly. "Jezebel, you silly thing. Don't you know that while we were in college, I was secretly envious of you? I wanted to be you so badly, because you were so perfect. In fact, I used to pray to my fairy godmother, asking her every night to make me more like you."

Jezebel sniffled. "Really?"

"No, of course not. Boy, you really are stupid, aren't you? Look, Jez, it doesn't matter what I think. Or what the magazines think. Or what anyone thinks other than you and the man you're about to wed. And he really loves you. You just need to love yourself, and everything will work out."

Jezebel wiped the tears off of her face and stood up straight. "Were you always this much of a bitch?"

"Yeah. But I'm right."

"But I don't love myself, Alice."

"Wah wah wah crying little baby." Alice grabbed Jezebel's shoulders and gave her a shake. "You've never heard the expression fake it till you make it? First comes action, then comes motivation. A journey of a thousand miles begins with a single step. Don't look a gift horse in the mouth. A stitch in time saves nine. A bird in the hand is worth two in the bush."

"What are you talking about?"

"Just put on the goddamn dress and stop your whining, or I'll stab your eyes out."

The best friends took the stairs to the Lord and Ladies Chamber, which was positively crowded with roses, which should have made Jezzy feel like a Broadway diva on opening night, but instead exaggerated her inadequacies. Alice helped Jez into her silvery white, strapless mermaid wedding gown. The fabric had a pearly quality about it, so that when Jezebel turned this way or that, it caught the light and different hues of color in the room. The clinging satin showcased her womanly curves, while leaving her shoulders bare. Her blonde hair was arranged in ringlets framing her face and cascading onto her shoulders.

"You look absolutely dazzling, Jezebel." Alice stood behind her wearing a puce bridesmaid's gown with hideous leg of mutton puffy sleeves and an awkward length. She clapped a hand to her chest, her eyes sparkling with tears. "You're the most beautiful bride I've ever seen."

"Thank you," Jezebel said, gazing into the magic mirror. "But, I don't know…"

Jezzy turned this way and that, studying her reflection. Another doubt niggled at the back of her mind. Did she really look that good? Or was the magic mirror tricking her eye into seeing her ideal self?

Just then the mirror became wavy and translucent, and a voice from within the mirror said in a soft, feminine voice, "Jezebel, you are exactly as beautiful as you believe."

Another one of those enigmatic comments.

This time instead of smiling and nodding, Jezzy frowned and turned to Alice. "Did you hear that?"

"Hear what?"

The voice came again. "Jezebel, you are the most captivating bride in the castle."

Jezzy frowned. The mirror had to be taunting her. "But I'm the only bride in the castle."

"Are you talking to yourself?" Alice asked.

"It's the mirror. It's talking to me."

"That's how I feel, too! I love watching myself in mirrors. And this is like one of those mirrors in expensive boutique dressing rooms. I look great from every angle. Well, I usually do. Did you go out of your way to pick the ugliest bridesmaid dress in the world?"

"Yes," Jezebel said. "But this is about me right now, not about you."

"Still," Alice said, ignoring her, "if anyone can pull off this look, I can."

Alice turned and twirled, admiring herself, until she lost her balance and nearly fell.

Jezebel steadied Alice, keeping her friend from tumbling through the looking glass.

"Oh, thank you!" Alice said, swishing to the other side of the room. "I'm so clumsy sometimes. You wouldn't believe what happened the last time I fell into a mirror."

As soon as Alice moved out of earshot, Jezebel leaned in close to the glass. "Mirror, mirror on the wall, am I the bride Jack deserves?"

But apparently the mirror had nothing more to say, because even though Jezebel's reflection was perfect, the mirror remained silent.

And then it was time for the wedding. After gathering their extravagant bouquets of roses, Alice and Jezzy headed down the twisty turny stairs. When they emerged from the keep, they strolled under the barbican (not to be confused with the bartizan, stupid fucking complicated castles) and into the courtyard, where several hundred people sat in uncomfortable folding chairs. A string quartet played from the bandstand,

and Jack stood waiting under the floral arch, so handsome in his white tuxedo that Jezebel couldn't move.

When they'd met, he'd been a waiter at a restaurant. And ever since he'd presented Jezebel with magic beans that grew into a giant beanstalk, he'd swept her off to ecstasies she hadn't known existed. They'd had many ups and a few downs, but they'd survived it all to be here today. He was so handsome, so sweet, so adventurous, that even if he wasn't rich and famous, Jezebel would love him.

Staring at all those expectant faces, the flashes popping, the cameras recording, Jezzy wished more than anything that he wasn't rich and famous.

Jezebel looked at her matron of honor for support, but Alice was texting.

Why am I even friends with this bitch?

Jez took a deep breath and steadied herself. Then, too soon, it seemed, the music began.

Alice gave her a smile and a little squeeze of the hand, then began a slow, measured walk down the aisle.

Step, feet together. Step, feet together. Step, feet together.

Then it was Jezzy's turn.

On trembling legs, Jezebel took first one step, then another. Her palms broke out in a cold sweat, her hands slippery on her bouquet. Her mouth went dry. She caught a glimpse of Hatter and Hare on the sidelines, where they held up a large, intricate sign that read UNWORTHY LOSER in huge letters.

When did they have time to make that?

Alice reached the floral arch, stepping to the side, and Jezebel focused on Jack.

In his face she saw so much love that Jezebel's stomach flew into her throat. Her feet faltered. Her breath caught. Her heart seemed to stop in her chest.

She looked at her husband-to-be, a man she didn't deserve. She looked at all of the guests and watched, dismayed, as their smiles turned to confusion.

Everyone is watching me. I'm not perfect enough. I can't do this.

Jack stepped toward her, his brows dipped low. "Jez..."

Her cheeks burned, and tears blurred her vision.

"Jez, please..."

"I... I'm sorry," she whispered then turned and ran, stumbling over the cobblestones in her haste to get away. She tripped, causing Hatter and Hare to laugh.

Recovering, Jezebel raced to the keep and up the twisty turny stairs. When she reached her chamber she fell to her knees in front of the mirror. The glass grew wavy, but she couldn't tell if the cause was magic or simply the tears swamping her eyes and streaming down her cheeks.

"Mirror, mirror... what's wrong with me? I went to the Hellfire Spa, I'm blond and toned and look beautiful, so why do I still *know* I'm not good enough?"

"You will know what you believe."

Jezebel stared at the mirror, anger and frustration roaring in her ears. "That shit again?"

Echoes from her stay at the Hellfire Club Spa reverberated through her memory.

You will be as perfect as you feel.

You will feel as confident as you are.

You will be as beautiful as you know.

"And now this?" she yelled out loud. "You will know what you believe? That makes about as much sense as all that Buddha mumbo jumbo. Bare told me to be a lamp to myself, but she didn't even care enough to come to my wedding."

"She's getting chemo," said the mirror.

"She's being selfish. Tell me, mirror, what is all that stuff supposed to mean?"

But again the mirror fell silent.

Jezebel tossed her bouquet against the glass. Everyone at the spa told her she was beautiful. Her adventures taught her to be confident. And deep down, she knew there was no such thing as perfect. But she still didn't feel good enough. She didn't believe.

Could that be my problem?

"Will I never know that I'm good enough because I don't believe in myself?" she asked the mirror.

The mirror began to warp and wave again, and then a scene became clear in the glass. It was Jezebel, climbing up that beanstalk years ago. She had been so selfish then, but she'd put her own wants and needs aside and risked the wrath of Lucinda to break a terrible curse the witch had put on Jack. And in the end, Jezzy had learned to be giving and kind.

Then the scene in the glass changed to show Jezzy putting her own feelings for Jack aside to help find him the perfect wife. She'd learned then that she'd still loved Jack, but she'd put his happiness ahead of her own. At least that's what she'd told herself. And when it turned out the happiness he sought was a marriage to her, her life had seemed complete.

Finally, the mirror revealed Jezebel at the Hellfire Spa, competing with the spinning king, getting the bukkake facial at the food orgy, taking it up the ass, going down on the bitch, Alice, taking part in so many different sexual adventures, feeling brave and powerful.

The images faded, and the reflection was again hers, right now, sitting on the floor in her wedding dress while all the guests waited and wondered below.

"You okay, Jez?"

Jezebel turned from the mirror and focused on her fiancé standing in the doorway. He looked a little lost, a little sad, and very, very worried.

"I'm so sorry, Jack." She stood up, smoothing her dress with her palms. "I don't deserve you."

He stepped across the threshold and joined her in front of the mirror. "What happened out there, Jez? Don't you want to get married?"

Jezzy's eyes filled with tears. "More than anything."

"Then what is the problem?"

She let out a heavy breath. Hadn't she just been asking the mirror that very thing? Wasn't she still struggling to sort through the answer? "I tried so hard to be perfect for you, Jack. But I just can't do it."

"I don't need you to be perfect. I just want you to be you."

Jezebel opened her eyes wide, so tears wouldn't spill down her cheeks. "I love you, Jack."

"I love you too, Jez. And I want to marry you. And I think you are perfect." He kissed her, then took her into his arms, holding her, swaying a little as if they were dancing. "Look at yourself, Jez. How could I not want to marry you?"

She stared past Jack at the magic mirror. The reflection of a beautiful blond woman in his arms stared back.

She was not too fat.

She was not too thin.

She was just right. And very, very hot and confident and powerful.

And then Jezebel realized the blonde was her.

Jezebel shook her head, her body shuddering with a barely held back sob.

Jack pulled back and looked into her eyes. "What is it?"

"I look great in a magic mirror. I just wished I looked like that in real life."

"The mirror isn't magic."

"What?"

"The mirror isn't magic, Jez. It never was. I just thought the idea of a magic mirror was romantic. But it's an ordinary old mirror I ordered from Amazon.com. They're the Everything Store, you know."

Jezebel felt dizzy. She stared at the reflection of the perfect woman, trying to make sense of it all. "Not a magic mirror?"

"Nope."

"But if the mirror isn't magic, then why was it talking to me?"

"What?"

"Never mind." Jezzy glanced at Jack. Was she crazy? She must be.

Crazy to let my stupid insecurities get in the way of marrying the man I love.

Also, years ago I was diagnosed with paranoid schizophrenia. And with all the wedding planning, I haven't taken my clozapine in weeks.

"I'm the problem, aren't I?" she said to the mirror, no longer caring if it was really able to hear her or not. "Not the color of my hair or the weight of my body, or any of my other imperfections, but my belief in myself. That and my paranoid personality disorder."

And this time the mirror didn't answer, but then it didn't need to.

Jezzy had been bold, she'd been brave, she'd been confident. She'd done things she'd believed were beyond her, and yet come out on top. Why was she letting her fears get in the way now?

She looked back at the non-magic mirror, at her own beautiful reflection, a reflection she somehow couldn't recognize until this moment.

Be a lamp to yourself. Be your own confidence. Hold on to the truth within yourself as to the only truth.

And take your damn medication.

The truth was, she wanted to marry Jack.

The truth was, she loved him and she knew he loved her.

She looked at Jack, her sweet Jack, the man she adored with all her heart. "Do you think the wedding guests are still down there?"

A smile tweaked the corners of his lips. "You want to get married? You sure?"

"I'm sure." Jezebel took Jack's hand and felt truly happy for the first time in her life. "Let's get married and live happily ever after."

And that's exactly what they did.

Then they had sex.

Two weeks later, Jez murdered Jack because the voices told her to.

THE END

Peterson, Sharp & Konrath Bibliographies

EROTICA

Make Me Blush series
MISTER KINK (Book 1)
FIFTY SHADES OF WITCH (Book 2)
SIX AND CANDY (Book 3)

Alice series
FIFTY SHADES OF ALICE IN WONDERLAND (Book 1)
FIFTY SHADES OF ALICE THROUGH THE LOOKING GLASS (Book 2)
FIFTY SHADES OF ALICE AT THE HELLFIRE CLUB (Book 3)

Jezebel series
FIFTY SHADES OF JEZEBEL AND THE BEANSTALK (Book 1)
FIFTY SHADES OF PUSS IN BOOTS (Book 2)
FIFTY SHADES OF GOLDILOCKS (Book 3)

Sexperts series
THE SEXPERTS – FIFTY GRADES OF SHAY (Book 1)
THE SEXPERTS – THE GIRL WITH THE PEARL NECKLACE (Book 2)
THE SEXPERTS – LOVING THE ALIEN (Book 3)

CODENAME: CHANDLER
(ANN VOSS PETERSON & J.A. KONRATH)
FLEE (Book 1)
SPREE (Book 2)
THREE (Book 3)
HIT (Book 4)
EXPOSED (Book 5)
NAUGHTY (Book 6)
FIX with F. Paul Wilson (Book 7)
RESCUE (Book 8)

Tracy Sharp Bibliography

LEAH RYAN SERIES
REPO CHICK BLUES

FINDING CHOE

DIRTY BUSINESS

RED SURF

JACKED UP

LONG GONE

THE LEAH RYAN BOX SET: 1 - 3

INTRUDERS SERIES
INTRUDERS: THE INVASION

INTRUDERS: THE AWAKENING

INTRUDERS: DECEPTION

STAND ALONES
SILVER AND SHADOWS

CAMILLA

SOUL TRADE

KILL HER GOODNIGHT

SPOOKED

WEEKEND GETAWAY

Ann Voss Peterson Bibliography

VAL RYKER THRILLERS
PUSHED TOO FAR (Book 1)
BURNED TOO HOT (Book 2)
DEAD TOO SOON (Book 3)
WATCHED TOO LONG with J.A. Konrath (Book 4)
BURIED TOO DEEP (Book 5)

SMALL TOWN SECRETS: SINS
LETHAL (Book 1)
CAPTIVE (Book 2)
FRANTIC (Book 3)
VICIOUS (Book 4)

SMALL TOWN SECRETS: SCANDALS
WITNESS (Book 1)
STOLEN (Book 2)
MALICE (Book 3)
GUILTY (Book 4)
FORBIDDEN (Book 5)
KIDNAPPED (Book 6)
THE SCHOOL (Book 3.5)

ROCKY MOUNTAIN THRILLERS
MANHUNT (Book 1)
FUGITIVE (Book 2)
JUSTICE (Book 3)
MAVERICK (Book 4)
RENEGADE (Book 5)

PARANORMAL ROMANTIC SUSPENSE

Return to Jenkins Cove
CHRISTMAS SPIRIT by Rebecca York (Book 1)
CHRISTMAS AWAKENING by Ann Voss Peterson (Book 2)
CHRISTMAS DELIVERY by Patricia Rosemoor (Book 3)

Security Breach
CHAIN REACTION by Rebecca York (Book 1)
CRITICAL EXPOSURE by Ann Voss Peterson (Book 2)
TRIGGERED RESPONSE by Patricia Rosemoor (Book 3)

Gypsy Magic
WYATT (Justice is Blind) by Rebecca York (Part 1)
GARNER (Love is Death) by Ann Voss Peterson (Part 2)
ANDREI (The Law is Impotent) by Patricia Rosemoor (Part 3)

Renegade Magic
LUKE by Rebecca York (Part 1)
TOM by Ann Voss Peterson (Part 2)
RICO by Patricia Rosemoor (Part 3)

New Orleans Magic
JORDAN by Rebecca York (Part 1)
LIAM by Ann Voss Peterson (Part 2)
ZACHARY by Patricia Rosemoor (Part 3)

J.A. Konrath Bibliography

JACQUELINE "JACK" DANIELS THRILLERS
WHISKEY SOUR (Book 1)

BLOODY MARY (Book 2)

RUSTY NAIL (Book 3)

DIRTY MARTINI (Book 4)

FUZZY NAVEL (Book 5)

CHERRY BOMB (Book 6)

SHAKEN (Book 7)

STIRRED with Blake Crouch (Book 8)

RUM RUNNER (Book 9)

LAST CALL (Book 10)

WHITE RUSSIAN (Book 11)

SHOT GIRL (Book 12)

CHASER (Book 13)

OLD FASHIONED (Book 14)

LADY 52 with Jude Hardin (Book 2.5)

JACK DANIELS AND ASSOCIATES MYSTERIES
DEAD ON MY FEET (Book 1)

JACK DANIELS STORIES VOL. 1 (Book 2)

SHOT OF TEQUILA (Book 3)

JACK DANIELS STORIES VOL. 2 (Book 4)

DYING BREATH (Book 5)

SERIAL KILLERS UNCUT with Blake Crouch (Book 6)

JACK DANIELS STORIES VOL. 3 (Book 7)

EVERYBODY DIES (Book 8)

JACK DANIELS STORIES VOL. 4 (Book 9)

BANANA HAMMOCK (Book 10)

THE KONRATH DARK THRILLER COLLECTIVE

THE LIST (Book 1)

ORIGIN (Book 2)

AFRAID (Book 3)

TRAPPED (Book 4)

ENDURANCE (Book 5)

HAUNTED HOUSE (Book 6)

WEBCAM (Book 7)

DISTURB (Book 8)

WHAT HAPPENED TO LORI (Book 9)

THE NINE (Book 10)

CLOSE YOUR EYES (Book 11)

SECOND COMING (Book 12)

HOLES IN THE GROUND with Iain Rob Wright (Book 4.5)

DRACULAS with Blake Crouch, Jeff Strand, F. Paul Wilson (Book 5.5)

GRANDMA? with Talon Konrath (Book 6.5)

WULFS? with Talon Konrath (Book 9.5)

TIMECASTER

TIMECASTER (Book 1)

TIMECASTER SUPERSYMMETRY (Book 2)

TIMECASTER STEAMPUNK (Book 3)

BYTER (Book 4)

STOP A MURDER PUZZLE BOOKS

HOW: PUZZLES 1-12 (Book 1)

WHERE: PUZZLES 13-24 (Book 2)

WHY: PUZZLES 25-36 (Book 3)

WHO: PUZZLES 37-48 (Book 4)

WHEN: PUZZLES 49-60 (Book 5)

ANSWERS (Book 6)

STOP A MURDER COMPLETE CASES (Books 1-5)

MISCELLANEOUS

65 PROOF – COLLECTED SHORT STORIES

THE GLOBS OF USE-A-LOT 3 with Dan Maderak

A NEWBIES GUIDE TO PUBLISHING

MISTER KINK

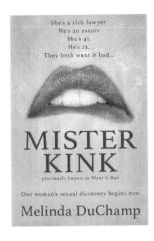

Carla thought she had it all together.

Then Jake moved in next door.

She never expected to fall for someone half her age. Especially Jake, an escort who specialized in very kinky sex.

But Carla was curious. And rich. And when Jake accepts her as a client, they each may have gotten more than they'd bargained for...

MISTER KINK mixes erotic romance with laugh-out-loud humor. Sexy, funny, and outrageous, this is the book you've always wanted to read. A smart, older woman goes on a journey of sexual discovery, and somewhere along the way finds love. Or at least something equally as tasty.

MISTER KINK
It begins where 50 SHADES OF GREY left off...

MISTER KINK is a 64,000 word contemporary romance by bestselling author Melinda DuChamp. It's hot. It's playful. It's more fun than the last ten books you've read.

Try MISTER KINK. You won't be disappointed.

FIFTY SHADES OF WITCH

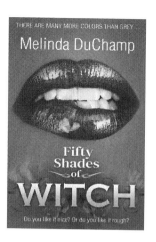

Here It Is, Nice And Rough…

This is the story of a witch in New York.

Actually, it is two stories.

The first story is an adult paranormal romance. Sweet. Sexy. Funny. It has some steamy parts, a heroine you can root for, and a Happily Ever After.

The second story is erotica. Rude. Hilarious. Filthy. It has a lot of kinky parts, and the heroine goes through quite the edging ordeal.

Whether you want a spicy, romantic adventure, or a wicked trip down a very naughty road, FIFTY SHADES OF WITCH has got it covered…

THE COMPLETE FIFTY SHADES OF ALICE

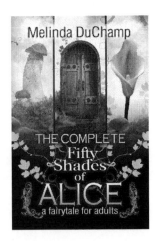

Eighteen-year-old Alice is sexually unfulfilled. But then she follows a very special white rabbit to places beyond her wildest erotic imagination. There are no nice boys—or girls—down here. Only those who indulge in secret, forbidden, kinky fantasies.

From escapades in a sexual Wonderland, to some hot encounters through the Looking Glass, and on to the infamous Hellfire Club, this isn't the fairy tale you grew up reading. This adults-only story is for those with sinful desires, who wish to explore erotic excess beyond the plain vanilla of everyday life.

The bestselling erotica trilogy is now compiled into a single, full-length novel, for only the most adventurous readers.

THE COMPLETE FIFTY SHADES OF ALICE

It's erotica for smart people who like to laugh, just like you.

Follow Alice down the rabbit hole, if you dare…

SIX & CANDY

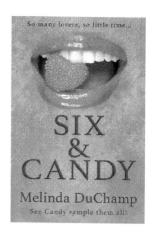

Candy is all set to become the CEO of her family's billion dollar company… but first, her grandfather demands she be married by her thirtieth birthday.

Candy can accept that archaic, sexist demand, but her cheating fiance just left her, and time's almost up.

Can Candy find a life partner in just a week? Or will all of the unconventional sex wear her out before she can say, "I do""?

SIX & CANDY by Melinda DuChamp

See Candy sample them all!

Printed in Great Britain
by Amazon

44221599R00188